Emma Henderson

Emma Henderson lives in London and is currently working on her second novel. *Grace Williams Says It Loud* was shortlisted for the Wellcome Trust Book Prize.

Emma Henderson

SCEPTRE

First published in Great Britain in 2010 by Sceptre
An imprint of Hodder & Stoughton
An Hachette UK company

First published in paperback in 2011

4

A CIP catalogue record for this title is available
from the British Library.

ISBN 978 1 444 70401 3

Typeset in Sabon by Ellipsis Books Limited, Glasgow

Printed and bound by Clays Ltd, St Ives plc

Hodder & Stoughton policy is to use papers that are natural, renewable
and recyclable products and made from wood grown in sustainable forests.
The logging and manufacturing processes are expected to conform to
the environmental regulations of the country of origin.

Hodder & Stoughton Ltd
338 Euston Road
London NW1 3BH

www.hodder.co.uk

In memory of Clare Curling Henderson (1946–1997)
and
Philip Casterton Smelt (1956–2006)

I

1987

When Sarah told me Daniel had died, the cuckoo clock opened and out flew sound, a bird, two figures. The voice of the cuckoo echoed, louder than the aeroplanes overhead, and opposite the clock, evening shadows stirred.

II

A shadow made me start as my mother's face loomed towards me where I lay, eight months old, tongue-tied, spastic and flailing on the coarse rug, on the warm lawn, in the summer of 1947 – in an English country garden. My father was playing French cricket with Miranda and John, and I could hear a tennis ball – in his hand, in the air, on the bat. Sometimes I saw the balling arc and even the dancing polka dots on Miranda's dress as she raced after the ball, or John's dusty brown sandals and grey socks when the ball rolled on to the rug and he came to retrieve it.

My mother's breath was toffee-warm. Her skin smelt of lemon soap, and her thick dark hair of the Sarson's malt vinegar she rinsed it with to make it shine. She kissed me on the cheek, put a palm to my forehead, then scooped me up. She hugged me tight, but she couldn't contain my flailing. She cooed and cuddled, I whimpered and writhed. We were both wet with sweat.

The next day – it could have been yesterday – my tongue was clipped. 'A lingual frenectomy'll do the trick,' they said. Lickety-split. Spilt milk. Not Mother's, no. The nurses gave it to me, clean and cold, in a chipped enamel mug with a hard blue lip. My loosened tongue lapped feebly, flopping against the smooth inside. The mug upturned.

When I came home, Miranda tied string around my tongue, my enormous, lolling tongue, with which I was learning fast to bellow, suck and yelp.

'Doctors and nurses,' she said, clucking like Mother.

I was in my cot, rolled rigid against the side. A wonky foot had wedged itself between the bars. My face was squashed to the mattress – mouth open, tongue dry and rubbing roughly on the sheet. Stench of starch, and particles of dust tickling my cheek, prickling the inside of my nose.

'I'll make it better,' said Miranda, and wrapped the string around my tongue in loops and big wet knots. She worked away without a word, breathing heavily, her own pink tip of a tongue flickering in the corner of her mouth.

'There.'

The ends of the piece of string were tied in a neat bow. Miranda stood back and surveyed her work, frowning. She must have been just six at the time, frilled eyes level with mine – two pairs of small set jellies.

'I'll tell you a story,' she said, backing towards the door. She had one hand on the handle and the other on the door frame. I didn't want her to go. I wanted to hear the story. I grunted and knocked the front of my head against the bars of the cot. Miranda swung backwards and forwards, holding both sides of the door frame now. At the end of a forward swing, she suddenly stopped, taking all the weight with her arms. Shoulders jutted, elbows locked, tendons strained.

'Once upon a time, there was a girl called Grace—'

A ski-jumper, a snow-bird in mid-flight.

But somebody shouted, 'Tea's ready. Come on, Miranda.' Then, 'Where's she got to, that child?' And Miranda pulled herself upright, backed out of the room and shut the door quietly behind her.

The string soon slipped off as I tossed and dribbled. It fell into the dark gap between cot and nursing chair and wasn't found until we moved house several years on.

Miranda was the silk-haired love child, so the story goes, pretty as a pixie, naughty as a postcard. Solemn John came along less than a year later. John was the quiet one, the clever one. At the age of three, he added spectacles to his round flat face and began to read books. At mealtimes, he would gaze at me in those long periods while my parents finished eating and Miranda picked fussily at her food. John's eyes behind his specs were tiny, grey and unblinking.

The eyes of strangers blinked or looked away.

After we moved to London in 1951, only when my mother was feeling brave, would she take me with her to the parade of shops at the end of our street, for meat, fruit and veg, a loaf of bread and, on Fridays, fish. 'Two and six, Mrs Williams. Filleted?' The fishmonger slipped the fish from bucket to board, or sloshed them noisily from their trays of ice.

I had learnt to walk, after a fashion. Without the support of another person, I sometimes tumbled and often splayed, but with an arm, or palm, on one side, I tottered quite nifty-shifty along.

We must have been an odd sight, my mother and I. She done up and efficient in her lightweight macintosh, home-sewn skirt and sensible, low-heeled shoes. Me lop-sided and limp, but buttoned nevertheless into my bristly blue coat with its dark, soft collar. A matching beret on my head. Knitted, patterned Norwegian mittens hiding my buckled fingers.

After helping me down the steps to the pavement, Mother would stoop to hook an arm through mine. She'd draw me close, adjust the shopping basket on her other arm, and start to chant and march us.

'*Left. Left. I left my wife with forty-five children and nothing but gingerbread left. Left.* Come on, Gracie. You can do it. Definitely.'

I frequently slipped and broke the rhythm, but Mother gamely improvised, '*And it serves them jolly well right.*' Hop-skip. '*Right.*' Pause.

So began our walks – hop-skip gavottes along the street. Often we paused. I needed a rest, she guessed. People stared, but kept their distance. Mother stared at the houses as we passed, or paused. What lay behind those painted doors, she sometimes wondered aloud? Why paint them at all? There's nothing wrong with wood, Grace.

The reds and blues were pop-eyed, she said, popping her own dark eyes, making us both laugh. She was snooty about white – unimaginative, she said. The only colour she openly envied was a deep olive-green. There were just three of these in our street, but we often seemed to stop by them, and Mother would frequently tell me, on those days, about a journey she once made in Italy. Not all at once, of course, just snippets and fragments, but something warm and wistful would enter her voice as she talked, and gradually I was able to spread my own Mediterranean around me, heady and potent, whenever she began. Like this.

Once upon a time, before the war, there was a very clever girl, whose cleverness was marked, first by her ma, then by the school her ma managed to send her to aged four. Six, eight, ten, twelve, fourteen years passed by. At the age of eighteen, instead of going on to higher education, as school and ma had hoped, the girl became engaged to a handsome Scandinavian named Joe. But the next we know, she's off to Italy, leaving poor Father – Joe – in Maida Vale, sharing flea-ridden digs with two penniless violinists.

Meanwhile, there was this giddy girl, gadding about in an open-top car, she and the Isadora Duncan of a girl-friend she went with, scarves trailing, leaning, waving, whooping at the bemused Italian boys. It was early spring 1939. Adventures with spaghetti, language and wine. Other tastes – other tongues in your mouth, Grace. Tattered Penguin paperbacks. And two hungry English girls, giggling in the gondola on their way back from the Lido in Venice so loudly and lewdly that the gondolier poled back to the landing stage and ordered them to disembark for their own safety. Florence, Rome, right down to Naples and beyond to Pompeii, where one of them lost a shoe somewhere in the volcanic ruins. Further even, a tiny fishing village with a luscious long name – Santa Maria di Castellabate. They spent the night sitting on the quayside there, watching for dawn, chatting with a young man from Durham, of all places – an archaeologist, a field trip. A field day, Grace.

Mother returned to England and married our father, who'd finished his studies by then and worked as a music librarian. Wagner was his thing. But 'My tastes are eclectic' he'd reply if asked and, if pressed, 'I'm partial to Grieg, naturally. Sibelius, Söderman, especially the *lieder*. Holst, Handel, Schumann...' Sometimes he'd simply say, 'Anything that sings.'

Hitler invaded Poland. Miranda was conceived and born, then John, then me, all wrong. Not just not perfect, but damaged, deficient, mangled in body and mind. Mashed potato. Let's take her photato. What shall we do with the crumpled baby, early in the morning? Put her in the hospital with a nose drip on her, early in the morning. What shall we do?

Return to our own pale green front door. Shut it quick. Shut us up.

My London room adjoined my parents'. My cot was against a wall, and on the other side of the wall was their double bed, with its swishing, soft-slipping eiderdown and clackety old headboard. When I couldn't sleep at night, I thought about the head of their bed, framing, protecting them both. I often heard my father's voice, grave, entreating, explaining. The response from my mother either yawning and bored – a flick-a-tut page-turning – or bitingly quick, which put an end to the talking, but led to heavings, sighs and the leaping sound of two grown-ups crying.

Bedtime, playtime, poo-time. You-time, me-time, teatime. Bread before cake. You before me. Bread and butter sprinkled with pink, sugary hundreds and thousands. Boiled egg and Marmite fingers. Soldiers, said John. Chicken and egg. There were millions of eggs in Mother's ovaries, he said. Why was Grace the rotten one?

For Christmas 1956, John, fourteen, was given the *Concise Oxford Dictionary*, Miranda, fifteen, a red Baedeker guide to Europe. I, still tiny at ten, received a baby swing.

The swing hung in the doorway between the kitchen and dining room, and I hung there in it, day after day, the soles of my stiff leather shoes tapping and scuffing as I swung and jerked. She loves it, they said. She can see what's going on. It makes her feel a part of things. But my feet were cold and my toes, in the inaccurately measured shoes, bunched and scrotched. I came to loathe that swing. The wooden bar at the back itched and irritated, and although I squirmed, my squirming merely slid me lower in the seat until the bar between my legs thudded and bumped, flinging me sideways or forwards. Eventually Mother would come to the rescue and readjust me. When we had guests, she placed my good hand on the rope, moulding my fingers into curls and making an empty triangle with my elbow. In my hair, which was blonder than Miranda's and wavier than John's – your crowning glory, darling – she sometimes tied a bow of winter velvet or satin summer ribbon.

Summer started early that year and built itself a burning climax towards the end of August. On the Sunday before Bank Holiday, Mother cooked roast beef, despite the heat. And this little piggy had none. Roast beef, roast potatoes, Yorkshire pud, runner beans and gravy. Mother's face was red as she flustered crossly around the kitchen. Our cousins were coming to lunch. Father was in his study on the top floor, with *Rheingold* streaming out through the open door. John was in his bedroom, Miranda in the garden, but the smell of burning brought her running, barefoot, along the hall.

I had fitted.

While the roast beef crisped itself to a cinder, I fitted. Again and again, convulsions battered my unresisting body. When they finally stopped, the charred remains of lunch were rattled from the oven, a note hastily penned and pinned to the front door for our cousins, and I was laid across the back seat of the car while John and Miranda half crouched on the floor, half perched on the seat. My father sat in the passenger seat. My mother drove to the hospital.

It's a mild sort of epilepsy, they said. Very mild in origin, but with the complications of being so spastic, and a mental defective to boot, it seems much worse than it is. Try not to worry, Mrs Williams. Relax. Think about the new baby.

I roared and I roared, but it made no difference. Not even when I roared so much that there was the crashing of glass, or six big, strong hands holding me down and shit and piss in my knickers, on my legs and through the white cotton socks, running all over the seat of the swing, then drip-drip-drippings on the tiles below, where my shoes turned the mess into strange and changing swirls of liquid and semi-solid.

Unbearable. Hopeless. Think of the others.

A place was found for me at one of the better Welfare State mental institutions. The Briar. My home for nearly thirty years. Can you imagine? They must have thought I was contagious. Can you blame them?

Off we went, one September afternoon, two months before my eleventh birthday. Just me this time in the back of the car, propped upright with cushions and an old tartan rug, thin and holey. Father and Mother in the front, him puffy in a greenish overcoat – white chicken-skin neck, sparse, straight, light-grey hair, badly cut, hanging like icicles on the collar of his coat. Her brittle now, and tweedy, pregnant, in a man's navy anorak, with an old headscarf knotted at the jaw. Through the gap between the front seats, I could see her left hand gripping the steering wheel. The ring on her wedding finger bit into the flesh, making a wealy red line. All of us were silent for most of the journey. Occasionally Mother would look over her shoulder and ask was I warm enough? Did I need weeing?

When we'd left London behind and were heading north through faded brown and orange countryside, my father produced a map and read out place names and road numbers from it. A411, A41. Barnet, Borehamwood, Bushey. Mother said there was no need for that, she knew the way, and pressed her lips so firmly together that they became a dark, dangerous slit. She tapped her ring finger on the steering wheel. Left, left.

I forced my eyes away from the rear-view mirror and towards the side window. Grey skies hurting my eyes. Grey smell of warm plastic and bananas. And nothing but ginger-bread left, hop-skip.

'Wake up, darling. We're nearly there. Don't cry.'

Scarcely any traffic now. Scraggy, turfy fields on one side of the road, brick after brick of wall on the other, until we came to a pair of enormous black gates set into the wall a few yards back from the road. My mother turned the car and we stopped. A man – a dwarf – fairy-tale-like except for the telltale shabby grey jacket and bleached corduroy trousers, too big. Also, his over-large face held no fairy-tale sparkle. It was puckered and pocked, and whoever had shaved it had left hairy tufts and messy patches of brown bristle. This face appeared at the driver's window.

My mother wound down the glass. My father picked up his briefcase from the floor.

'Williams,' he said, removing a letter from the briefcase. Mother took it from him, snatchy-swiftly, and passed it out of the window. The little man nodded, passed the letter back, then glanced at me, before pottering to the gates, easing them open and, one by one, pushing them wide enough apart to allow our car to pass through. I wanted to turn round, as you used to see children do, kneel on the back seat and wave a smile at the man. I wanted to be one of those children. But it was far too late for that.

We drove in a slow hush for another minute, our breath misting the windows, before my mother stopped the car next to a long, low, still building with a corrugated-iron roof. There were eight windows, paintwork pale and cracked, a few steps, with a handrail, and a door at the end nearest to us.

'Here we are,' said my mother.

Here we are. Here we are.

She didn't turn and try to smile.

My father was clearing his throat as if to say something when the door opened and two figures came out, one tall and male, dressed in a dark, shinny-shiny suit, the other tall, female and large, wearing a nurse's uniform. Car doors opened and closed. My case was taken from the boot and carried by the tall, suited man. My mother and the nurse manoeuvred me out of the back seat. I stood, queasy, uneasy, unsteady. There were soft, chilly cheek-kisses from my father. A quick hug and neck-peck from my pushing-me-away-from-her mother.

It began to rain. My parents hurried back to the car, furry and distant in the damp September dusk. The nurse took my arm and I, unaccustomed to the stranger's gesture, tripped. The nurse stooped to help me up and I caught a glimpse over her shoulder of the car and of my parents, in the car. The sound of the key turning in the ignition. My mother turned her head and began to back the car down the drive. Reversing.

So vivid is my memory of those final moments that it is not hard to imagine myself reversing also, going back, towards – and, with the smallest of imaginative leaps, to – a very different life, belonging to blue-eyed baby Sarah, the bouncing bundle who arrived home in a taxi which had stopped on the way for Mother and Miranda to choose the biggest, proudest pram available, the loudest one.

Sarah was born in a large London teaching hospital. Not taking any chances this time. She was born at three a.m. Several hours later, as a blustery March morning dawned, Mother held Sarah in her arms for feeding. She looked at the healthy infant and disgust swept her body. She wondered, briefly, whether the baby felt the same. The baby's body seemed to shudder and recoil, but Mother soon forgot to wonder, and she thrust the baby from her breast, distressed. Sarah was quickly removed and taken to the nursery, where she screamed for four hours. Then, again, she was brought to Mother for feeding. This time, Mother, half expecting the instinctive, sickening revolt, forced herself to let the child feed. She couldn't bring herself to look. A nurse came by. Sarah did her best to suckle, but Mother's breast was old and loose, its nipple tough and rubbery. Gracie – me, I – had worn it out. Sarah pursed her lips and wrinkled her brow in concentration. Sourpuss, muttered the nurse. Sarah screamed more loudly than ever. She kicked her legs and beat her arms so wildly that the tight hospital swaddling came undone. Mother saw the screwed-up, angry face and the lively limbs, but she didn't respond.

The following evening, Miranda and John went with Father to inspect the new baby. Sarah screamed, which upset John, but pleased Miranda.

'I know. I'll make it better,' she said. 'I'll take her for walks. Let's get a new pram for her, Mother.'

So it was out of Mother's indifference and Miranda's enthusiasm that the plan for a brand new pram was hatched.

The pram features prominently in the few remaining photographs of Sarah's early months. There she is, lying in it, under an apple tree in blossom. There it is again, in the distance this time, on the beach, with towels hanging on the handle. In the park, being used as a backrest by John as he reads – Miranda holds Sarah up to the camera. And here, in the London garden again, Sarah is sitting in the pram. She's wearing a white dress embroidered with rosebuds, a white matinee jacket, reins. Fat hands grab the sides of the pram, almost as if she is rocking it with mirth, for yes, for once, Sarah is beaming, chortling, in fact, with laughter, and her eyes are wide and surprised, a light, pearly shade, the colour that in black and white photographs is actually the most colourless. They called her Baby Blue-Eyes, but her eyes were no bluer than mine, and I saw them sea-green sometimes. They called her Sarahkins, *elskling* and all sorts of other nicknames. Everybody marvelled at her oomph, this speedy little sister of mine. At three months Sarah rolled over, by five she was crawling, and at eight months, she walked.

Sarah says that the story of her walking so young is apocryphal, but I know otherwise. I saw Sarah's first steps. It was 10 November 1958, my twelfth birthday. Mother and Father brought Sarah to visit me.

Miranda couldn't come, they explained. Too busy studying. John ditto. So it was just baby Sarah. Too young to notice, Matron had said, ticking the 'yes' on the Visiting Relatives Request form.

They came by train, my parents said, because of the pram, and because of the forty per cent reduction on third-class tickets for visiting relatives. I was allowed to hold

Sarah, first in the day room, and later, because it had stopped raining, outside. Mother put Sarah in the large black pram. Sarah began to cry.

I was weaker than I used to be – muscle wastage, they said – so they attached me to Father's arm on one side, and Mother clutched my other wrist with her hand, meanwhile pushing the pram with her free hand. Sarah screamed, the wind blew, the grass was muddy. By the time we'd hobbled across it to the old cricket pavilion on the far side, we were all bad-tempered and exhausted. Father sat me down on a damp wooden bench, then went round the corner to light his pipe out of the wind.

'Do you want to take her again?' Mother asked as she lifted the wailing baby from the pram. 'Here.' She put Sarah down on my lap and set about readjusting the hood of the pram for the return journey. Sarah squirmed easily out of my hold. She stopped screaming and stood, looking up at me, one arm balanced on my knee. Her skimpy hair was lifted so high by the wind, you could see the thin, blue-lined skin of her scalp underneath.

Sarah gestured towards the distance with her other arm, thrusting out her thumb and index finger in an L-shape, an invitation. And then she walked. She walked across the rotting wooden floorboards of the cricket pavilion. She tripped at the edge, down on to the muddy grass, but she hoisted herself up and continued to walk. Our mother, of course, saw her, shouted to Father, and they both ran after Sarah to make her stop.

What a performer my sister is.

Daniel was a performer too.

I met him the day after my arrival at the Briar.

III

1957

I met Daniel at school. School was two rooms in the Children's Occupation Unit, which stood between the girls' and the boys' wards. There was a room for the children under ten, a room for the rest of us and a dining room, which we shared. But there wasn't any school as such, because the old teacher had left and the new one hadn't arrived. Nevertheless, the nurses installed us on chairs, behind desks. Some people were strapped in, some slumped, some slept. We were all given blue exercise books and banda-copied sheets of paper with violet ink that smelt of spring to smudge and drool over. The nurses bickered and bartered about who should supervise us.

Daniel was already seated at the front when I entered the room. Head bent, he was reading, so I only noticed, at first, the short, straight hair, tufty on his forehead. Daniel liked to draw himself tall, paint himself dark and say he was handsome – debonair's the word, Grace – but my eye spied that day a sandy boy, looking up from his book with curious, changeable eyes and a silly, girlish grin on his old man's face.

I bit Daniel's leg at playtime when he knelt and tried to steal the car I'd taken from the toy box. I was lying on my side, on the floor – a fish in the bottom of a bucket – curling and uncurling my limbs. I didn't see Daniel coming. His bare shin felt, smelt and tasted rough and homely, like old bread. Daniel bit back, on my bad arm, but it didn't hurt. It was more suck than bite. More kiss. More please.

The boy had bruised, scratched, pebbled knees. He knocked them or they knocked themselves together.

'You're not old enough to drive,' he said, rocking backwards, standing up. Then, 'XK 140. Rack and pinion steering. The best. I'll show you.' He pawed at my layout of battered cars.

'Corgi, Dinky, Matchbox,' he chanted, moving the cars into groups with the tips of his shoes.

I was, and still am, good at layouts – arranging things, sorting, placing, polishing. A darn sight better than some. I kept the car in the fist of my good hand and scrabbled to my feet. I spat at Daniel, who tooted with laughter.

'Blow me sideways. A girl who likes cars.'

He step-leapt closer. I started – funny-bunny legs he had, and close, close up he was taller than me.

'Give us a lift, then. Let's go for a drive.' And Daniel bowed, a low bow – his nose must have touched his knee. The scruffy hair at the back of his head flipped over so I saw the hidden bit of his neck underneath. It looked like a bat's wing, except it was white, and I didn't want to puncture it.

But I couldn't help myself – I guffawed. The boy had no arms. No flipping arms at all. The short sleeves of his Aertex shirt dangled and wobbled like the flaps on Miranda's knapsack.

'Come,' said Daniel. He jerked his head, twisted his feet and started hoppety-clopping across the room towards two nurses who were standing by the door. One of them had a cup and saucer in her hand, with a cigarette between her fingers. The other was absent-mindedly swinging the long key-chain that hung from her waist.

Daniel cleared his throat.

'May I show her around, nurse?'

'I don't see why not. She can start learning the rules.'

Daniel turned and nodded, and I bobbled after him, out

of the classroom, through the lobby, into the dining room, which was empty and still wet on the floor from cleaning.

'So when did you get here? I didn't see you at breakfast.'

Too bad. Daniel didn't see me at breakfast because I wasn't there.

Mother and Father drove away, and what happened next is anybody's guess, but I'm telling you now, it was a bloody mess.

'Temper,' said the nurse, raising her scratched arm and slapping me on the cheek with her hand.

I crouched at the door and saw naked, dim, electric lights, two rows of empty beds, and, in the distance, the tall man, smaller and smaller, carrying away my case. His steel toecaps echoed on the bare deal floor and I could feel them through my cheekbone when I lay on the threshold and thrashed it with my body until my brain was still.

They woke me up at five to seven the next morning. The nurse's watch was upside down on her boosy, but it swung near my face, and I smelt, for the first time, the nursey tang of Woolworths' perfume, Woodbine cigarettes and Briar sweat.

'Five to seven.'

'Nil by mouth for this creature.'

'Get up, slug-a-bed.'

I struggled to sit, still groggy from the pill I'd swallowed the night before along with choking doses of water. Along with suddenly dozens of other girls.

This morning the ward was empty again, except for me and the nurses. The beds were unmade and rumpled, with bundles of sheets, stained yellow and brown, on the floor at the ends of them. I was indignant when the nurse who had woken me up said, 'Shall we toilet or pad her?'

I wasn't a baby.

They took me to the toilet, a stuffy room at the far end of the ward, and I weed with pride and pleasure.

Oh, weren't we proud and pleased, the Williams family, when Gracie – nearly three – achieved an almost acceptable level of bladder control?

'Normal, Joe. Normal, I tell you! There's hope yet.'

Father smiled and told Mother it was down to her. She was a good mother.

'Good enough,' said one of the kinder specialists we trekked to see, up in Great Ormond Street.

But my bladder and bowel control remained only, ever, almost acceptable.

'No,' said the nurse when I tried to reach for the damp pile of torn newspaper on the floor. 'We're short.'

She pulled me to a standing position. The warm drips of wee caught between my thighs, and Mother would have clucked. In public toilets, in the past, before the polio and the iron lung, Mother used to hold me over the bowl.

'Step out of your knickers, Grace.'

We put my arms around her neck. She put her hands under my knees and lifted my legs around her waist. She held me in mid-air while I pooed or pissed, and she never once told me to hurry up. She wiped my bum from front to back and lowered me gradually to the floor for redressing. She called it doing knick-knacks.

No knick-knacks at the Briar. The nurse was about to lead me out of the toilet when two large, pink, muscled women appeared at the doorway, each carrying a pile of clean, folded sheets. The nurse told me to hold on to the wall. She walked over to the laundry women. I saw her hand out cigarettes, and the three of them strolled away to join the other nurse. There was the sound of matches striking, women talking, smoking, coughing.

I waited. The wall was dark-painted enamel, cold and smooth. The enamel of the toilet bowl had been cold and wet. My nightgown touched the ground. I clutched it at the waist with my good hand, so it didn't get wet like my feet. But by the time the nurse returned, the coldness had made another piss come, and this time in all the wrong places – along my legs, in the folds of the gown, right over my toes. The nurse, when she did return, was in too much of a hurry to notice.

We walked the length of the ward, through the open door, down the steps and out into the hospital grounds. I still wore the light-blue gown they'd given me last night. It was tied at the neck, but flap-dappered at the back. As I had no shoes, my feet were pimpled and streaked with purple, like the windy, early sky. The sun was pale and low but shone on the soaked lawn, on the nearly bare, waving trees and on the roof of the main hospital building in the distance. It made me squint, that rising sun, and through my squinty eyes and windy hair, the hunched chimney stacks on top of the hospital roof turned into a line of limping me's.

The nurse hurried me along a path, across wet grass lapping with dead leaves and brown squelch between the flagstones, which my feet didn't reach in time, so there was brown on my feet too, then on my legs, and heaviness on the hem of my nightgown.

A figure appeared ahead of us. He was dressed in clothes like the gatekeeper's, but he was tall and thin, and his trousers and the sleeves of his jacket were too short for his long skinny arms and legs. His bare feet stuck out at an odd angle. He held a spindly hoe in his hands, and was poking with it at an empty flowerbed. As we approached, he stopped poking and leant on the hoe. He was singing, 'I love coffee. I love tea,' and his big open mouth was grinning toothlessly.

The nurse ignored him.

'He's not smiling at you, dimwit.'

The man stopped grinning, stopped singing.

'What the heck,' I heard him say.

To make me go faster, the nurse pulled me by my bad hand. We stopped, she pulled, we started again.

We stopped outside a double door with wire diamonds in pitted glass. The nurse unlocked it, using one of the keys dangling from the chain around her waist. She fumbled and swore. She let the jangling bunch drop and then swung it against the small of my back. I squealed and tried to twist away, but the nurse clamped her hand around my head, and so I entered, for the first time, the main hospital corridor.

I soon got used to it. I soon knew the nooks that took so long to dust, and the crannies that could never be clean enough. That morning, however, I scarcely noticed the doors on one side leading to locked wards and punishment rooms, and the high, barred windows on the other which let in slishes of morning light. We were moving fast, the corridor was long, and I gave up counting the black numbered doors, the patterns on the floor made out of squares of grey-streaked linoleum, and the fat, shiny fire extinguishers with their red hoses marking every wing and corner.

After the corridor, there was the refectory, the laundry, offices and, finally, the grand entrance hall with its big, gold mirror – a gift, I discovered later, from Daniel's dad – two curly coat racks and some upright chairs with spotted leather seats. Nobody entered here except our parents, doctors and official visitors. There were five shut doors, each with a bright brass knob, plus the extra-large dark front door. The floor was polished wood in long straight lines, smooth and warm underfoot.

We went through one of the doors and up a staircase. More corridors, narrower, shorter, until we arrived at a door that said Medical Examination. The nurse knocked and we went in. A balding, freckled man with black-rimmed specs and a tired frown looked up from his desk.

'Nil by mouth?' he asked, leaning back in his chair, folding his arms across his chest.

'Grace Williams. Nil by mouth, doctor.'

'Let's get on with it then.'

The nurse removed my gown. The doctor examined me. Weighed, measured, surveyed. Height, head, wrists, ankles, waist – which made me snort with laughter because he reminded me of Mother, kneeling there on the floor like that with his arms around my waist. Like Mother when she made me skirts and dresses. Her firm hands first stretched and flattened the tape measure. She would reach round my back and bring both ends of the tape measure to my belly-button, tight at first, then two fingers' width apart.

'I'll have to elasticate,' she would mutter, her head bent as she peered at the inches – eighteen, twenty, back down to seventeen last month, when she made three skirts for me, all in one day. She sat at the table in the corner of the sitting room by the window, furiously turning the handle on the taxi-black sewing machine. It had royal-gold writing on its side, rolling cotton reels, spools like jewels, and a secret compartment where Mother kept her needles and the engagement ring that no longer fitted her finger.

As she worked, Mother's jaw was taut, and the machine and the material juddered alarmingly. I lay on the couch, dozy on the Omo-smelling cushions, and watched as she turned the material this way and that, flipped the lever, snipped the two ends of cotton. She was rougher than usual when it came to measuring for the waistband, but I still enjoyed her vinegary closeness, the hot, lemony skin, faintly greasy, and her grumbling voice.

'Damn it, Grace. You're thinner again. They'll think I've been starving you. Blast. Dropped a pin.'

Mother held the pins in her mouth. I could see the white-ness of her scalp through her dark brown hair, which was short and wavy, puffed up by the hairdresser only that morning. In places, even the roots showed – tiny, pricked-out stalks, like her dibbered seedlings in the garden shed.

I looked at the doctor's bent head. There wasn't much hair, but there was glistening and freckles. I'd never seen a freckled head before. I dabbed at it. The doctor stood up quickly and moved away to his desk, where he wrote on a form, frowning so much that even the skin on his bald head, especially at the front, went wrinkled like the sea, or like the material of my skirt by Mother's sewing machine, on the table.

Next I had to walk around the room while doctor and nurse watched. Naked and dizzy, I wobbled and tripped but made several laps before the doctor told the nurse to stop me. He stayed behind his desk, writing away. I stayed where I was, warm now, at least on one side, since I'd stopped near the fire. Leg, bum and back must have been nearly as red as the doctor's head.

'Good,' he yawned. 'Placing form – done. Section Three – complete. Free from infection certificate – I'll do that next. Check her reflexes at the same time.'

The nurse tied a clean gown around my neck. It was grey and shorter than the first. She sat me down on a chair, opposite the doctor. He looked in my throat with a light and, like they always did, gave me a wooden spatula to hold while he poked in my ears, using his cold metal rod with the tiny torch on the end.

'Blocked,' the doctor stated.

He peered in my eyes, up my nose, tapped my head and my shins, put me on the couch – off with the gown again – and listened all over with his swaying stethoscope. I lay as still as possible. When he tickled the soles of my feet and brushed his finger along the hairs of my arm, I held my breath.

The doctor sighed, returned once more to his desk, and wrote and spoke at the same time.

'Unresponsive. The patient has considerable sensory impairment. In the course of today's physical examination, I detected a greatly diminished sense of pain, indeed of any feeling.' He paused, looked up at the nurse. 'Not uncommon in spastics. You know that, don't you, Nurse Hughes? More than thirty per cent, I believe.'

'Yes, doctor. And perhaps it's a blessing for them.'

'Perhaps, perhaps,' the doctor replied, and continued to write, but in silence now. He dotted the final full stop with his Parker pen – a pen like Father's, but bluer, newer – and clicked the top carefully back into place. He seemed to relax after that.

'A fairly clear-cut case.' He glanced at the pile of papers in front of him. 'Physical and mental deficiency. Since birth, it seems. The notes begin at eight months. Club foot. Mangled face. Malformation of the skull and spine.'

The doctor flicked through the wodge of letters, forms, reports – Williams, G., aged three, five, six and a half.

'Ah. Polio, aged six. Spastic paralysis in left arm and upper left leg.'

The doctor looked over to where I was standing with my good arm extended – how Mother had taught me – a railway signal, to help Nurse Hughes retie my gown.

'There's something so ghastly, so animal about them, isn't there, nurse?'

He looked down, then up again, and nearly caught my jelly-fish eye. I bulged both my eyes, blew up my cheeks and let the air in them out through my lips. Saliva splattered down my front.

'Monstrous,' the doctor added. 'There's no other way to put it. You can see the mental deficiency at a glance, can't you? No speech, I assume?'

'Not as such. A few sounds. Some of them might be words, I suppose.'

'I doubt it. Is Bulmer bothering to test?'

29

'I'm to take her over to him from here.'

The doctor leant back in his chair and folded his arms.

'The outlook is indeed, as our good County Medical Officer concludes –' he nodded at the sheaf of papers – 'bleak.'

Dr Bulmer was in a meeting, so I missed being tested by him. I was glad, because I was hungry and I didn't want to miss lunch as well as breakfast.

I missed ECT – the electrics – too. The generator was down. But that's why Grace slug-a-bed Williams was nil by mouth and hadn't been at breakfast.

Daniel didn't know all of this back then, because I didn't tell him, not in so many words. But I liked the questions he asked, and most of the answers he filled in, so I shook my head and tried my widest smile, which made Daniel laugh again, and when he spoke, it was as if I'd spoken.

'You're right. We should have met earlier in our lives, my dear.'

He turned to face me and did his odd, low, sweeping bow before continuing, 'Perhaps, perhaps. Perhaps you're right. What a life we might have had! What love, what passion! But I'll tell you a secret, my dearest one – it's never too late.'

The words Daniel spoke, the way he said them, coupled with his old man's face and damaged body, were so idiotic I had to laugh again. So laugh we both did, Grace and Daniel, squawking and squeaking in the echoey room. We slid to the floor and wriggled on the wet shiny lino, hugging ourselves, hiccupping, flipping like fish in the morning sun. Our legs tangled, and we rolled ear to ear. Nearly canoodling, hootled Daniel. And nobody could see or hear us, so we went on for as long as we could, and it made us gasp, like Miranda and her friends at the rec when they used to dip their heads in the fountain, full of cold water. They'd hold their breath for as long as they could. When they came up, they were red and spewy with relief.

Eventually, we both stood again, Daniel, funnily, more quickly than me.

'Well, *chérie*,' he chirruped. 'That was jolly good fun, but now I must run.'

Why? I flicked a finger on my two floppy lips, then did the same to Daniel's birdy beak.

Daniel bent and mimed looking at the time on an imaginary watch, the wrong way up on my boosy. He twisted his head upside down. This nearly set us off again, but Daniel said in a more level voice, 'Seriously, I don't think I've enjoyed myself so much in a month of Sundays.'

Lopsidedly I shrugged, lopsidedly I grinned, and my tongue plopped out like a great stupid dog's. I tried to haul it back in.

'Nor me,' I said.

We stood for a moment looking out of the window. It was raining again. There were several men now picking at the flowerbeds with rakes and hoes. One of them, a black giant with a minute, bean-shaped head, was digging with a spade. The wet earth flew up and some of it landed around him in a lumpy mess, but most of it rolled back into the hole. Two nurses straggled along the path towards the main hospital building, their capes whapping, their hair loosening. From the left, in the distance, a small figure hurried across the sodden lawn. You could see that she had stout boots on, but she wore a light, beige macintosh knotted neatly at the waist, and her shins were thin and pale. Around her head was a scarf, tied in a tidy bow under her chin.

'Miss Lily,' said Daniel. 'Her day off.'

I watched Miss Lily scurry towards the trees and disappear.

Daniel and I went back to the classroom, and I played

some more with the cars in the corner while Daniel talked to a tall boy with big, flame-red hair. The two boys wore identical brown shoes, lace-ups, with thick, grey, woollen socks, like my brother John's before he went into long trousers and I didn't see his socks any more. They both wore baggy shorts, grey pullovers and short-sleeved Aertex shirts. Daniel's was faded blue, the other boy's green. Children's clothes, yet the boys looked like men the way they stood, the way they talked. They could have been my father and a colleague chatting on the terrace before dinner. It wouldn't have surprised me if one of them had lit a pipe. It didn't surprise me when the boy with red hair turned towards me and wobbled out the words, 'Welcome to Sputnik, Miss Williams.'

Simultaneously, Daniel looked at me and nodded his head, slowly and deliberately, a bit like my father – his way of acknowledging me in a crowded room – and it made up for the silky-tight ribbons and the stiff dress with the scratching poppers. It made up a bit now for the empty feeling in my belly.

I nodded firmly back, all the while wondering why the boy with big red hair was allowed to grow it so long. The rest of the boys had close-cropped hair. All the girls in the classroom had short hair too, chopped at the ear and near the hairline on their foreheads.

The nurses cut mine, after tea, in their office. They did the job quickly, with the largest pair of scissors I'd ever seen. The ends of cut hair prickled inside the vest, inside the dress they'd put over my head. Afterwards, they gave me a brown paper bag containing my hair and told me to take it to the workshops.

'And bring back some wood while you're at it.'

'She's too feeble. Another boggin' polio-no-hoper,' said Nurse Jameson. Nasty words, but spoken low and not unkind. 'Look at her arm.'

'Too bad,' said Nurse Hughes. Then, to me, 'Go on. Shoo. I'm fed up with you. What are you waiting for?'

Daniel. At the bottom of the steps to my ward. It was already dark, but Daniel shone in the light from the open door. I shut the door and Daniel went grey, except for the white bits in his eyes and a white piece of paper poking out of the top of his pullover.

'For the workshop?' he asked, nodding at the bag clutched between my bad hand and my chest. 'Come.'

We turned left towards the Children's Occupation Unit, and then on past the boys' ward, which mirrored the girls', except that two of its windows were broken. The main hospital building was a long way over to our right. I could see its narrow bands of dim yellow light, jittery through the branches of the trees, which moved with the wind and spat leaves. Few leaves remained on the trees. There were more in the air, and more and more on the ground, which was damp, but no longer wet. At least not the piece that Daniel led me to, deep beneath the branches of a cedar tree.

'That's the Maitlands' house,' said Daniel.

Before we ducked under the branches and everything dimmed, I had time to spy a thick hedge, and behind it, a good twenty yards back, inviting light, squaring warmly through reddish-curtained upstairs windows.

'The Maitlands' house,' Daniel repeated, ducking. 'The Medical Superintendent. Avoid him if you can. Mrs is all right, and they've a girl, Eleanor.' Daniel twisted round and looked up at me. 'Come. I'm Daniel, by the way. Smith or Dumont. You choose.'

Daniel smiled and raised his eyebrows at the same time. Then he turned, continuing to chatter, and disappeared underneath the branches. I couldn't hear a word, so I ducked and followed.

We sat side by side against the tree trunk, which was

wider than the both of us put together. Daniel was still talking about Mr Maitland.

'He wears bedroom slippers. Not always. But if he wants to skulk about without being heard. Slippers and a Jermyn Street suit. Barmy.'

I tugged the blue dress over my knees, and Daniel used his feet, like hands, to do the same over his knees with his pullover, which made the white piece of paper fall out. It was a newspaper, or part of a newspaper, folded long and flat.

'I've just finished work,' said Daniel.

With his feet, he spread the newspaper on the ground and began to unfold it.

'In the workshops. Back there.' He glanced over his shoulder.

All I saw were grey branches and, beyond them, a dark expanse of wall.

'Shoes.' Daniel lifted his feet from the ground and shook them so that his too-big shoes swung like doctors' handbags. The brown lace-ups were old, and I could see recent black stitching where there probably used to be brown.

'Mending shoes. That's what I do.' He tapped the newspaper importantly. 'Will, that's Will Sharpe, the man I work for, lets me have the newspaper. If he's finished with it by the time I leave. You should know what the world and his wife are up to, Will says. Plus ...' Daniel paused to make sure I was listening. 'Plus, I'm an autodidact, like him, he says. I like that. Sounds as if I like cars. Which I do.'

Daniel and his cars. How his squashed bauble of a face glittered at talk of bodywork, bonnets, mph and horsepower. He would gabble at full throttle to anybody interested, but especially with his French-speaking dad, both of them racing and listing – Porsches, Daimlers, all types of Jag. Italian Lamborghinis. They frilled the 'r's with the backs of their tongues – *Citroën 2CVs, Renault Juvaquatres, Renault Dauphines*.

Cars were just cars to me then. Taxis, now – I've always liked them. But there in the darkening shelter of the cedar tree, the only response I could think of was to open the brown paper bag still tucked between my chest and my bad hand.

'Beautiful hair,' said Daniel, eye-nodding first at the hair in the bag, then, again, at the hair on my head.

That's what everybody said, and Mother liked to hear it. Perhaps because it was the thing about me that was the most different from her – she of the dark, olive-tree hair – that and my pale Norwegian skin, blue, white and thin as new ice.

My head felt airy, my skull exposed, particularly behind the ears. Last time my hair was cut short like this, I was six. I was sick and in my iron lung, sucking and sighing with poliomyelitis. I scarcely noticed. Usually, Mother trimmed my hair. Nothing special. A snip and a sliver. But she was a good cutter, holding the hair between two fingers of her left hand, pulling and flattening it until the ends showed like broken reeds. Then, with a single snip, neatening the jagged points into a solid line. Mother had a pair of scissors she only ever used for haircutting. She kept them in the box in the hall with the spare front-door keys. They were long and loose, and one of the handles had a pretty curl for her little finger. They made a swish, like feet on snow, when they cut. Sometimes, Mother made the swishing noise over and over again, in the air.

'Just for fun, Grace,' she'd say, her mouth as wavy as her hair, her eyes as shiny as the scissors.

Afterwards, she would hold me up to the mirror.

'There, darling. All done. What do you think?'

And I would nod, clinging with an arm around her neck, prolonging the moment.

There weren't many mirrors at the Briar. But here was Daniel, skewing his body, turning his head from left to right. He kept his gaze on me, and when his head steadied, and our eyes swivelled, met and focused, I saw dozens of reflections in Daniel's eyes, including dozens of different me's. Daniel's inky-black pupils were enormous in the shadow of the cedar tree, but they still shone, and the thin bands of greenish-grey around them made them look like the pictures of planets in my brother John's *Encyclopædia Britannica*.

'Beautiful hair. And with a name to match. I know now you're Grace. I asked Matron. Grace Williams.'

Daniel lifted the newspaper and put it on my lap.

I stared at it.

'Grace,' Daniel urged, putting his nose right up to mine. 'Tell me. Can you read? Can you tell the time?'

Why was it important? I put my thumb on my nose, which was cold, and then on Daniel's.

Thumbelina dance, Thumbelina sing. Thumbelina, what's the difference if you're very small?

I was very small when I sat on my father's lap in the warmth of his study. We listened to music, and I heard Father's heart, my heart and the music tapping into them. We listened so much, but never enough.

'More, more!'

Never enough, but we sang along. And when it was time for me to go, when Mother knocked on the door, or John called us to come down for tea, Father picked me up. He balanced me carefully while he bent over the radiogram to turn it off, and I saw the record, black and shiny, like brylcreemed hair. The records looked the same, but Father showed me how each one had a different name.

'*Thumbelina*, Grace. There we are. And here's *Copenhagen* – you know that's in Denmark, don't you? Scandinavia.'

Wonderful, wonderful Copenhagen. Father's mamma came from Norway. But he felt an affinity, he said, with everything Scandinavian.

'There are so few of us,' he said. 'I sometimes wonder whether we mightn't all fit into Trafalgar Square, say. On New Year's Eve, perhaps.'

He'd proposed to Mother there, he told me, down on one knee in the dirty snow. It was dark. He was worried he might lose the engagement ring. The temperature was dropping, he remembered, and fresh snow was just beginning to settle on the bronze lions, the granite plinths and the black rims of all the fountains.

'There wasn't a Christmas tree in those days,' he told me. 'After the war, though, not long after you were born, Grace, Mamma's people gave the people of London a gift – a magnificent Norwegian spruce, every year, for Trafalgar Square. One of our finest. Fifty years old, at least, and always more than fifty feet tall. The queen of the forest.'

The King's College Carols. 'The Holly and the Ivy'. Father sang along merrily.

And when things went from bad to worse with me, 'Mustn't be down in the dumps,' he'd say, almost cheerfully. Then he'd light his pipe and put on one of his favourite songs – 'Mad Dogs and Englishmen'. Or sometimes one of mine – 'Thumbelina'.

I took my thumb away from Daniel's nose, and Daniel moved back, resettling the newspaper on my lap. I couldn't read what Daniel put in front of me that wet September night. My eyes were teary because of thinking about Father's study, his radiogram and wonderful, wonderful Scandinavia, Oxfordshire, London, him, home. Plus the damp night air in the Briar's chilly garden had smudged the print.

There was a picture of a space machine on the front of the newspaper, I could see that much. One shiny metal barrel inside another, with a ball on top and a silver capsule

37

on top of that. Like a giant Christmas decoration, except there was a dog inside the little barrel, inside the big barrel.

'Laika.' Daniel nodded at the newspaper. 'And Sputnik. It's the new space age, Grace. Space race – that's what Will says. As to cars –' Daniel sighed – 'and the road, it's the end of an era, I fear.' He began to refold the paper. Three speedy flips with his feet. Well done.

'I learnt to read by reading road maps,' he continued. 'For my papa.'

And that was all he said that day. But Daniel and his papa began a journey of stories, the likes of which you'd never believe, and I didn't either, not all of them, for Daniel told the tallest stories, the biggest whoppers. The best.

'Follow, Grace.' Daniel stood up. I ducked and followed again, tucking the newspaper under my bad arm, clutching the paper bag tight in my good hand.

Daniel moved quickly now, along a path that led to a door in another long, low building, this one dark and deserted. The door was ajar. Daniel nudged it open, then jumped back, bent down and swept his head from side to side, as a doorman would with his arms, sweeping royalty inside.

'*Mademoiselle*,' he said. '*Entrez*. Isn't my French exquisite?'

His mother was French, he said. Her name was Marie Dumont.

'She danced.' Daniel cancanned his legs and nearly toppled us both over.

'Maman,' he continued, 'was a famous actress. In Paris. She died.' Daniel looked past me, frowning. I noticed, for the first time, the small scar on Daniel's forehead, round, like a sleeping spider, with lines like legs that only showed up sometimes.

I went inside, past Daniel, who flicked a switch with his shoulder, making a light come on. I was in a lobby. There was another door to the interior of the building. The lobby contained nothing but a wooden box on casters.

'Go on. Put it in.'

I emptied the paper bag into the box. Immediately my hair was lost in the dull spill of other people's hair. The box was nearly full. I looked more closely. There were curls and colours, but you had to look for them. Otherwise the hair was dead and greyish-brown.

I screwed the paper bag up in my fist.

'No. You need to give that back.'

Trouble, and I forgot the wood too, what with the muddle of saying goodbye outside my ward.

'*Au revoir. A demain. Fais des bons rêves*,' Daniel said.

I couldn't make head nor tail of the piping, sandy boy, so I put the side of my head to his, and we rubbed bristles like a couple of doormats. Then I turned away and began to haul myself up the steps, gripping the rail with my good hand. Daniel's voice, behind me, went trilling on as if I were still there.

'Don't forget. Our drive, Grace. *Demain*. Where shall we go?'

'Oy. Smith.'

I twisted my head and saw Daniel hobbling towards the boys' ward, where a male nurse stood in the lit doorway. The nurse had a hand on his hip, waiting, and you could see the stick all the male nurses carried in his other hand, waiting too.

Daniel glanced back at me.

'See you tomorrow, Grace.'

Daniel disappeared into his ward, followed by the nurse with the stick. I opened the door to my own ward and stepped inside.

I was sent off again immediately to fetch the wood, this time alone. It wasn't far. Only round to the back of the building. But I didn't like the trip. Daniel seemed long gone. The trees made creaking sounds. The wood was wet and heavy, with bits of bark that kept sliding off. I carried two pieces, one on top of the other, balanced on my bad arm, but held with my good hand. There was dirt on my hands and down the front of my dress when I deposited the logs in the crate next to the nurses' fireplace.

'Filthy girl.'

I stood in the doorway, looking at the fire. Invite me in, I wanted to say. Make me marshmallows, buttered toast, honeyed crumpets. More, please. Don't tease. It'll be enough.

'Get out. You're disgusting.'

I turned and started walking back down the ward. Something sheered the skin above my ear. A piece of bark. Jeering.

The bits of cut hair inside my vest prickled for the rest of the evening, and all night. My head fizzed on the pillow and I wondered again about the boy with red hair before my thoughts returned to Daniel – his dangle-dancing body, his changeable eyes and his endless questions. I'd replied with my feeble two words. I'll never achieve an acceptable level of speech. Not good enough. Not normal.

I shivered. My two word replies were ever so meagre. Yet Daniel had conjured worlds from them. Journeys, at least. Cars, maps, departures. A revving-up.

Red-haired Robert, I soon discovered, had an unshorn head because he was the hospital messenger. It went with the job – a privilege. He rode a bicycle. He rode it along the corridors, around the grounds and, once a day, out of the gates and down the road to the village, then back with the post. Toby, the gatekeeper, had learnt to recognize the crunch of Robert's bicycle tyres on the gravel drive. He would waddle out from his small house, then hurry to pull open the iron gates before Robert crashed into them, which he did on a number of occasions.

Robert and Daniel were best friends. But I got to know Robert because of the oranges.

I didn't go home for Christmas that first year. Visits and visiting for Grace Williams wouldn't begin for some months. Best for all, they thought. They medicated. We waited. She'll settle, they said.

From December on, I spent a lot of time unwrapping oranges from large wooden boxes. I had to flatten the squares of tissue paper and put the squares in a pile. Another patient would skew them on to safety pins and they would be hung in the toilets for bum-wiping. The boxes had pretty coloured labels with writing in a foreign language stuck on their ends.

Robert was sometimes my safety-pinner. He hadn't gone home for Christmas either. His mother, he said, was having a room taken out of her tummy.

'A bloody drag,' he spluttered.

Robert didn't talk, he exclaimed and leapt from topic

to topic. Fom Earl Grey tea in white bone china teacups, something about Miss Lily – and why was it grey, what made it grey? – to the forty-nine constellations of the universe, with Orion spied, he said, with his stark, staring, naked, bonkers eye, night-fishing for salmon in Scotland. Then on to the smell of roasting rabbit, shot by his granny on her Highland estate, and prepared by a servant in her warm, flag-stoned kitchen. It was only his granny and his mother at home, he told me, in bursts, twisting an orange with his hands.

'Odds on I can do it,' he enthused.

The orange split apart in two squished halves, spraying juice across Robert's shorts and on to his freckled thighs. I didn't want to get sticky. But Robert sucked and swallowed the lot, turning the peel inside out to chew the last bits of orange from the pith.

'I'm a great fan,' he declared, trying to toss the two empty halves into the air like a juggler.

Robert simply wasn't very good at the job. He was always dropping the box of safety pins, wriggling forwards to reach my pile of tissue squares. Often, he jabbed hopefully at the tissue with the pin, but missed and tore the paper. Or jabbed his hand. Or the unravelled cuff of his thick, red, hand-knitted sweater. Robert wasn't very good at very much, but what he was good at, he was very good at – riding the messenger's bike, for instance.

'Tell us about it,' Daniel begged. 'The biking.'

But Robert's gob didn't gab like Daniel's. He talked with his limbs and his big hairy head – a scarecrow scaring nobody.

'Give us a ride, then.'

Then Robert would sweep Daniel up, an arm around his waist, and fold him on to the bicycle's crossbar. He'd pedal as fast as he could, up and down the gravelly orange drive, knees splayed, hair wild, Daniel pale and tiny, grey and pink, between Robert's long arms.

Daniel taught himself to ride this bike.

I should have known. But Daniel would always have secrets, even from me.

Robert, like Daniel, was a clever-headed, clumsy-bodied epileptic. Both twelve years old, they were juniors on Eric's engineering team.

Eric was an engineer, but he was also in charge of a ward of adult epileptics, male. This ward was separate from the rest of the adult wards, separate and different. The men had converted it themselves, supervised by Eric, from one of the disintegrating Nissen huts standing leaky in the hospital grounds. The hut was to the side of the main hospital building, by the store rooms, next to the tool-shed. Inside, it was a hot, safe place, full of men-things and smells – Father's study gone soggy. Each man had his own clothes and a tea chest next to his bed for keeping them in. The men tore pictures from magazines and tacked them to the wall. Nudey women, women with clothes on, cars, motorbikes, aeroplanes, soldiers, sailors, sunsets, but mostly nudey women. Eric, who slept in the Nissen hut too, had a shelf above his bed. It was stacked with thick engineering manuals and the blue school note-books he used for making sketches and plans.

Eric wasn't a nurse. He was a mechanic, already quite old by the time I arrived at the Briar.

'Both World Wars. Fleet Air Arm. Decorated twice, court-martialled once,' he liked to boast.

Very, very old by the time I left.

'No goodbyes, Grace, just God bless.'

Nevertheless, the nurses left him to it with his crazy fitters. That's what we called Eric's elite epileptics. Crazy fitters.

And what shall we call Robert and Daniel? Bubble-headed boobies, plucked eggheads, silly billies, mates, noodles. Loony boys zooming.

And memories of them zooming too.

Robert cycling in his underpants and shoes and socks on Easter day 1958, the coldest Easter for half a century.

'I'm pretending it's summer,' he yelled, waving and joggling as he passed the girls' gammy-legged crocodile. 'I say, ladies. Won't you join me for a Highland fling? Hey! Watch me dance the Hooligan's Jig.'

He reeled across the lawn, tipping his bike and bobbing his woolly red head at us.

Daniel, in May the same year, falling off the crossbar of Robert's bike – crikey – right outside the chapel, right in front of the fat soprano from the local operatic society when she came to sing with the hospital choir.

'*Désolé*, *Madame*, or should I say Maria Callas? My apologies. I'm French, not Greek.'

And then another zoom – to Eric.

'Ill or sane – as far as I'm concerned that's just a narrow gap.' He'd strike a Swan Vesta and light his roll-up.

Eric was always saying this, and because he believed it, he taught his team to watch out for each other. He taught basic first aid, how to deal with convulsions and fits, and how to keep busy, to keep out of trouble. He showed the men how to cook on the wood-burning stove he installed in the hut – great, stinking fry-ups – how to work hard, and also how to play. Cards, darts, drinking games.

Yes, there was drinking in the crazy fitters' Nissen hut. Bottles of beer on a Friday night if Eric was pleased with their work. Drinking and gambling. Songs, stories and, occasionally, me, wrapped between Daniel – or Robert – and Eric, snug in the smell of greatcoat, my slidey-wide eyes wet from the smoke, the tales, the male, animal warmth.

Worlds within worlds – a world away now.

Here's Robert again, crashing open the double doors of the refectory with the sturdy front wheel of his bike. We all jumped. But here he comes, rolling neatly between the tables, holding a buff file, tied with brown string, on his lap – look, no hands. Back-pedalling to brake. Gliding to a standstill in front of Miss Blackburn, our tall, strict, big-bummed teacher.

'For you,' he gasped and clasped his heart with one hand, the file waving wildly in the other. Robert never grew out of his crush on Miss Blackburn.

Daniel, standing on his chair to get a better look.

'Look. No hands.'

Daniel staring and staring at Robert.

Me seeing but not. Seeing Daniel, but not what he saw – no hands.

And here are all three of us again, inside the Nissen hut. Smuggled and snuggled. Robert's red head in the firelight, nodding, his freckled fingers wriggling, then still. Daniel, winning at pontoon, which he called *vingt-et-un*, fanning the cards – pretty – with his feet. Fumes. Cheers. Unshaven smiles. We stayed very late, and Eric carried me back to my ward, over his shoulder, a firm, fire-warmed hand on my neck, close but not tight, my bare feet dangling, toes on his thigh. He didn't pass me over at the door to the ward. He went on carrying me all the way to my bed, lifting the sheet, like Mother, tucking me in. The bristle and whisper of a kiss.

'Not goodnight, Grace, just God bless.'

Wards overflowed in those days. Even on the children's wards, you had to clamber over other people's beds to get to your own. I always made a point of stamping on the bed next to mine. It belonged to fat Ida. I had a run-in with Ida early on. She and I didn't see eye to eye over a plate of biscuits. I took. She grabbed. We both bit.

In June, dark-suited men carrying briefcases came to the Briar. They counted our heads, shook their own. Daniel said they were trying to divvy up illness and handicap.

But, he continued, illness and handicap – Jack and Jill – go hand in hand. Physical and mental. Mental and mental. Up the hill or round the bend, we were all the same, he explained. Pale and watery. Crappers, wets, bennies, spastics. Nameless. Just all these people standing around, shaking and dribbling.

Soon after the visit, a few of the adult patients left the Briar. For good. A dribble, a trickle. One day it would be a stream, Daniel said. Eventually a flood. Even I have taken my bow now.

Back then, though, it meant slightly less overflow for a while, that's all. And Eric's ward of crazy fitters continued as before.

As juniors on Eric's team, Robert and Daniel spent three afternoons and two evenings a week working with the adult epileptics. This in addition to school, delivering messages and mending shoes. Most of the jobs for Eric were routine. Many of them involved the hospital's enormous, steaming, groaning boiler. It had to be serviced once a month, cleaned once a week, and given the once-over every day. There was also a list of minor repairs for the entire hospital, typed by Miss Walsingham, updated regularly. Robert delivered it to the Nissen hut. Eric folded it and put it in the deep pocket of his thick overcoat, which he wore in winter done up, in the summer undone.

Eric believed in progress. He was always planning improvements to the Briar. Soon after I arrived, he turned the old airing courts into a rock garden. Mr Peters, who was in charge of the hospital grounds, grumbled and said it was a waste of space – he could do with the land himself – but Eric got his way. Eric usually got his way. He said it would be a good place to sit and think, quietly.

'Peace, Mr Peters. Two world wars. It's the least we can do.'

The rock garden was made, and soon much used. The crazy fitters, who knelt and tweaked at the hard earth, month after month, to keep things growing, didn't give anyone any trouble when they went to sit in it, quietly.

Eric had landscaped the rock garden with dips and hillocks. From the bench on the highest hillock you could see beyond the cricket pitch, beyond Mr Peters' farmland, to open country – fields, hedges, greens and yellows, flattish and soft, with trees in hearty dark clumps. One of the crazy fitters told me that on a clear day, you could see the London skyline from that bench.

I sat there sometimes, when winter turned into spring, Sarah was born and the blossomy Briar settled, drifted and began to blur the pictures of home in my head – the rooms with Mother, Father, Miranda, John, and now the new baby, Sarah.

Matron read me a letter from Father. In it, he said that I had a new baby sister, who cried a lot – 'rather a lot' – and I wondered what that meant. As much as me?

One day, Daniel sat with me on the high-up bench, and we canoodled.

It started as usual with our moving legs, which swung and rubbed, smooth on rough, but, 'Imagine I'm Humphrey Bogart,' said Daniel.

I flipped my lips with a finger.

'Don't ask why. Just shut your eyes, Grace. I mean Ingrid. Or Ilsa.'

I didn't know what or who Daniel meant, but I shut my eyes and waited.

'We can be private here, without being punished,' he explained, slucking my ear with his lips and tongue.

We began to meet on the bench frequently. I never canoodled with Robert. He wanted to, but, 'Not you,' I tried. And Robert replied, 'Just not your thing, I suppose.' Each time.

In the summer of 1958, Eric decided the hospital should have a pets' corner. He'd been talking to Will Sharpe, who'd shown him cuttings about other mental institutions and their experiments with pets. A children's home in Surrey had dogs on some of the wards. Two hospitals in the north had thriving pet schemes run by local volunteers.

Never one to be outdone, Eric set his team to work. Cages were built, hutches knocked together, and the old tool-shed, where Robert kept his bike, turned into a mini-menagerie. Rabbits, guinea pigs, a tortoise, some parrots and several budgerigars were bought or acquired, and Robert and Daniel were put in charge. They had to keep the place clean, feed all the animals and make sure they didn't escape.

Daniel claimed to have overheard the budgerigars devising an ingenious escape plan. It involved the birds dressing up as rats. The rabbits would provide the fur.

I knew he was joking. Robert said it wasn't funny.

We three often talked about escape, or running away.

'Where shall we go, then? Ballymackey? Ballymenoch or Barton-le-Willows?'

This was Daniel, to Robert and me, in front of the big map of the British Isles on the wall of Miss Blackburn's classroom. Daniel put his nose to the map and moved his head in an arc from Tipperary to North Yorkshire by way of Scotland.

'The stars,' said Robert. 'I want to go the stars.' He raised both his arms, waggled his wrists.

'You and the stars.' Daniel stood back and laughed. 'You can't bike to the stars, Rob. You'd need a rocket. What about Mars? It's red, like your head, at least. And closer.'

But Robert shook his head, and his shoulders shook too.

'No. The stars.' Craggy, shaking, certain Robert.

'Grace?'

Bushey, Borehamwood, Barnet? No.

'To Rome,' I said, partly because I'd seen it on the bigger map in the visitors' hall, partly because Mother used to mention it and I liked the way she opened her mouth to say the words – Colosseum, amphitheatre, Vatican City, Rome. But mostly I said it because it rhymed with home.

Another time, just Daniel and me. 'Let's jump on a train, Grace – Gretna Green.' Cheering me up. 'The Nevada desert, Katmandu.'

It was a Saturday afternoon. Drizzling rain. Daniel and I were two of the half-dozen children waiting in the day room for visitors who didn't come.

Visitors came to the tool-shed. Every Sunday after chapel, there was a queue of children waiting outside, while inside, Robert and Daniel supervised stroking, poking and some-times near-strangling of the birds and animals. Squeals of pleasure could be heard coming from the tool-shed if you happened to be nearby. I tended to avoid the area. Animals really aren't my thing. I don't mind birds in the sky or the garden, but they look stupid in cages. Also, it made me cross that Robert and Daniel sometimes chose to go to the tool-shed instead of coming to find me.

Visiting the zoo, as they started to call their tool-shed, became increasingly popular, and not only with the younger patients. Some of the nurses, who hadn't been keen at first, brought groups of adult wheelies, swivelled them into a line on the gravel drive, and plonked guinea pigs on their laps or let parrots perch on their shoulders. Everybody was happy. I was bored.

It all came to a sorry end because the animals escaped one night. Not hard to imagine those ragamuffin boys forgetting to shut the door to the shed, is it? Harder, though, to account for all the doors to the cages and hutches found swinging on their hinges the next morning, isn't it?

The birds flew away and were never seen again, all

except one budgerigar, discovered, dead, later in the day, on the window ledge outside Dr Young's office. Nobody liked Dr Young.

'That bird was definitely the leading strategist in the escape plan,' Daniel said, continuing the joke weeks later, but nobody was laughing by then.

The tortoise was spotted ambling along the drive towards the main hospital gates. A night nurse, on her way home in the early hours, reported this. She'd thought nothing at the time. The tortoise made it out of the gates and on to the open road, but then we heard from Toby that it had been found, crushed by a delivery van, a few hundred yards further along the road.

I don't know what happened to the guinea pigs. But the rabbits have a lot to answer for.

It was August and very hot, so some of the unlocked wards had their doors as well as their windows open. I woke up in a sweat with my bad arm clamped the wrong way round.

'Go back to sleep, Grace. It's half past four.' Nurse Jameson's voice.

Light was already seeping into the summer sky. I could see the quiet, round clock on the nurses' desk, next to the nurse's quiet, round face.

Two rabbits, one grey and large, one smaller and black, were bumping softly along the central aisle of the ward. They didn't look so idiotic out of their cages. Their twitching whiskers which, in the tool-shed, made them seem nervous and dim, were alert and curious now. I cried out in surprise.

My cry woke the rest of the ward. Chaos. We tumbled and bounced from bed to bed, pretending to catch the lolloping things. Who cared where they came from, or why? Pretending to be frightened. Us, not them. We thrilled to the chase, chased each other, fell in heaps and dirty sheets.

Ida caught the grey rabbit and squeezed it like a third

boosy between her own enormous two. The rabbit scratched her. Ida yelled and let go. The hunt was on again. Up and down the ward we ran, burrowing under beds, hurrahing at each other, ignoring Nurse Jameson's feeble calls.

'Stop it. You'll pay. I'm warning you.'

We didn't want to go for breakfast, not even when Matron was sent for, and then a gang of male nurses, who shooed us away with sticks and the threat of fists. Then fists and not pretending – being frightened. Rabbits.

I wasn't frightened, however, when I was summoned to the Medical Superintendent's office a few days later. I thought it was because of the rabbits and making too much noise.

I put the fingers of my good hand on the edge of his desk. I still wasn't frightened. I knew plenty of others had done this plenty of times. I clutched the underside of the desk with my thumb.

'Both hands.'

I turned my head to Nurse Jameson, who sat on a chair by the door, which was locked. The Medical Superintendent stood up, leant across the desk and wrenched my head back.

'Keep still. I said both hands, imbecile.'

'She can't, sir.' Nurse Jameson stood up. 'It's stuck, the other one. Paralysed. Useless.'

From the corner of my eye I saw her take a step, protective, towards me.

'Fetch the redhead.' The Medical Superintendent spoke curtly, as if my manky body was yet another mark of my hanky-panky tendencies. Oh dear. What had I done? Spat? Nattered? Shat? There were holes in my bucket-head – I knew that much.

Nurse Jameson unlocked the door, opened it, motioned Robert to enter. Robert came and stood next to me at the Superintendent's desk.

'I want you to watch, redhead,' said Mr Maitland, putting his face up close to Robert's. 'Carefully. Afterwards I want answers.'

The Superintendent spread my fingers on the desk, using the ruler to flatten them, like Mother with her palette knife when she iced cakes – pressing, patting, tapping. He turned the ruler on its side, lifted it, whopped it through the air and down on to my fingers. 'Smith – where is he? Speak, girl.'

And when I kept my gob shut, to Robert, 'Daniel Smith. Where's he gone?'

And when Robert kept his gob shut, to Nurse Jameson, 'Fetch the pizzle, nurse.'

Which nearly made me laugh, because it sounded like a kiddy word. But that's what Mr Maitland called the short, fat, nastiest of whips hanging on the curly coat rack in the corner, next to his dark grey coat and two longer, leaner leather-handled floggers.

Daniel had escaped. On the bicycle. And I knew nothing. I couldn't speak. There was ow across my knuckles, but something much worse in my head, or my heart, or skittering in between them. Where was Daniel? Why had he gone? Why didn't I know? Why couldn't I speak?

'I just wanted to know what it felt like, Grace,' Daniel told me later. After Nurse Jameson had bandaged my fingers. After Robert had been pizzled and his bum went red. After Miss Walsingham had phoned the Medical Superintendent from her home in the village to tell him Daniel had been found – he was safe and sound with her. After Daniel had been frog-marched the two and half miles back to the Briar, a male nurse on either side of him, one of them wheeling the bicycle. After the week in the pads – the first stage of his punishment.

When Daniel emerged from the pads, his eyes looked bruised and he had trouble walking.

'I wanted to know what it felt like,' he repeated.

We were sitting in Eric's rock garden. I wound my leg round Daniel's. My calf bulged white above its dark blue ankle sock and next to Daniel's blueish shinbone.

'I couldn't resist.'

I tightened the grip of my leg, and we swung for a while. Then Daniel flung back his head.

'It felt bloody fantastic. You should try it.'

He laughed, and how did he laugh? Simply, happily, like a boy in a storybook having an adventure. He leapt to his feet.

'Like this.' He closed his eyes, tilted his head. Silence.

'Like this.' Silence. Then, urgent,

'The wind in your hair. The tarmac, the earth underneath, the whole bloody universe beating in your feet. I cycled to the stars, Grace. Do you believe me?'

I stared at the pale little person in front of me. Only his closed eyelids, like folded wings, flittered. Yes, I believed him.

'The speed. My knees. The wheels and the pedals. Up and down, round and round. In time.' Daniel opened his eyes. 'An AA man, wearing a yellow cap, passed me on a motorcycle with a sidecar. He saluted.' Daniel grinned. 'That was the best bit.'

Daniel sat down and asked me to put my bandaged hand between his thighs.

I've seen how butchers bash at meat. That's what my hand felt like, a limp lump of battered meat. I was glad that Daniel couldn't see it, because it was ugly. But I wanted him to see it too, to see how he hurt me, going away like that, without a word.

The pressure of Daniel's leg muscles increased.

'I'm sorry, Grace. That's how I am.'

I know.

We heard the sound of Robert's bicycle bell and turned

our heads. Robert was pushing his bike up the path with one hand, waving with the other. He was hurrying. His legs seemed longer and thinner than ever, bending out at the knees, even though he was walking, not riding. He arrived, breathless, leant the bike on the bench.

'Eric wants to see you,' he panted, flicking his fingers at Daniel, at me.

'Now? Why?'

'No. Later. All of us. A fry-up.' Robert pumped his arms and twisted his head from side to side, which made his hair seem longer and redder than ever. 'In the hut. After lights out.'

'How's your bum, Rob?'

'Bad.'

Robert pulled down his shorts. Daniel gasped.

In fact, the streaks on Robert's bum were already beginning to fade. Daniel hadn't seen Robert last week, in the infirmary. Robert didn't cry by my side in the Medical Superintendent's office, where he was brought to watch my hand being rulered and then had to bend over and stick his freckled bum in the air. But he howled and squirmed like a puppy later, when the nurse dabbed cold water then yellow iodine on the reddening weals. Nobody believed that we knew nothing about Daniel's escape. We scarcely believed it ourselves.

'But not that bad.' Robert pulled up his shorts, took hold of the handlebars of the bike again and thrust the bike towards Daniel. 'Come on. I want to know how you did it. Spill.'

'Not now.'

'You owe us.'

'Yes.'

Later that night, when the fry-up had been eaten and the fire in the stove was pink and grey embers, Daniel took us on one of those journeys of his. To Paris.

He waited until the noise in the Nissen hut had almost died down before wriggling his bum off the bench and standing as tall as he could. He stood between Robert and a grown-up fitter called Charlie. Robert and Charlie shifted their bums into the gap left by Daniel. I sat opposite, next to Eric on one side and a pillow, folded in half, on the other. Let's give that arm of yours a rest, shall we? Eric had said.

'I was five,' Daniel began. 'Five and a half, to be precise. The trees were in blossom on the Champs-Elysées.'

He moved his head in a swivel – slow and controlled, not a twitch in sight – around the circle of fidgeting listeners. Somebody whistled.

'There was a gentle, southerly breeze,' Daniel continued calmly. 'Parisian petals, pink, white and stripy, swirled on the wide grey boulevard.'

'Boulevard?' boomed Charlie. 'Wassat?'

Shut up, shut up, shut the fuck up, Charlie, and Charlie, for once, shut up.

'I was learning to ride a bike,' Daniel went on. 'Dad gave it to me. Second-hand. Nearly new, Dad said. It had stabilizers, for balance. 'When can we take the stabilizers off, Papa?' I remember asking, over and over. 'Soon, son, I promise,' Dad always replied. But this particular spring morning, I asked and, 'Today, son,' said Dad.

'Dad held the saddle. He ran alongside. "*Vas-y, Dani,*" he shouted. "Don't grip so hard. Loosen your arms. Relax your fingers. Let the bike do the work. Imagine you're driving a Lamborghini." Dad and I were both out of breath.'

In the pause that followed, Daniel's shoes moved, just an inch or two. Odds on his toes were curling, like his fingers once curled around the handlebars of his bike on the Champs-Elysées.

Suddenly, '"*Vas-y, Dani!*" Papa let go of the saddle. "*Vas-y,*" he yelled. "*Pédale, pédale, pédale. Bravo, petit bonhomme*".'

Bravo, bravo. The Nissen hut filled with cheering.

'It was easy,' said Daniel, stepping back. He shrugged and sat down, squashed but unruffled, between Robert and Charlie. 'I remembered, that's all. I'd done it before. In Paris. I watched. I practised. Something like that. Mostly – look, no hands – I imagined.'

I'd seen him watching, I realized. When Robert rode all the way into the refectory, I'd seen Daniel watching and thought he was jealous.

So when had he practised?

'Oh, now and then.'

And did he really remember, or was he just good at telling stories?

Daniel would always have secrets, even from me.

The second part of Daniel's punishment was banishment from the engineers' team. Eric objected.

'There are maps in that boy's mind no one gives him credit for,' he insisted. 'In fact, someone clever enough to plan and execute such an escape is, in my opinion, clever enough to live outside.'

These words skittered – ow – but Eric, as usual, got his way, and by the end of September Daniel was back on the team. Daniel, however, never rode the bike again, not even on the crossbar, because red-haired Robert went and died in mid-October.

'No goodbyes, boys, just God bless.'

Mr Maitland suggested that Daniel take on Robert's job. Hospital messenger, a brand new bike, a privilege? No.

1958

The afternoon that Robert died, I was dusting the Briar's grand entrance hall. It was my job on Thursday afternoons – dusting. An extra job. It meant favours. It meant that the orderly who should have done the dusting could go and smoke or chat with his friends. It meant that the same orderly might help me slip out to meet Daniel and Robert.

I liked dusting and I was good at it because Mother had taught me how to do it. I was a real professional.

'Here, Gracie. Put this on.' Mother would lift one of her home-made aprons over my head. They were cut from her old summer dresses. She folded the apron once at the waist to shorten it, then wrapped it under my arms, bringing the ties round to the front and making a long bow with them in the middle of my chest.

'Let's roll those cuffs up.'

This was way before the iron lung. So I held both my forearms out, and Mother turned the cuffs of my sweater one, two, three times, nearly up to my elbow. First one arm, then the other. She'd usually give the sweater a tug, or my sides a pat, before placing a faded yellow duster in my right hand.

'Off you go, darling, a real professional.'

I felt funny but important swaddled in Mother's apron, as if it would make me behave like her. I dusted everything – window sills, ornaments, pictures, the skirting board, even the rungs of our dining-room chairs. It gets everywhere, dust.

Mother, who wore an apron too, switched the radio from the Home Service to the Light Programme. She Ewbanked the carpet, shook out the rugs, swept the floor and turned the volume up on the radio when Winnie Atwell and her piano came on.

'All the way from Trinidad to the Royal Academy. That's quite a journey, Grace.'

At the Briar, I always dusted the mantelpiece above the marble fireplace first. There was never anything on there, so it didn't take long. A swipe with the duster, which was identical to Mother's, one way, and a slower rub back the other. But I stood for a mo, envisaging cards and invitations – Grace Williams, At Home, We request the pleasure, You're invited, RSVP, a concert, a lecture, Come to our party.

Next, the narrow table, also bare, and the framed map of Europe beside it. Saggy-sock Italy, knobbly Britain, confusing Scandinavia. No Trinidad, though.

After the map, the mirror opposite, which I dusted quickly, trying not to look at the me reflected in it, but seeing me anyway. Why do mirrors always make things smaller than they really are? I'd like to be nine feet tall.

Daniel's dad's mirror was square, about five foot by five, each side alone longer than me. It had a thick gold frame with leafy curls, like a picture frame. Where did it come from? I knew it was old. Daniel's dad dealt in antiques.

'He imports and exports,' said Daniel importantly.

Daniel had talked about marble from Milan, tiles, leather and woodcarvings from the Alps and furniture from the flea markets in Paris. All packed into the back of a white Commer van.

'And then the road.' Daniel paused, and the spider on his forehead crawled. 'Before the plane.'

That aeroplane.

I gave the yellow duster a shake.

I dusted the brass door handles and the painted wooden beading on the insides of all the doors. I avoided the banister. Robert had discovered you could unscrew the knobs at either end of the brass banister that ran all the way up the first flight of stairs. The banister was hollow. Things could be poked up from the bottom or dropped in at the top. Last week, Robert had filled the whole banister up with conkers. He'd chosen conkers just small enough so they didn't get stuck, then he'd deliberately left the knob at the bottom end loose. You can imagine what happened when the Medical Superintendent put his hand on the loose brass knob at the bottom of the banister and it came off. I could. I can. We laughed. I laugh now.

Last, because it was the dirtiest, I dusted the outside of the black front door.

When I opened the door that afternoon, I saw Eric with a group of crazy fitters, mostly juniors, and including Robert and Daniel. They were on the visitors' lawn, which was already half-covered in fallen leaves. Even though it wasn't windy. Even though a gang of patients had spent all morning raking the leaves into piles, and the afternoon wheeling them, in metal barrows, to Mr Peters' compost heap

The crazy fitter boys were collecting conkers, filling their pockets and brown paper bags with them, making a right old racket, shouting, crunching and kicking at the leaves, blowing up the paper bags and bursting them.

There was a conker-fight league table pinned to the wall in the Nissen hut. Robert and Daniel were at the top of it. Everybody was bonkers about conkers that year.

Daniel called them Indian chestnuts. He soaked his in vinegar stolen from the kitchen, then he gave them to Toby, who carried them into the gatehouse and baked them for Daniel in his oven.

Robert's collection of conkers was small. In fact, many of his conkers were small too, wrinkled and unruly. He spent a long time choosing his conkers, though, refusing to break open their spiny green shells, taking only conkers that were already loose, already on the ground. And Robert kept his conkers all over his body, not just crammed into his pockets, but twisted into the sleeves of his shirt, tucked into his socks, and once, just to see if he could, dropped like toffees into the curls that crackled on his head.

I stopped pretending to dust, and stared. The boys had formed themselves into a semicircle now, around Robert and Daniel. A conker fight was about to begin.

Robert couldn't keep still. He twirled his conker on its string above his head and windmilled his other arm at the same time. Daniel sat on the grass and emptied his collection of ready-stringed conkers from their paper bag. He removed a shoe and sock, inserted his toe into the loop of a piece of string, then leant back and raised his foot. A large, round conker dangled from the end of the string.

Eric put his hands on Robert's shoulders, calming him, bringing his arms down to his sides. Robert nodded enthusiastically and knelt on the grass with his knees together but his shins splayed and his head still nodding.

Eric tossed a coin and Robert took first shot at Daniel's conker.

Daniel's turn. Then Robert again.

I knew that Daniel's glossy conker was a mere fiver, whereas Robert's was already a twenty-fiver. The winning conker, Daniel had explained, would become a thirty-oner. Its owner would be at the top of the league table. But neither conker won.

Robert conked out. Keeled over. Died. Just like that.

I saw Daniel take aim again at Robert's swinging conker. Waiting for the swinging to stop. He flicked. Missed. The string caught the string of Robert's conker. As the two strings twisted and knotted, Robert let go, and at the same time he fell forwards. From where I was standing, it looked as if Robert was praying, his two arms uplifted, his hands reaching for the conker entwined with Daniel's. Robert's arms came down and he seemed to stare at the ground in surprise before toppling sideways, staying like that for a few seconds, then rolling slowly on to his back.

The two conkers bounced away together across the lawn, and I saw one of the crazy fitter boys pick them up and pocket them both. Robert's hair caught the autumn sun, and he didn't look uncomfortable lying there, glowing among the leaves. No waving limbs, no fitting, hiccupping body. But no Robert either. Just his name echoing in the still October air, Daniel calling it again and again.

It was a couple of weeks after this that Mother and Father brought baby Sarah to visit me at the Briar. My twelfth birthday. The day that Sarah walked. Nobody talked about Robert.

But a few days after that, I had another visitor.

'So you're Grace.' Robert's mother, as wiry and red as her son. 'Lena Macintosh. Delighted to meet you.'

We were sitting opposite each other on chairs in the grown-up day room. Robert's mother had moved the chairs away from the wall and turned them to face each other. She took my good hand between her two better ones. Our knees touched. Lena Macintosh wore grey trousers with a ridge up the middle of each leg, and a matching jacket. My arm rested on her leg and I felt firm, unladylike muscles through the soft material of her trousers. I looked down and saw that she had a pair of men's black lace-ups on her feet, which were thin and very long.

'I've heard so much about you.'

Robert's mother peered at me, making me look up again. She wore speckle-edged specs, and her eyes behind them were small and slatey. She had a pale face, and her Robert-hair was curly, but shorter and thinner than Robert's.

'Robert was a great fan,' she continued.

My own blue jelly-eyes slipped when she said this. Salty slicks down both my cheeks.

Buddy Holly? Oh, I'm a great fan. James Dean? Botticelli? Oxford United? Grace Williams? Oh yes, I'm a great fan. Yes indeed. I could imagine posh Robert gesticulating with those long arms of his, spindling the words from his tripping mouth.

She was arranging a memorial service, Robert's mother went on, as if we were sisters arranging a birthday party. Here in the hospital chapel. She wanted suggestions, help. She wanted to involve people.

'You're invited,' she might have said. She definitely said, 'He had a heart attack, Grace. I paid for a private post-mortem. There's no blame.'

She should have tried saying that to Daniel, who didn't speak for a very long time, and when he did, he had no doubt that the blame lay with him.

He told me so, eventually, as we sat on one of the abandoned rabbit hutches in the tool-shed, which is where Daniel went to be silent, this time.

It was dusty and warm inside the tool-shed. Eric had removed the bird cages and fitted shelves and a fold-down work surface along one side. He was thinking of making a darkroom, he said, a photography club.

Robert's bike leant against the timber wall, opposite us.

When Daniel spoke, 'How will I ever know I didn't pull, Grace?' he asked. 'Pull him? Pull the string, I mean?'

Daniel's face was shrivelled and bloodless, his voice raw and dry from hiding it away for so long.

'I know,' I said, putting my good hand on the back of his neck, smoothing it down round the hunch of his shoulder.

Daniel moved away an inch. He didn't like me touching him there. So I stroked his neck again, keeping my fingers still, but rubbing and pressing with my thumb on the warm dip at the back. As if it were the palm of a hand.

I knew none of it was Daniel's fault. I was there, I was watching, I saw. Plus, I knew by now about the heart attack. I told Daniel about that too then, and I remembered Robert's mother's words – 'no blame' – exactly.

The memorial service took place two weeks after this, two weeks before Christmas. There we all were, including Daniel, packed into the chapel, almost silent at first, because Robert's mother wanted it that way. It wasn't silent, but it was quite, quite quiet. Until the singing. 'Lord of All Hopefulness', chosen by Eric, who had helped sway the decision in favour of the service. The doctors were against a memorial service for Robert, saying it would renew all the upset. And people were upset. Miss Blackburn cancelled school for several days. Toby wept and kept opening the gates at the wrong time. And Eric, when he wasn't swaying decisions, stayed, unusually inactive, in the Nissen hut.

The crazy fitters chose 'All Things Bright and Beautiful' for the memorial service, because the line about creatures great and small made them chuckle, remembering the zoo. And we also had 'When a knight won his spurs, in the stories of old'. Miss Blackburn did a high, birdy singalong when it came to the thumping castle of darkness and power of the truth in the last line. I don't think she can have chosen the hymn, though, because she told us she didn't believe in God.

There were flowers, including a twiggy wreath with autumn leaves made by Mr Peters' team, and there was a single candle burning on the altar, which I'd dusted that morning along with the pulpit and the tops of all the pews, aligning the pale red Books of Common Prayer on the shelves underneath. No speeches, no sermons. Eleanor Maitland played quietly on the organ, the chaplain gave a quick blessing, then Robert's mother stood up and said refreshments and a surprise were waiting for us in the refectory. We bustled eagerly out of the chapel, across the grounds, and in through the side door that led, via a dark corridor, to the main hospital refectory.

Last year, all of us had helped decorate the refectory, ready for Christmas. We'd been herded into the grown-up dining room to find the tables covered in hundreds of red and green strips of paper.

We had to sit down, and those of us who could had to make circles out of the strips of paper by licking the sticky end and pressing it flat on the other end. The nurses clustered in a far corner of the room, dithering around the Christmas tree and the men putting it up. We, meanwhile, stuck and pressed, stuck and pressed, and nobody remembered to tell us we were supposed to loop each ring through another.

Paper chains. I would become an expert, but not immediately. Torn and spit-sodden strips of paper soon began to litter the floor as well as the tables. It wasn't until Major Simpson arrived in the refectory that order was restored.

Everybody liked Major Simpson, even the nurses, who usually sneered at volunteers and called them a nuisance, nosey-parkers, or worse. The Major visited several times a week. He coached the Briar's cricket and football teams. He also ran the games room, including a gluey hobbies section and a quiet corner, with trestle tables for chess and stamp-collecting.

In the refectory, the Major bossed and coaxed, setting the nurses even more afluster with his good-humoured huffing and puffing.

'Nonsense, pretty sister.' This to a lowly orderly, not

pretty, not a sister at all. 'There's plenty of time. Let's get these decorations hung.'

He made some of the nurses sit down next to us and help. He sent the men to fetch ladders. He told us to keep up the good work. Circles, he said, were AOK. However, he whisked a few of the children off to a special table, where he taught them how to thread a flat strip of paper through one that had already been made into a circle. Then, how to lick it and link it. Dainty Daniel, the Briar's clever cobbler-boy, was whisked, of course. But Robert went too. This didn't seem right. Robert hadn't a clue when it came to fiddly, fingery things.

I could do the oranges and I could do the paper chains. So I did. Big Ida saw. She couldn't do any of it. Heavy arms like bags of flour and doughy hands that would never unwobble enough to thread paper chains. It was easy for me, because of my bad arm. I hung the circle of paper on the rigid fist of my useless hand, and it hung there so still, it wasn't hard to poke the next flat strip of paper through the hole in the middle. Nor was it hard to bend the paper, lean, dribble, wipe and stick it.

Ida didn't like this. She lunged at the growing pile of red paper chain between us. At the same time, she pushed back her chair and stood up. The paper chain went up in the air and, for a split second, looked very pretty hanging there – a giant version of Robert's hair. Then it fell back down to the table, collapsing in on itself, and Ida hauled it towards her boosies, grabbing and scrunching the paper circles as she hauled.

But Major Simpson had glimpsed the prettiness I'd made. 'Out,' he ordered, and Ida obeyed. She simply turned away from the table, the mess, me. She walked out without a word, and nobody went after her until Major Simpson signalled at Sister, the real sister this time, to follow. Then he came over to where I was sitting and put his fist on my head. It was a heavy fist – a bit too heavy, but I don't think he meant it to be.

'What's your name?' he asked. And when I didn't reply, 'Well, Nelson, I think you'd better come and join the experts.' He led me to the table where Robert and Daniel were busy-boying happily, squadging the paper chains into all sorts of noodly shapes. I sat down. We worked as a team, and Daniel officially baptized my bad arm Nelson. Without Nelson, he said, we wouldn't have made nearly such a good team.

On the day of Robert's memorial, the refectory was bare and cold. No paper chains and no sign of the promised refreshments. The only difference from every other day was that the upright piano, normally pushed back to front in a corner, stood open against the wall, and a table had been placed alongside it. On top of the table was one of the low chairs from the COU.

The nurses were unable to settle us. Major Simpson walked up and down the aisles, wiping his forehead with his square white handkerchief as if it were summer. Robert's mother stood nervously by the piano. The nurses hushed and shoved, and some of them, out of habit, swung their sticks or keys warningly.

Only Daniel didn't need shushing. He sat by himself, composed and quiet, at the far end of one of the tables, not, for once, with the crazy fitters, but with the boys from his ward, and close to Miss Blackburn, who was in charge of the table. She looked grim and sad, not unlike Mother on my birthday last month. At school recently, Miss Blackburn often paused and looked out of the window, frowning – not cross, but as if puzzled by something.

Suddenly the double doors of the refectory crashed open and, for a mo, I half-expected to see Robert himself cycling through them, but no, it was Eric. He was carrying a small boy over his shoulder, like he carried me, just as firmly, just as gently. Silence fell as Eric made his way across the room to the piano.

The boy, who looked about eight years old, wore a smart shorts' suit with empty sleeves tucked into the pockets. He had bare legs and feet. His dark hair was razored short at the back and sides, but slicked shiny and long on top. I saw brown berry-eyes, a small nose, neat white teeth and a smiling mouth over Eric's shoulder as they passed my table.

Eric sat the boy on the chair, and almost before Eric had straightened up again, the boy started playing the piano. Bang, bang, bang on the out-of-tune keys. Bang, bang with his feet went this cheerful little chappy.

Daniel, like before, when Robert delivered Miss Blackburn's parcel, stood on the table and stared and stared. Look, no hands. But today Daniel wasn't the only one to leap on to a table. The boy played jazzy tunes with a ragged beat that got people going – stomping, thumping, singing and clapping.

The double doors opened again, and this time no fewer than six bakers, wearing tall white bakers' hats, walked into the refectory. Each was carrying a pile of boxes. The boxes contained cakes – fairy cakes, cup cakes and slices of Battenberg, doughnuts, iced buns and whirls of Swiss roll. Nobody mentioned sandwiches again. Everybody tucked in except the boy, who went on smiling and playing.

'Eat as much as you like,' called Lena Macintosh above the hubbub. 'Dance. Enjoy yourselves. It's what Robert would have wanted.'

Grown-ups danced with children, and nurses danced with patients. Daniel, still standing on his table, looked across the room at me and did his making-up-for-things nod. Robert's mother went over to Daniel's table and whispered in Miss Blackburn's ear. Miss Blackburn whispered back. Robert's mother stretched her arms out to Daniel, and Daniel, believe it or not, jumped right into them.

1959

i

'Believe it or not, I enjoyed myself that day,' Daniel said later. Several wintry weeks later. We were sitting in the classroom, discussing holidays. Miss Blackburn had popped out to get paper. 'Shhh, though. It's a secret,' Daniel added.

Daniel had said the same about the recent Christmas holiday.

'Believe it or not, I enjoyed myself here at Christmas. Shhh, though. That's a secret too. Secrets and stories – yours, Grace, and mine.' Daniel tapped my shoe, once, with his.

He'd devised a system of taps, he said, based on the pipe-tapping done by some of the adult patients in the main hospital building. He described how the pipes spread out from the boiler room, like veins or arteries, along the corridors, through the walls, ceilings and floors to all the wards. If you had friends in the ward next door or above or below you, he said, you could talk to them by tapping.

'As simple as that.' He tapped my shoe again. 'Tap back, Grace.'

I did.

'See? Easy,' he tapped. 'Let's call it G for Grace. Tap back.'

I did.

'And D for me. Good. It means we can share, secretly.'

Daniel hadn't left the Briar at all over Christmas. But he'd secretly been all over the place, he said.

'And I learnt to type as well,' he added. 'Tappety-tap. What do you think of that, Grace Williams?'

'The truth?' I asked. I knew by now that Daniel didn't always tell things straight, or whole. Mostly over-whole and flowery.

He said that the office ladies had started leaving the administration block unlocked at lunchtime. He'd nipped in and had a shot at using one of the typewriters.

'It's not as hard you'd think,' he said. 'I use both my big toes. I'm making progress.'

One day, Miss Walsingham came back earlier than usual. She was accompanied by Mr Shipman, the young assistant bursar. Daniel didn't hear them open the outer door of the office. The inner door was a large, glass-panelled affair. They could have been watching him for ages, Daniel said. When the inner door opened, Daniel stopped typing and froze, with his heels resting on the desktop. He felt the soft, hot pressure of hands on his shoulders.

'Miss.' He jerked his head round and up in fear.

'Don't panic,' said the secretary. 'It's Daniel, isn't it? Don't be frightened.' Her hands moved down his back, then up again, then down both his sides.

'She squeezed and rubbed, stroked and pumped. I expanded like a loaf of bread.'

Miss Walsingham's closeness and warmth, her damp, summery, country smell turned the inside of Daniel's head, he said, into a luscious southern landscape of low hills, distant seas, white villas and wine-drenched meals on shaded terraces, with lemons, big fat melons, black olives and cold, fruity pink wine – the best *rosé*.

'I replaced my clothes,' he said, jiggling the empty sleeves of his too-big, not-too-clean jumper. 'I replaced them with a white linen shirt, fine and cool, with grown-up cuffs and silver cufflinks. A grey silk handkerchief. Pressed, dove-grey trousers and Italian shoes, handmade. I put my feet on the floor, sat bolt upright in the chair and looked Miss Walsingham in the eye. Debonair.'

'You're the boy who tried to escape, aren't you? On the bicycle. I'm Joan, remember? Joan Walsingham.'

Mr Shipman sidled off at this point, and Miss Walsingham set about discovering exactly how well Daniel could type and what he was typing. By the time the rest of the pool returned from lunch, Miss Walsingham was overflowing with excitement. She was very young, Daniel said, twenty, twenty-one at most. Miss Bradshaw, Mrs King and Miss O'Donnell were older, sceptical at first, but Miss Walsingham showed them Daniel's work.

'It was just lists, Grace. You know – cricket scores, makes of car, people's names. That sort of thing. You should have seen their faces, though.'

Daniel raised his eyebrows, made his eyes big and opened his mouth, all at the same time.

'Miss Walsingham leant over me to pull the sheet of paper out of the machine,' he continued, 'and the top of her bare arm touched my cheek. It was so soft. Like a boosy. But damp. Whiffy with soap and lawn, newly cut.'

Miss Walsingham, he said, let him rest his cheek there while she turned the knob at the side of the typewriter until the piece of paper came free. She took it out and put it down next to the typewriter. Then she inserted a fresh piece of paper at the back, and turned the knob until the paper curled underneath, round and up at the front. She told Daniel to type something else.

'I obliged. "Take a look at this," she said when I'd finished, passing the piece of paper to Mrs King, who read it aloud.'

Lists of football teams, types of aeroplane, all sorts of leather.

'"Mocha, morocco, levant," Mrs King recited. She sounded so funny, Grace. Like the chaplain, reading a prayer. "Chamois, cordovan, cabretta, chevrette. Skiver, slink, rawhide. Gracious,"' Daniel imitated, '"Goodness gracious me, I think he's spelt them all correctly too."'

Mrs King thought they ought to report it immediately. Miss Walsingham begged her to wait. Mrs King looked at Daniel's typing again and said they'd have to see, it was the holidays, after all, she supposed it was harmless, but for now, Daniel must return to his ward.

Daniel went back to the office the next day, and the next, and whenever he wanted to after that, because the typing ladies decided to keep quiet about their discovery.

'They've adopted me,' he said. 'They let me sit in their office and type or watch them type and work.'

Often they stopped working, though, Daniel said, and started chatting instead. He joined in and asked questions that made them laugh. Miss Walsingham fed him buttery bits of shortbread and little squares of home-made fruit cake. Every evening, before putting on her cardigan and coat to go home, she dabbed her neck and wrists with perfume.

'"Blue Grass", it's called,' Daniel said. 'On Christmas Eve, she put a drop on my forehead and under my chin.'

Daniel had spent Christmas day with Eric and the left-over fitters in the Nissen hut. Some bottles of wine from Mr Maitland's wine cellar found their way to the Nissen hut, and everybody had a sip. It was purple and stained your lips, Daniel said. Probably Burgundy. Papa would have known. But Papa, Daniel said, was *en panne* in Kent. A tyre on his white Commer van had burst. On the road out of Dover. The hilly A20. He'd been obliged to hole up with a mate down there.

'But he sent me this. From Paris.' Daniel toe-pulled a handkerchief, silky grey, from the sleeve of his dirty grey jumper, like the magician with his top hat who performed on the children's wards just before Christmas.

A clown came too, but I missed him. I, Grace Williams, by written request and with written permission, did go home for Christmas that year.

Sarah was everywhere – into everything, as everybody said. She was nine months old. Her eyes were blue and often fierce. Sometimes they turned into the eyes of a cold wet fish, trapped, not in a net – Sarah could wriggle her way out of anything – but in a strange, blue-green sea-world of their own.

By Christmas, Sarah rarely fell. She made for whatever she had her blue eye on with noisy shouts, one arm, or both, held out in front of her. Ah, she would sigh, when she reached what she wanted. She would sit down on the floor to explore the brick, the doll, the teaspoon, John's book – don't tear it. Father's pipe – don't suck it. Mother's blue Murano vase – too late.

Sarah wanted to explore me that Christmas. She clambered all over me when I lay on the couch, resting. She prodded my gob with her bickiepeg fingers, tried to uncurl Nelson, using both her hands, and touched or tugged my pudding-basin hair. My hair had coarsened. It was darker and straighter than before. There wasn't often shampoo at the Briar, and when there was, it definitely wasn't Vosene.

Sometimes Sarah touched or tugged her own baby-thin hair afterwards, thoughtfully, and then her eyes went fishy. If I was lying on my side on the couch, there was nothing Sarah liked more than to squirm her body next to mine, nose to nose. When she settled, she would suck her thumb, keeping her elbow bent, sharp, and her arm wodged, tight like my Nelson, to her side. Then her other hand would creep over my shoulder to my back, where it just reached my hump. She would stroke my hump, her fingers as light as eyelashes, and we would lie there, entranced, eye to eye.

But when Sarah cried, she didn't sound hungry or tired, just angry or awfully sad, and nobody knew what to do. Father held her with his back to the window.

'Look over my shoulder, *elskling*,' he'd say.

Miranda tried the pram. John read aloud. Mother, at the end of her tether, went to bed.

All in all, I didn't see much of Mother over Christmas. She took a lot of tablets. 'And not just Rennies,' whispered John to Miranda.

Miranda, home from abroad for the holidays, danced and pranced like a creamed cat, making private long-distance phone calls on the phone in the hall when she thought no one could hear.

'*Oui. Moi aussi, je t'aime*, cherry-pot. Oops. Sorry. Got to go. *Maman descend les* stairs.'

But Mother did hear, more than once. She shouted and burst into tears, while Miranda burst into tears and flounced. Out of the house, sometimes.

When this happened, John would set off for his bedroom, a stack of *Scientific American*s in his arms, so big and heavy he often dropped them on the stairs. More tears.

On calm days, John went into the kitchen. He was painting a wooden box in there.

'I'm banning the bomb,' he said, sandpapering carefully.

He painted the box white with a large black sign on the side. The kitchen was cold and smelt of turps and paint, not marmalade and turkey. The paint dripped. It dripped down the side of the box and on to the floor. The sign was spoilt, Mother's lino was a mess and Mother was so cross, she knocked John's box over, breaking the lid. An accident, she said. John, sobbing in hiccups, went to his bedroom without his magazines.

Most days, I lay on the couch in the sitting room, with Sarah mucking around on the floor, and Father in the armchair, reading, or at Mother's sewing table, working –

always forgetting to light the gas fire at four o'clock, which is when Mother told him to.

'No, Sarah,' he'd sigh patiently, moving the squiggly music manuscripts away from the edge of the table, giving Sarah a dangerous silver bobbin to play with instead, or once, daft man, Mother's heavy pair of pinking shears.

Mother took a turn for the worse towards the end of the holiday. I think Father forgetting my bed-wetting pills had something to do with it. And because Father didn't drive, due to his dicky heart, and no one could be found to look after Sarah for the day, I went back to the Briar in a taxi. Not all the way, but for some of it, and by myself. A nurse was sent to meet me and three other patients at King's Cross, but from our house to King's Cross, I travelled alone and peaceful in a black London cab.

The driver didn't talk to me. It was bitterly cold outside, with flurries of snow in the midday grey. There was a radiator in the cab, though, sending out hot air and a summery drone, like Mr Peters' bees. I was tucked between the soft black arm of the seat and Miranda's old knapsack. She'd given it to me to put my things in, instead of the cardboard box I'd come home with from the Briar.

'Keep it, kitten,' she'd said. 'I need a new one, anyway. I'll be off again soon.'

Feeling more like a queen than a kitten, I sat up straight in the back of the taxi and stared straight ahead. But the taxi didn't go straight at first, and I couldn't help woggling my eyes, then my head, at icy London, to my left, to my right. The people were bright against the dull buildings, and many of them were hurrying. We stopped for traffic lights – 'bloody Marylebone Road,' said the driver. A man standing in a queue – 'bloody Madame Tussauds' – smiled and waved at me. He flapped his arms over his chest to keep them warm. He was wearing a knitted black hat pulled down over his ears, and a long yellow scarf wound twice around his neck. I waved at the man, not queenly at all, but woolly and warm, inside and out. I'd have preferred to be travelling in the opposite direction, but I enjoyed that cab ride very much.

Back at the Briar, before Miss Blackburn reappeared in the classroom, Daniel told me that Robert's mother, Eric and Major Simpson between them were planning to raise enough money, through private donations and charitable organizations, to start a holiday fund for the children at the Briar.

'The armless little piano player caused quite a stir, Grace.'

He was, it turned out, the son of a friend of a friend of Eric's. Nobody special. Nothing wrong with him. Just born with no arms, God bless. Nor did he really have any great musical talent.

'But,' said Daniel, 'he has sweetness, innocence and a smile that melts hearts and opens purses.'

Eric's friend of a friend was letting his son be used as a gimmick, a sort of mascot to help with hospital fund-raising.

We never saw him again. I've never heard of him since.

Daniel said it was a wool-pulling scandal, letting people think that the Briar was full of cute, piano-playing kiddiewinks, but he was the first to admit we'd benefited.

'Those cakes, Grace. Remember? Oops.' Daniel twiddled his bum on the seat, put his feet straight and neat on the floor as Miss Blackburn swept through the door. 'Shhh.'

I remembered with relish. Especially the bloody red doughnuts – their sweet gritty skin and curdy insides. Squittering jam on our lips and tongues. Ditto our faces, the tables, our clothes. My clothes in the knapsack, my holiday at home.

And now another holiday to look forward to.

Margate or Hastings – where would it be? Bournemouth, Sidmouth or Southend-on-Sea?

'Good out of bad,' said Daniel. 'That old Indian chestnut.'

And then, as the trees changed colour again and again, the holidays to talk about – Bognor or Barnstable, which was better? Whitsun in Whitstable or September in Weston-super-Mare?

And now the holidays all rolled together. Pevensey, Clacton-on-Sea, and let's not forget Torquay '63. Three cheers for the Macintosh holiday fund.

In the end it was Eastbourne, that first, memorable year, but I always adored those jolly, if not sunny, Briar holidays by the sea.

Sitting beside Daniel on the coach or train, swapping sandwiches – meat paste for Marmite – sticky thighs, itchy heads, scorching hard windows, and the nurses' quick hands as they helped us out. The flighty, sweaty heat of them. They always asked permission to leave their uniforms behind. It was always refused. Nevertheless, there was a mufti lightness in their step, a saucy brightness in their eyes, and even Matron sometimes smiled.

Look. The sea, the sea, there was the sea. Often, because it was low-season June or early October, livid and full of heaving, breaking waves. A spray-shock on my face, eye-sting – cold – and a surprised tongue of salt, making me mashmack my lips and spew with my mouth.

Daniel said he didn't like the sea – it made him claustrophobic. He said the sea was a grave, and a watery one at that. Drowning is meant to be a pleasant, painless way to die, Daniel said, but he believed it must be like being buried alive, only worse. Imagine the pressure of all that water – the airlessness and then, when your body and all your insides are nothing but silence and dark, that terrible sinking feeling.

I knew that feeling, but I didn't agree, and anyway – hip hip hooray – Daniel liked the other sides of the sea. He liked the seaside. Like everybody.

When it was sunny, we sat on the stony beach. Bony buttocks on the tartan rugs donated for this very purpose by the kind Friends of the Briar. We all wore hats – caps, berets and knotted hankies – which frequently blew off, making us splutter and chunter after them. Only Daniel had a proper straw sun hat – a college boater, Grace. How he acquired it he refused to say, even to me.

Our legs burnt easily, unused to so much sun. The nurses were supposed to drape our legs with towels, but they often forgot. Hip hip hooray. The hot sun pinned us in the glassy landscape for what seemed a happy nearly ever after. The towels made us sweat and fiddle. Without them, I could sit and see the sea, see the people paddling in the sea, see the man's rolled-up trousers, how he held them, ridiculously, at the knee, prancing like a horse. The woman was wearing a spotty swimming costume, baggy at the belly. She might have been pregnant. The woman was holding a child's hand. The man took the child's other hand. One, two, three and away. The child was swung high up over the shallow, lapping water. She shrieked with pleasure and fear, her parents smiling at each other above her head.

After finishing our sandwiches and toing and froing to the public conveniences, we usually moved into the shade of a high, sparkling wall which ran all the way along the beach. We were made to lie down on rugs and towels for a rest. Lots of people went to sleep, including the nurses. Nurse Jameson snored so loudly once that Matron pinched her nose, then pushed her jaw up to close her mouth, but it kept falling open again, and Nurse Jameson went on snoring and snoring. It wasn't until Matron bellowed in her ear that she woke up. Usually so round-faced and pretty, Nurse Jameson was squished now, too pink, and there was a dribble of saliva down the side of her chin.

In the afternoon it was particularly hot, and, while I lay

on my back, Daniel turned on his side and whispered in my ear.

'Keep very still, Grace.' His breath was hotter than the air.

Then he blew in my ear and whispered the names of the winds that he knew. Over and over, a flurry of words. Trade winds, east winds, the cold north wind, which the French call the *bise*. Kiss, kiss. And he was off. Foehn, mistral, tramontane. Bora, levanter, harmattan. Chinook, sirocco, willy-willy.

Giggle-giggle. But he continued all the same, on and on, blowing and whispering.

'In the eye of the wind, you can be anywhere, Grace. Honolulu, Madagascar, St-Tropez. Imagine Australia, Japan, the U.S. of A.'

Santa Maria de Castellabate.

I was lulled like a cradle, the song of my limbs, usually off-key and jerky, stilled in the soft wadding of the sand to the half-forgotten lilt of Father's grey-flecked jersey, watery shadows and a creamy white ceiling, the big wooden radiogram playing, over and over, the black crackled records of German *lieder*, light opera, flitty-ditty songs sung in English by men with deep, freeing voices. Wonderful, wonderful Copenhagen, Englishmen in the midday sun and tiny Thumbelina, who grew to nine feet tall.

Nine feet tall, the nasty deckchair man who suddenly stood in front of the long row of more or less seated but squirming, twitching bodies.

'Who's in charge here?' he asked.

Matron stood up. The man touched his cap, respectfully, except it wasn't respectful.

'Deckchairs, ma'am?'

'No thank you.' Matron had her back to us. She smoothed her palms over the tight material of her uniform, which had damp patches on the bum. Then she put her hands on her waist, and I saw, through the strong, firm curves of her arms, the sea, the sea – two halves of a heart.

The words of the man were a wheedling, needling sing-song.

'I'll do you a deal. How many of them mentals d'you have there? Fifteen? Eighteen? I'll do you three for the price of two. What d'you say?'

'We like sitting on the ground,' said Matron firmly.

The man glanced along the line of us, where several nurses were leaning forwards listening. Some of the children were gabbling and starting to flap. Daniel had stood up.

'Suit yourself,' said the deckchair man. 'You'd look less of a sight, though.'

'No. Thank you.'

'Well, don't change your mind, love. You won't catch me back here in a hurry. What a job. I don't envy you, Sister.'

'I am Matron,' said Matron. 'And I'm proud of the job I do. Good day, young man.'

She turned round then and came back towards us. Her small bare feet were red and swollen in the pebbles, and they made puffs of heat and dust with each scooped step she took. Daniel cheered and some of the squirmers tried to join in, but Matron told them sharply to stop. She reprimanded the nurses for eavesdropping – shame on you, girls – and she told Daniel to expect extra breakfast duties next week. Nevertheless, Matron was a heroine. That hot day, at least.

Someone would invariably get burnt, be sick or need the toilet again, so we rarely sat on the beach for more than an hour at a time. We would loiter along the seafront, and when it rained, we trooped into a tearoom, with steam rising from the damp Formica, from people's wet clothes and from our dripping hair.

'Soaked to the bone,' chortled the nurses cheerfully, ordering flowery, rippling cups of tea which spilled in the saucers and dripped on the table-tops, dulling the scattered sugar-grain glitter.

People were always getting lost on holiday, so it wasn't a surprise when Jesse failed to answer to his name one afternoon roll-call. We carried our shoes, with socks rolled or stuffed inside them, up some steep steps, which had only a rope-rail to hold. I closed my eyes and the world went red, with wavy lines scorching through my eyelids. When Daniel turned round, lumpy at the hips where I'd stuffed his shoes into the pockets of his shorts for him, I laughed. Daniel laughed back and said I looked drunk. What shall we do with the drunken sailor?

Return to that esplanade above the beach. It was wide and patterned with flowerbeds, phone booths and stripey pastel kiosks selling candy floss, ice cream and pink rods of rock.

The nurses sat us down on benches on the esplanade. We were told to keep our eyes peeled while some of the staff went to search along the water's edge. I put my good arm across Daniel's back and let my hand rest on his waist, like we did when the grown-up day room turned into a makeshift, night-time cinema, which it did every third Saturday of the month. As soon as the lights were switched off, we copied – aged twelve, fourteen, sixteen – the grown-ups canoodling on the screen and, semi-unseen, on the chairs around us. We watched lots of good films and bad films, and many films again and again – Fred Astaire and Ginger Rogers, *Casablanca*, Rick and Ilsa, *Brief Encounter*, *The Wizard of Oz*. But mostly, that year, westerns, goodies and baddies. That's how Jesse got his name.

It was Daniel, naturally, who christened him.

Jesse was simple and rickety. He was the son of a Welsh sheep farmer. He'd only been at the Briar a few months.

I wondered why he couldn't be simple and rickety at home. He was a twin, and his real name was James. James Jackson. But when you asked him his name, he looked at the floor and said, 'Frank.'

'Frank what?'

'Jackson. Jackson. Jackie Jackson's twins. Daddy Jackie. Daddy's good boy. Daddy's bad boy.'

He refused to answer to the name of James, and at first he was teased. He loved the westerns. He went to the day room straight after tea on those Saturday evenings. He took one of the hard wooden chairs from behind the nurses' desk, carried it close to the screen, then turned it round and sat with his stick-legs and Charlie Chaplin lace-ups in zigzags down each side. His hands, white and knubbly, clutched the top of the back of the chair. And he stayed like that all evening. Afterwards, he would burst with energy, bouncing up and down on the chair, shouting, trying to run around the room. We all had our heads full of moll-toting, gunslinging goodies and baddies. The nurses hated every third Saturday of the month and did deals to change shift.

One evening, on our way out of the day room, people were talking and jostling as usual, some of the boys were yee-ha-ing, and Jesse was lassoing with his arms and braying. The screen was still illuminated. Jesse ran in front of it and stopped. Big black letters stretched across the screen, announcing the cast. First up was Jesse James.

'Look,' said Daniel. 'Jesse James. Hey! Jesse. What do you think? Cowboys. Heroes. Villains. Frank and Jesse James.'

At the word Frank, Jesse stopped running, turned towards us, nodded solemnly, then walked as quiet and good-boy as John to school, to join the queue. The name stuck.

So Daniel found Jesse a name, but in Eastbourne, Jesse was nowhere to be found, and two of the nurses were sent to fetch help.

The rest of us continued to sit on the wooden benches. Daniel linked his left foot round my right and swung his leg back and forth, rough-scudding our heels on the warm paving stone. Matron was on the other side of me, half turned away, talking to the nurse on the end of the next bench. Matron's back was vast and blue like the sky, but solid, alive and warm on my cheek when I let my head and my neck droop blubbery-sleepy next to it.

The two nurses didn't come back for a long time. When they did, accompanied by a policeman, they looked dull and creased, like at the end of a long night shift. Matron, Sister and the nurses formed a group around the policeman standing in the stripey shade of one of the confectionary kiosks.

It was hot, they were hazy and I was thirsty now. My canvas hat had become too tight and Daniel's leg-swinging irritating. Sister and some more nurses walked away with the policeman, but we continued to sit on the benches. When the younger children began to whimper, one of the remaining nurses went to the kiosk and came back with ice lollies, Orange Maids, for everybody. She had to make several trips, but she didn't seem to mind. She talked to the man behind the counter, who leant over, then pinched the nurse's chin between his thumb and index finger. The nurse threw back her head and laughed.

When she'd finished handing out the lollies, the nurse told us there was a special method for removing the wrapper and she would show us. First, she said, you had to put the bottom of the lolly – like this – the stick and a mouthful of wrapper, into your mouth, and blow.

'Look. Off slides the wrapper. Go on. Try it. Watch me. Here it comes. Now you must lick it. Quick.'

The Orange Maids, damp in their wrappers, demanded to be licked. But the nurse's method was impossible for some – Daniel for one, me for another. So we peeled and pulled and eventually sucked away the sodden shreds of paper. My mouth lost its flabby droop, though, as the cold of the Orange Maid pierced my tongue, my gums, my throat. I became a suck suck sucker of sweetness, holding the little wooden baton and sucking that too until it splintered – thumb and fingers sticky-stick-sticks.

Daniel stood up and sidled behind a man with a camera. 'Grace's lolly holiday,' he jollied the man. 'Do take her picture.'

A nurse told Daniel to sit down and stop being silly.

'Solly,' he said, and bowed to the nurse, to the man, then to his own black-hatted shadow, tilting towards the pier and beyond.

Much later, the nurses helped us put our socks and shoes back on. We trundled to a police station, where we were given lemon barley water to drink in thick, white china mugs which smelt of coffee and had brown stains on them. We sat on chairs attached to the wall, girls on one side, boys on the other. I swung my legs, but even with my shoes on, neither of my feet touched the concrete floor. It was dark when we were herded on to the coach and back to the Briar, without Jesse.

Whispers went round the wards – drowned, murdered, kidnapped. But the mystery was never solved. Jesse had, quite simply, disappeared.

His family came to the Briar, right into the classroom. Mother, father, shy big sister, healthy twin brother Frank and a brand new Bronwyn baby. More policemen. The rustle of newspapers and scandal.

Daniel joked that Jesse must have met Frank and Jesse James. I preferred to believe he'd swum far, far out to sea, way out into the middle of the English Channel, which wasn't grey-green, rough and deadly – I pictured it as colourless except for the tides, which looked like hair, and which measured time by the names of the winds. Jesse swam a slow, elegant crawl, like the fly on Miss Blackburn's map, but pausing now and then to float on his back, flapping his wrists to propel himself westwards, past the Isle of Wight, the Portland Bill, past Start Point, Prawle Point, the Lizard, thrusting right, round Land's End, and then north, in a willowing arc, across the gaping mouth of the Bristol Channel to the Gower Peninsula, Land of our Fathers and strong, sheep-farming Jackson boys.

The Chair of the Governors made a special mention of Jesse in his speech at the summer fete, which took place at the end of July. Daniel said it was meant to impress the press and starve the gossip-hungry. It ended like this.

'His wasn't much of a life,' he said. 'But it was a life, nevertheless, and that life has been respected. We have searched for James. We have prayed for James. Now let us allow James, wherever he may be, to rest in peace.'

The hospital band struck up 'Rule, Britannia!'

The sinking feeling came.

ii

We went back to school, everything went back to normal, and Jesse was rarely mentioned, except by the nurses on outings – 'Don't you dare do a Jesse,' they used to say.

Daniel continued to work for Eric, but spent more and more time with Will Sharpe in the shoe-repair workshop. I was busy scrubbing and dusting. We met at school and at mealtimes. That's all, officially.

Secretly, though, we rendezvoused often. Sometimes we went to the tool-shed. But the shed – a photography club now – smelt like the pharmacy, not of rabbits or Robert. Sometimes we crept under the branches of the cedar tree or made our way to the rock garden. Occasionally, we climbed up to the old library on the top floor of the main hospital building.

The old library was never locked, and, because of its location, it was rarely visited. Most of the books had been moved to the new library on the ground floor. There remained a few strewn remnants of furniture, out-of-date medical text books on the shelves, some cardboard boxes full of paperback novels with ripped covers and torn pages, a stack of old files containing government papers, health authority reports, minutes of meetings from decades ago, and a pile of women's magazines, five or six years old. Daniel and Robert used to peep and squeal at these, especially the advertisements. Bronco toilet paper was one of the funniest, they thought – a drawing of three white bums and the unanswerable question, why is Bronco so popular with the hygienically minded? They also enjoyed looking at the brassieres.

'What do you get with a Beasley's corset?' Daniel would ask, pretending to peer over a pair of half-moon specs, like Miss Blackburn when she looked up at you from the reader. 'What do you get with a "c" and a "c" and a "p", Robert?'

'Comfort, confidence, poise.' Daniel hooted with laughter.

And a picture of a half-naked lady with curves like Miss Walsingham.

'Poésie.'

Sniggering, wriggling boys.

Up in the old library, alone now, Daniel and I canoodled. But more than usual. Rubbing bodies. Skin licking. I undid the buttons at the front of my frock, letting two tight boosies pop out, and when Daniel lowered his head and it hovered like a buzzing bee, I popped a boosy into his mouth and let him suck.

It wasn't long before we took all our clothes off. One of us – usually me because I could steady us both with my good arm – lay face down on the ground. I would spread my arm like the wing of an aeroplane, while Daniel lay on top of me, face up. Back to back. Soft hair, warm scalp, hard head on my hump, two skinny bum-knobs squashed on my thigh and two rough calves rubbing on the sandpaper soles of my feet. If it wasn't too cold, we stayed like that for up to half an hour. In the library, we timed ourselves by the chimes of the clock in the tower above us.

Mutual masturbation, Dr Young called it. Perverted.

Disgusting, spat the nurses.

'October 3rd, '59, Sunday. Caught masturbating, 10.00 a.m., with Smith again, on the old library floor.' Nurse Hughes wrote it up in my notes.

I was often in trouble in those early years at the Briar. I used to kick up a right old fuss, busting stuff, blubbering, clouting the other children. If I didn't like the food, I tipped it on the floor. If a nurse slapped me, I slapped back. When they forced semolina or semi-cooked mash between my teeth, I sicked it on to their uniforms.

I didn't like my bed. It was narrow, draughty and difficult to climb into. Between it and the bed next to it, there was scarcely room to stand sideways. I didn't like going to bed. I'd cower in the knicker cupboard, crawl under the nurses' table, run up and down the ward, naked and hollering, until Sister was called and came, but never before I'd thwacked somebody – sneaky, cross-eyed Sheila, who'd goody-two-shoe up to me and try to reason, or Mary Jardine, because she spat when I tried to touch the corners of her too-square head.

I frequently fought in the classroom. Often with big Ida, who was nearly fourteen and weighed more than fourteen stone. Nobody liked Ida, but you left Ida alone. Not me, though, not one bitter winter's afternoon with the wind blowing flurries of dark sycamore against the uncurtained windows. When Ida placed herself in front of me, blocking my crazy lap-loops, I went head first into her.

'Like an aeroplane into a cloud,' said Daniel admiringly afterwards.

With my good hand, I clawed and scratched at Ida's back. She lifted me off my feet, but I clung on and dug my teeth into her belly. Her red cotton nightdress, which she wore as a day dress, was thin with wear but stiff from the laundry and dry in my hot mouth, soapy on my tongue. I pressed and felt warm, soft, rounded flesh through the material on my face. Then I bit. The cotton came out like a mouth with lipstick. Ida screamed louder than me.

If you fought, you usually went into the punishment room. This was a small room at the back of the ward, between the toilet on one side and the nurses' office on the other. The nurses could put us in there at the drop of a hat – in you go, good riddance, slut, nutter, fuckwit, dunce.

Ditto into the isolation rooms, which were in the main hospital building, although a doctor was supposed to okay that. The isolation rooms were high-ceilinged and cold, with nothing to sit down on or look at. There were six of them in a row, echoing, even in the corridor outside, with the yelling of the patients within.

Worst of all was to be sent to the pads – two triple-locked cells built on to the side of the back wards. The Medical Superintendent had to be called to unlock these. I never went into the pads, and they were pulled down in 1962, soon after the old workshops.

I didn't mind the punishment room on the girls' ward at the Briar. It was private and peaceful in there, like the chapel when you were meant to be cleaning it and nobody else was around. The room had no windows, just the one locked door, but it was warm, and there was a bench, which you could sit on if you didn't have to lie on it, strapped down.

I liked lying on the floor because if you lay a certain way

you could see out beneath the door. That's not true. You couldn't see out exactly, but there was a wide gap, because the orderlies needed to be able to push plates back and forth under it. And through the gap came shadows. I saw shadows accompanying the sound of footsteps toing and froing to the toilet and office. Fainter shadows, moving slowly, followed the morning shifts of light. Then, in late afternoon, the flashing on and off of electricity. Darkness at night, except for the glow and flutter of the night nurse's lamp. Sometimes, in the daytime, when the children and nurses were in the COU, the ward was empty but for me, on the floor, in that room. Then, through the gap, I might see the shadow of a branch on the sycamore tree as the wind bent it across the sun. The night of my fight with Ida, there was moonlight, and that same sycamore bent its bough to me.

Daniel bent his head to mine, and his hair brushed my cheek. It was surprisingly soft, for such a cocky boy.

We were at breakfast and weren't meant to sit girl-boy, girl-boy. It was my first full day back on the ward following the library incident. I don't know what Daniel's punishment had been, but I flipped my lip – why? – when I saw the gash on his ear and a blackberry bruise nearby.

'Because Maitland hates me. Still, he missed my eye.' Daniel smiled. 'And I missed you.' He tapped my shoe. 'Bloody hell. Here comes Matron.'

The dining-room doors of the COU swung shut behind Matron's wide, tight bum as I tapped secretly back.

'Grace Williams.' Matron plodded across the lino towards me, making her ankles bulge above her short, fat shoes. 'A postcard.'

She sniffed and dropped a postcard on to the table next to me.

'Look at the stamp.' Daniel nodded in excitement.

'Foreign,' said Matron, and sniffed again.

The postcard lay there, upside down, as Matron turned to the nurses and began issuing instructions. The postcard lay unnoticed.

'Quick,' said Daniel, 'hide it.'

Where? Up my sleeve, down my knickers? I wasn't wearing socks today.

'Give it here.' Daniel curled forwards as if to lick his plate. But he slid his head sideways instead, and lipped up the postcard. Then he uncurled himself and adjusted the card in his mouth. He flattened his chin to his neck, and – *comme ça* – the card disappeared. Almost. I could still see a corner poking out of the neck of his sweater. But nobody else saw anything at all. Not even the leg-hugging Daniel and I managed to do under the table before it was time to hold our dirty spoons up in the air for counting and part for our separate wards.

Later, again, in the lunch queue,

'You must hide it, Grace.'

Yes, but where?

'Haven't you got a special place?' Daniel sounded surprised. 'I'm off to mine, right now. I'll tell you about it later. If you're lucky, I'll show you.'

It was an afternoon with no school, no duties, few must-dos. Daniel went to help Will Sharpe with the shoes in the workshop. Some of the older girls on my ward were invited to tea at Miss Lily's. The rest of us were sent to Major Simpson's games room.

I thought about special hiding places all afternoon. Why didn't I have one? Because, until today, I'd have had nothing to put in it.

I sat in the games room playing tiddlywinks with a new boy called Rick. Being deaf and dumb as well as new, Rick was quiet and seemed happy enough at first. I tried not to hear the plickety-click of the ping-pong balls on the ping-pong bats. I blocked out the chatter and clatter of the kiddies on the floor with their scattered marbles, cars and bits of Meccano. And I ignored the laughter, loud in the hobbies corner, where Major Simpson was helping two mong-girls turn a broken drawer into a doll's house.

I did know about hiding places at the Briar, and not just for people, but for things. Precious, private things. String, scraps of paper, tobacco, stones, bits of material, wool, rubber bands, food. Coats and trousers had pockets. People bulged at the Briar. People hoarded. Women, and men too if they could, carried handbags stuffed with stolen goodies. Broken pencils, torn dusters, gritty slivers of soap, discarded paper clips, safety pins, bottle-tops, buttons.

I'd listened to dozens of conversations about secret places at the Briar. There must have been thousands of personal treasures hidden in the hospital grounds. In hollowed-out tree trunks and dens made from bushes. In mounds of branches and woven twigs. In flowerbeds, between the stalks of the flowers. But mostly just buried, in bundles of cloth, brown paper or cardboard.

Whenever the owners had the chance, they visited their secret place, dug up their secret things and, not secretly at all, counted and fondled them.

Mr Peters, as head gardener, knew what went on – 'I make it my business,' he said – but he let it go on. It was harmless enough, he said, and anyway, the cloth and the cardboard would eventually rot. The problem was, people forgot where they'd buried their things. They often dug somebody else's treasure out of the soil, which led to trouble and fights if the real owner got wind.

Inside the hospital, floorboards were levered up, window casements eased apart, the hems of curtains unpicked and then resewn with all manner of tiny oddments tweaked into them.

Built at regular intervals along many of the indoor walls

of the hospital were air bricks with fine, zinc, fiddly-to-dust gauze coverings. Each air brick had a sloping lip sticking out several inches from the wall. These were cleaned – by me and a team of expert cleaners – but not very often. They made ideal hidey-holes. There was a waiting list for them, though. The list was administered by a fat, vicious boy called Ray who had tuberous sclerosis – nodules on his brain, which, said Daniel, made his brain as useless as a brown paper bag full of worms. The nodules had also turned Ray's skin green in sharky patches and made lumps the size of rice grains under his skin. Daniel said it was best not to have anything to do with Ray or his dodgy deals.

This was way before the days of lockers. I never wore the skirts that Mother had sewn. I never saw the contents of my suitcase, carried away by the man with echoing feet. I doubt I saw half the cards and presents sent by my family during the years I spent at the Briar. Envelopes and parcels tended to go astray on their way to the wards from the main office. Daniel described how Miss Walsingham sorted the post every morning into three wire trays – admin, medical, personal. The personal tray didn't contain much, he said, and it didn't often reach the right patients.

Presents from home were booty for the staff. Likewise gifts from the public. There was a big noisy television in the nurses' lounge, donated to the patients of the Briar by the St Albans Boy Scouts in 1953 so that patients could enjoy the televised coronation celebrations. But Daniel, already a patient, aged seven back then, told me they'd all crowded round the ancient wireless in the day room, listening to the clop-clopping up the Mall of the golden carriage with its seven grey horses, and later, trying to imagine fireworks exploding and moonlight silvering the sky above the river Thames.

Major Simpson, who had organised the donation, was furious when he found out. There'd been a showdown with Matron.

'Damn it, woman, they're not animals,' he'd been heard to say. 'Set an example, or get down on all fours yourself.'

Daniel still imitated him, making us laugh, whenever Matron was unusually mean.

But the coronation television, as it came to be called, stayed in the nurses' lounge, and Daniel's imitations merely earned him hours in the punishment room on the boys' ward.

'Dad gave me a coronation carriage, though,' he boasted. 'Matchbox, the best.'

Spats between us were frequent.

My car. Mine's the best. No, mine. We pretended to mind.

I did mind, in the games room, when Rick tipped the tiddlywinks on to my lap, took a box of matches out of his pocket and tried to set fire to the hem of my skirt. The wool shrivelled and frizzed. Shrieking, I tweaked at it with my good hand, but that just made a stink of smoke and uproar in the games room. Major Simpson waved his white handkerchief for calm, then calmly rolled it into a sausage and spat on it, several times. Everybody watched, gobs shut, while he wrapped his hanky round the hem of my skirt and stopped the smelly smouldering.

Major Simpson confiscated the matches and sent Rick back to his ward.

The tiddlywinks had slipped to the floor, and Major Simpson asked me to tidy them up before tea.

'Atta girl,' he said. 'I know I can rely on you to do a good job.'

To the gawpers he said, 'Mind your own beeswax.'

Nobody minded their own beeswax at the Briar.

Even Robert used to grab willy-nilly at the pile of toy

cars – 'I'm a Corgi boy, see, the ones with the windows.' He'd hopey-poke his fingers into their bodies. Fling himself, laughing, backwards. Always surprised there wasn't a single car, Corgi or otherwise, that had all its doors, let alone windows, intact. As if we didn't know that.

'Oh, blast. Never mind. All the better for hand signals, eh, Dan?' And he would flap an arm, twist a hand, push-tapping Daniel to make him get a move on. 'Be fair, Daniel. My car. Divvy up fair.'

'They're goners. It's the garage again for these old bangers,' Daniel would usually announce. Then he and Robert would go off to an imaginary repair shop, full of oily mechanics in oily overalls, stinking of oil and petrol, open twenty-four hours a day, seven days a week, with a secret Jaguar workshop at the back. Only a few experts knew about that, they said. Ditto the roadside café next door.

'With the best bacon butties in the world,' Daniel would add. 'Chivvy along, Grace – you'll love them. You need to change gear, old girl.'

I made layouts with the cars the boys spurned. I grew fond of a particular Triumph Herald.

'Dinky. Die-cast, Cambridge blue,' Robert informed me.

'When it was new,' Daniel corrected.

The car had lost most of its paint, except for a horizontal white stripe along each side. It didn't run very well, because it only had one tyre. The other three wheels caught, even on lino. I liked holding the car. I stroked its ridged metal underside. I tickered its wheels with my fingers. I envied the speedy spin that Daniel could do with his toes, even on the wheels of the battered old milk van – Bedford, number twenty-nine, Grace – with pretend pints of milk, like the ones Mother used to fetch in from the front doorstep. She'd tilt them to mix up the cream in their necks, then press and pop off their silvery tops – milk before tea, Grace.

After tea, Daniel said he'd show me where he hid his things. He hopped impatiently from foot to foot.

'You must find a special hiding place. Come. I'll show you mine. Come. Quick. We've ward check in twenty minutes.'

Daniel and I short-cut across the grass to the workshops. We slipped through the lobby, where the hair box, I noticed, was full, almost overflowing that day. We hurried through the carpentry rooms, past the upholstery workshop, which had two giant-sized mattresses leaning up against the wall.

'For the pads,' said Daniel. 'Wait here a sec,' and he disappeared round the corner.

'All clear,' he said, returning. 'I thought Will might be working late.'

We entered Will's workshop, or at least Daniel did, jigging ahead like a jerky Fred Astaire. I lingered at the door, overcome by the smell of leather, leather glue and shoe polish.

'Here, Grace,' called Daniel from the far side of the room. 'You're drunk on shoe. Come. Over here.'

I staggered cautiously across the lino, past a workbench stacked at the back with piles of shoes – big black doctors' shoes and smaller nurses' ones, old walking and work boots, kitchen galoshes and laundry slippers, and there, at the very back, what could only be our shoes, the patients' – a wobbly wall of laceless clod-hoppers.

There were more than two thousand inmates at the Briar in those days.

'The size of a small village,' said Daniel, proudly.

He hopped backwards, lifted his toe, and, with a magician's flourish, plucked open one of the drawers underneath the workbench.

'*Voilà*. The tools.'

The drawer was divided into compartments, with the tools arranged in size order. I bent down and thought, for a mo, I was looking into Mother's silver drawer at home.

'Reach for a teaspoon, Grace,' she would say, balancing my bum on her forearm, tucking her other hand under my armpit. 'Hang on a mo.' Adjusting me. 'I know you can do it. Go on, Gracie. Please.'

Along the front of Will Sharpe's drawer glinted a row of tiny swords, or daggers. I poked one of them with the tip of my middle finger.

'No,' said Daniel. 'Don't touch. They're the sharpest. Twin blades – for slitting tiny sections of the vamp from the shank. Funny words, eh?'

Rude words.

'Vamp, tart, lady of the night, streetwalker, *pute*, woman of ill repute – I like that one,' Daniel laughed as he listed, opening more drawers.

Scrubber, slapper, slattern, slut. I didn't like those ones.

There were hooks, hammers and punches, several pliers, awls and two whole rows of different-sized knives.

'Burnishers, bevellers, bone-folders. And look at all the studs and tips. Tom Thumbs, they're called. Blakeys and segs. Which do you like the best, Grace?'

In one drawer, near the packets of needles, a group of strange pointed instruments caught my eye.

'Bodkins,' nodded Daniel, moving away to the far corner of the room.

'This is where I work,' he said, standing tall and formal like an old tin soldier, his back rigid and no arms to wobble the sleeves of his tight, dark-blue knitted jumper with its two folded triangular flaps at the collar, and the edge of my postcard peeping out between them.

I made my way, more eagerly than before, towards Daniel, past a stack of brown wrapping paper and several bundles of newspaper.

'And these are the shoes I'm working on.' Daniel nodded to the pile of shoes at the back of the low bench.

The pile of shoes wasn't as big, nor as neat, as the one

on the main workbench. The shoes were roughly sorted into men's, women's and children's. All of them were worn and tattered. Some still had mud on them. Daniel's job was to clean the shoes and prepare them for Will. That meant scraping and wiping all the dirt off, he explained, then unpicking the stitching around the part to be restitched.

Daniel showed me the unpicking hook he used for the job. He removed his own shoes and socks, not soldierly at all, but lying on the floor, kneading his mouth to loosen the semi-tied laces, his feet to push and kick his shoes off, and his toes to unpeel his socks and drop them into his side-by-side shoes, neat as eels into buckets.

He demonstrated how easy it was to unpick, using one of the shoes from the pile.

'Cobbler, cobbler, mend my shoe,' he chanted, standing and knocking another shoe to the floor. 'And my feet, while you're at it, too.'

He danced over to Will's sewing table, which was by the window. There was a miniature pair of soft grey pumps on the table. Daniel lifted his foot and slid a toe into one of the exquisite things. He pointed his toe.

'Eleanor's,' he said. 'Resoling. They're only her school shoes – indoor shoes – but it's all got to be done by hand. Will says it'll take most of tomorrow afternoon.'

Daniel returned to his corner.

So what was he hiding? And where was his special hiding place?

Daniel tipped his head towards the pile of shoes.

Shoes?

'Inside them. In the heels, in their soles.'

I was disappointed. I must have imagined a shoe box or biscuit tin stuffed with stamps and bus tickets, sweet wrappers, a half-smoked cigarette, conkers, of course, an old box from a Matchbox car, and probably a pencil stub or two – a Jennings and Darbishire, boy's own world that

Daniel had read and told me about but would never inhabit. Not shoes, not smelly old shoes.

Daniel toed a shoe at random from the pile – a small brown shoe, scuffed but clean and repaired, a child's or a young maid's. He propped it against a fixed block of wood on the low workbench and held it in place with his foot. With his other foot, he took a sharp curved knife and, in a few swift movements, split the soft leather from its harder sole.

Dozens of tiny strips of paper fluttered out.

I remained unimpressed. Not a very clever place to hide things. The shoes would fall to bits or be thrown away, sooner or later, and sooner than that they would go back to their owner, taking Daniel's pieces of paper with them.

'That's the whole point. That's the joy of it, Grace,' insisted Daniel. 'Don't you see?' He took a man's sturdy boot and kicked it up in the air, catching it again between his chin and chest.

'Me here. Me there. Me every blimmin' where.' He let the boot drop, then flicked it with his toe, sending it skimming across the floor.

'Ice-skating. See.'

Daniel walked across the room, kicked the boot again, and, this time, it went up and nearly hit the ceiling.

'Look. Flying.'

He put his foot into the boot and pretended to walk it up the wall.

'Now I'm climbing Mont Blanc.'

He took another shoe, a doctor's brogue, then another, matching. They were too big for him and made his bare, skinny ankles look as if they were about to break, but he walked stiffly up and down in them.

'Lawyer, doctor.'

Suddenly Daniel stamped and shook the shoes so they fell off.

'Cannibal chief.'

We both laughed.

'Grace, I even get to play football.' Daniel had never sounded so serious. 'Once every six weeks, we get the Watford Football Club boots to patch up. You know, like our laundry does their shirts.'

As to the bits of paper, Daniel said he collected them, that was all.

Were they stolen? No, they came out of waste-paper baskets, Daniel said, from the school rooms, from the offices. He tore them, or cut them up with one of Will's knives. He couldn't manage scissors.

And wrote on them?

'Lists and things. Nowadays,' debonair, 'they're typed.'

I stared at Daniel. A strange sort of hoarding, this. My brother John, with his blue dictionary and his big red encyclopaedias, might have understood. John used to stammer lists of words – definitions and explanations from his books. When he was upset, he recited them as if they were poems, or prayers.

As I stared at Daniel, I noticed my postcard more than peeping, nearly popping out of his jumper.

Daniel removed the postcard, plucking it out with his mouth, ducking his neck, making the hair on the crown of his head – due for a haircut soon – fur up like a yellow-grey chick's.

Daniel let the postcard drop to the bench. Neither of us said a word while we both looked carefully at the picture of the dark-haired, dark-clothed top half of a woman. She had a flat, smooth face, soft-looking skin and eyes like Mother's when she was thinking about smiling.

'Read it,' I said, sweeping the postcard up with my good hand and holding it in front of Daniel's face.

'"For Grace. From me, in gay Paris,"' rhymed Daniel. '"Love, Miranda."'

That was it, or would have been, but for Daniel filling in, 'Paris. *La ville lumière*. Where I was born. I wonder what she's doing there. Do you think she's swum in the Seine, Grace?' Daniel sat down on the floor and tweaked and wriggled his socks back on. 'Danced in the Jardin du Luxembourg? Skied the Champs-Elysées? I bet she's climbed the Eiffel Tower.' Daniel slipped his feet into his shoes and stood up, leaving the laces undone. 'From the top of it, Papa says, on a clear night, the city looks like the sea. A great, glittering sea-mirror of the starry sky.' He sighed.

After showing me the polishing machines, which he wasn't allowed to use, and the newspaper cuttings, which he tore out, under Will Sharpe's instruction, and pinned to a board made of crumbling cork, Daniel said we'd better get going. He tidied the scattered shoes, gave the drawer with the tools a quick toe-tap to close it, and clopped ahead of me to the door.

We trotted like horses, one behind the other, down the corridor, through the lobby, and out into the hospital grounds.

'Horsepower,' said Daniel, slowing to a walk, panting beside me as we reached the path next to the orchard. 'It doesn't exist, you know. It's a pure figment of the imagination.'

I stopped walking altogether and pulled at Daniel's jumper to make him stop too. I was sure Mr Peters, crossing the orchard, passing the apple-house in the distance, wasn't a figment of my imagination. He had a torch in his hand, and every time he stepped forward, it lit up the ends of his black wellies.

'Oh, blimey. Don't move, Grace.'

I froze. We watched.

'Can't be many apples in there at this time of year,' whispered Daniel, and I wriggled nervously, first with held-in laughter, then with held-in thoughts.

We were lucky. Mr Peters didn't see us.

Daniel left me, safe and sound, at the girls' ward, gave me a wet lippy kiss – *bonsoir, chérie* – and off he galloped.

And off I galloped, early next morning before breakfast, to investigate the apple-house. I bribed Sheila to do my sheets for me. I promised to show her my postcard, which I had, in the end, put down my knickers. It stayed there all night, and was still there the following morning, sticky on the skin below my belly-button.

I was lucky. The only person I saw on my journey to the orchard was bag-head Ray, and he was a long way off, lumbering along the path towards the laundry. He must have been on dirty-duty, because he had a sack on his back that looked heavy from sodden sheets and shitty nightclothes, even at this distance.

I left the door to the apple-house open, and, in the faint light, began to explore.

There weren't many apples, Daniel was right, just a few large cookers on the shelf by the door. I put my fingers, my nose, then the palm of my hand to the big old Bramleys. I sniffed their rich, over-sweet stink. I ran my hand along the rough slatted-wood shelves. I poked my toe into the spidery corners. There was a bucket in one and a pile of splintering strawberry punnets in another. I stood still, in the middle of the apple-house, and, as the damp, dusty air settled around me, I decided the apple-house was as good a hiding place as any.

In my happy-apple state, I clean forgot to take the postcard out of my knickers. I was more than halfway back to the ward, quickety-skipping across the grass, before I remembered. I lifted my nightgown and pulled out the postcard. Just then, Ray, wearing only a pair of tight pyjama bottoms, bombed out of the boys' ward and headed towards me. He was followed by two other boys, naked and shouting. They chased Ray, but Ray, a surprise for his size, was a fast mover, and the boys soon gave up and went back inside.

Ray came to a standstill in front of me. He simply looked with his drooping eyes at Miranda's postcard in my hand, and I simply passed it over. All I wanted was for Ray to go away. No dodgy deals.

Ray held my postcard up, then tore it in two. He put the pieces back together and tore them into four, eight, I don't know how many shreds.

I attacked Ray then, with my good hand, snatching at his huge fists and scratching his wrist as the last bits of postcard fell to the ground. The rice grains under Ray's skin made the blood come in dots, not lines. I tried to join them by drawing my fingernails all the way up Ray's bare arm. But the lumpiness, his smell, our closeness, made me too tight inside.

Ray freed his arm with a single jerk. He grabbed my hair. A hank in each hand. He pulled backwards, cranking my neck and twisting my face to the sky. For a second, I saw the pale blue of my favourite car with a thin film of white nylon cloud, and a bird, like the ghost of an aeroplane, flying high on the other side of the white. But only for a second, because Ray stood over me.

He was so big that he couldn't bend very easily, and his face was still some distance away, but I could see that it had pustules on it, yellow and crusty, with beads of dried blood, as if he'd rubbed his face on a brick.

Ray kept hold of my hair with one hand, gripping it close to my scalp, harder than ever. He bent down, and with his other hand, he clawed at the torn fragments of postcard on the ground. I was tugged by my hair left and right, up and down, as Ray silently pincered the muddy scraps.

When he'd finished, Ray tweaked me straight and forced my head back up again. He stuffed the bits of postcard into my mouth, then shoved his ricey hand over my chin, closing it, like the nurses sometimes did with food or pills. He pushed his palm against my lips.

'Apples,' he hissed. 'You'd better watch it, Grace Williams.'

He kicked my legs, which were clutched, shin to knee, knee to thigh, all the way up, as tight as my toes, my fingers and all my innards. I fell backwards on to the grass, and when I opened my eyes, I saw Ray running off towards the cricket pitch, chased, this time, by two male nurses.

I was choking – from the fall and from the card and mud in my mouth and throat – when the nurses left Ray to it and came over to me. One of them picked me up, turned me upside down and shook me. Sick and postcard fell out in grey splatters, like bird shit. I was led back to my ward and handed in to Matron, who said she'd decide what to do with me later, she didn't have time to hear the details now, it sounded like mismanagement on the boys' ward again, and anyway that boy Ray needed to be found, he was on her ECT list today.

In the course of the morning, news of my fight with Ray spread. I was quite a heroine. But I didn't tell anybody about the postcard, nor what happened to it.

I met up with Daniel, briefly, at lunch.

'So,' he said. 'Have you found a good hiding place for your postcard, Grace?'

I shook my head and pointed to my mouth, sore and full of mash.

'OK. I understand.' said Daniel. 'Keep it a secret, Grace. Even from me.'

I kept my gob shut then.

1960

'Open wide.'

There wasn't a dentist at the Briar, but there was a dentist's chair. Everybody sat in it once a year and my turn usually came in March, when clouds of winter-flowering jasmine, even on the shady north wall, made the walk across the hospital grounds pleasant, soft and yellow, despite the wind.

The first time I went in the chair, I was thirteen, and Nurse Jameson still held my hand, my good hand. She squeezed it tight and said in a voice that wasn't Mother's but sometimes tried to be, 'This won't be nice, Gracie.' She knocked on the door with its two white words, 'Medical Examination'.

I already knew that door. We were medically examined twice a year. I knew its brown flaked paint and its bumpy beading, which furrowed your cheek, when the nurses let you slump against it. A slap on your cheek when they didn't, but you slumped anyway.

No waiting that warm spring day. The door opened, and there was Dr Bulmer, washing his hands in the corner-sink. Catching the light on the desk by the window, two matching pairs of silver pliers, a dark green bottle and two small tumblers – new, unusual, unlike anything I'd seen before. Where was the long, high table with its menace of a stethoscope coiled at one end, which they called a couch, wrongly – a couch had cushions, smelt of Omo, Vosene, home, me? The table, or couch, had gone. The chair had arrived.

Dr Young, who'd opened the door, told Nurse Jameson to go, scat, fetch the next patient.

'We haven't got all day, woman.'

'It's only spastics this afternoon.' Dr Bulmer's voice.

I'd seen a dentist's chair before, once, when Mother took me to Mr O'Brien's, but then I sat on her lap while Mr O'Brien tickled my cheek and made funny faces. He said I had the loveliest hair he'd ever seen. He said I was as good as gold, and if I opened my mouth wide enough, he'd pop a golden sweetie in it later. I knew he meant a barley sugar – I'd seen the jar in the hall – and I loved barley sugar. Hard-boiled Lucozade, John called it. So I leant back on Mother's lap and let her hold me like a chair, the most comfortable chair. Arms, legs and all the rest. Dissolving.

It was summer, so Mother was wearing one of her airy poplin blouses. She was clammy, which made her more melony, less lemony. My hair at the back splatted on her chest, above her boosies, her blouse unbuttoned there because the bus had been late, we'd rushed along the street, and when we got to Mr O'Brien's, Mother said she'd murder for a glass of water, not to drink, but to pour around her neck, and she undid the second and the third buttons of the blouse, flapping the material which had stuck to her skin.

Her boosies, moist and giving, lapped my neck. She put her palm to my forehead, flannelly, and stroked backwards, flattening my fringe, like she did the time I fell out of the swing and the sweat on my head went red from the blood, and although it hurt and I yelped, everything was fine because there was kissing, stroking, washing, dabbing, soothing and bandaging. And everything was fine at Mr O'Brien's, warm like the weather and the drift of Mother's voice, sirocco in my ear – it's all right, darling. I'm here.

Hear, hear.

The dentist's chair at the Briar had new leather straps, stiff, which Dr Young buckled across my arms and over my chest, breathy-sharp. It also had padded flaps, like horse blinkers, which were fastened on either side of my head, covering my ears, pressing them into my skull. The flaps muted sound and stopped my head from moving. I moved my eyes instead.

'Oh, Lord.' Dr Bulmer seemed bored. 'Not a fitter, is she?'

'No, sir. The notes. I checked.'

'And?'

'The occasional fit, but not epileptic. Occasionally violent, but we increased her Largactil in January. Physically and mentally defective. Obviously. A complete imbecile.'

'Obviously.'

I grunted, rolled my eyes, closed them, then opened them again, slowly – a blinking frog. The chair unfolded, my body went flat. There was the sound of running water, a window opening. The movement and murmur of doctors playing dentists.

Their voices and the familiar smell of leather were reassuring. I opened wide when they told me to, giving those men my best, barley-sugar smile.

Dr Bulmer's rinsed fingers were cold on my lips, quick on my gums, soap-scented and deft. Like Mr O'Brien, he felt, tapped and prodded. Metal, enamel, skin. That was reassuring too.

'Take a look.'

Dr Young's face appeared beside Dr Bulmer's. The men were the same height, but Dr Young's face was pink, pale and thin, with dim grey eyes and pin-prick pupils. Dr Bulmer's face was patchy and rutted, with thick black hairs – single short ones on his chin and cheeks, longer clumps coming out of his nostrils. Above the brown, bony nose, two close-set eyes, blue and beautiful as snow.

'But the palate,' said Dr Young. 'What a mess.'

'Yes. Not a success, that experiment.'

'Why bother?'

'Good question. They had her tongue done too. D'you see? I'll clamp her. You'll see.'

I never saw. Not the clamps. Dr Bulmer must have slid them in from underneath, but I pictured clothes pegs, because of their size and the way they sprang open, straining my mouth like a pair of knickers in the wind on the washing line – big, puffed, inside-out knickers.

Kneading my tongue against the mess of my palate, using one of his thicker than lolly-stick spatulas, Dr Bulmer put a finger in my mouth, pointing. His fingernail scratched.

'See the clipped bit, Young? Come up close.'

Up close I could see the flutter of fear in two grey eyes.

'Indeed.'

Dr Bulmer removed the spatula. My tongue flopped and spread across Dr Bulmer's finger. He left his finger in my mouth while he chatted away. Idly, his finger moved from side to side – a suckling expanding – not tickling. My nipples prickled.

That was all, the first time.

I was unclamped, unbuckled, unharmed. Nurse Jameson stood at the door with fat, ratty Janice behind her.

'It's Janice's front teeth, doctor. They're making her bottom lip bleed. You said you'd see about taking them out today.'

'Yes, the rodent. I remember. An interesting case. Rather extreme. Dr Young, will you do the honours?'

'Delighted. Gas?'

'Hardly worth it. They don't feel a thing. Brandy, Young?'

'Thank you, sir.'

Nurse Jameson led me out of the room to the clinkle of glass and a green chink of memory – Father, the terrace, cheers, sipping – slipping away already.

We walked through the hospital grounds in the weak spring sunshine, Nurse Jameson swinging an arm, my good arm, swinging and singing.

'I love coffee. I love tea.'

Cheers. I loved walking, swinging, Nurse Jameson singing in clouds of yellow. There. And back.

I rattled then pushed on the door of the apple-house.

Nurse Jameson had left me outside the Children's Occupation Unit. I was still in time for lunch, she said. But for once I wasn't hungry, and as soon as she'd gone, I walked away from the COU, back across the lawn, past the gatehouse, through the orchard, to the apple-house. It was the first time I'd been there since the day I discovered it. I was frightened of Ray, worried about Mr Peters, and anyway, there'd been no more postcards.

The door gave, and I stepped into the dark. I didn't close the door behind me. I felt my way to the far wall, sat down with my legs outstretched and my head resting on the uneven stone. I shut my eyes, but opened my mouth, letting the air seep through my throat and nose, wash over my tongue and gums and swish through my lungs, as if I were dirty on the inside.

Light, uneven footsteps and a scrabbling noise made me open my eyes and shut my gob. My eyes were two inches from Daniel's.

'Grace,' was all he said at first.

He was kneeling. He touched my nose lightly with his, sat back on his heels. He looked at my mouth, then my eyes, then my mouth again. He shook his head sadly.

'You don't know the half of it yet, my love. Not half.'

And he shuffled closer, bent over and buried his face in my lap.

I stroked his hair, which was short now and prickly as thistle.

Daniel sat up then and smiled.

'You're not very good at keeping secrets, Grace Williams,' he said. 'So this is your special hiding place, is it? Not bad.' He bobbed and nodded, all around. 'I saw you, though. From the dining-room window. Heading towards the orchard. I followed you.'

Still I kept my mouth shut.

'Good place, though. Well done. Now we can share.'

Tap, tap.

'Places, secrets, everything.'

Daniel told me that Mr Peters had built and thatched the apple-house himself. It was only about ten foot by six, and couldn't have been more than six foot tall. Daniel stood up and paced. Its cob walls and thatched roof were extra thick, said Daniel, making it warm in the winter, cool in the summer. From October, every shelf would be lined with apples, arranged one by one so as not to touch and spread rot.

'Now, Grace,' Daniel said. 'Good news. There's a meeting for all of us this afternoon. Robert's mother's here. She's in with Maitland now. It's about this year's summer fete.'

Robert's mother – Lena Macintosh – was in charge of the Friends of the Briar. She oversaw the organization of the Briar summer fete in 1960. She sat on committees, like the Major and Mrs Maitland, but she was also hands-on, as Eric put it. For the fete, she hired a van and drove it herself to collect jumble, tents, tables and folding chairs. She had served with the First Aid Nursing Yeomanry during the war, Eric informed us, driven ambulances – a FANY, God bless – and she wasn't a bad mechanic, either, for a woman.

At the meeting, Lena Macintosh asked for volunteers to help prepare for the fete. I was allocated to Major Simpson's team, along with Daniel and some younger children. For the next three months, every Saturday afternoon, if we didn't have visitors or go home for the weekend, we helped Major Simpson.

A few days before the fete, Major Simpson showed us how to assemble a game he'd prepared called Fish the Fish and left us to it, saying he had important business to attend to.

Sitting on the grass in the blowy morning shade of one of the marquees, next to five grizzly kiddies, sticking magnets on to cut-out cardboard shapes of fish, was tiresome. Daniel lay on his back a few yards away. He was using his toes to thread length after length of thin black waxed string through the small holes the Major had made in the ends of twenty short bamboo sticks.

'This is a doddle,' Daniel declared. 'The eyes of my sewing needles are a fraction the size. Will's are even smaller. His stitches are tiny. Incredibly neat. He says the best shoemaker in Northampton stitches sixty-four stitches to the inch.'

Daniel stopped threading and closed his eyes.

'Must be an elf,' he muttered.

My legs grew stiff. The squirty glue kept sticking my fingers together. I wasn't sorry when Major Simpson reappeared round the corner of the marquee, wiping his head with a large white handkerchief.

'Everything all right? Nearly done? Good work,' he chuffed. 'You can finish off later. I want you all – now – in the front drive. Marching orders.'

We followed the Major along the side of the cricket pavilion, through the orchard, across the lawn and past Toby, who was standing, gnome-like and important, outside the gatehouse, discussing parking arrangements with Mrs Maitland.

The sight that met our eyes, when we turned into the drive, made Daniel piss himself, which was rare, except after a fit.

'Shit. Sorry, Major. Ladies.' Daniel clutched his blue shorts where the wet was seeping along the thin cotton weave like ink.

The cause of the piss was the arrival, in the grand, circular sweep outside the main hospital building at the end of the drive, of a small, but dazzling, fairground ride.

'Blow me sideways. Bumper cars,' said Daniel, regaining his chirrup, but not even trying to be debonair. 'Come, you lot.' And he set off at a running, lolloping hobble that nobody could keep up with.

Eric was standing by the lorry from which the last of the shiny bumper cars was being lowered. Mr Peters, next to him, was complaining that the dodgems would ruin his privets. He pointed to the turdy green blobs – topiary, he called them – hedging the edge of the gravel circle.

'Too bad, old chap.' The Major, who had brought up the rear, rubbed his hands on the white handkerchief and put it in his pocket. Eric added, 'Don't fancy a ride on the dodgems, then, Mr Peters?'

Mr Peters walked off, his shoulders hunched. 'Runners need picking,' he grumbled away.

'Daniel,' said the Major. 'Eric's list fell out in the van. Hop up and find it for me, will you? There's a trooper.'

He and Eric exchanged amused glances. Daniel and I exchanged confused ones. How did the Major know the list had fallen out? Why couldn't Eric nip back up himself?

But Daniel obliged. And he did look like a trooper. Stiff knees. Tappety shoes on the wooden blocks that Eric had piled up as steps. At the top, Daniel stopped. I thought he was going to topple and have another accident, but no.

'No, but I'm surprised I didn't really shit myself, Grace,' he said later.

Inside the lorry, and, a second after, outside, was Daniel's father, tall in his shirtsleeves, wearing sunglasses and a white sun hat with green lining. He was in a cloud of his own cigarette smoke, but you could see that he was smiling, Smith-style.

Daniel's father picked the little trooper up and carried

him down the steps. At the bottom, he put Daniel on the ground but kept him close to his side. The bulge of his bicep was against Daniel's shoulder-bowl, and his thick forearm pressed all the way down Daniel's side. It looked as if they were holding hands.

'Next job, Major?' he said, winking at me and blowing a smoke-ring in my direction.

That was my introduction to Daniel's dad, because, although he visited regularly, he didn't come on regular visiting days. He had a special arrangement – something to do with a delivery to St Albans. He came to the Briar, on his way to St Albans, every third Thursday of the month. The rest of us were usually in the COU then. But if Miss Blackburn sent me on an errand, and if I dilly-dallied on my path, taking the longest detours I could think of, I occasionally glimpsed Mr Smith's white Commer van parked outside the main front door and, once or twice, bumping along the gravel drive with Daniel, pale and minute, on the seat next to his dad. 'Smith & Son. Fancy French Antiques', it said on the side of the van.

We all said hello to Mr Smith, and we all tried to say our names, even the lispiest, littlest kiddy.

'Pleased to meet you, Miss Williams,' said Mr Smith, picking up my good, right hand and holding it in his left. He swung my hand firmly, as if we were about to go skipping together. Whiffs of Gitane in my nose – 'but we call them jits, me and Dad.' And eau de cologne like Mother's at home. The sprinkle – her fingers – on Father's white cotton handkerchiefs before the fizz and press of the iron.

The kiddies went back to the Fish the Fish game. But Daniel and I spent the rest of the day with the crazy fitters, plus Eric, Major Simpson and Daniel's dad, helping set up the dodgems. By the end of the afternoon, we were ready to try out the lights. The lights worked, but because it wasn't even teatime yet, their green and orange bulbs didn't glow very strongly, and some of the pink ones were missing. They should have spelt out 'Roger's Dodgems. Drive 'em if you dare', but the 'dod' had gone from dodgems, and the whole of the word 'if'.

Browbeating, tempers, dirty white handkerchiefs, much cursing in French and English, and several bottles of Eric's brown ale, which I helped carry back and forth, full then empty, to the Nissen hut. But by evening, the bumper cars and all the lights worked.

'Like a dream,' said Mr Smith, taking off his sunglasses and putting them on Daniel, who kept them there for as long as he could by tilting his head back, like the chaplain when he sang 'Allelujah'.

We watched from the sidelines as Mr Smith climbed into one of the cars and Eric into another. The Major, who sat in a wooden booth by the edge of the ring, switched on the machines that set everything going.

'Ducks on a pond,' shouted the Major.

'Skaters on ice,' whispered Daniel with glittering eyes. His limbs flittered and his toes twitched.

No touching, no climbing into, no driving the cars, ordered Mr Smith, by our side again. Not without his permission. The dodgems were precious, dangerous and he'd borrowed them from a mate in Hastings who thought they were on loan to the Hertfordshire flower show, not a bunch of bloody nutters. But you could tell he was proud of his *coup*, as Daniel called it. As proud as Daniel.

A few days before the fete, Robert's mother asked the secretaries to write reminder letters to all the parents of the children at the Briar encouraging them to attend. She sat on a deckchair in the middle of the visitors' lawn and added a handwritten PS to each one – 'I know so-and-so would be particularly pleased, were you able to come. He – or she – will be –' and then, 'playing the triangle in the band', or 'helping with the sandwiches', 'manning the tombola', 'hoping to be well enough to watch the cricket'.

When Robert's mother saw me walking across the lawn with a bundle of bamboo fishing rods, she called me over. She told me to sit down on the grass while she finished her letters. She scratched and dotted, and then used quiet blowing noises to dry the ink, instead of blotting paper, like Father.

'There, Grace. Done.' Robert's mother uncrossed her ankles, bent her knees and folded her feet under the deckchair. 'Would you like to hear what I've written? To your parents, I mean?'

She read aloud the PS she'd written to Mother and Father.

'"I know Grace would be – blah, blah. She will be –" you'll like this, Grace – "assisting Major Simpson in operating the dodgems".' Lena Macintosh paused, smiled at me over her specs. 'Oh dear, I do hope it's a good turnout,' she said. 'We could do with a jolly good turnout.'

The Williamses turned out, as did more than two hundred others.

People came in cars, by train, taxis and a special bus from the station. The bus had 'Briar Mental Hospital' written on a piece of cardboard and taped to the windscreen. One couple arrived on motorbikes. Another family, whose car broke down three miles away, walked. The little girl got blisters and the heel of the mother's shoe fell off, but they arrived red and cheerful, the father carrying a pig under his arm. When the father tried to shake hands with Mr Maitland, the pig slipped and ran squealing into the bushes and flowerbeds.

My mother and father came in the old black Ford, bringing not just baby Sarah, but grown-up John and Miranda too.

I didn't see them arrive in their car. I was already busy with my dodgem duties. Daniel was supposed to be helping too, but he was whizzle-head excited, unable to concentrate on a thing. He couldn't keep away from his papa, who wore a crumpled white suit today, and a white hat – all the way from Panama, Grace – with his sunglasses.

Mr Smith sauntered about, chatting, offering cigarettes, listening to Mrs Maitland's jumble arrangements, congratulating the Women's Institute ladies on their home-made cakes and could he buy some cherry buns, discussing the recent Grand Prix in faraway Florida with the small man and his wife who had arrived on motorbikes.

'Ida's mum and dad. Nice couple. Ida a friend of yours?'

Mr Smith passed the Major and me a cherry bun each. The Major and I were squashed together in the wooden booth. There were two upright metal chairs with splintery seats, but I preferred to stand. Otherwise I couldn't reach the switch I was in charge of. When the Major told me to, I flicked the switch one way, releasing a voice with a drumbeat in the background. 'Ladies and gentlemen, girls and boys. Roger's Dodgems. Dodge 'em if you dare. Six pence a ride. Three rides a shilling.' At the end, I turned the switch off, without needing to be told when – after the last drum flourish.

I'd just flicked the switch – off – when my family came into view around the corner from the visitors' car park. Father, carrying Sarah on his shoulders, walked next to Miranda, whose head came up to Father's chin now. Mother, wearing a new summer frock, walked a few steps behind. John lagged even further back, looking uncomfortable in white cricket trousers and a dark blazer, and small because he was carrying a large picnic basket.

I huffed and hurrahed, chuffa-choked up that my whole family would be part of the jolly good turnout Robert's mother was hoping for.

Father waved. I waved back.

Matron must have seen my family too, because she

hurried over and shook hands with Mother and Father, then led them to the booth, where Major Simpson put his fist on my head and told me to scarper, I had leave of absence.

'Atta girl. Go and enjoy yourself,' he said.

I took my family, first of all, to the corner where Major Simpson had organised apple-bobbing, Fish the Fish, and Shove Halfpenny. Miranda fished the fish and won a tin of spam, which she put in the picnic basket that John had given Mother to carry.

'Let me take it,' said Father. 'Sarah can walk.' And he lifted Sarah from his shoulders and put her down on the flat, mown grass. Sarah started to inspect me – face, hair, bad arm, short leg – then she lost interest and set off towards the coconut shy. She'd nearly made it, with Miranda running after her, when the rest of us were waylaid by Robert's mother.

'Grace, Grace,' she called from her temporary post as Mrs Smartie. 'Come and say hello.'

Ida and Janice were supposed to be in charge, Robert's mother explained.

'Guess how many Smarties. You know, Grace – easy.'

I nodded.

Robert's mother shook everybody's hand, including Sarah's, who was with us again now, squiggling in Miranda's arms. The trouble was, said Robert's mother, Ida kept swiping the Smarties, and she indicated the half-empty bowl she'd filled with sweets.

'I was trying to tempt people to stop,' she said, then laughed. 'I've sent Ida and Janice to do the egg-and-spoon race. They can work off some of those Smarties.'

Mother asked if there was anything she could do to help. Robert's mother said no, but she knew the cricket match was about to start – looking at John – so why not wander over and take a look?

'Kind woman,' said Mother as we made our way towards the cricket pitch. 'I wonder who she is.'

We stopped to admire two men from the disturbed ward tossing the welly, paused to buy a binca mat made by one of the ladies in Miss Lily's sewing group, and stopped again for all of us to have a go at Eric's home-made hoopla.

'Five hoops a shilling.' Eric's always rough voice was croaky from shouting. He was red in the face, and the strap of the camera, which hung round his neck and poked out from his open overcoat, had nicked the coarse skin above his collarless shirt.

'One each,' said Miranda eagerly.

'One each,' I repeated, lifting my good arm as high as I could, like I did for Miss Blackburn if I knew the answer to one of her questions.

But Sarah wanted a hoopla too. She started crying. Father tried to reason with her. Mother offered Sarah the hoop, which she, Mother, held sadly in her hand now. She had been about to throw it. A smile still lapped her lips. But Sarah shook her head rudely and opened her hoopla mouth even wider. John and Miranda both stared at the ground and John tapped a foot – an echo of the frightened or excited hopping he used to do as a little boy. Sarah's crying wasn't just noisy, it was quacking, pitiful and agonized, as awful to listen to as anybody's on the ward at night. You'd have thought she was being tortured, accused of a crime she didn't commit. It reminded me of Mother. Mother crying. And ducks, eiderdowns, drowning. A drowning-out.

Sarah stopped crying when Daniel appeared. He was wearing a hoopla around each of his ankles. He waddled and flippered, making the hooplas spin and wobble. Sarah hiccupped, gurgled and laughed louder than any of us.

Crying forgotten and hooplas returned, we all moved on. Daniel tried to skip at the right pace to stay next to John.

'Cricket,' he said. 'Now there's a thing. John, do you play?'

And when John didn't answer, 'Silly me. Of course you do. You must. I like the shoes, don't you? Cricket shoes, I mean. I expect you have a pair. Calfskin, are they? Don't you?'

Daniel twittered on for I don't know how long, and about flip knows what, but John wouldn't be drawn. He withdrew, stiffening, into his shell, coughed, adjusted his specs, almost skipped himself, trying to catch up with the others.

Daniel, downhearted, slowed and walked with me.

Nobody spoke until we all stopped in front of a flashing, buzzing, looped piece of wire. You were supposed to pass a metal ring along it without letting the edges of the ring touch the wire.

'No punters, Ged?' said Daniel.

Ged was the electrician at the Briar. He was so quiet, he was almost invisible. His stall at the fete had nothing to tempt people to stop. He hadn't even given his stall a name. Nobody, so far, had managed to loop the metal ring more than three inches along the wire. The second the ring touched the wire, a buzzer went off, the wire sparked and lights flashed. I wasn't surprised that Ged didn't have any punters.

'D'you want a go, boyo?' Ged's voice was damp and round at the edges, like Jesse's. 'I could put it on the ground.'

But Daniel shook his head.

'No. Thanks, Ged. I know my limitations. I'd never be able to control it. Not for long enough. With my needles, I'm in and out, quick as a fish.'

John, however, said he'd like a try. Ged nodded. With pleasure, he said. And I saw him nodding with a different sort of pleasure at John's firm grip and steady movements.

John nearly reached halfway. Miranda was shouting, 'Come on, John,' and Mother, Father and Daniel were all watching. But John suddenly seemed to lose his confidence. The hope in his flat, moony face shrank to despair, and he let the metal wand drop, setting off the ear-splitting buzzer and the lights.

'Never mind,' he said. 'Butter fingers, me.' And he laughed nervously.

'Well done, all the same,' said Daniel, genuinely impressed.

John turned his unwavering, speccy gaze on Daniel for the first time.

'Thank you,' he said quietly.

Daniel said he'd better get back to his dad. He made a pretence of looking in horror at an imaginary watch on an imaginary wrist, making us all smile, and causing Sarah to laugh and stamp her foot. Daniel let the imaginary watch fall to the ground, then fake-stomped on it with his foot. Baby blue-eyes pretended to pick it up. Ah.

'I look forward to seeing you later,' said Daniel, taking in everybody with his eyes, but letting them rest on mine, Smith-style, before scooting off.

We, the Williamses, sat in deckchairs at the edge of the cricket pitch and ate Mother's picnic.

Afterwards, Mother and Father went to the big marquee to listen to the hospital band. Miranda and John said they'd come with me, back to the dodgems.

'We'll find you there later,' said Mother, waving goodbye.

Sarah walked between Mother and Father. She took hold of both their hands. One, two, three and away.

Back at the dodgems, it was as busy as ever. Daniel, in the queue, called us over.

'Here, Grace. Come.'

When we reached him, Daniel said it wasn't pushing in because his dad was the boss.

'The bumper cars belong to him,' he added.

'Really?' said Miranda. 'Are you sure?'

'As sure as eggs are *oeufs*. That's him, over there,' said Daniel, nodding towards the wooden hut. Mr Smith was leaning on it sideways, listening to the Major, who was trying to tell him something above the racket. Mr Smith nodded, several times, and smiled in our direction.

Daniel's dad had been as good as his word and had let us all have a ride on the dodgems the day before. I hadn't liked any of it. Not the cramped, tinny car. Not the way it jashed my neck and bumped my hump against the metal rung at the back. Not the sparks, which flew like mad, blue birds on the ceiling. And not the noise. I'd begged to be released.

So now, when we reached the front of the queue, I shook my head, even though Miranda said she'd keep her arm around me all the time.

In the end, Miranda went with Daniel. Then she went with John. Then John said he wanted to drive. So Miranda got out, then into another car and drove alone. Daniel, meanwhile, climbed in with driving John.

I stood and watched. Mr Smith caught my eye, and the next time the music stopped he wiggled his way towards me through the jumbled cars. He paused by Miranda's car, bent down and whispered something in her ear. He nodded to John and Daniel and said something to them, which made them nod too.

'I'm letting them stay on, Grace,' he said to me, arriving by my side. 'Boss's prerogative. Can't I persuade you to join them?'

I shook my head.

'I'll be very careful. We'll keep our eyes on the road.' He paused, lit up.

I shook my head again, then hung it. There was a bubble of tears behind my eyeballs, and I didn't want it to pop.

'All right, *ma puce*. It doesn't matter. What shall we do with you, in that case?'

I didn't have any choice. Mr Smith picked me up and carried me all the way round the edge of the circle of dodgems to the wooden booth.

'Here, Major,' he said, shouting up to the plastic window. 'Pass us a pew. The little lady's tired. She needs to sit down.'

Mr Smith took the metal chair that the Major passed out of the door. He placed it firmly on the walkway ringing the dodgems, and bowed.

'Take a seat, *mademoiselle*,' he said, just like Daniel. 'And don't budge. If you need anything, let me know. Wave. I'm busy, but I'll be on the *qui vive*.'

So I sat still as Miranda and John, with passenger Daniel, drove, raced and crashed their cars. Mr Smith lounged, chatted, walked around the circle of cars, winked at me from time to time, smoked. The back of my chair was against the wooden booth. A loudspeaker hung above the hut. The music was very loud.

I looked at Daniel, and, as John grew more confident and quick with the steering wheel, I saw thrills of pleasure flick across the blur of Daniel's face. Lights flashed and sparks rained from the electric cables above the bumper cars.

'Miranda, John.' Mother's voice, sharp and panicky. 'Oh, Grace, there you are. Have you seen Sarah?'

Father, white and worried, was right behind Mother.

Sarah had wandered off during the concert, he said. They couldn't find her. They'd searched everywhere.

A false alarm, not a Jesse. If it hadn't been for the noise and the smoke, the heat, the lights and the bright summer sunshine in my eyes, I might have heard or seen my naughty little sister hauling herself up the steps behind me to the Major's booth. It was only a matter of seconds before the

Major saw the fearful faces of Mother and Father, and he came out of the booth, carrying a smiling Sarah in his arms.

'Thought I'd hang on to her. Knew you'd come for her sooner or later. She was a dab hand with the switches. But –' the Major smiled at me – 'I missed my expert.'

There were exclamations, and lots of thanking – the Major, the Lord – and goodness, what a fright we had. Mother took Sarah from the Major, but Sarah fussed, so Father took her from Mother. Mr Smith, meanwhile, strode over to see what was going on.

The grown-ups chatted. The weather, the fete, the Grand Prix again. I sat on my chair and and listened politely.

'Fuck,' said Mr Smith suddenly, not politely.

He leapt past me into the busy dodgem rink.

When I turned round, it was as if my innards exploded, messy and blue, all the way through the smoky air to the place where John and Daniel's car stood alone and stationary at the far end of the ring. The passenger seat was empty. But in the driver's seat, Daniel lay flung across the steering wheel. His small sandy head was still, his neck was at an even funnier angle than usual, and his back sagged.

My own head dithered and flickered like the overhead lights as Mr Smith fuck-fuck-fucked his way across the floor to his son. He puffed fierily on the jit between his lips.

When he reached the car, he didn't pick Daniel up. He knelt down at the front of the car and leant across its feeble bonnet. He put his face up close to Daniel's drooping head.

The music stopped. Major Simpson must have gone back into the booth, because next, all the machines were switched off too, making it seem quieter than it really was. Too quiet. I heard Mr Smith's breathing and the clicking of the cooling electricity. Then the wispiest of voices,

'*Excuse-moi, Papa.* Sorry, Dad.'

There was a burst of voices and cheering.

Mr Smith carried Daniel over to us. But he didn't stand him down on the ground. He kept him, like a baby, on his hip, steadying Daniel's back with his arm. Daniel clenched his knees around his dad's waist. We all stared, but Sarah, in Father's arms, stared most of all.

'Now, *fiston*,' said Mr Smith. 'Explain.'

Daniel didn't explain then, because he fitted again – a whopper – and had to go to the infirmary. Pale, straight and unmoving on the stretcher Eric fetched, he looked like one of the bodies we occasionally saw sliding out of a side door near the back wards into a long, black, windowless van. I tried to follow the stretcher, but Eric shook his head. I tried to say Daniel's name – scream it, I mean – but the rushy grown-ups shushed me, and only Major Simpson spoke to me.

'Be brave, Grace,' he said. 'There's a trooper. He'll soon be better.'

By the time Daniel was better, the dodgems had gone, and all that remained of the fete was the churned-up grass by the marquees, soggy bunting and a pile of semi-dismantled stalls next to the old tool-shed.

1961

Nearly a year passed before Daniel even mentioned his epilepsy to me. It was the day of the dare, a May day.

We were up in the old library, lounging and smoking. Cigarettes were allowed and encouraged at the Briar, rationed and used as rewards by the nurses. The crazy fitters stockpiled theirs, turning them into gambling chips. Eric made his own roll-ups with tobacco from Virginia. He gave his old tobacco tins to Ged, who used them for storing fuses and fuse wire, and also cigarette butts, which he'd give you if you asked quietly and kept quiet about the price – 'a Welsh snog', a wet snog.

It's all Silk Cut, cutting down, low tar these days. If you've never felt untouchable, you won't know what I mean, but smoking for me is like touching – from the inside.

Inside the library, it was hot and airless. I was hot and restless. Not much had happened during the last year. There'd been Christmas, of course. Major Simpson dressed up as Father Christmas – that was funny. And in March my eye teeth were pulled – that wasn't so funny.

The trip to the dentist had seemed much the same as the previous year at first. Except it wasn't one finger but two, this time.

'Such large gobs, Young. Have you noticed? And such over-productive salivary glands.' Dr Bulmer parted his fingers under my tongue. Heat forked. The scarred, clipped tissue stretched.

Dr Young said he'd noticed we slobbered and spat a lot.

Below the leather straps, my chest ached and I noticed my cunt fizzed and dribbled a lot.

'Take a look at that gum, Young.'

'Eye teeth?' squeaked Dr Young.

'Skew-whiff,' yessed Dr Bulmer. 'They need a tweak.'

There was a pushing on my cheek. The doctor's dick, thick through the thickness of interlock underpants, tweed trousers and a white butcher's apron splattered and stinky with mouth-blood. The softness of the pushing. The softness of the cloth, overwashed, on the skin between my nostril and the leather flap. And the hardness within, much bigger than a finger or two, or three.

'Just a tweak. Thank you, Young.'

And it was. Just a tweak or two, or so. No need for the nitrous oxide. Dr Bulmer was nimble-fingered indeed. No need for the student nurse, who'd stayed to watch, to screech so.

'Good God, woman. Be quiet.'

Then, at Easter, Miss Blackburn started extra classes for some of the children. She was preparing them for a test, to see if they were clever enough to go and live somewhere else – a new residential training school for handicapped adolescents and young adults that had opened near Cambridge, she told us.

'It's ridiculous.' Mr Maitland, in the lobby outside the classroom, with Miss Blackburn, was almost shouting. 'Spastics – sitting exams. Your correspondence simply doesn't convince.'

'They may have spastic bodies, Mr Maitland,' Miss Blackburn replied, 'but some of them have the most plastic, malleable, marvellous minds I've ever come across – in more than twenty years of teaching.'

She swept back into the classroom, leaving the door

wide open and Mr Maitland, flustered and uneasy in its entrance.

Five children were picked for the special class. I wasn't chosen, because I couldn't read well enough yet. Miss Blackburn didn't mince her words.

'You've a step to go, child. But keep trying. You'll get there.'

And Daniel wasn't chosen, by announcing he didn't wish to be.

'May I ask why not?' Miss Blackburn's nostrils flared. She was a fair woman, as strict and firm as her ruler. Her mutton-leg jaw and mushroom-cap of hair made her mannish. So did her jacket and brogues. But her wool or cotton-skirted bum was a wonder. Softly up and roundly down it bounced when she wrote on the blackboard.

Daniel smiled. Always best to be debonair in a tricky situation, he informed me later.

'I suppose,' he said to Miss Blackburn, but looking at me, 'I'm hoping for better.'

'I see,' said Miss Blackburn, and I bet she was thinking the same – silly-billy Smith – as me, but, 'It's up to you,' she said. 'My offer remains open.'

Daniel and I were in a tricky situation up in the old library that bothersome day in May 1961. As well as hot, I was cross and sorry for myself. My chest was tight and wheezy. My gums, where Dr Bulmer had pulled out my eye teeth, still hurt and, worst of all, my name had finally come up on Matron's electrics list. ECT for me – no more reprieves – tomorrow morning.

I didn't like the sound of the electrics at all. Daniel called them the etceteras, but that wasn't much better.

I'd managed to avoid them up until now. First the machines weren't working. Then the fire alarm went off just as we were trundling in our nighties, nil by mouth, to the infirmary. Next there was the muddle about whether or not I'd eaten, and I was sent back, along with several others, to the ward. This was shortly after one of the catatonic ladies who sat, like Mr Peters' topiaried privets, around the radio all day long, choked to death from not being nil by mouth before the treatment.

A more recent inquiry into overcrowding had led to the whole of the girls' ward being off ECT for months.

But this morning, Matron had said if I was well enough to blow raspberries at her, I was well enough to go on her list, and she took out her biro.

Daniel said it wasn't too bad, ECT. But I knew he was lying. His egg-shaped head always appeared longer, and his eyes scrambled like a bust kaleidoscope, after his own occasional shocks. Few of us ever had regular electrics. Increasingly, we were treated with colourful cocktails of pills. The only patients who still received regular ECT were the adult skitters, the lady catatonics and a group of curled, withdrawn, lost-looking men called DPCs. Daniel said they came from abroad, from camps. If they spoke at all, they spoke in a mysterious mix.

'A cocktail, Grace. Russian and Polish. I asked Papa. Serbian too. And some of them understand French.'

Daniel tried to befriend the men. 'They're displaced people, Papa says.'

Parlez-vous français? For a while, the nurses on the overcrowded DPC ward enjoyed parroting Daniel. If any of the men said *oui*, nodded or stirred, the nurses said they could be moved out of the ward and on to one of the equally overcrowded general wards.

'It's a crime against the spirit.' Daniel was back on the subject of ECT. 'That's what Eric says. And Will Sharpe,' he added, 'calls it a controlled type of brain damage.'

Up there in the library, Daniel wouldn't look me in the eye.

'Honestly, Grace. It's not too bad, though,' he repeated

uncomfortably, trying to settle his neck more comfortably on the rolled piece of old carpet we were using as a pillow. 'It's just the headaches. They're quite bad. Splitting, actually. But they don't last long.'

'Not true.' I pinocchioed my nose.

I knew. I'd seen for myself. Sometimes, if there weren't enough staff to keep an eye on us, we girls were distributed, singly or in pairs, among the women's wards. It meant we got off cleaning because there weren't enough staff to oversee that either. But it also meant a numb bum from sitting for hours on a hard chair by the door to the nurses' lounge.

One such afternoon, I was sent to the peepos' ward. Peepos, said Daniel, were post-partum psychos – ladies who'd lost their marbles along with their babies. Some of the peepos were scarcely more than girls themselves.

'Better fetch the peepos.' A nurse yawned, got up from her armchair and put the kettle on, ready for another cup of tea when she came back from the ECT rooms.

The peepos were allowed to lie on their beds in the ward after their ECT. Most of them merely flopped half asleep, moaning and muddling. But one, a strong, horsey-looking thing with thick, dark hair, dark skin and wide, flashing brown eyes, sat bolt upright in bed and glared into the nurses' lounge. The nurses were stirring their tea, smoking their cigarettes, dunking their biscuits. Ignoring me. I scooted over to the woman's bed and offered her the leftover piece of biscuit I'd snitched earlier and kept hidden in the nook between Nelson and my chest.

The woman took it and thanked me.

'Rape,' she croaked. 'It's rape. Of the soul.'

Her voice was deep and her eyes flickered with fury, but she was a gorgeous sight, that horsey lady, I can assure you.

Up in the library, Daniel was still trying to reassure me.

'Think of it like going to sleep, Grace,' he said. 'That's what I do. Imagine someone's telling you a story. Or reading to you.'

He toed an old book across the floor – *Physical Order in the Mentally Disordered* – opened it at random, read aloud.

'"*Cri du chat, café au lait*, maple syrup." They call us ugly, but at least they give our deformities beautiful names. It's not all bad, Grace.'

Hydrocephalus, scaphocephaly, phenylketonuria. Subnormal, deficient, retarded, impaired.

Patients still ate their own vomit, drank from the toilet bowl, shivered in shit in cold, chipped bathtubs. I pushed Daniel's foot irritably away. The book thudded, and I heard its open pages crinkle and crush. Daniel, however, remained uncrushed.

'Tay-Sachs, Waardenburg, Laurence-Moon-Biedl,' he continued, as if by citing or reciting he could make things better – or different, at least. The point is, he could. Up to a point. That was Daniel. That was what he did. Point. Paint. Brighter pictures.

'Rubella, Talipes, Amsterdam dwarfism. Autism, asthma, eczema, epilepsy – the Sacred Disease. Moth madness, Papa calls it,' said Daniel. 'The epilepsy. Papa used to say I was his little *papillon de nuit* – because of how I fluttered and got the shakes.'

Butterfly of the night. It suited him. I twisted my head and looked at Daniel's pale, never-still face in the dusty gloom.

'That and because we drove so often at night. Me and Dad. In the white Commer van. He let me dip the headlights. Before the accident.' Daniel's whole body shuddered, but he raised one leg and paddled his foot in the air.

'The switch was on the floor, next to the clutch. I had to slide my bum off the seat and hold on to it with both hands, pressing with my right foot – like this – on the switch.'

Daniel prodded me on the cheek with the unlit cigarette in his mouth.

'Give us a light, old girl. You're nearly out.'

I placed the burning tip of my cigarette to the tip of Daniel's. He breathed in until the tip lit up. We were both experts at this.

'Dad used to boast he could drive the route blindfold. "Do you dare me?" he'd say and pretend to put a hand across his eyes. And once, "Don't you dare," when I turned the knob on the dashboard which switched the headlights off altogether. I was always trying to impress him.'

Daniel tried, and failed, to blow a smoke-ring. He went on trying until he was out of puff. I took the butt from his lips, inhaled deeply, spewed as I blew out and Daniel went on.

'I suppose I was trying to impress your brother John last summer. Do you remember? I wanted to swap seats. He wouldn't. He said I couldn't. "You can't drive," he said. "Let me try," I begged. But he wouldn't. In the end he got out. Just walked away. I don't know where he went, but, "I'll show you," I thought, as if he'd dared me.'

Daniel flicked his head suddenly sideways, to face me.

'Grace,' he said, 'do you dare me?'

Do what? I ground out the cigarette on the upside-down saucepan lid we'd found near Mr Peters' compost heap and smuggled up here. The lid clanged on the floor as I stubbed. Ash slid and fell through the hole in the middle where there used to be a knob.

'Go and see Dr Young. Ask him to postpone your ECT. Tell him about your cough.'

I shook my head.

'I would, you know. I bet I could persuade him. You

know it's my forté.' Daniel sat up, rocked to his feet, knees bent, before knocking them straight.

I shook my head again. Nobody liked Dr Young.

I held out my hand, my good, right hand, ever so lady-like. I coughed, not so ladylike. Daniel bent forwards and took my fingers in his lips.

'Let me at least help you up, ailing Grace, my lovely, ladylike darling,' he said, and I could feel the 'l's quiver across his tongue and flitter, scaly-winged, through the nails of my fingers.

I stood up.

'Think about it,' said Daniel as we left the library. 'My offer remains open.'

It was still warm when Daniel and I met later that evening on a bench behind the laundry rooms.

We were barefoot, following a wart inspection. My hump rested on the wooden back of the bench which had soaked up the heat of the day from the wall behind it. We were both wearing shorts, cotton vests and grey cardigans. Daniel said that wearing a cardigan made him feel like a girl. So what? Wearing shorts made me feel like a boy. We sat close together. Our bare legs touched. We stretched them out as far as we could. My longer leg was the same length as Daniel's, but paler, fleshier, rounder, definitely female.

Daniel pulled his bare foot all the way up my leg and tweaked at the hem of my shorts where it lay in a loose fold between the bench and my thigh. His toes curled and gripped the thin material, but he couldn't twist his foot enough to poke it up inside.

He swung on his bum and lay down flat on the bench, keeping his feet on my legs.

'Copy me, Grace,' he said. 'Mirror me.'

I hitched myself round and leant back, letting the armrest of the bench take some of my weight, via my hump. I pushed Nelson against the wooden struts at the back of the bench and moved my legs until my longer one slotted between both of Daniel's.

Slowly, we each slid a foot up and under each other's shorts.

I wore underpants. Daniel didn't.

'Press,' said Daniel, pushing and squeezing the knickered curve of my cunt with his toes and the arch of his foot.

I pressed lightly on Daniel's bare, crinkling sex-skin beneath my foot. As the flesh hardened, I pressed more firmly, remembering the bamboo rods at the fete last year and Daniel running his feet over them. I remembered John rolling an old rubber ball under his bare foot, backwards and forwards on the terrace one evening. Mother, in socks, on the rungs of a ladder. Or was that Miranda? And my own, bare baby feet, safe in Mother's good hands.

'Press, Grace,' she used to say. 'Go on. See if you can push me over.' And she'd pretend that I had, falling backwards with a hurrah. 'Fantastico, Grace. See, there's nothing to be frightened of.'

Daniel suddenly withdrew his foot, pulled back both his legs.

'How frightened are you really, Grace? Of the ECT, I mean.'

So frightened, I felt sick, I felt wheezy, I knew I wouldn't sleep and I would probably wet the bed. So frightened. I flicked myself round and sat up in a panic.

'Let me go and see Dr Young.' Daniel swung round too. 'Please, Grace.'

'You dare?'

'Wait here,' he said, and he'd gone before I could protest.

Daniel went one way. I went another. Sneaky-deaky with curiosity, I crept along the side of the building, past the closed offices, past the shuttered stationery store and the dark front door, further and further along until I came to the big bay window of Dr Young's office.

The curtains were undrawn and I could see the tall, narrow room with its skimpy furnishings and its skinny inhabitant.

There was a plain metal desk on the left facing into the room, with one upright chair behind it and three in a row opposite. You usually sat on the middle one of these when you came to be punished. On the far wall was a door and a line of one, two, three, four, five grey filing cabinets. Scratchy carpet on the floor, staring portraits on the wall chained to a high, chipped picture-rail. And a standard lamp behind the peasy-green easy chair placed at the bay end of the room, half turned to face the window.

Dr Young was sitting in this easy chair. He was reading a book. Each time he flipped a page, shadows rippled briefly in the ring of light on the ceiling thrown by the lamp.

Dr Young closed the book and put it down on the arm of the chair. He put his left hand on top of the book. He drummed his fingers, slowly, as if counting, or thinking, or choosing. 'Eeny meeny miny mo – catch a spastic by his nose' was one of the doctor's favourite chants as he nabbed a child, grabbed a stick and dab-thwackled on our crappy arses.

I drew back from the window because I thought Dr Young was looking at me. He wasn't. With both hands, he loosened his tie, which was blue-black, thin and glistening. Then he took something out of the shiny inside pocket of his blue serge jacket. A letter? A photo? I stepped right up close to the window. There was a dip in the turf there, where the earth was once removed to make the foundations of the building. I could balance very well, like one of Daniel's mythical mountain goats – dahus, he called them – with my longer leg in the shallow moat and my good arm leaning on the wide window frame. It was warm through my cardie, moss-damp and woolly, like me down below, a hand – or toe – in my knickers.

Dr Young sat with his skinny thighs and knees together. His calves and feet splayed, like the light from the lamp. He held the letter – or was it a photograph? – cupped in his hands, on his lap. His shoulders were relaxed against the back of the chair, but his head had dropped forwards, and he was looking closely at the photograph or piece of paper in his hand.

In a minute, Daniel would open the door. But before Daniel arrived, I saw a Dr Young I'd never seen before, and one I would never tell Daniel about.

The doctor continued to look at the paper or card, and there was no scary glint in his eyes any more, no pounce, no flare, no flouncing muscle. He looked sad. The light had silver-dotted the grey bits in his hair, and I could see a small oval of pink scalp at the back. The lines on his face, which were usually straight and grey, were thicker, blurrier now, and all his skin looked softer, whiter, puffier.

His hands, normally big with holding the stick which scutched our skin, were surprisingly small at rest. Chubby, dimpled baby hands. The doctor looked very sad. Like Father, at the end of a visit, when he thanked the nurses for looking after me. Like Miss Lily, when she came back from her day off. Like me, when I saw myself in the mirror in the visitors' entrance hall.

Daniel entered and went to stand – and I could see he was standing as upright as he could – with his back to the desk, his shoulder blades pulled together. We knew Dr Young had been a doctor in the war, so maybe Daniel thought a military pose would impress. I was impressed.

Daniel had scarcely begun to talk when Dr Young got up, crossed the small space between them and slapped Daniel on the cheek. The doctor sat down again on the easy chair, and tugged it forward. Daniel continued to stand, but he was no longer speaking. His long eggy head was beginning to twitch. I saw him tense the muscles in his neck, tight – tighter, Daniel – trying to control it. But the doctor's hands were at Daniel's trouser fly. They undid the buttons. Just three, and the flimsy shorts slipped to the floor. With difficulty, Daniel stepped out of them. His knobbly buttock creased on the edge of the desk as he cringed backwards. Dr Young stretched out his right hand towards Daniel's dick, which was brown and shrivelled in his hairless crotch, but looked wet like the worm-casts on Margate beach. Daniel's legs were brown too, crooked mirrors of each other, stiff, bandy, dirty and thin. Daniel looked ridiculous in his tight vest and overwashed cardigan, fastened with just one button, and in the wrong button-hole. I wanted to laugh. I wanted to bang on the window and make him laugh. Break the window. Would I dare?

There was no banging or breaking from gawping, gaping me. Dr Young came over to the window and pulled both curtains shut at once. I couldn't see Daniel, but Dr Young's flannelly thighs were level with my eyes. I looked up, and before the curtains closed across the column of light, I saw the straining fly of Dr Young's trousers and his white, unbuttoned shirt-tails open and loose around the bulge. His thin tie, undone now, shone black against the dull, naked skin on his ribs. I saw his pink ostrich neck, long and ragged above the open shirt collar, and then, finally, his scared, mad, grey-eyed face. I know he didn't see me, because the stare in his eyes was blind, and because he shut the curtains so quickly.

The following morning, before breakfast, I was sent to stand in the nil-by-mouth queue. Matron handed Nurse Ellis the ECT list.

We trudged to the infirmary. We lined up in the infirmary corridor.

'In.' Nurse Ellis ticked the list on her clipboard as we filed past her, one by one.

I slept. No stories, no dreams, no memories at all. The last thing I saw was Nurse Ellis's face flirting up to handsome Dr Jack, a trace of pink, off-duty lipstick on her open bottom lip.

The first thing I saw looked like a lip, but wasn't. It was a fat, pink fold of flesh. A fat, pink neck. Ida's.

'Blimming heck.' Ida woke up too. 'Not you?'

Yes, they'd put us in a bed together in the recovery ward.

All that spring and through the summer they put me with Ida after the electrics. For more than three months, we were ECT regulars, Ida and I. I got used to waking up next to Ida. Came to like her heavy, sweaty, soft-skinned body. I got used to the electrics too, but I never came to like them. For ages afterwards my head buzzled like a cross, stuck wasp. They didn't seem to do me any harm, though. 'Calmer,' wrote Nurse Ellis in my notes. Ida said they did her good. Daniel said I shouldn't take too much notice of what Ida said. He said I was one of the lucky ones, that's all. I didn't mention the dare, and nor did he, ever. But I saw him slip off to Dr Young's office a number of times after that, so I suppose such business paid off occasionally, dared or not.

In September, Miss Blackburn wrote the word 'Audition' on the blackboard and explained about the end-of-term play. There was talk of grease-paint, green rooms, wardrobes, dresses, rehearsals. I longed to be the mermaid in the Christmas play that year – *The Little Mermaid*, 1961. I'd been in the audience three times in the past – *The Little Match Girl*, *Cinderella*, *Snow White* – envied the costumes and make-up, not to mention the applause, even if some of it was pretend.

'And now,' Miss Blackburn told us, 'you're old enough to take part.'

One whole end of the refectory, where the performances took place, became a blizzard of noise and colour in December, especially when the chorus was brought in to be drilled. We had wood sprites one year, nymphs another. Mice, fairies, elves, goblins. Singing, dancing dumbos and spazzos.

While Miss Blackburn directed, Eric built flats and scenery and got the crazy fitters painting crazy rough seas with sea horses as big as people, and a golden palace with gauzy slits for windows and lights that lit from behind. Ged sorted out the lights, Major Simpson put together a team of stagehands and Miss Lily was in charge of costumes. Her hussif went everywhere with her in December. She would untie it, unfold the fabric panels and spread open the soft material, rippling a finger along the lines of needles and pins, over the tape measure, the poppers, the buttons and the small silver hook which she called a quick-unpick, until she found what she needed.

I needed a part. I auditioned, I hoped. Miss Blackburn gently but firmly explained that they needed somebody dry, and who could be relied upon not to improvise. That's how she described my occasional talking aloud to myself

– stop improvising, please, Grace. However, she gave me a small part as one of the mermaid's attendants, and she said I managed it very well. A girl called Missy – pretty Missy, some people called her – was the main mermaid. At one point we all had to squirm across the floor in our sacks, which Miss Lily had covered with tin-foil scales. Missy's sack kept slipping off. Mine didn't. Nelson was helpful. I could have done Missy's part. I'm sure I could. I knew all her lines off by heart.

Oh, but the following year, I was the Sleeping Beauty in the Christmas play. Half. Daniel was the prince. They had pretty Missy be the princess before and after she goes to sleep, but they chose me to be the sleeping Sleeping Beauty. I was good at sleeping by then, because of my cocktail. Who cares if they only chose me for that reason? I was the one who was kissed. And in front of everybody.

During rehearsals Daniel misbehaved. In fact, for much of the year, between *The Little Mermaid* and *Sleeping Beauty*, Daniel misbehaved.

It all began in January 1962 with the pulling down of the old workshops.

There was no warning. One day, Will and Daniel were sewing away as usual in their cobblers' den. The next day, bulldozers came, and cranes with gigantic balls attached by cable to them.

We were out for the afternoon at Watford Public library when they arrived – an educational trip, organized by one of the new student-volunteers. Miss Blackburn was really in charge, and Eric came too in order to hoik the wheelies up the library steps.

The library was lovely and warm. Lovely and quiet. Shiny and bright. Daniel and I moved from section to section, shelf to shelf, reading the spines aloud. If Daniel liked the sound of one of the titles, he nodded, and I took the book out. If I liked the look of one of the titles, I took the book out, and Daniel nodded. We talked a lot. Probably too much. The student-volunteer shrivelled with worry. People, especially the smaller kiddies, were beginning to twaddle aimlessly around the islands of books. Miss Blackburn had to take over. The last straw was Ida putting her fat hand in the pocket of her smock, which you could tell was meant for a pregnant lady, and pulling out a library book, along with a boiled potato she'd saved from lunch, and a handful of carrot, squashed and brown with gravy. The librarian had words with Miss Blackburn, and we left soon afterwards.

When we returned to the Briar, the workshops had already half-gone. The bulldozers and cranes were still there, but immobile, abandoned among large dark mounds of brick, earth and rubble.

As the coach drove slowly along the gravel drive, everybody fell silent and turned their heads to look out of the window at where the workshops used to be. There was a chill, dull January mist in the late-afternoon air. The mist hung above the demolition area, making it look like a theatre – scenery, flats, wings, waiting in them – not the familiar grounds of the Briar.

The coach came to a standstill and the driver opened the door. Daniel hopped down and legged it – not fast exactly, because his feet weren't steady and his upper body bucked – across the grey lawn. He stopped by the first mound, and I saw Will Sharpe emerge from behind it.

We were supposed to form two queues – girl-girl, boy-boy – ready for going back to our wards. However, Eric and Miss Blackburn had set off across the lawn, their almost identical brown walking shoes indenting the grass, squishing the wetness, revealing darker pale-green underneath. Daniel's uneven footprints beside theirs were scarcely visible.

The volunteer-student didn't know what to do. The wheelies were left sitting on the cold gravel, waiting for their wheelchairs to be unloaded. The mongs began, gradually, to spread out across the hazy lawn – strange, squat, moving creatures. The rest of us simply stood, unqueued. Everybody stared, a few of us shivered.

Will Sharpe was talking to Daniel, still now and with his back to us. Will wasn't a tall man, and he didn't bend down to talk to Daniel. He stood with his arms loose at his sides and his leather satchel slung in a broad diagonal from shoulder to hip. The only way you could tell Will was talking was from his shrugs, which made the satchel swing. Once or twice, he glanced over his shoulder at the earthy hillocks behind him.

Will Sharpe didn't move when Daniel flitted to the right and started hop-running, like a wingless insect, round and round the lawn. Eric and Miss Blackburn tried to block him, but he dodged them, time after time. Miss Blackburn began to look quite unlike herself, holding out her arms, flapping and moving much more quickly than usual. Eric zigzagged grimly, attempted to rugby-tackle, fell sprawling to the ground. His overcoat had damp patches, white, on it from the ice-wet grass when he stood up. But by then, Daniel had gone, stumbling and flailing, worse than I'd ever seen him, towards the demolition site.

Until now, there had been no noise. Even the mongs, milling around on the lawn, were silent, some of them stepping tippy-toed as if playing hide-and-seek, others seeming to search on the ground for something lost, moving like dreamy astronauts drifting in space.

The silence was broken by Will Sharpe shouting 'No' to Miss Blackburn and Eric, who were both heading straight after Daniel. At the same instant, Will held up his two hands calmly, as if surrendering. For a mo, he looked like a cowboy, and I imagined the mist was gun smoke. But although I wished this was a film, or Miss Blackburn's amateur dramatics, I knew it definitely wasn't.

The cold air and the hard ground made Will's voice carry clearly under the mist across the thirty yards of grass to where the rest of us remained agog.

'Let him be,' we heard Will say.

And when Miss Blackburn shuddered as if to say something, and Eric gestured towards the mounds of earth 'No,' again, and 'Leave him.'

All three grown-ups turned, and all of us, plus the volunteer-student and the coach-driver – who'd unloaded the wheelchairs but left them empty on the drive – continued to watch as Daniel went as mental as they come, running round and round the mound.

'Anti-clockwise,' he explained later. 'I thought if I ran fast enough I might be able to turn back time.'

Round and round and round Daniel sped, the saddest ragged rascal you'll ever see.

Eventually, his hobbledehoy legs slowed, then stopped. I saw him – side-view, his small nose tilted – glance at the empty space where the workshops had once stood, and I bet the spider on his forehead crawled. His head started to twitch. Then he dropped to the ground, lay on his back and kicked his legs. I expected a fit. But the pain that usually silenced Daniel as it threw him to the ground, while his legs jerked and spun like broken pistons, for once, the pain came crying out of his mouth in ugly sobs that smashed the still, iron-cold January air.

The sobs didn't stop when Daniel disappeared into the main hospital building, dragged then carried by three male nurses. I heard them, hiccupping echoes, across the hall, down the long corridor, around the corner at the far end. Further and further away. To the pads.

When Daniel came out of the pads, he was woozy and slow for several days. Some of the nurses took advantage and taunted him.

'Think you're better than the shit on my shoe, do you?'

'Cobblers, Smith.'

'I'll show you what putting the boot in means.'

Daniel didn't retaliate.

'Drugged up to the eyeballs,' said Eric. God bless.

A few days later, Daniel's dad came to the Briar. We saw the white Commer van parked outside the main front door. Mr Smith rarely bothered with the visitors' car park. But it wasn't a Thursday, and Daniel hadn't been called to see his dear papa.

'Maitland. I bet he's seeing Maitland,' said Daniel.

We went and stood, then sat on the floor by the door to Mr Maitland's office.

'Disordered. My foot.'

'More than disordered, Mr Smith. Your son's becoming unmanageable.'

'*Merde alors*,' spluttered.

'Uncontrollable.'

Snorts of 'I don't think so's and French 'r's of disbelief as Mr Smith repeated the word 'uncontrollable'.

'It's very difficult. Yes, Mr Smith, he's bright. No one's denying that, but. What did you say? Fifteen?' Mr Maitland paused, then went on lower and slower, not every word clear.

'The brain. New research. Convulsions, seizures, lesions. Damage. Dangerous.'

'Dani's not dangerous.'

'We were wondering. Surgery. Reversal. Improvement. New surgical procedures.'

I heard a chair being pushed back and took hold of Daniel's sweater at the baggy, ribbed bottom-edge of it.

'*Ça? Non, mon Dieu.* You're wasting your time, Maitland.'

I held on tight.

'Let me just explain, Mr Smith.'

'If you must.' Mr Smith's voice was clipped and impatient.

'A study, hereditary. Surgery. Improvement. Lobectomy.'

'What?'

'Anterior temporal lobectomy.'

'No. Absolutely no. Dani will not be operated on again.'

Daniel pulled his knees up and pressed his arm-socket into my shoulder.

'Good for Dad,' he whispered, and we relaxed our bodies against each other.

'Let me just ask you, Mr Smith . . .' Mr Maitland's voice snaked out again. 'Statistics. A study. Genetics.'

His voice quickened with questions, and Mr Smith's answers flipped back as bouncy and fast as tennis balls.

'That's what I mean by debonair.' Daniel nudged me with his hip.

But then, 'Don't you know who the boy's mother is?' we heard the Medical Superintendent ask.

And Mr Smith's lobbed, debonair reply, 'Lord, no. Some French tart. She left the moment Dani was born.'

Daniel started, then slumped like a puppet over his knees. I heard the word 'No' leak from his mouth, and then nothing. I nudged him, crooned and poked.

'You dead?' I said in the end.

'Dead head,' I tried, then 'Grace here,' and 'Wake up.'

Daniel was warm, but as floppy as a nearly dead mouse, and when he lifted his head, which he did when the door to the Medical Superintendent's office opened, his eyes had gone floppy too.

After that, Daniel avoided me and began to spend time with Ray. They stole from the stationery store – six dozen lead pencils, HB. They chucked the pencils at the gerries on their way to the sluice-rooms. They stole from the doctors' private toilet near the boardroom – swathes of soft toilet tissue from the roly-poly holders in there. They wetted the strips of tissue paper and flicked them on to walls and windows, where they stuck and hardened like mouldy bits of cauliflower. They detonated the French bangers Daniel had secretly saved from his dad's Christmas package – in the front drive, in our faces, in chapel, in the middle of a sung 'Amen'.

Floggings were frequent that month.

Eric came across me loping and moping one afternoon on the lawn near the cedar tree. We went to the Nissen hut, where Eric brewed a pot of tea, served us each a big, sweet, saucerless cup of it, and we settled back on the hard chairs by the wood-burning stove.

'I was thinking,' Eric began, 'of making Daniel boss of the new boys on the team. Three of them. A handful. But it might be good for him. Time he had some responsibility. What do you think, Grace?'

'Me too?'

Eric looked at me and shook his head.

'No, Grace. You wouldn't like it. They're wild cats, these boys. Maitland's been swinging the medication again. Didn't get his way over that surgical appointment. All the epileptics, across the board, are having a rough ride at the moment.'

Eric was right. I didn't like it. Daniel became bossy and bullyish. With me. The new boys he wooed, cruelly. But I didn't keep away, either.

First it was snails. Not racing them, not pretending, like Daniel and Robert used to pretend – this one a Porsche, that one an Aston Martin. Daniel got the crazy fitter boys crushing them, tweaking them out of their shells, trying to slice off their wobbly wet horns.

The boys loved it, and Daniel was their hero in no time.

The cockroach farm that came next wouldn't be so bad, I thought, as Daniel showed the boys and me the enclosed runs he'd assembled out of tins and cut-down cardboard boxes. Next he showed us the cockroaches – shiny and clean-looking in a black rubber bucket where they scrabbled on top of each other. Finally, Daniel produced a tobacco tin with tiny silver dressmaking pins hidden in the ash and stubs. The cockroaches were removed from the bucket one by one, by Daniel. The boys gasped at how neatly his toes pincered each insect. Daniel passed the cockroaches to the boys, who – instructed, encouraged, applauded by Daniel – pinned them through their middles, then pinned or propped them in the farm, so their legs could still move, but they couldn't go anywhere.

'Kill, kill!' yelled Billy, the smallest of the new-boy crazy fitters.

Billy was pale and chunky, with a hard nut of a head, spiky sharp hair, a flat face and wide-spaced eyes that you could tell had always swum in the wrong direction.

Thomas was skinny, limby and long. He had murky grey eyes and pointy little eye teeth coming through on either side of his gappy front teeth. He'd be getting them seen to soon, no doubt, by Dr Bulmer, and remembering how, when my eye teeth went west, I'd screeched and spewed blood all over that doctor-cum-dentist, I pitied Thomas. He was feeble and limp, but he exploded easily into kicking and fisticuffs and was the most enthusiastic insect-torturer of them all.

The third fitter, Rick – tiddlywink Rick – had soft, suedy-brown eyes which matched his light brown skin, and dark brown hair, cut short but with the look of a curl because of how the ends went different ways. Rick's epilepsy was the least of his problems. He was violent, as deaf as a post and an incurable pyro. He'd arrived at the Briar with an army sack stuffed with toy guns and real knives, matches, candles and kindling. Nurse Illingworth tittered at Rick's prettiness and called him mulatto. Other staff called him half-caste, tar-brush, scum, mongrel. Rick was a bed-wetter too.

'Not uncommon in pyromaniacs. You know that, don't you, Grace, I mean, Nurse Williams? More than thirty per cent, I believe.' Daniel taking the piss – not a blessing for anyone.

I often came across Rick in the laundry in those days. The nurses had decided that those bed-wetters who could should wash their own sheets. I quite liked plunging the soggy yellow cotton up and down in the enormous sinks, watching as the piss blended with then disappeared into the warm, soapy water. But I could tell that Rick was embarrassed by the way he wouldn't do any eye-to-eye with me, and by the way he did his plunging – quickly, carelessly and quite ineffectually.

One afternoon, Daniel produced a magnifying glass – pinched from the stamp-collectors, he said. He placed it over a small pile of brown leaves. We all watched. Nothing happened.

'The leaves must be damp,' announced Daniel. 'I'm sure the sun's strong enough.'

We were into February now, and it was still very cold, with grey frost on the shaded parts of the grass and in patches on all the trees, hedges and nearly empty flowerbeds. Yet there was sun – pale and small, but giving a white glare to everything and hurting your eyes if you turned towards it.

Daniel sent the boys to find the driest leaves they could. While they were gone, he stayed squatting on the ground, fiddling about with his feet, the leaves and the magnifying glass. I sat on the upside-down bucket and made a noisy show of buttoning my lip – flap-flop – but Daniel ignored me.

Billy and Thomas came back empty-handed. Clever Rick had sprinted all the way to the cricket pavilion. He mimed what he'd done, getting down on his hands and knees, crawling and blowing to show us how the wind had blown last autumn's leaves underneath the deck of the pavilion, keeping them dry and hard.

'Perfect,' said Daniel when Rick showed him the leaves he'd brought.

Daniel took the pale leaves and put them on a flat stone. Slowly, he passed the magnifying glass over them. This time, almost straightaway, the leaves crackled, crisped and began to smoke.

An ant treadled on to the stone and into the white light made by the magnifying glass. Daniel tilted the glass and made a tiny, concentrated bullet of heat. The ant's legs – and you could see that it was a common or garden worker ant – crinkled. Then, half quick, half slow, like your hair on a gas flame, the ant's six legs and two antennae shrivelled. I could almost hear them frizzle and fry. Next time I looked, the whole ant – head, big belly, small belly, all – had gone.

Rick grabbed the magnifying glass and started searching around for more ants to burn. The other two boys jumped up and down, begging Daniel to let them have a go.

'We need to be methodical,' said Daniel, imitating Miss Blackburn. 'The most important thing to know about the *Lasius niger*, the common ant,' he continued, 'is that it does not live alone as most insects do. It is, like us Briar termites, a social insect. To damage one is to damage the whole community.'

Being methodical involved dislodging stones and prodding earth until ants scurried into the open, where they met their undignified, hot, magnified deaths to the accompaniment of increasingly energetic war-dances and whooping from Daniel and his gang. I remained sitting and silent on the upside-down bucket, wondering whether I should tittle-tattle to Eric. Daniel was definitely misbehaving. Plus, Rick had acquired a dangerously fiery glint in his soft, chamois eye.

Over the next few days, the cold but powerful sun continued to shine, and, one lunchtime, the boys' ant-burning activities moved to the south side of the chapel. Daniel had discovered that the yellow gritty stone of the chapel wall made an even better surface for setting fire to the ants.

There was a shout from behind one of the buttresses. Billy appeared, followed by the two other boys.

'Look what I've found,' shouted Billy, waving a floppy black shape in his hand – a dead bat.

'Must've fallen off the roof,' said Daniel.

Rick put his hand on Daniel's shoulder and turned him towards the chapel. Daniel looked, then turned back to Rick, and a spark of understanding passed between them as they both put an innocent one and one together, making a wicked two.

Daniel, Rick, Thomas and Billy headed for the front door of the chapel. I followed, slowly. Once inside the chapel, we all stood for a moment, letting our eyes adapt to the dim light. Daniel and Rick were both staring upwards.

There was no upper level to the chapel that you could see, but to the right of the main entrance there was a small door which Rick opened to reveal a staircase. Rick led the way up it. At the top, a narrow passage with another door at the end opened into a space the size of the apple-house, but with a much higher roof – the roof of the chapel – and it was lighter than the apple-house, having two dusty skylights which you wouldn't have known were there from the ground. The floor was wood and solid enough, but along one wall was a gap, and when we all, except Rick, peered over it, there were the hollow tops of the organ pipes.

Rick nudged Daniel and pointed to the ceiling on the opposite side to the skylights. A row of folded bats hung in the safety of the shadow up there.

Billy was sent to fetch stones, pebbles, pins and knives. An orgy of destruction followed, with stones hurled to make the sleeping bats fall. Many of them didn't fall but started swooping as madly as the boys themselves. Those that did fall had their wings stretched until they split or were punctured by the boys with their stolen knives. Rick pricked holes with Daniel's sharp pins in the wing of one of them, in the shape of a star. When Daniel showed it to me, I knocked it from between his feet and set off down the stairs. As the heavy chapel door swung shut behind me, I heard Daniel's laughter unhinge and join the frenzied laughter of the younger boys.

That night, Rick leapt out of a window in the boys' ward. How quickly he must have climbed the small staircase of the chapel, sat down on the floor up there, emptied his pockets of dried leaves, twigs and empty cigarette packets and struck one match after another, setting his silent world alight and bunging bits of it into the hidey-hole pipes of the organ.

The chapel didn't burn to the ground, and the organ wasn't badly damaged, but the roof of the chapel did catch fire. The Watford fire brigade came. The whole hospital – staff, patients, gerries, disturbed, everybody – was marshalled on to the lawn in the pitch-black, freezing cold. A few of the nurses tried to do a head count, but half-heartedly because it was so dark and people kept moving about. Plus it was hard, even for them, not to keep looking at the chapel. Smoke seeped out of most of the upper windows, grey against the black sky, and there was a spreading red glow on the roof near the door.

When the firemen unwound their hoses and pelted the chapel with water, many of the patients, unable to contain themselves, started cheering, running towards the chapel, ringing it, shouting and waving. Matron managed to keep the girls and most of the boys in order, but I had a clear view of Daniel breaking free from the grip of a male nurse. Daniel went up to one of the firemen and started speaking to him. The fireman shook his head. Daniel hobbled away from him and in through the open door of the chapel. He nearly got swept off his feet, I saw, by the force of the water jetting through it as he disappeared inside. There were yells of alarm, but it was the hiss of the hoses I listened to – the magnified sound of sizzling ants.

A different fireman followed Daniel at a run. Firemen, patients and several staff began scudding all over the place. But I still managed to see through a gap when the fireman who had followed Daniel reappeared with Daniel next to him and what could only be Rick in his arms. Daniel slipped into the crowd and stood by my side. He was dirty and silent, looked worried but definitely alive.

Rick looked dead, but he wasn't. Blankets, torches, flames and shadows, Dr Jack's night-duty face flashing past me, nurses and patients pushing and shoving, then the lights and whine of an ambulance.

As the ambulance drove off, Daniel scuttled towards the Nissen hut. Eric lumbered after him. Gradually, the flames on the roof of the chapel turned to smoke and it became clear that the firemen were beginning to get the fire under control. The nurses managed to sort us back into wards, then lines, and as we were led off, there were just dirty, smouldering puffs coming from the roof of the chapel and melting into the wintry dawn.

1962

i

Alexandra Rose Day. Rose Day, Rose Day. The words were on everybody's lips from March onwards. At first it was rumour. Then it was real.

Ten thousand ladies selling wild roses on the streets of London, way back in 1912, Miss Blackburn told us. Charity.

The chaplain announced it formally at Easter. The Briar had been chosen as a special anniversary beneficiary. Fifty rosy years of charity. We were honoured. We repeated the words – Rose Day, Rose Day. They fluttered around the wards. People intoned and burped them. They were parroted, lisped, stuttered and muttered. It didn't really matter. We didn't really matter. We nattered – we nutters – and nattering away to the tune of Rose Day changed our grey, difficult, painful world into a joyful splosh of colour. That mattered. Preparing for Rose Day mattered.

Always an event, the fete that year was planned and perfected like never before. Roses were everywhere – in the hospital grounds, in the vegetable garden, even out in the fields, beyond the cricket pavilion.

'That's that, then,' Mr Peters lamented. 'No more home produce. And I'll be out of a job.'

Daniel said he was a prophet of doom, but probably right.

Nevertheless, it was this prophet of doom who saved Daniel's bacon shortly after Rick returned to the Briar with burnt legs and long hair. I was right, Rick's hair, long, was curly, and as shiny as mine used to be in the Vosene days. His legs were a mess, though – blistered, scaly, ruckled and ridged. He walked as if his skin was too tight for him.

Daniel apologized to Rick. I don't know what he said. To me, he said he felt responsible, but not guilty. Not like with Robert and the conkers.

'We were mates, that's the point, Rob and me. It was different with Rick. I was just bloody stupid.'

Bloody stupid. Eric had used the same words to Daniel,

'We all have a hard road to hoe, Daniel,' I heard him say. 'Believe you me. But that's no excuse for being bloody stupid. Now. Listen. Here's my plan.'

Mr Peters had been told way back in September the previous year to prepare the hospital grounds for planting roses where there were usually vegetables, fruit and his own choice of flowers. He had been told to keep quiet. Now, Alexandra Rose Day necessitated weekly trips for Mr Peters to Covent Garden. The Briar management committee was bent on producing the most magnificent display of roses any Alexandra Rose Day had ever seen. Mr Peters was provided with a blue Morris Minor, a petrol allowance, a map and a list of roses.

Gruff Mr Peters was really very timid, and I believe he was relieved when Eric announced his plan – that Daniel accompany him on his trips to London. At first Mr Peters spluttered and objected. He stood in the middle of the Nissen hut clutching his cap, looking around at the gathered crazy fitters as if afraid they might all want to come with him. But it didn't take Eric long to persuade Mr Peters that Daniel would be no trouble. He might even be an asset, he added. He could navigate, he'd be company, he could read the tiny labels on the roses. Everybody knew – except, it seemed, Mr Peters himself – that Mr Peters' eyesight was bad. It accounted for the cross look on his face, even when he wasn't cross.

When Mr Peters said yes, all the crazy fitters cheered, and when Charlie and another man lifted Daniel, like a football champion, high above their heads, I joined in.

So Daniel got to go to London every Friday morning. He left very early before anyone except Mr Peters and the night nurses were up, and he was back before lunch. I don't know how Eric wangled it, and I can't say I didn't mind. But I enjoyed the stories Daniel returned with. Most of them concerned the mishaps on his journeys with Mr Peters, who not only had weak eyes and no sense of direction, but whose driving, Daniel said, also left much to be desired.

'He pranged the Morris Minor turning into Floral Street. So now he always pretends to miss it – as if you could with a name like that and the market spilling out everywhere. We go careering off down Garrick Street, all the way to the Strand. Before you know it, there he is, going round and round Aldwych, grumbling away that it's my fault we're lost. When we're not lost at all. I know that part of London. From the van. From Papa.'

We were all impressed by the Smith-style account of the city where Nelson waved and Eros pissed, and I clustered round with the rest, yearning for more.

The best, Daniel always said, was the flower market itself.

'There are more colours than I knew existed. Seriously. Each week I see umpteen new ones. And the air – heavenly. Scented, like . . .' He would roll his eyes around the crowd, then up at the ceiling or sky. '. . . a million damp Miss Walsinghams – that's what it smelt like.' He would sniff and shiver with pleasure.

But the best was when Daniel shivered with a different sort of pleasure, alone with me in the apple-house.

'It's a corsage, Grace,' he said, standing in the doorway, nodding at his pocket where some greenery drooped and the head of a flower dangled. 'For you. Take it.'

Petals fluttered in the space between us as I pulled out a fat, floppy flower as pretty and soft as whipped cream, with yellow watercress stalks in its middle. Its edges were rusty, and the green surrounding it wet and webby.

'A camellia,' muttered Daniel, putting his face on my chest between my boosies. 'That's what Mr Peters says it is. We found it on the ground.'

With his teeth, Daniel undid two buttons of my cardie, then pressed his pointy nose flat on the flattish bone there.

'That's where it goes. Right there.' He kissed the bit he'd pressed, and stood up.

'Would you like to be a rich Parisienne, *ma belle*? The belle of the ball. You'd be wearing a long satin ball gown – what colour, Grace? – with a corsage to match. Not a silly old camellia. The best, most beautiful red roses in the world. And on your feet, high heels. A perfect fit. We'll dance. All night, we'll dance. And we won't stop, not even when dawn comes. Can you imagine?'

I can. And Daniel in the suit he described – *le smoking*, 'With a bow tie – black silk. Mother-of-pearl dress-studs – seven altogether, says Papa. And fine Italian handcrafted shoes – black, naturally.'

The flower market, Daniel told me, was as busy as the refectory at the Briar on a Saturday dance-night.

'People shouting, whistling, hustling. Muck all over the place. Squashed heads of flowers. Seas of leaves, a dozen different greens. Mr Peters always tuts. What a waste, he says.'

Mr Peters tended to tut. He'd been instructed to speed up with his work in the grounds of the Briar. He was offered a bigger team of helpers. He was offered a stronger team. He was even offered the crazy fitters. He tutted, said thank you but no, and, in the end, mustered the oddest team of farm hands. He chose a few of the older mongs. Then he plucked out some of the snail-like creatures from the back wards – soldiers and pilots, still shocked in their shells, or cracked and weeping. Finally, Mr Peters took on the new lock-ups – pale, shy, unfit men, moved to the Briar from Broadmoor last year. A scandal, said Daniel, who'd read about it in Will Sharpe's newspaper.

None of Mr Peters' men cared to talk, or if they did, nobody cared to listen. Mongy Simon gathered imaginary roses and placed them on an imaginary grave, but nobody seemed to notice. Benjamin from Broadmoor sang about roses – in Schubert songs, with Goethe words – but nobody ever responded. I only heard him because the work-gang passed the Children's Occupation Unit every day on their way to work. I recognized the songs, the words, the tunes and the slow churning up of a creamy white room, sunny afternoons, Father and me, the shadows on the ceiling, Thumbelina and the radiogram. But I'd stopped believing the stories behind or between the simple words and the lilting tunes. The naughty boy who picked the rose and got pricked by the rose. The madman in love, seeking a rose in the snow. Even Thumbelina dancing was really very small now.

And the soldiers didn't march. They crept out of their wards and trailed along the path on the other side of the COU. We saw them from the classroom window, and although Miss Blackburn explained about war and peace, roses, poppies, kings, countries and freedom, none of us knew what to make of it. None of us knew anything about Rose Day, really. Just rumours of royalty and Rose Day, Rose Day, ringing and ringing.

Things changed in March with the official announcement. A frenzy of preparation began, and increased week by week.

Between March and June, Mr Peters' team patrolled the roses in the visitors' garden with buckets of soft-soap, carried between them or poured into waterproof canvas sacks which they lugged on their backs. They pumped the soapy liquid through rubber tubes and brassy nozzles, squirting it over the roses and over each other. Gloomy Mr Peters predicted black fly, then white fly, and expected mildew, even in May. Soft-soaping the roses, he said, was an essential twice-weekly preventative measure.

Sometimes, if I was on laundry duty, I helped to mix the frothy buckets. First the water – warm, not hot – then the soapflakes. I spooned them in from the tub under the sink using a metal ladle hooked over my bad arm, and swung with the other.

We played with the ladle and the big wooden spoons meant for stirring. We pretended they were cricket bats, golf clubs, lolly sticks, roses, dicks, dollies, Sarah's Barbie, Dr Young, all of the nurses, mummies and daddies. Often they fought, making a slippery mess on the laundry floor. More often we drowned them, clanging their heads on the sides and the bottom of the bucket. But drowning them, dropping them in, was also an excuse for getting them out again. Because that meant a hand, or hands, in the bucket. I wasn't supposed to stir, but unless Ida was in charge, I usually managed to get my hand in, just for a mo.

So did anyone who had the chance. Daniel was snooty, but even he dipped a toe in occasionally. The soapy water bubbled on top, but underneath it was as smooth as Mother's stocking drawer, and afterwards my hand was silky clean, all the dirt from the edges gone, all the cracks and lines wiped out. Everything wiped. I wish it was, that Alexandra Rose Day.

By June, all pretence of routine was abandoned. Daniel and most of the junior crazy fitters were transferred to Major Simpson's team. Every afternoon, they raced around the grounds making a lot of boy-noise, putting up tents and taking them down again, fetching tables, lining up chairs, lining up in front of Major Simpson.

I helped Miss Lily with costumes for the pixie's pageant. The youngest children were to mime the adventures of the White Rose Queen, the loss of her crown and the finding of it by a small pixie. Miss Lily had been helping me and Missy with our frocks for the Rose Queen parade. The Rose Queen would be crowned at three o'clock. Later on there would be dancing at the Rose Queen ball. There would be Daniel, who Miss Lily called my *beau*.

The Rose Queen parade and, later on, the dancing. That was how it was supposed to go. These would take place in the visitors' garden. I wouldn't forget.

'I'll see you there,' Daniel winked. 'The first dance is mine. Don't forget. And the last.'

I won't.

My new built-up shoes were ready and waiting. My new built-up shoes were a surprise for Daniel. Will's suggestion.

The industrial units that had sprung up to replace the old workshops did make space for Will's cobbler's tools and equipment, but they were relegated to a small corner of the grand new leather-works section, where Will Sharpe was to oversee the making of a range of leather belts for a nationwide retailer. From now on, Daniel explained, most of us were going to be fitted with plastic shoes that had rubber soles glued to them.

'Cheaper,' said Daniel. 'Cheapskate, says Will. From a manufacturer in Peterborough. And when they wear out, we'll throw them away and get a new pair, not bother sending them for mending any more.'

Daniel was right, and over the next few months the hospital became much quieter as plastic and rubber replaced leather, and muffled padding or heavy flapping replaced the echoing tap-clip-shuffle of steel and leather on lino, stone, rough deal and smooth, slippery, polished wood.

I was one of the people unsuitable for such shoes. I was measured for them along with everybody else, lining up in the refectory, putting my socked feet, one after the other, on the flat metal plate of the measuring slide, waiting while the small stranger from Peterborough nervously buckled the measuring strap and slid the measuring nut into place. Afterwards, I had to walk to the door of the refectory and back while the Peterborough man watched and wrote things down in a little red notebook.

Not being suitable for the rubber-soled shoes, I was sent to Will Sharpe in the new industrial units. My short leg had got shorter, and I was walking more and more bent. But the stout pair of built-ups – one thicker than the other – that Will managed to make for me put an end to the bends. I wasn't upright, and my hump made me hunch, but once I got the hang of the built-ups, I swanned.

All through May and June, I practised walking in my new shoes, with Will helping me, him clopping, me clop-pying, across the bare concrete floors of the half-finished industrial units. Will taught me how to turn, how to stop and even how to kick a football. He called my kick the Williams' welly and showed me pictures in his sports' pages of penalties, goals and corners, teams, flags and supporters. Spurs, Wolves, Burnley and Liverpool, Watford, Pompey and the Cobblers. I became a great fan.

I was to wear my shoes for the first time on 26 June 1962 – Alexandra Rose Day. I was ready. Mother and Father couldn't attend the celebrations that year, but I scarcely cared. I was fifteen. My heart was beating.

Alexandra Rose Day dawned, pink and full of promise. The nurses rushed, as keen as us. We were taken for break-fast to the main refectory in our nightgowns and barefoot, so that the whole ward could be stripped and tidied earlier than usual.

There were too many people in the refectory, too many grown-up men and women. There was joshing and pushing. When it was time to carry our plates to the end of the room for washing, the joshing and pushing got worse. A man, wearing boots, stood on my bare toe. I tripped and swore. I knocked into a nurse I'd never seen before. She started shouting, first at me and then at Nurse Halliday, who was new and young. Nurse Halliday looked to Nurse Hughes for help, but Nurse Hughes was busy with Ida, who was trying to steal slices of wet bread from the slop bucket.

Nurse Halliday said I'd have to be punished, and on our way back to the ward we stopped by the COU. Nurse Halliday unlocked it and told me to go in and wait. I was to miss the trip to the laundry to collect clean underwear, and I was to miss the treat, after that, of going back to the refectory for orange squash and biscuits provided by the Friends of the Briar. But they would collect me later, in time to get dressed for the fete, in time to prepare for the Rose Queen parade.

I sat for a while in my usual seat, behind my desk, and stared at the blackboard where yesterday's date was still written clearly in the top left-hand corner. The rest of the board had been cleaned, but not very thoroughly, and there were traces of sums, spellings, a diagram, two plants – roses, no doubt.

I went up to the blackboard and pressed one finger on its chalky surface. I moved my finger slowly to the right, making a thick, dark smudge. Miss Blackburn kept the chalk for the board in her desk drawer, along with her specs and her sandwiches. I took the chalk from the drawer – just one stick, but it broke into two – and carried it back to my seat.

I drew on my desk, wiped the mess with my arm, let the chalks drop to the floor, let my head drop to my arm, my arm asleep on the desk. Pins and needles. Deadhead.

I awoke with a start, needing a wee, and cold. I went over to the reading corner, sat in Miss Blackburn's reading chair, crossed my legs like nearly-pissing Daniel did. I waited, suspected, checked – wet. I shivered.

I sat on the floor, tweaked at the woolly bits on the reading rug, counted the books, counted the pages, dozed some more, woke up again. My belly rumbled. I could hear the hospital band. Alexandra Rose Day had started without me.

I slept. I woke up. It was almost dark. I could hear voices faraway. Laughter. Then, some time later, music from one of Major Simpson's dance records. I'd helped him choose them earlier in the week. Looking for gavottes. Finding foxtrots, tangos and any number of waltzes. We all enjoy a waltz, Grace.

I tore up the books, I shat on the floor. I took all the chalk from Miss Blackburn's desk drawer and stamped on it. I ripped off my nightgown. I knocked on the door and scratched at the window. I pulled out the fingernails of my bad hand and made a pattern with them on the windowsill. I plunged my good hand into the squelchy shit. I pressed my shit into the wool of the reading rug, smeared it across the books, dribbled it through my fingers, scrawled my hand, both sides, along the blackboard, wiped my fingers through my hair – your crowning glory, darling. I bangadanged my head on the wall, making my hair flip like a pizzle.

I slept some more.

'There she is. Oh, my lord.' Nurse Halliday's voice.

'Grace?' Miss Blackburn's voice, but quieter than usual. I opened my eyes. Nurse Halliday's face, next to Miss Blackburn's. Both faces peering and wary.

'Do you know what time it is, Grace?'

I raised my swollen eyes to the clock above the board. At first it was blank – look, no hands. Then it hung upside down on the hard, starched boosy of the wall – nil by mouth for this slug-a-bed. Eventually it settled, and its hands waved in their usual, friendly fashion.

'Grace, it's late,' said Miss Blackburn calmly. 'I'm very tired. We'll sort this out in the morning.'

Miss Blackburn wrapped me in one of the blue satin cloaks from the pixie-pageant. She'd brought a pile of costumes and props back to the classroom, and she finished storing them in the cupboard at the back while I stood by the door. Nurse Halliday was sent to inform Matron that Grace Williams had been found. Miss Blackburn told me to move my legs and arms to keep warm, but I didn't because of the shit all over me and now all over the blue satin cloak.

When she was ready, Miss Blackburn helped me out of the COU and into the hospital grounds. The stink of shit came with us, but it mingled with the smell of a hundred different varieties of rose which the damp night air had deepened and released.

There were still lights on in several of the hospital buildings. There was even music, very soft, popping out from one of the ground-floor nurses' rooms, and as we passed the visitors' lawn I heard stifled laughter and voices. It was too dark to see anything, but I know I heard Daniel's voice and I know I heard Missy's.

Crack, went my heart, even though I clutched Nelson tight – tighter, Grace – with my good hand.

'Come.' Definitely Daniel, and in his dipsy, husky, film-star voice.

Then a giggle. At a pinch, it could have been any young girl's. But, 'Come, Missy.' Daniel again, filmier than ever. He sounded like the doctors when they flirted with the nurses.

'Don't, Daniel dishy Smithy.' Missy, for sure, but why she got it into her head to call him that, I've no idea.

And then the real cracker.

'Give us a kiss, pretty Missy.' Sing-song. Pretend?

Miss Blackburn's pace increased, and she talked about what would happen tomorrow.

'There's going to be the most God-almighty hoo-ha, Grace. You must be aware of that. But,' she went on, 'not tonight. Not if I've anything to do with it. Tonight, at least, I intend to keep an eye on you.'

We didn't pause at the door to the girls' ward, where all the lights were off except for the tiny globe of the night nurse's lamp. We took a path that led across the lawn, past the cedar tree to the main drive and the gate-house, where Miss Blackburn and Miss Lily shared a flat on the floor above Toby's. The entrance to the flat was up a spiral iron staircase at the back of the gatehouse, and as I took a step up, I tripped on the long cloak. Miss Blackburn unwrapped it from my shoulders and stayed behind me, close. I could feel her breath on my filthy, hump-backed skin as I hauled myself up the steps. At the top, she stepped past me, opened the door, and I followed her inside.

In a few weeks' time, and certainly by the time of the *Sleeping Beauty* Christmas play that year, I would know some parts of that small flat like the back of Nelson. But on the night after Alexandra Rose Day, I didn't notice much.

Miss Blackburn woke Miss Lily, who was lying in a double bed piled high with quilts and a pink crocheted blanket. The women whisked me into the tiny bathroom off the bedroom, stood me in the bath, and soaped and shampooed me, using a jug, until the water ran clear. They wrapped me in a towel and helped me, naked, into the bed, which was still warm from Miss Lily's body. Miss

Blackburn told Miss Lily to sit with me while she went to make sandwiches for all of us.

My costume for the Rose Queen parade hung alone on its hanger above Miss Lily's dressing table. On the floor by the door were my smart new built-ups. No prizes for guessing who'd won the Rose Queen crown.

I fell asleep before Miss Blackburn returned with the sandwiches. When I woke up it was morning. The sandwiches were still there, on a blue and white tree-patterned plate, so I ate them – egg and cress – and they tasted very good.

The official hoo-ha started as soon as I went back to the ward. It wasn't as bad as I'd feared – two days in the punishment room, followed by two weeks on toilet-cleaning duty. But Nurse Halliday masterminded an unofficial hoo-ha, and she turned out to be a very nasty piece of nursey work.

'You're a disgrace, Grace Williams. A filthy fucking pigface. Stick her head in it.'

I licked the shit from the wet enamel of the nurses' toilet. I deserved it, they all agreed.

But I was a big girl by then – nearly sixteen – and, despite the crack, my heart was still beating. I didn't scream, not even when Nurse Halliday poked the rubber tube into my mouth with all the laundry girls laughing. Nor when it went into my belly, and the soapy bubbles broke like glass inside me. Ten thousand women on the streets of London. Remember that, Grace. Ten thousand wild roses. And Mr Peters, who knew about these things nowadays, said that wild roses grew on the highest slopes of the Himalayan mountains. Apples and pears did well there too, apparently, and wheat and potatoes were grown in great quantities. The air, he said, was scented by the wild roses, which grew in large bushes covered with hundreds of cream-coloured blossoms.

'Itchy feet. That's all it is, was. Don't get in a tizz-wozz, Grace. I've got itchy feet. Forgive me.'

Daniel said Missy might be pretty, but, 'She's prissy and silly. And I prefer Grace. My Grace.'

As to his itchy feet, he added, 'I miss the outside world, Grace. More than I can tell you. Misbehaving, messing around like I did with Missy, being bloody stupid. They're just ways of trying to forget. How much.'

We were standing at the gates to the Briar, watching them open and close for the postman, a delivery van, Major Simpson in his Ford, like Mother's, Mr Maitland in a Bentley saloon. Major Simpson waved at us and saluted Toby, who saluted back.

'One day,' said Daniel, going right up close to the gate, 'I'll escape. Properly.' He pressed his narrow forehead to the bars.

Fear ziggered up my spine as I joined him at the gate.

'Me too?' I said.

'No question.' Daniel knocked his head on the bars, tapped his shoe against mine. 'I'd never leave without you, Grace, and if I did, I'd come back.'

I tapped.

'That's right. Secretly. As soon as I could. I'd always come back for you.'

Just then Miss Lily came into view, hurrying towards the Briar on the road from the village.

'I wonder where she goes. I think she goes for a walk, that's all. But some people say she has a lover in the village, and some people think she's a witch.'

Miss Lily thanked Toby for opening the gate and said hello to Daniel and me. Her mouth, like most of her, was small and exact.

'By the way, Grace. Daniel,' she said, turning to go, but

not by the way at all. 'You're invited to tea. With me. Next Friday.'

There was an outbreak of chickenpox at the Briar that summer, so my first ever Friday afternoon tea with Miss Lily didn't take place until September.

While I was in the infirmary, scratchy and crotchety, Daniel, who said he was immune, visited regularly. He told me that Miss Lily was a lovely lady.

'Although she says her name is White. "My name's Miss White," she told us, "Lily Madeleine White. But call me Black, if you prefer. Call me Blanche. Call me Bianca, or Irish Lil. Call me the Lily White Virgin of Dublin's fair city. It's all the same to me," she said. Miss Blackburn calls her Maddy.'

Call her mad. To most she was Miss Lily, the hospital seamstress, and Miss Lily's Friday afternoon teas were a hospital legend. She had an arrangement with the ward staff which meant a group of us were sent, or taken, to her flat, to do or learn, I don't know what. The names of all her swathes of fabric? Muslin, serge, kersey and merino. Seersucker, shantung, crêpe de Chine. A veritable family, she'd say. Silk, Swiss cotton and the softest viyella. Yet each and every one unique.

Miss Lily taught me manners, that's for sure, but much, much more besides. She taught me how to lay the table and reminded me how to hold a spoon properly. How to sit, not shit, eat, not spew, drink without dribbling. I even learnt to open the tea-caddies and measure out the tea. Miss Lily called it scooping the scoop. Oolong, Souchong or Darjeeling? I think we'll have Earl Grey today, Grace. She called it the cut and thrust of etiquette. She called it our ticket to heaven. The outside world. Above all, though, she taught me what Daniel called alchemy.

'Word alchemy, Grace. Changing things.'

Miss Lily's afternoon teas certainly made a change,

and I looked forward to them more than anything that autumn.

There were three boys and three girls in my Miss Lily group. Wetness in the air and puddles islanding the new gravel path that led from the COU, past the industrial units to the gatehouse. The exterior spiral staircase, which we helter-skeltered up, had rusty patches and a lumpy, bolted handrail that wobbled when you held it.

The six of us arrived on the threshold, out of breath and with damp, dead leaves clinging to our shoes. The door opened and there was a smiling Miss Lily. She helped us in, off with our coats – wipe your feet well, mind – and had us sitting in no time. Three on the settee, deep in its pink and green cushions. Two, including me because of my size, squashed on to a dark blue velveteen armchair which tickled and pricked the skin between my socks and the hem of my dress. The piping tucked neatly into the crease behind my knee. I liked pinching the piping with the thumb and forefinger of my good hand. Daniel sat on a low redwood stool next to the fireplace.

Tea was already laid, but not on the table, on a teak sideboard. We were instructed, one by one, and each one differently, each according to our abilities, on how to take a plate, unfold a napkin, use a saucer. When Miss Lily was satisfied, 'That's the ticket,' she'd say. 'Help yourself.'

And the spread was good. Yesterday's bread but with strawberry jam, home-made, or molasses, which looked like Matron's nasty radio malt but tasted as sweet as Mother's marmalade, and china cups of tea with tea leaves the size of tiny twigs. The twigs formed a brown pattern on the bottom of your white cup, and if you were lucky, Miss Lily read your fortune. It was only pretend – merry old make-believe, she called it.

When winter came on, when it was already dark outside before we arrived, Miss Lily lit a fire and lamps, and tucked us into rugs and shawls, muted purples and mauves with sudden silver streaks or hemmed with thick gold thread. Shooting stars, Arabian nights, Scheherazade's stories. Best believing.

Daniel scoffed. Miss Lily smiled. Daniel was always one of the first to finish his tea and raise his cup hopefully.

'No, Daniel. Manners. You must ask. Politely, please.'

While we ate, pin-thin Miss Lily, who ate not a morsel herself, talked. She rarely sat down, even though there was one other chair in the room – a dining chair, plain enough in shape but softly rounded at the top, like a heart, and crossed by a single bar with a carved rose in the middle. Its legs tapered, and the seat was wide and curved.

'Like the curve of the earth,' said Miss Lily, smoothing her hands over the creamy cambric, which was fastened to the wood with studs covered in the same rough off-white fabric.

'Ecru,' she announced. 'French polish. A rose by any other name.'

She was quite, quite mad. And everything, especially the strawberry jam, was quite, quite delicious.

Miss Lily talked until it was time to put down our teacups on their saucers – neatly, quietly, please, ladies and gentlemen – and start the real business, as she called it, of the afternoon. We took it in turns to sit on the cream-covered chair and play Miss Lily's game.

Miss Lily's game had no name. Not even Daniel managed to invent one. It was simply Miss Lily's game, and it was very simple. While you sat on the chair, you had to be somebody or something else. There were no other rules. If you had trouble choosing, which was rare, the rest of the group helped. Conversation, directed and presided over by Miss Lily, continued as usual, except for the change in identity, which had to be respected at all times, of the person sitting on the chair.

First of all, that first afternoon, we had Matron, I think, then Queen Elizabeth. Daniel, to be different and make us laugh, chose to be a dog – the poor old collie from the village who sometimes wandered lamely into the grounds and buildings of the Briar, pissing in the laundry, stealing from the kitchen.

My turn next. I chose Wilma Rudolph.

Daniel had brought me the newspaper cutting ages ago – the Olympics in Rome. He knew I'd like the picture of the Colosseum with the whole British team posing in front of it. Blazers in the blazing sun. I also liked the story of the tall dark lady from Tennessee sprinting her way to gold in both the one-hundred- and two-hundred-metre races. Quite a journey. That cutting went in my secret collection, such as it was. I bunged it in a corner of the apple-house, under the strawberry punnets, along with a get-well card from Mother and Father, the remains of my camellia corsage and the scraps of red and orange wool that I pulled from people's jumpers whenever I could because, put together, they looked like Robert's hairy head.

Miss Lily nodded encouragingly at my choice, and for the next few minutes her questions ran me out of my crippled body and into Wilma's. She asked me what it felt like to run so fast, what it felt like to win, to stand on the podium, hearing the cheering people? How many hours a day did I train? Would I give up running if I married, had a husband, children, family? What did I intend to do with the rest of my life?

I believed in it all so much that when Miss Lily nodded in the very particular way she had, to indicate that it was time to return to my place, I sprang up from the seat unusually quickly, as if I still had Wilma's powerful limbs. My shrivelled leg gave way and I toppled clumsily to the floor. As I tumbled, I glanced backwards and I saw, right in the middle of the white cambric chair-seat, a spreading, red-brown stain.

Miss Lily came to help me up, and, as she bent over me, I saw her see the stain too. It was dark, jagged and ugly.

'I die?' I shrieked.

'Calm, calm,' said Miss Lily, calmly. 'You're not dying. Sit down and I'll explain. It's moontime.'

Miss Blackburn, who had come into the room, alerted by my shriek, led the other children away.

I sat and bled and worried about the stained fabric, while Miss Lily talked about months and the moon, seeds ripening, bleeding, babies and nature's cycles.

'Walls inside us, Grace. Waxing and waning. Thickening and shedding.'

She mentioned Adam and Eve, eggs, napkins and, several times, the colour red. Then she opened a drawer in her rosewood cabinet and took out a wodge of fabric squares. Their edges were pinked, and they were every shade of red.

'Which is your favourite?' Miss Lily lovingly flicked and patted the pretty squares.

'Henna, oxblood, sorrel, terracotta? Take your pick, Grace. Titian, burgundy, cerise, puce? You choose. You say.'

Her small, exact mouth tremored with pleasure at the words it formed.

There were no anatomical details. They came later, when Miss Blackburn returned. But there was alchemy. There was escape. In great, mad, Miss Lily-ish dollops. I was made to feel a lady. In a story. In a way that would never again let me be merely fuckwit Grace – spastic, menstruating Grace bloody Williams who had to be taken later to Matron for sanitary rags.

Matron and the nurses called the bleeding the curse, but

I went back to the ward that night with my head, like my womb, ripening and shedding. Ripening, reddening, readying. I went to bed a Sleeping Beauty.

A few weeks later, the auditions took place, I was chosen and rehearsals began. And Daniel began to misbehave again. But did I care? This time, no.

As soon as Prince Daniel had kissed me – 'Let me kiss your sweet lips,' the wake-up cue – it was Ged's job to dim the lights. While it was dark, I was supposed to nip off the bed, then hop-skip quickly off the stage in time for Missy to enter, take my place and steal the show with her pretty, fake waking-up.

But Daniel always went on kissing me and kissing me, so that when the lights came back on, he was still kissing me, and Missy was standing there, looking an ass, not knowing what to do. What a to-do.

What would Daniel do when we acted our play in front of our parents and visitors? Daniel's dad wasn't coming – Smith-business, shrugged Daniel, it's brisk, this Christmas, in Paris – but Mother and Father were due, and Matron said they were bringing Sarah too.

On the afternoon of the performance, however, Daniel was helpful in the green room and he was quiet backstage, setting a good example to the younger kiddies, princely and charming to all. When the moment came, on stage, for him to kiss me, he did it efficiently, then, in the darkness, helped me off the bed. No whispering or fumbling. I scarpered. From the wings, I saw him turn to Missy as the lights came back on and smile. But it wasn't Smith-style. Not his usual grinning thing. Just pretending. I could tell.

And at curtain call, when in rehearsals I often fell, I stood proudly on one side of Daniel. Missy was curtseying prettily on his other side. I couldn't curtsey, so Miss Blackburn had told me simply to try and stand still. Daniel bowed – his low, sweeping bow that didn't make his hair flip today, because Miss Lily had greased it flat. When Daniel stood up, he kissed me – in front of everybody – and everybody clapped.

'And they all lived happily ever after.' Sarah shut the Ladybird book of *Sleeping Beauty* and put it down on the table.

'Sarah's learning to read,' said Father, later, in the COU dining room, where Miss Blackburn had organized tea and mince pies for the cast and their relatives. 'She knows her favourite stories off by heart. Don't you, *elskling*?' He ruffled her hair, which was still as wispy as a baby's. Sarah was four and a half. Four and three-quarters, Sarah corrected.

'Don't you?'

Don't we all?

Sarah nodded but didn't look up. She'd crumbled the mince pie with her spoon, and now she was pushing a finger around in the brown slime, making patterns and shapes and a mess.

'Don't do that,' said Mother. 'What on earth's the matter with you?'

'The others are,' muttered Sarah, looking around the room. Two mongs opposite us were squeezing their mince pies in their hands. The raisiny insides of the pies dripped through their fingers in sticky dark blobs. And there was Ida, by the serving hatch, using her fat hands to snatch at the mince pies as they came through. She stuffed them into her gob, but wet mucky lumps dropped on her boosies and dripped to the floor.

'She is,' Sarah added, looking at me. I was eating neatly with my good hand, but there were flakes of pastry on my frock, around the Nelson area, and my sweet lips were smacking and spliced with pieces of pith and gluey sultana.

'Besides,' Sarah went on, jabbing a mincey finger at the picture of the princess on the front of *The Sleeping Beauty*, 'Grace doesn't look a bit like she should.'

'That's enough,' said Mother, and hauled Sarah off the bench, with Sarah wrestling and protesting.

'But it's true,' Sarah was shrieking now. 'Grace is ugly. It's horrible here. I want to go home.'

Mother had to drag Sarah, squirming, screaming, scratching at Mother's arm, out of the room. It reminded me so much of me that I couldn't help chuckling. And I wasn't the only one. The two mongs opposite us went on laughing so long that Miss Blackburn had to come over to shut them up.

'Wasn't Grace good?' said Miss Blackburn to Father.

'Yes,' said Father 'Jolly good.' He didn't ruffle my hair, which was just as well because I was still wearing my crown, made from a plastic hairband with silver cardboard stuck on. My hair had loosened from the plastic spikes, and I was worried the whole thing might fall off. But Father did try to smile and patted Nelson.

'Jolly good,' he repeated.

'Are you going home for Christmas this year, Grace?' Miss Blackburn turned to me.

Mr Maitland had advised against it. Erratic behaviour, he'd written on my report. Frequently sexually inappropriate.

Father cleared his throat.

'That reminds me,' he said hastily. 'Christmas. We've presents in the car for you, Grace. I'll fetch them.'

By the time he came back, Mother and Sarah had returned. Mother said they'd better get going. Snow was forecast, and the roads would be slow.

As soon as they'd gone, a male nurse swiped my presents.

'I'll put them somewhere safe,' he said.

But Daniel spotted them later in the male nurses' sitting room. With Eric's help, he organized a rescue mission, and I was given my presents on Christmas day in the Nissen hut.

'You're an honorary crazy,' said Daniel.

It was snowing, and every time a crazy fitter burst through the door, feathers of snow blurred the air and stayed on the men's hair until the men came near the stove and shook or rubbed their heads. The Nissen hut was smoky, and my belly full of Eric's turkey fritters. Also, my head was fuzzy from a new lot of drugs – libido-lesseners, laughed nasty Nurse Halliday. Nevertheless, I was almost sure the parcels on the floor by my feet weren't mine. They didn't look at all the same as the ones Father had left in the COU dining room. And when I opened them, they turned out to contain two pairs of mens' underpants, two pairs of itchy, thick-knitted socks, two checked hankies and a pouch of tobacco.

While the fitters went on crazy-Christmasing into the dark afternoon, Daniel and I slipped out of the Nissen hut, my good hand clutching, and Nelson piled with, the funny presents. We slid and thumped through the thick-ening snow to the apple-house.

It wasn't cold at first.

'Snow insulates,' said Daniel. 'Wait long enough, and we'll be in an igloo.'

Plus we were wearing our new duffel coats.

We were ever so chuffed with our thick, tartan-lined, camel-coloured duffel coats. Eric had acquired them from a friend of a friend down in Portsmouth with a brother in the Navy. The brother diverted some of the Navy's stocks of postwar surplus duffel coats our way, along with a box of black woolly hats.

The woolly hats went to Mr Peters' gardening team. Sailors all over the world wore them, Eric told us. They could be bought in ports all over the world. Admirals, deckhands and bosuns wore them. Carpenters, petty officers, able seamen. Everybody.

Everybody, children, adults and even some of the younger male nurses, wanted a duffel coat. But Eric was in charge and he asked Miss Lily to shorten and adapt the smallest of the coats for us. Daniel's even had the arms properly cut off and two circles of matching duffel inserted at the shoulder. The duffel coats were still enormous, but all the better for that. They kept our legs warm, and although you couldn't move very fast in them, you felt protected.

Daniel liked the large outside pockets with covering flaps. He often asked me to stand behind him and put my good right hand into his right-hand pocket and pat his hip through the thick material. He said he always used to keep his hands in his pockets at the Paris markets in winter, to keep them warm.

I was a fan of the toothy toggles. There were four, and one of them was in just the right place to be held and stroked by my good hand, like the Triumph Herald, Miranda's hairslides, Mother's clothes pegs, Father's corkscrew – its smooth handle, his big white hand on top of my whiter, smaller one pretending to pull out the cork, then mine on top of his, feeling him really pull. The sound of pouring and Father's voice pouring over me – cheers, santé, skål, Grace.

'Don't be sad, Grace.' Daniel's voice was quiet in the apple-house.

It was difficult to do more than kiss with the duffel coats on, but we kept them on and managed as best we could. Eventually, though, the cold got through. Daniel's face was blue, and my boosies, especially the tips, as hard as light switches.

We decided to leave the apple-house, but when we opened

the door, we found the air foggy and stripier than ever with snow.

'We must dress for the occasion,' said Daniel solemnly. 'We're not going back to our wards, Grace. We're not going back to the Nissen hut. Imagine you're in Alaska. The Alps, Siberia, the Arctic Circle. We're traversing a snow field. Visibility nil. Blizzards expected.'

He toed a pair of underpants towards me.

'Balaclava,' he said. 'Put it on. Time to go.'

I struggled a bit pulling the underpants over my head, but it was easy doing the second pair over Daniel's because they were extra large, and his head definitely wasn't. The pants covered our heads, our necks and our shoulders, leaving just our faces poking out through the dick-slits.

'Excellent,' said Daniel. 'Next. Skins.' He lay down and began to wiggle his shoe-ed foot into one of the socks. 'Sealskin. That's what they use. These will do perfectly.'

When we were ready, 'This way,' he said.

And we set off, socked, balaclava-ed and duffeled, including the hoods.

'Where are you, Grace?' asked Daniel a few minutes later as we slopped blindly through the snow in the orchard. 'Tibet? Tromsø? Kilimanjaro?'

I was trying to recall our Oxfordshire garden, puffy then slushy with snow. Me in the old pram. The pram wheels sticking and sliding. Mother laughing. Miranda and John rolling over and over. The smell of Father's pipe smoke. Memory-blobs, soft and disappearing as the snow itself.

'I'm in Switzerland, Grace,' said Daniel, hopping ahead of me like a snow hare now we'd reached the gravel drive. 'Well, not quite. I'm at the border, still in Germany. I'm a spy, carrying secret information. I'm escaping.'

He stopped by one of Mr Peters' snow-covered topiaried privets.

'Shhh. Here we are. The border.'

Daniel launched himself head first into the bush. I could hear a muffled chortling, and when I was near enough to see nothing but a mound of leafy snow with a pair of itchy, thick-knit socks sticking out, I joined in, full blast.

1963

i

We escaped together in 1963. Not for ever. But to Torquay. For two whole weeks.

The news came in April, on the day of my first-ever trip to the hairdresser. As I set off from my ward with Nurse Ellis, there was still snow on the ground and on the branches of all the trees at the Briar. It was that cold. 1963, the coldest winter since 1740. Will Sharpe's newspaper had pictures of icebergs floating in Lowestoft harbour, and beaches where huge blocks of ice had formed when the waves broke and their spray froze.

I knew about snow long before I saw it at the Briar, and I liked it. But snow was one of Daniel's passions. His stories were full of snow. My favourite, even though he never finished it, was about a beautiful girl who lived in the tiniest village perched in the highest mountains in the furthest corner of south-east France. When she grew up, the girl went to Paris to become a dancer and make her fortune. But she met and fell in love with a handsome Englishman. He promised to help her career, and it wasn't long before the young woman fell pregnant. What should she do? A child would ruin everything. She waited until her belly was too big to hide, then she hurried back to her mountain village, and one dark September night, with the first big winter snows curling down from the peaks, through the trees, and settling on all the houses and fences, barns, hedges and fields, she gave birth to a perfect, dark-haired baby boy. The next evening, when it had stopped snowing, she wrapped the baby warmly in a woollen shawl and carried the bundle all the way to the forest, which spread from the banks of the icy river, up the hillsides to the mountain pastures. The snow in the moonlight glittered shadowy blue and silver-grey. Trees looked straighter, mountains clearer.

The girl reached a glade in the forest where the snow was soft, the air unmoving and quiet. She laid the baby in the earthy dip of a tree and kissed it farewell. Then she retraced her steps to the village, to Paris, to a dazzling career in the capital's theatres and dance halls. But she never saw the handsome Englishman again.

Sometimes Daniel stopped, ending the story there. Sometimes he merely paused.

What she didn't know, this beautiful girl, he'd then continue, was that she was not alone in the forest. A poor woodcutter was out cutting wood by the light of the nearly-full moon. He came across footsteps in the snow, faint, small, human footsteps, and he followed them. They grew even fainter as fresh snow began to fall, but eventually the man came to the clearing. He stood still. No more footprints.

'Shhh. What can you hear?' Daniel would say, and people would chip in, hooting like owls, flapping their clothes. 'No. Listen. What do you hear? A baby's breath? The touch of a feather on a single hair of your skin? The heartbeat of an injured bird? The movement of your mother's milk? Not even as loud as that. The woodcutter hears. He's a patient man. He waits.'

We waited. Not very patiently. But Daniel never finished this story.

Why not rescue the perfect boy from beneath the flipping tree, I wondered, scooting along the icy path with

Nurse Ellis towards the main hospital building and my hairdressing appointment.

There had been a hairdressing salon at the Briar for more than a year. It was on the first floor of the main building in what used to be the doctors' digs. It was for female staff and female adult patients only. The hairdressers were real trained hairdressers, and there were U-shaped basins, oval mirrors and giant-sized space helmets for drying your hair. It was a place I liked a lot and visited a lot, later, when I became an adult patient and had my own spending money. This first visit, when I was still on the children's ward, was a reward for spring-cleaning all the store cupboards on the ward. It was a job the nurses hated because of the old hoarded food in the cupboards – mouldy, smelly, stuck to the wooden slats and difficult to clean off. You had to use your fingernails, and bits always stuck underneath them.

I followed Nurse Ellis, who was having her hair done too, into the building and up the stairs. When we entered the salon, there was Ida, who'd moved to a women's ward after Christmas, installed on one of the wheeled chairs in front of a mirror. Ida seemed bigger than ever. She wore a pair of men's work trousers and work boots, but most of her was covered by a pink overall – pink with splatters of red and orange, flowers and buds. Ida was bigger, but better – she took no notice of me. She was deep in conversation with the hairdresser, who stood there with a permanent smile on her face, winding Ida's hair into rollers and dabbing at it with a wet, flat brush. Next to Ida, a young nurse was having her hair washed, and Sister from the children's ward sat opposite, under one of the hairdrying helmets. Sister nodded hello to me, and Nurse Ellis sat me in a wheeled chair two along from Ida.

I watched us all reflected and multiplied dozens of times

in the dizzying mirrors, until the hairdresser finished rolling Ida's hair and came over to me.

'Shampoo and set?' she asked, running her fingers through my hair, like Miss Lily through her silks.

'Like you,' I said.

The hairdresser's hair – masses of it – puffed and swooshed on top of her head.

'That's a beehive,' she said, and patted her piled-up hair proudly. 'You can't have that. It's shampoo and set or a dry cut for you.'

I chose shampoo and set. Wouldn't you?

When my hairdresser went to rinse Nurse Ellis's hair, leaving me with my rollers taut and crackling, I stretched out my hand and stole Nurse Ellis's powder compact from where it lay on the shelf next to her lipstick and the hairdresser's combs, scissors, lotions and sprays.

After my own rinsing and the removing of the rollers, I scarcely recognized myself curling away in all those mirrors, so it surprised me that Daniel didn't comment when he found me later on the high-up bench in the rock garden. I was busy examining my face and hairdo in the small round mirror inside the powder compact. I was pleased with what I could see of my hair, but I had to move the mirror and my eyes in semicircles and study a section at a time. The stiff, lifted waves of hair definitely made me ladylike. My skin was grey in the dull light and, close-up, holey. I liked the shine on my nose and chin, but I dabbed a bit of powder here and there – just for fun, Grace. Then I tried to look at my eyes in the mirror but the mirror was too small, and when I put my face up close, my eyelashes brushed uncomfortably against the silver glass.

Daniel flapped an envelope against my face.

'Marry me, Grace Williams,' he said as he approached. 'I've booked the honeymoon.' He dropped the envelope from his mouth to the bench.

I closed the powder compact and put it in the flapped pocket of my duffel coat. He still hadn't noticed my hair.

'I will,' I said, knowing Daniel was joking, but not poking fun.

'We're going to Torquay, Grace,' Daniel continued. 'In the summer. High summer. With the kiddies. They want me to look after the youngest fitters. Well, help, at least. It's my last chance, Eric says, for getting on the team.'

'And me?'

'You?' Daniel turned and smiled.

'Beautiful hair, Gracie. You, my darling, fair-faced, hair-dressed Grace, Grace, darling, Mademoiselle Villiams, are going to be a farmhand, a land girl, a dairymaid, a cowgirl. Look. It's all written here.'

I picked up the letter and studied it. 'Torquay 1963' it said at the top, and then a long paragraph explaining about the Variety Club of Great Britain and a caravan site with special facilities at Luscombe Farm. Coaches to London, and trains from Paddington to Torquay, with a single change at Exeter. It was a letter to all the parents and guardians of the youngest kiddies about their summer holiday, which would take place at the end of August. Two weeks. Peak season. And the joy of it was, I was going too. Forget Cinderella and the ball. Fuck the Rose Queen. Piss on Missy. Grace Williams was going to Torquay.

The last paragraph concerned staffing arrangements, and there was mention of 'a few hand-picked adolescent girls or boys' to help with the children and any extra work on the farm.

'That's us, Grace,' said Daniel, tapping the piece of paper with the tip of his shoe. 'Hand-picked. Don't you love it?'

Summer '63 – two weeks in Torquay. *Fifty-Five Days at Peking*. We saw four films, three shows, the Paignton zoo and Bertram Mills' circus too. The Variety Club of Great Britain had connections. They did us proud. We saw Bruce

Forsyth, Miss Thora Hird and the Merseyside wonders at the Princess Theatre. Major Simpson bought everybody programmes.

'Keepsakes,' he said. 'Records. Important.'

We saw *The Great Escape* and *Mutiny on the Bounty* at the Colony cinema, *Doctor in Distress* and *Fifty-Five Days* at the Royal Odeon. Miss Lily bought boxes of Black Magic, which she passed darkly along the rows. We gobbled the chocolates, bobbling like royalty in our red velvet seats, tipping them, flipping them, sitting on their tops.

'Top layer first,' Miss Lily instructed. Manners, etiquette. Important.

Tickety-boo went the tap-dancers' shoes at the special show a group of retired dancers laid on for us at Torquay Rotary Club.

Plickety-plick went the teaspoons in the blue cups in the Sea Breeze café which overlooked the beach. The cups matched the Toby jugs for sale on a shelf behind the counter. The niece of one of the Variety Club members had a summer job as a waitress in the Sea Breeze café, and when the café wasn't busy, we were welcome there. Samantha wore a very short skirt, and you could see her knickers – a different colour every day – when she bent to sweep the floor. Her bobbed hair swung and gleamed like a polished car as she hummed her way around the tables. *Sweets for My Sweet*. We all adored Samantha, and she seemed to like us, sneaking us extra teacakes and Nice biscuits, which Daniel called 'niece'.

Flick went the wheels on the old-fashioned tricycle with the red and white box on its back which trundled along the promenade behind the beach. 'Stop me and Buy One' read the banner on the side of the box. The man who rode the tricycle and sold the ice cream wore a white cap and a white vest which showed his brown glistening shoulders, bulging biceps and forearms like Popeye's. With one hand he gripped a straight, iron handlebar. With the other he rang a bell, which made the dippier kiddies think it was dinner-time. Some of the nurses went sad and soft, saying they remembered the tricycles from their youth. They often stopped and bought dark, sweating choc ices from the man, or yellow rectangles of vanilla ice cream slapped between two wafers. There were flaps around the top of the red and white box, and when the man opened them, fumes fled up from the slot in the middle.

'Close your purses, nurses,' the man would sometimes say. 'Ices on me, and have a good day.' And he would hand out frozen triangles of flavoured ice – penny Sno Fruits – to all of us before letting the lids flap shut.

Click. The Major's wife, Mrs Simpson, using the camera Eric had lent for the holiday. There she is, framing her husband with sea, sky and two tall palm trees. The Major salutes and puts his heels together. He looks very short in his khaki shorts. Daniel imitates him, and Mrs Simpson clicks the camera again. There's Miss Blackburn, frying sausages on an open fire outside one of the caravans. She's squatting. She too is wearing shorts. The muscles of her calves squidge beneath her thighs, and you can tell that she's smiling, even though it's a side-view shot.

Here she is again, Miss Blackburn, in a large black bathing costume now, on the beach. She's carrying somebody in her arms. Miss Lily. Even at a distance you can see Miss Lily's pale skin and how pink and sore it is. She's limp in Miss Blackburn's arms until they reach the sea. Then Miss Lily starts thrashing her pinny legs. Miss Blackburn wades through the shallow waves until the water laps her bouncing bum. She drops Miss Lily into the sea, splat on her back. Miss Lily sinks, comes up laughing. They splash each other, batting and scooping the water with both hands.

Clap your hands. We were happy and we knew it.

Love-fucking with Daniel.

The love-fucking started in Major Simpson's car, a new, shiny, black and grey Rover. He'd driven down with Mrs Simpson in the front, Miss Lily and Miss Blackburn in the back. They were staying in the farmhouse, bed and breakfast, but Major Simpson didn't want to risk the pink rutted lane that led to the farm, so he parked his car in the car park by the beach.

After we'd helped put the kiddies to bed in the caravans, Daniel and I walked back down to the car park, deserted now except for the Major's Rover. We were to fetch Miss Lily's hussif, which she'd left by mistake in the glove compartment.

'Here, Gracie, you drive,' Daniel joked.

We were sitting in the front of the Major's car, facing the sea, me in the driving seat. Daniel had the car keys in his mouth. I tried to take them, but Daniel clenched his teeth around them. I leant across the gap between our seats. The handbrake jabbed my hip and I toppled against Daniel's empty arm socket.

'Keep still, Grace,' said Daniel. 'I'm going to give them to you.'

I wriggled round until my bum was on the driver's seat and my feet rested on the closed window on the driver's side. Nelson was where he always is, and my good arm was by my side. My head lay on Daniel's lap.

Daniel bent his head, folded at the waist and leant his body until all I could see were the keys coming towards me. I opened my mouth and told my tongue to stay inside. There were two keys, on a ring, and then a flap of leather, which Daniel kept between his teeth. He was so close now that I could see the letters RAC printed in gold on the leather, and a black stain from Daniel's saliva.

Both keys went in my mouth at once, slowly, tasting of money.

'Suck,' said Daniel.

I sucked. Spittle came into my mouth. Daniel pulled back slightly on the flap of leather. I liked the way the ridges of the keys pressed against my tongue. But the keys went too far back and I had to cough them out. They fell. Then it wasn't keys any more, but Daniel's teeth in my mouth, his tongue, salt, and enough spittle to sink a battleship. And the lap wasn't a lap like mother's. No napping here. It was more like Father's, in his study, with the radiogram and the big windows that let in the rivery smell of mud and beer and made the leafy shadows on the ceiling move. A watery kaleidoscope. And Thumbelina spinning. And singing.

Daniel kept his lips on mine. His dick beneath the thin summer shorts was puffy and pulsing at the back of my head. He opened his legs, so my head tucked between them, and my cheek lay against the buttonless fly of his shorts. We stopped the kissing then, and Daniel sat back. His eyes had gone swimmy, and he said that mine had too. He said he loved my eyes. Loved my hair, my mouth and, most of all, my voice.

'I love you, Grace,' he said.

And she loves you. She loves you, yeah, yeah, yeah.

In the end, we love-fucked like doing knick-knacks with Mother, facing each other, Daniel sitting, me clinging around him.

I took Daniel's shorts off. I pulled his pants off. Slowly. With difficulty. I had to squirm over, round and then to the floor, on my knees. The hump of my back rubbed hotly against the glove compartment. Twice Daniel slid down the seat, tangling with me on the mat. But I was the queen bee, bossy boots, honeymooning me. I had to be.

I heaved and pushed Daniel back into a sitting position. His hips twitched towards me, involuntarily, and his dick lurched, drunk and needy. Still kneeling, I took it in my good hand, rubbing like Aladdin.

'Not like that, Grace. Ow. The other way.'

Now it was a giant finger, a funny Thumbelina. I circled it with my own fingers and sucked – a sour Orange Maid. Yeah, yeah, yeah.

I scrabbled up off the floor and we put Daniel's dick in my cunt, or rather my cunt around his dick, me slicking down on to him. A foxglove over a finger. I rested my good hand on Daniel's shoulder, letting Nelson press against his bony tummy. We bucked, licking and noseying each other's faces, and I let my hand trickle down to the forbidden bit by his shoulder. Daniel had never let me touch him there before.

Under the loose short sleeves of his shirt, the empty half-orbs where there should have been arms were oddly smooth. I'd expected bumps and jagged scars, but the hollowed skin felt almost polished, like the insides of the ashtrays at the Sea Breeze café made out of scallops. Curved like them too. Oh, the sea, the fucking sea. Yeah, yeah, yeah. I wet my finger with spittle and circled the skin of each socket. A spiralling motion. Like Daniel spiralling a boosy with his tongue.

Just before our bodies juddered still, there was a scream, or squawk, and you couldn't tell whether it was coming from Daniel or me, or the hundreds of seagulls flying across the bay on the evening wind.

Afterwards, we sat side by side, in the Major's black and grey Rover, smoking, looking at the sea but not really seeing it, because Daniel was talking about the other side of it. Normandy. He was telling me about the accident. His father's old Commer van. Fog on the Normandy roads. Driving home, through the night, from Paris.

'We were late. The plane left for Lydd at six.'

'How late?' I asked, winding down the window, letting out the smoke and the sexed smell of our bodies. This sounded like the beginning of another of Daniel's stories, except his voice was unusually level and toneless.

Daniel and his father drove to Paris every two months to buy fancy French goods – antiques – for his father's shop in London. The van went on the plane from Lydd to Calais, then, after Paris, back across Normandy and over the cuff of sea from Calais to Lydd.

'We drove the van on to the plane through its nose, or mouth, Gracie. Can you imagine?' Colour and warmth crept back into Daniel's voice. 'Like being swallowed. Dad called the plane a flying whale. And Jonno, the pilot, Jonah.'

In Paris, they slept in his Dad's old flat on the place Pereire, rising at dawn to drive to the market.

'Dad would say, "Let's take the scenic route, son," and we'd loop south through the empty streets to the Seine, past the Louvre, around Notre-Dame, before heading back north, up to the ninth.'

Daniel lifted his feet on to the Major's dashboard and wiggled his toes, slipping them in and out of the bow-loop on Miss Lily's hussif, which I'd taken from the glove compartment and put there, so as not to forget it.

'I knew those avenues and boulevards like the whorls on my thumb,' Daniel said. 'It used to get soggy, my thumb. I sucked it so much. Papa stopped me sucking one day. "You're my co-pilot, Dani" he said and gave me a map showing the cobwebby streets of Paris, and another with all the roads in France on it.'

I glanced at the spidery scar on Daniel's puckered fore-head.

'I became Papa's eyes, more navigator than co-pilot. He needed me when he'd been drinking.'

It had been a good trip, Daniel said. The van was packed with lamps, clocks, marble urns and carved fireplaces for the warehouse in Battersea, the shop in Fulham.

They ate in a restaurant near Montmartre, where the waiters wrote your order on the paper tablecloths. Daniel said he remembered being given boeuf bourguignon to eat and watered-down red wine to drink, even though he was only five.

His father swigged two bottles of wine, then another with a lady-friend at the next table. A couple of nightcaps and one for the road.

'Papa held my hand when we walked back to the van. He used to press on my knuckle-joints and waggle them so they knocked into each other.'

Daniel said he and his dad often skipped like girls along the midnight streets. Sometimes Mr Smith danced – sometimes the rumba, more often the tango or cancan.

'He tried to teach me the steps. At the end we'd bow to each other. He's very tall, isn't he, my dad?'

Daniel turned in the car seat to look at me. I nodded.

'But you know what? Papa can bend right over and sweep the ground with the curls of his hair. A doddle, he says. He taught me how to do it, how to place my forearm across my waist. "You've got to envisage a cummerbund, son" he'd say. "Black tie, white shirt and a splash of red, for courage, across your belly where you bend." I used to practise, when he went off by himself on private business, in the huts behind the market stalls.'

So it had been a good trip, but, 'We were late,' Daniel repeated. 'Not very. Papa wasn't worried. We'd make up the time, he said. I sat up front, same as usual. Next to Dad. Co-pilot.'

Reading the map, sucking bonbons, sipping Orangina. Jit-smoke, tired eyes, peering at the fog, feeling blanketed, not blinded by it.

'I was never frightened with Dad.'

Reading the map. Reading out place names. Making them up. Listening for the growling noise in the engine which meant they had to stop, cool down and top up with water from the bottle his dad kept in the back of the van.

'We weren't far from Abbeville. We were planning to stop for a piss and fill up near there.'

A wind had sprung up from the east, Daniel said, turning the fog to rain. The wind blew the rain in smacking gusts across the windscreen. One of the windscreen wipers was bust and hung down like a black eyelash. The other had lost its rubber and squeaked each time it swiped the wet black glass. Daniel said he remembered having trouble hearing the engine properly above the wind and the rain and the dodgy windscreen wiper. They were forced to slow down, and his dad became irritable.

Lighting cigarettes for his dad, passing them to him. Passing him one.

'Just then, I saw headlights coming towards us. On the wrong side of the road.'

Swervings, an oncoming car, the speeding van, the rain.

'Dad always drove fast. But he was a good driver. The best.'

Just then, in Torquay, the sun went down for the night. It had been doing its happy-holiday sunset show, making the row of pink, cream, light blue and green houses by the harbour look like icing on a birthday cake, the shop-bought sort. Now the houses looked dull, and the harbour dark, empty and cold.

'After another swerve, the van tilted and stopped.' Daniel hesitated. 'It's hard to remember the rest.' The steering wheel spinning. His father's arms in the air. The lit cigarette arcing through the broken windscreen into blackness.

And much, much later, cool-handed nuns at the hospital in Abbeville. Their prayers. The word 'amputation' spoken quietly.

'I was born with a funny-shaped head and dangly legs, Grace,' he finished. 'And I was born a crazy fitter. Papa's *papillon de nuit*. We were making the best of a bad job, me and Dad. Smith and son. But this –' he nodded with distaste at each shoulder in turn – 'this was too much. And my fits got worse after the operation. Doctors began to think it was brain damage. Dad began to believe them.' Daniel paused. 'So that's how I ended up at the Briar. Do you see?'

I saw the spider on his forehead crawl.

'A shard of glass from the windscreen. That's all.'

Very small.

We forgot Miss Lily's hussif after this. I remembered it as we walked quietly back along the road to the farm, but it didn't seem important. I put my good arm across Daniel's shoulder and slipped the palm of my hand into his empty shoulder socket.

As we turned off the lane and started up the red, mud-hardened track, Daniel said, 'Let's try your ma's old march. Come, Grace. Left. Left. I left my wife with forty-five children, and nothing but gingerbread left. Left.'

We couldn't link arms, so we linked legs instead, which made a nonsense of the nonsense-words. My left leg became Daniel's right, and vice versa. But it enabled us to establish a decent tempo, and we stomped along at a fair old marching pace.

When we reached the gate to the field with the caravans, we unwound our legs and said goodnight.

'And it serves them jolly well right.'

Tap tap.

ii

Sarah cartwheeled across the visitors' lawn.

'You,' she said, stopping in front of me for a moment, 'can't do that.'

No, I shook my head. No. I can't do that.

'Watch me.'

Off she went. She raised one knee, high and proud like

a horse, and both her arms, one in front, one behind. She balanced. She looked over her shoulder at me to make sure I was watching, me, her audience of one – Mother had gone to fetch the car, Father was saying goodbye to Matron – then she whirled, or tried. It turned into a dive, and all I saw for a while was an overexcited starfish of arms, legs and elongated hairy head.

Sister Sarah, five years old. Starting school next week. Blue-eyed, twirly Sarahkins, changing all the time.

It had been all change back at the Briar after Torquay.

Daniel, as expected, was given a place on the crazy fitters' team and went to live in the Nissen hut.

'On one condition,' said Eric. Daniel was to attend Miss Blackburn's special classes.

I, not at all as expected, was transferred to a women's ward. Several girls were transferred – some to the ground-floor Beech Tree ward with me, some to Fir Tree, and a few to Ward Eleven on the first floor. No more school for any of us, but, said our new Sister, we were to start work, paid work, in the industrial units, very soon. As soon as we'd had our patient reviews.

Beech Tree ward were called for reviews a couple of weeks after Torquay. Weeks that we spent being tested, medically examined and under observation in the industrial units, where we had a go at everything – assembling toys, television aerials and tinsel Christmas trees, label-stringing, radio-making and bundling pens using a holey template to count to twelve. Some people even manoeuvred the levers in the leatherworks section and operated the big polishing machines in there.

'Still very small, isn't she?' commented Dr Jack at one of my medical examinations.

My boosies were bigger, and so was the hump on my back. Only a smidgeon – don't worry, Grace, said Daniel.

I weighed five stone but was less than five feet tall, even

at a stretch. They measured me flat, on a board marked with feet and inches and fitted with pulleys to straighten you out. The board left lines on my bum and hump. My left leg, they said, had shrunk again.

But my right leg had grown so long, I could touch the floor in Mr Maitland's office as I sat there between Mother and Father opposite the desk. Sarah was in the admin office, where Miss Walsingham had promised to keep an eye on her.

'Patient Review. Grace Williams', said the pale brown file on Mr Maitland's desk. Mr Maitland opened the file and turned the pages.

'We're here to discuss long-term provision,' he began. 'Grace's persistent bed-wetting. New drug therapies.'

Mother was worried about the bed-wetting.

'We think it's often deliberate,' said Mr Maitland. 'When she doesn't get her way. Obstinate, the nurses say.'

Father wanted to know about the new drug therapies.

Mr Maitland read out the names of the pills I took and what each one was for. At the end, he talked about sexual maturity, danger, protection, and better to be safe than sorry.

'That's why we've put her on the Pill,' he said.

'We're putting you on the Pill,' a nurse had sniggered only a few days ago. 'A preggie Gracie wouldn't be funny.' She pushed a beaker through the hatch in the wall of the pharmacy. The beaker was made of metal, and the tablets rattled in it like dice.

Everybody was worried about long-term provision.

'It's a new initiative,' said Mr Maitland, 'setting them to work at sixteen. If they're capable. It's a job for life.' He hurried on, 'Grace will have a home for life, here at the Briar.'

'But . . .' said Father.

'What about . . .?' Mother.

'There's no point your daughter staying in the COU any longer, Mr and Mrs Williams. I know Miss Blackburn claims there's been some progress with her reading, but our recent tests suggest, at best, a sort of mild echolalia. Usually Grace just pretends, makes things up. Two words, if you can call them that – two animal sounds – at a time.'

Mr Maitland glanced in the file again.

'She remains ineducable,' he said.

Mother flinched.

'On the other hand,' Mr Maitland continued quickly, 'she's not Ward Eleven. Not OT only. Occupational Therapy. Her manual dexterity's surprisingly good. Sharpe wants to try her on radios in the industrial units. With your agreement.'

Questions from Father interrupting the Medical Superintendent's long answers. Mother's silence, broken only by her 'I don't know's.

'Oh, Grace. What's to become of you? I just don't know.'

Eventually sighs, signatures. Closing the file.

We went to collect Sarah. As we approached the administration block, we heard her crying.

'The button of her shoe came off,' explained Miss Walsingham. 'She's terribly upset. I'm awfully sorry.'

Sarah lay on her back on the floor, kicking her legs, one shoe on, one shoe off.

'I've sent Daniel to Will with it. To get it sewn back on. He won't be long. I'm awfully sorry,' Miss Walsingham repeated.

Don't worry. Absolutely nothing you could have done. She gets like this Mother and Father fussed and reassured.

We waited, but there was no sign of Daniel. Sarah went on crying, despite Mother picking her up off the floor and Miss Walsingham offering her some fruit cake.

'It's a lovely sunny day,' said Father. 'Let's get some fresh air. It'll do us all good. I'll carry you, Sarah. Then you can take your socks off and run around barefoot.'

When we reached the visitors' lawn, Mother removed Sarah's other shoe and her socks.

'The grass tickles,' Sarah complained. But she stopped crying.

We walked all the way to the orchard, where Miss Blackburn and Miss Lily were picking Victoria plums. Nobody held anybody's hand or arm. Sarah darted about, snatching at flowers – not the roses, Sarah. At the branches. She'll hurt herself, Joe. At the air – they're dandelion clocks, *elskling*. Mother and Father walked far apart from each other, both of them slowing and stopping, but not at the same time, for me to catch up.

I was tired when we reached the visitors' lawn again. I sat down on one of the benches at the edge of it. Sarah was told to sit next to me.

'Stay there while I fetch the car,' said Mother. 'You can be putting your socks back on, Sarah, and this shoe.' She turned to Father. 'Joe, go and let them know we're off. And fetch the other shoe.'

'Are you sure they'll be all right?' Father looked from Sarah to me.

'We'll only be five minutes. You'll be fine, won't you, Grace?' Mother hesitated. 'You're a grown-up now.'

I nodded.

'Sarah?'

'One, two, buckle my shoe.' Already busy with her socks, Sarah nodded too.

As soon as Mother and Father had disappeared from sight, Sarah, wearing just her socks, stood up from the bench and started cartwheeling.

The bottoms of Sarah's white socks were stained green from the grass. They were short cotton socks, thinly ribbed, the sort that folded over at the top. But Sarah must have unfolded them, and, as she cartwheeled, they sagged up and down her spinning shins, giving her legs a boyish, bony look. She wore a sailor-suit skirt, blue, pleated and neat when she arrived with Mother and Father, but now – as she cartwheeled freely across the lawn, showing her knickers, which were so white they must have been new – the skirt flipped over like an umbrella with broken spokes, and the navy-blue top with the square white collar slipped this way and that as Sarah turned, making a pale, rotating circle out of the taut, bare band of her tummy-skin, hiding the back of her head with its flapping white collar.

Sarah's face spun featureless, except for the mouth, gashed, not its usual budding pout which opened and closed at will so winningly.

When Sarah reached the far end of the lawn, by the rose beds, where the grass was greener because of the shadow from the wall, she turned, waved and posed again, ready to cartwheel back.

Her shoe lay on its side, on the grass by the bench. A pretty shoe, a party shoe, with a strap and a button, not a buckle. Creased and worn, but definitely best. I used to wear the same. And socks like that, and clean white knickers, soft from the wash, warm from the airing cupboard. My knickers, mine, and my mother's arms steadying me as I stepped into them.

'Come on, Gracie. You can do it.'

One foot. Then the other.

'Lift your knee, darling. Come on. High and proud, like a horse.'

Done.

'Well done.'

A quick cotton tug up my legs, Mother's hands on my hips adjusting the twisted elastic, a pat on the bum. A pat-a-cake, pat-a-cake ache in my heart.

'Well done, my love.'

And ribbons in my hair. And singing in the kitchen. Before the mess on the swirling floor. Way back. Before the bye-bye sighing of the iron lung which let me breathe but left me with Nelson and my dahu leg. Such shoes wouldn't do any more. Such pretty shoes.

'Such pretty shoes.' Mother used to say it nearly every night. She told me that when she was a little girl, her own mother had to scrimp and save to keep the family in decent shoes.

'"Decent shoes – very important," my ma used to say. But you know what I say, Grace? Pretty shoes – very important.' And she would laugh at the streak of vanity, the glint of Italian chic that ran through her despite herself.

Once, when Mother was warning a departing Miranda about the dangers of hitch-hiking, she told us about a lorry driver she met on her trip to Italy before the war. The lorry driver gave them a lift, she said, she and her friend Isabella, dizzy Izzy, you'd adore her, bella Bella.

'You were hitch-hiking,' Miranda accused.

'No, we weren't,' lied a smiling Mother. 'And anyway, it wasn't the same in those days. Guess,' she said. 'Guess what he had in the back of his lorry, that lorry driver?' she invited us eagerly, distracted us easily. 'Shoes, darlings. Fine Italian handcrafted shoes.'

'So what?' said Miranda, but she paused in her hurry to go.

'Well,' continued Mother, 'the point is, they were all left-footed shoes.'

'Don't be ridiculous.' But Miranda couldn't hide her interest.

'The Mafia,' said Mother, lowering her voice and rolling her eyes. The Mafia, she said, were highwaymen, baddies, villains. The lorry drivers lived in fear of having their lorries flagged down and their loads unloaded and stolen by them.

'Or worse. Bang bang.' Mother pointed two fingers, a gun, to her head.

Dividing the shoes into left and right and transporting them in different lorries was the only way to outwit the Mafia.

'Ingenious, eh?' she laughed. 'But very funny too. Because the lorry driver was a twin. At least, that's what he told us. And his twin brother drove the other lorry.'

'Oh, come on,' said Miranda. 'You'll be telling us next that one of them was left-handed and the other right-handed.'

Mother laughed again.

'No. That'd be too good to be true. But there is some-thing else.' Mother put on her serious storytelling face. 'The lorry driver had different-coloured eyes. One eye was green. One was blue. I forget which was which. But he said his twin brother had the same, only the other way round.'

'I'm not sure I believe you,' said Miranda.

I do, I do.

'Best believing.'

Mother in a good mood – 'shoes off first, Grace' – at bath and bedtime. She'd lie me on my bed – my bed, not hers, not the double bed with the slippery eiderdown. That came after my bath. She'd lift my feet and clap my shoes together.

'Such pretty shoes,' she'd sigh happily and press my feet to her soft belly. Then she'd unbuckle the shoes – ambidex-trously, Grace, that's the way.

She lifted the shoes off and dropped them, any which way, to the floor. She held my feet and stroked their soles through my socks with her thumbs. Then she tweaked the toes of the socks and pulled them slowly off – so slowly that my legs were pulled into the air too, which made us both laugh.

'Okay. Let's sit you up, darling.'

Off with my sweater or cardie, blouse and vest.

Finally, flat on my back and legs in the air again.

'Come on, Gracie. One fell swoop,' Mother would say, and her hands would disappear under my bum and sweep away my knickers or tights and skirt, all at the same time.

Into the bath, soap and flannel, rub-a-dub-dub. A Sunday shampoo – 'Here, hold the sponge over your eyes, Grace, while I rinse' – and occasionally lemon juice, not soapy but sharp. 'Vinaigrette for brunettes,' Mother would say. 'But *limone* for my only blonde *bambina.*'

Miranda refused to have Sarson's poured on her hair. Her hair was neither blonde nor dark. If John called it mousey, she flew into a rage and said her hair was dirty blonde, very fashionable. Later, she experimented with egg yolk, honey and camomile tea, hair dye from a friend and henna from abroad.

After my bath, Mother would wrap me in a towel, hard and scratchy from years of washing and boiling, but warm from having been hung over a chair in front of the gas fire in Mother's and Father's bedroom. She'd carry me across the landing, past the stairs and into their bedroom for drying and dressing me, ready for bed.

'Ready, Grace?' Sarah's voice was shrill on the other side of the visitors' lawn.

Not yet. I'm still sprawled on Mother and Father's double divan. The eiderdown slithers and slides underneath my nightgown, but Mother fetches another warmed towel and puts it there. She draws the curtains across the dark London night. She sits on the edge of the bed, her feet on the floor, her body twisted to face me. I can hear the gas fire, and smell it. I can also hear Father in his study above – the squeak of his desk chair, the sound of him opening a drawer, clearing his throat. No music tonight.

'Oh, Grace.' Mother's whole face caves in on itself. 'What's to become of you?'

She puts her hands on the sides of my waist, picks at my nightgown, strokes the worn Viyella, embroidered with stars at the wrists and yoke, made by her, washed by her a hundred times or more. It used to be John's, and Miranda's, before. Smoothing it, soothing us, counting our fingers and toes a hundred times or more. Forty-five children. Her babies.

'I just don't know.'

And here are her strong, firm hands on my sides again. Spanning and holding. She heaves me higher up the bed until my head lolls flatly on the folded-over flap of the white sheet. She lies down next to me.

Mother takes the pillow from above my head and puts it on her chest, then over her face.

Then over my face.

The pillow smells of her and Father – her hair, its sweet, rich oiliness, and Father's dry, talcy arms – washing and neck sweat. Her neck – I love to splay my fingers at the collar of her blouse, stroke the skin there, suck my salty fingers afterwards.

The pillow rests lightly. I can hardly feel it, except with my eyelashes and in the heat of the air going in and out of my nostrils. Noisy air. That's all I can hear.

Then it stops. There's pressure on the pillow, pillow in my nostrils. No smell, just tightness across my eyes and hardness in their sockets. I open my mouth and something like sea rushes in. A heaviness fills my body. I know that it's dark and I can't move my eyes, but light splits behind them, pooling into colour, while sound is reduced to a single, strained wail in my ears. As I sink, I feel Mother's hands through the pillow, pushing, gushing. Her despair in my mouth.

Mother eventually removed the pillow and stuffed it

into her own mouth. Then she put me to bed without a word.

'Grace!' Sarah shouted. 'You're not watching.'

Oh yes I am.

I nudged Sarah's shoe with my own, levering it back the right way up. My built-ups looked enormous next to Sarah's pretty party pumps. The design of my shoes hasn't changed much over the years – plain leather lace-ups for spasticky ladies, not rose queens or pretty *bambini*. I didn't need a wee, but I crossed my short leg over the other one and swung my built-up back and forth. The Williams' welly – not even Sarah can do that.

Sarah stood in the shade of the old hospital wall, wreathed in roses – Mermaid, Albertine, Snow Goose roses – ready to cartwheel back.

Daniel came into the garden. He walked along the edge of the rosebed at the far end of the visitors' lawn until he reached Sarah.

'Hello, Princess,' I heard him say. 'One, two.'

'Where's my shoe?' Sarah laughed and cartwheeled away.

1963–64

Daniel passed the test for the residential training school for adolescents and young adults near Cambridge.

'In a matter of months,' said matter-of-fact Miss Blackburn.

'With flying colours.' Proud Fleet Air Arm Eric.

Congratulations.

'For he's a jolly good fellow,' sang all the crazy fitters.

He went away in February 1964.

'A weekly boarder,' he reassured. 'That's all, Grace. I'll be back in a flash. Before you know it.'

He was, every *Friday, it's five o'clock ... it's Crackerjack* – not very long after that.

What's more, Daniel and I had more time together than before. Now we were grown-ups, we had grown-up evenings and weekends, with pretend free-time. Men and women were allowed to mix. Bingo and singalongs on Friday nights. Socials on Saturdays, including dances. Sunday evenings, if you weren't on the list for a bath, meant extra telly or the Major's music seshes. Because I went to those so often, the Major called me his assistant and let me help him choose the records.

During the week, I was busy. Sister on Beech Tree ward had us all up and dressed by seven. Breakfast in the refectory took an hour, ward chores another. Then we queued with the men in the hospital grounds and made our way to work.

Five to Ten, Amen.

Flickety slot. Side-drop. Lock, sock.

I liked my time in the industrial units, where the radio played all day.

Ten thirty-one, Music While You Work.

I liked Will Sharpe, who was in charge of us all. By the time we arrived, Will would already be cobbling away in his shoe-mending corner, or bustling around, opening windows and drawers, switching on lights, machines, the radio on the wall.

Eleven o'clock, Morning Story.

I liked watching my good hand twist to pick up the pale blue transistor panel from the pile in front of me, how my hand slid the panel into the metal frame that my neighbour passed along. I'd push the panel with the flat of my hand, just hard enough to check the fit, then a bit harder to knock it into the waiting sock-shaped sack attached to my workbench.

Plasticky plop. Click, knock. Non-stop.

Voices, music, murmuring air. The whirr of work. Small electrical components. Small repeated movements. Tea breaks, wee breaks, fag breaks.

There was a clock on the wall above Will's lathe, but we didn't need it.

Four thirty-one, The Racing Results.

'You can go now,' Will said every day at four-thirty. But nobody went immediately, and if there was overtime, we all put our hands up, except on Fridays.

One Friday in April, everybody left in the usual rush, but I was slower than usual because Nelson had stitches, four, and hurt from a fall in the sluices – a small tussle about a plastic comb that led to a big muss on the floor, the comb-lady astride me like a jockey, me with my nose rubbing the tiles, and the comb wet and jaggy in Nelson.

I hung my work smock on the hook in the lobby, opened

the heavy industrial-unit door and stepped out into the hospital grounds.

It had snowed on Sunday, Easter Sunday, just last week. We'd come out of chapel to find the greening lawns, the budding trees and Mr Peters' pretty spring flowers sprinkled with white. More snow had fallen during lunch – enough for Eric to organize his crazy fitters into a team of snow-sweepers for the afternoon. Five days later, most of the snow had melted. There were just a few patches in the shade of the trees and the tall brick wall, and several small pyramids on the lawn where snowmen and snowballs had melted.

I trundled along. My Hillman limp, as Daniel used to call it, whizzling past me, with Robert – got a puncture, Grace? – in their imaginary Porsches, Jaguars, Daimlers, Morgans. I was making for the day room and the start of *Friday*, Daniel and bagging the best seat for bingo later.

I crossed the drive, near the gatehouse – no sign of Toby today, but I could see the jug Daniel had stolen from the Sea Breeze café and given to Toby on the windowsill of his kitchen window.

I was just passing the cedar tree when a wet lump of snow hit me on the neck. I turned round. There was no one in sight. But there was the sound of laughter coming from the cedar tree, and suddenly there were hands upon me. Two, four, six hands. Small, rough, quick hands. They pulled me to the ground and tugged me face down across the wet grass and underneath the branches of the cedar tree. They rolled me over and I found myself looking up at three black balaclavaed heads. No faces, just ovals of black, with holes for the eyes.

'Now what?' said the smallest of the three figures, nut-head Billy.

'Yeah. Now what?' echoed another, tall and wobbly. Thomas.

'I know. Now we fuck her,' replied Billy.

The third boy was standing silently at my side. He carried a knife, in a sheath, on his belt. I could see two light brown eyes through the holes he'd made in the balaclava. The eyes were clear, clever and ever so familiar. Rick.

'Not you,' I said.

A gasp from Billy, a half-laugh from Thomas, the silvery flick of a knife and, 'Now what?' wailed Billy as Rick thrust the knife so close to my eye it tickled the lashes.

'Not now,' I mouthed, staring straight into Rick's pupils – through my quivering eyelashes, past the long, grey glint of the knife, into the blackness of the woolly balaclava and the pinprick light at the back of his eyes that was gold and far too bright.

Rick withdrew, but he kept the knife in his hand.

Scallywag boys. They didn't know what to do. So they fought, but like puppies, not dogs. They argued, scrabbling, shouting, 'The knife, the knife, mine, no mine.'

'Mine.' Billy brandished the knife, tripped and fell on top of me.

Thomas straddled him and we rolled. Rick tried to yank Thomas off, but we were turning over and over – the knife, the boys, my face in the cold, damp earth. All of us rolling. The knife slipped. The boys lunged, and Rick got there first, but the others were on top of him, on top of me, and the knife went sideways between my legs, at the very top, right through my frock. Would it slice through my skin, my cunt like a peach? Sudden wetness? Blood like juice?

I saw black waxed suture cotton, and it was closing not my cunt, not Nelson, but my mouth for ever. I saw red.

I reached with my good hand for Rick's head.

'Not you,' I tried again.

Behind the back-to-front balaclava, my hand grabbed at Rick's hair – softness and dry, tight curls. I slipped the curls like rings through my fingers. I didn't pull, he didn't push, but my hand, his hair, head and him moved backwards, and I saw, not defeat in Rick's yellow-brown eyes, but a dimmer, less dangerous light. I removed my hand and plucked the knife, safe and silver, from between my thighs.

Rick, Thomas and Billy unknotted themselves clumsily, quickly. I couldn't help kneeing Thomas, the kicker, in the stomach, before he stood up.

Bed-wetting, fire-raising, no longer knife-wielding, deaf and dumb Rick looked rumpled and young when he removed his balaclava and dropped it on the ground. Thomas and Billy took their balaclavas off too, but put them back on again, the right way round.

'What now?' Billy looked from Rick to jumpy Thomas, who was clutching his leg with one hand and pulling on his long top lip with the other.

The three boys turned, stooped and stumbled away, swiping at the branches of the cedar tree.

I lay where I was and waited for my breathing to steady. No rush. I'd missed the start of *Crackerjack*. Plus I needed a wee and anyone could see that Nelson needed attention.

Eventually, I hoiked myself to standing and leant against the cedar tree. My head was throbbing, in time with my heart. Congratulations, Grace Williams, I said to myself. I wasn't an elite epileptic, I would probably never set foot in a special residential training school near Cambridge, I was less than five feet tall, smaller than nut-head Billy, but I'd dealt with those bully-boys and I felt as tall as the tree behind me. When I looked up at it, I couldn't even see the top, just fronds laced with shreds of surprising snow, and branches as dark and steady as Mother's strong arms.

Rick's balaclava lay on the ground like a dead bird. I picked it up and wrapped the knife in it. I tried to dig a hole in the ground. With my good hand, I scraped, raked, scratched and swept, but the earth was too solid to make more than a mucky saucer of a hole. Nevertheless, I placed the wrapped knife in the dip, sprinkled earth and twigs on top of it, and patted it neatly, nearly flat.

I pulled a few twigs from my hair, shook the loose earth and grit from my slushed frock, then, without a backward glance, I headed out from the cedar tree.

I strode across the lawn towards the main hospital building, but not in a straight line. I zigzagged from pyramid to snowy pyramid and I gave each small pile of dirty snow the biggest, most powerful Williams' welly ever.

I'm going to like being a grown-up, I thought, definitely.

1964

'Old Empires, son,' said Daniel's father as we approached Lydd airport. He hunched forward over the van's steering wheel and looked skywards. Daniel imitated him, pressing his chest against his bent legs, itchy feet nearly at rest, for once, on the sliver of flat, black dashboard, on top of the empty packets of pretty, gypsy-blue jits, and on top of the bonbon wrappers that crickled – so pretty – when Daniel jiggled his feet. Daniel's shoes were new.

'For the occasion, Grace.'

The occasion was my eighteenth birthday – a journey to the sea that might as well have been to the sky or to the flipping stars. We ate the best bacon butties in the world, on Tuesday, 10 November 1964, and Daniel's dad had baked beans too.

We all squinted skywards. The dawn light was white and low with ham-pink ridges of cloud. I could see the planes but not hear them. They were too far away, in a V-shape, like disappearing train tracks, but coming closer and closer, the lines breaking up into shivering specks – ants, fish, birds, planes.

'Blimey, hydravions, son.'

A buzzing, rumbling, roaring – louder and louder in zooms and squeals.

'Flying boats, Grace,' Daniel explained. 'From Hythe.'

Great, juddering aeroplanes, each with three, six – or was it nine? – tiny windows.

'How fast, Papa?' asked Daniel.

'Two-fifty, two-sixty. At least. Count them for me, Dani. Quick.'

There were eighteen. Eighteen hydravions.

If a day can be debonair, then Lydd must be that day.

Daniel's father collected us from the Briar at three a.m. Three a.m. Can you imagine? I don't have to.

'Planned and perfected,' said Daniel, 'with military precision. Daniel Smith, strategist *par excellence*.'

He'd been to see the new deputy Medical Superintendent, a Dr Green.

'He okey-dokeyed it on the spot,' said Daniel. 'He's a new-fangled type. Keen to be seen as open. I didn't give him all the details, though.'

Open was the word and the way, these days, according to Daniel. Open-door policies, opening minds. Closing wounds, rising hopes.

'Empty promises,' said Mr Peters, dour as ever.

'No, Mr Peters. It's empty purses. That's all,' replied Eric.

Three a.m. and as dark as the larder, but smelling of leaves, softening wood and a stinky excitement cutting through them, which Daniel said was fox. We were standing outside the black iron gates waiting for Daniel's father to pick us up in his van.

'We've been planning it for ages.' Grinning. 'Smith and son. But it was my idea, of course. All of it. For you, Grace Coming-of-Age Williams.'

He moved closer, so the thick, blue corduroy of his trousers rubbed against mine. I was wearing trousers for the first time in my life.

'I'm calling it my leg-over in Lydd,' he said, pausing for effect. 'With Grace.' Then, moving to face me, making mirrors with our eyes.

'And love.'

Toby hovered anxiously on the other side of the gates.

His wide dwarf-face was creased with sleep and straggled with beard, but he smiled and wished us well as Daniel clambered first into the van.

'Hop up, little lady.' Daniel's father stood behind me. He put two big hands on my waist and spread his giant fingers. Then he lifted me, a feathery fairy, on to the long, suedey-grey seat next to Daniel, who'd already settled in and was toeing the tin of bonbons on the dashboard.

As soon as we set off, everything – the noise of the engine, the shapes and shadows of the slipping-past world, and the air full of smoke and eau de cologne – was so warm and soft that we both fell asleep within minutes, the side of my head safe in the shell of Daniel's shoulder.

We awoke in Camden Town, next to a long dark line of railway arches.

'Picking up some bits,' Mr Smith muttered. 'From a mate.'

He climbed down from the van, shut the door, went round to the back and opened the doors there. Soon there was the sound of rattling crockery.

'Willow-pattern china,' whispered Daniel. 'The French love it. Posh dosh, Dad calls it.'

Why was he whispering? I blew air through my lips until Daniel laughed.

'I don't know,' he said. 'I suppose I'm trying to slow things down. I want us to remember this day for ever.'

There was a slamming of the van's back doors – cheers, mate, cheerio, *bon voyage*. A patting on the side window, and we were off again, thumping through London, which was empty, wet and inky, with traffic lights as bright as the lights on Roger's Dodgems. I sucked on the bonbon in my mouth and peered at the deserted streets.

'Kingsway, Aldwych, the Strand,' Daniel recited.

A few glistening figures scurried or loitered on the pavements. Right at Embankment, past the Houses of Parliament

– sandcastle-yellow, with rows of lit windows like the Briar, even at this hour.

'Time, Dani?'

Daniel twisted across me and looked backwards at the stoney, honey-coloured tower of Big Ben.

'Half past four.'

We picked up speed – sixty along Millbank. Then Grosvenor Road, with Battersea Power Station rising like an upside-down bed into the dark night.

Over the bridge we went, over the river, blacker than the sky, down long, empty side streets, then shorter ones, and finally a dead-end with a row of sheds and garages along one side and nothing on the other – just the four soaring towers of the power station in the distance, and their smoke.

Daniel's father went into one of the sheds.

'Fetching his passport and documents for France,' said Daniel as we both slithered down from the van and pissed on the ground behind it, giggling like kiddies at the different tinklings of widdle in the quiet night. My wee spread out on the cracked and grass-clumped concrete like a map of Europe. Daniel's was a torrent, as strong and dark as the river Thames.

'We're not going to France, Grace,' Daniel said when we were back in the van. 'Even I couldn't arrange that. I'm not a magician.'

I patted his corduroy thigh, then mine.

'First of all, we're going to wave Papa off. From Lydd airport. You've always wanted to, ever since I told you about it, ever since the first time we saw *Casablanca*, do you remember? Now you don't just have to imagine it.'

I ran my fingers along the velvet lines of my trousers.

'You'll see. Afterwards, old girl, we're going to hole up for the day in a hotel, an inn. A pub, actually. But it's all booked. Very correct, Papa says. A room with a sea view.'

The corduroy changed colour, like the sea with the wind on it, as I stroked the nap back and forth.

'Later, one of Dad's mates'll come and find us. He'll take us back to the Briar. O'Reilly's his name. He's driving up north with a van-load of pictures. He said he didn't mind dropping us off on the way.'

I stopped rubbing my trousers.

'It'll be very, very late, my dear. I hope I don't fatigue you.' Daniel nudged me with his hip.

I half-slept again after that, but I could hear Daniel and his father talking, being private, being family, smoking and joking quietly, in French and English.

'Don't worry, son. We're going to do the little lady proud,' I heard – '*Merci, Papa*' – and, as I drifted off, 'The Rising Sun. *Le soleil levant. Mon Dieu*, I can't wait.' My magician's voice.

Streatham, Norbury, Croydon. The open road until East Grinstead, and another stop just beyond it, this time for bacon butties, in a café called 'The Best in the World'. Someone had painted the words in wide, dripping red on to a metal panel outside the café. The dirty white sign was edged with rust. It swung and creaked each time a lorry went by.

Inside, smoke and steam mingled with the smell of frying fat and the voices of the two young women shouting orders, bored and brisk, through a hatch behind the counter. Tired men sat with their food at square tables which had dark wood-grain beneath the crockery, cutlery, ashtrays and smeared bottles of red and brown sauce. Some of the men read newspapers, damp and folded small. One man had the Holy Bible open like a screen around his plate. We sat at the next table along from him.

'No Sally today?' asked Daniel's father when the waitress came to take our order.

'Off sick,' said the young waitress. 'You got a message?'

'Just passing through. Give her my regards.'

'Smith and son,' said Daniel. Ever so gently, he brushed the waitress's stockinged calf with the dangling lace of his new shoe, and smiled.

'Of course.' She twinkled in an instant. 'Smith and son. I won't forget.' Then, turning to me, 'And who might you be?'

'May I introduce Grace?' said Daniel's dad.

'And where's your ma?' She said this to me, looked at Daniel, and then at Daniel's dad, who rescued us by announcing, 'Mum's the word, my lovely girl.'

The waitress wasn't lovely to look at, but she did prove to be a lovely girl.

Daniel's father lit a jit and blew a large, wobbling smoke-ring that hovered in the air between us.

'We're graced with the presence of this little lady today. It's her birthday, see? See no, hear no, say no more, my lovely.'

Another pretty, impressive smoke-ring, then, 'Now, more to the point, where's our breakfast?'

The bacon butties came, speedy and generous, on thick white plates the same as at the Briar.

'We could fetch the willow-pattern,' said Daniel, only half joking.

They were indeed the best bacon butties in the world. Would be for ever. They dribbled and oozed down our chins, and Daniel's father had to ask for extra serviettes because he used up so many feeding Daniel, who didn't want to remove his new shoes, and more trying to wipe us both. It wasn't his forté, he said. The waitress came back with a cloth that smelt of tea and drains but did the job. And she did the job, wiping me nervously, meaning well, leaning close to dab at my lips. Her face was greasy and thin, with pimples on her forehead and chin, skewed from the gum she chew-chewed crazily. Her hair, held back with a rubber band and kirby grips, but with loose bits spewing out, was greasy too. She poked her finger into the cloth and tickle-tappled along my floppy top lip, then the firmer, bottom one.

'It's like putting lipstick on my sister,' she said, sounding startled and happy.

'Yes, please,' I said. And before I knew it, what with Daniel and his dad being debonair, Sally not being there and this new, young waitress so kind and suddenly unbusy, I found myself swished up with those big, Smith hands on to the sticky wooden table-top, and before you could say Jack Robinson – or Grace Coming-of-Age Williams – there I was, having happy-birthday lipstick applied, ever so lady-like, to my sloppety, slickety lips. The waitress whipped a tube from the pocket of her pinny, unscrewed it, and set to, more confidently now, smoothing the tip of the stick along my skin. I grinned. It felt like Daniel's toe on my tit – sexy, waxy, let's have a look-see.

'Kiss me,' said Daniel.

We kissed, I laughed – Daniel's mouth had become a purple-red thumb-print.

I laughed even more when I saw myself in the rear-view mirror of the van. My mouth was maroon and so mammoth and glossy it looked like a balloon exploding.

'No, Grace. Don't say that,' said Daniel. 'It's more like a . . .'

'Cherry,' said Daniel's dad.

'No.' Daniel shook his head.

'A cowrie shell, *alors*?'

'No, Dad. Much darker than that.'

'Another sort of sea creature then.' Daniel's father blew smoke, quickly, in a fan, so it hit the windscreen and bounced back. 'A crimson sea anemone, *peut-être*.'

'Red rose,' I said decisively.

'Yes,' said Daniel and his dad simultaneously.

A22, A271. Battle, Baldslow and down to the A259, which is where we saw the hydravions. On through Brookland, Brenzett, Old Romney, New Romney and then right, towards Lydd and the coast, past a lone signpost that said 'Ferryfield'. It was almost light now, and all around the land was flat, grey-green and wet.

'To the west, Dungeness.' Daniel's father gestured with his cigarette towards a line of faint squat shapes on the horizon. Daniel and I were smoking too, not jits, but Eric's roll-ups – eighteen in a Benson & Hedges packet with a white ribbon tied around it – another birthday gift, God bless.

'Dungeness. Means 'dangerous nose'. They're building a nuclear power station. I told you about it, Dani.'

Daniel didn't reply because, 'Voilà. We've arrived,' he cried.

Lydd airport.

A low, white, angular building. Next to it a few huddled sheds, hangars in the distance, and an expanse of clumpy land with a runway cutting through it towards the sea, which was rutted today, a dark, foamy, faraway grey. The sun hadn't cut through the clouds, and because of the drizzle, everything was hazy and dim.

Two small aeroplanes lay wing to wing to one side of the runway. A larger plane stood on the runway and was alive with movement. Its nose, or mouth – Dad calls it the maw – didn't look dangerous, but it was very big. People were carrying boxes and the oddest of objects up a short ramp into it. There was a grand piano without any legs, a stack of wicker chairs, two bicycles tied together and an old-fashioned black and red rocking horse.

While Daniel's father strode around knocking on sheds, disappearing into them, coming out again, pacing up and down, lighting jit after jit, Daniel and I stayed in the van, watching it all like a programme on telly through the windscreen. We shared a roll-up, and, for once, Daniel let me put it to his lips for him. He smiled, then frowned.

'I can still remember, you know – having arms, having hands and fingers. Only just, or only sometimes, but I can, Grace, when you hold the roly to my lips like that.'

Daniel sucked in a lungful of smoke and let it out, in puffs, while he spoke.

'Dad let me smoke as soon as I was old enough to unwrap his jits for him. That's how it seemed, anyway. He'd give me the box, or his fag-ends to play with. All those hours on the road. I used to shred the ends and separate the unsmoked tobacco from the burnt. Tear and uncurl the papers, then flatten them. Sometimes I tried to fold the silly scraps into planes or cars.'

I let Daniel lip the roll-up again.

'One day, we stopped to fill up with petrol, and while Dad was out of the van, I took his Zippo and lit one of the fag-ends with it. Dad was impressed, and after that, he let me smoke as much as I liked. That's all I remember. Except for the burns in my cuffs, and the smell – the smell of smoke on my hands – and sucking my thumb for hours, trying to taste the smell. Oh, and poking my fingers into my ears to stop a fit coming on. I can't do that any more.'

But Daniel refused to let the story be sad. He added, 'And using my fingers to pick my nose, of course. Flicking bogeys at the windscreen. Dad and I had bogey contests.'

After that, Daniel and I simply sat, following the comings and goings, until Daniel's father walked back to the van accompanied by a figure half his height and twice as wide, with a blanket around her shoulders. The drizzle had turned to heavy spit. Mr Smith opened the side door to the van and said it was time to say cheerio.

'Mrs Perkins, hello,' shouted Daniel, nearly knocking me out of the van and tumbling down himself in his haste to get out. 'Mrs Perkins, Grace. Grace, Mrs Perkins.'

'Hello, Daniel.' Mrs Perkins was a large, oval, middle-aged woman whose broad, red face beamed open easily. 'How do you do – Grace Williams, isn't it?'

I slipped down from the van without any help, while Mr Smith murmured something in French to Daniel. I saw him slide a few bank notes into Daniel's trouser-pocket.

'Mrs P'll look after you. I must shove off, son.'

Daniel's father put his arms around Daniel and clutched him. Mrs Perkins stood next to me, close but not touching.

'Goodbye, little lady,' said Daniel's father then.

We shook hands.

'Thank you,' I said, remembering Miss Lily and her etiquette.

'The pleasure is all mine,' Mr Smith replied.

I put my hand to my mouth, and it smelt of jit.

Daniel's father climbed back into the van and drove towards the runway and the bulbous Bristol 170 Freighter waiting there.

'A high-wing monoplane, with fixed undercarriage and Hercules radial engines. Like the old Bombay bombers.' Daniel moved a few feet away from me and Mrs Perkins and stared after his dad. I sucked my fingers.

The short ramp at the open front of the plane had been removed, and there was a long ramp now, like a tongue, coming out of the front. A car drove up it and disappeared inside. Then another. Then it was the van's turn. Mr Smith hooted the horn, twice, as he drove up the ramp.

'See. Just like I said,' Daniel hopped from foot to foot. 'You must wave, Grace. He can see us, even though we can't see him.'

I waved, and went on waving while the maw of the plane closed and two men in overalls pulled the ramp away. A man – the pilot, said Daniel – was hoisted up and through a door in the side of the cockpit. The clam-shell door was slammed shut, engines started, and the plane began to move, turning slowly towards the sea, then setting off down the runway diagonally away from us, picking up speed, making the air around it whirr and blur. I went on waving, even though my good, waving hand tingled badly. Daniel tilted his head from side to side, goodbying too, and Mrs Perkins lifted her blanket and flapped it like a swooping wing. When the wheels of the plane lifted off the ground, my belly, chest, heart and blood all loosened and quickened. The plane rose higher and smaller into the diagonal French distance, leaving a trail of puffy dark grey, like the smoke coming out of the chimneys of Battersea power station. I wished, for a mo, I wasn't wearing trousers but a lady's big-buttoned suit, pale silk stockings, two matching, high-heeled shoes, and a tilted grey felt hat.

'Right, you two. Ready to go?' said Mrs Perkins.

Where to? I jerked in panic, suddenly so far away from everything I knew. Everything new.

'It's okay, Grace,' said Daniel. 'Mrs Perkins is the landlady of the Rising Sun, the Ritz of the south coast. She's going to whisk us there in a jiffy, aren't you, Mrs P?'

'Not unless my hubby gets a move on,' said Mrs Perkins, puckering her rubbery lips and glancing around her.

While we waited, Daniel told us that in the olden days, when he used to go on the plane with his dad, the pilot was a mate.

'Jonno, his name was. He used to let me visit the cockpit. Blimey it was cold in there. Windy. And everything shook. Jonno said the plane was nothing but forty thousand rivets flying in close formation.'

The spit turned to rain, and Mrs Perkins tried to keep us dry by wrapping her blanket around the three of us. It wasn't quite big enough, so she held it tight and we breathed into each other and squeezed our middles together. Mrs Perkins was fatter than Ida, and you couldn't tell where her boosies ended and her belly began.

A green Mini appeared from behind one of the sheds, drove over to us and stopped.

'About time, George. Where have you been? We're drowning out here,' said Mrs Perkins as a man even larger than herself wound down the window of the car.

'Sorry, love,' said George. 'Beer delivery.'

Mrs Perkins opened the passenger door. George tilted the seat forwards and told us to climb into the back. Mrs P fitted herself into the front seat. Her bum and George's were both so big that they met in the gap above the handbrake. Luckily, George didn't need the handbrake, because the land between the airport and the Rising Sun was as flat as the sky.

We were hurried out of the car, through the pouring rain and into the pub. Through an empty bar, past the kitchen, along a corridor with barrels stacked on one side, then up some back stairs. There was a landing at the top of the stairs with four doors leading off it. Mrs Perkins opened one of them.

'Toilet,' she said. 'Dodgy. Watch out for the flush. Nearly a goner.'

She opened another door.

'Here you are.'

We were shown into a room with two salt-streaked windows, a dark wardrobe, a table with a mirror behind it, a rusty ashtray on it and an upright chair next to it. There was also a double bed.

'I'll send some food up later. But now – bed. Mr Smith's orders.' She turned to go but looked back over her shoulder before shutting the door. She smiled. The blanket clung wet and heavy on her fat, round shoulders and was beginning to steam.

'The heating's on the blink again,' she said. 'Keep warm.'

There was a key on the inside of the door. When Mrs

Perkins had gone, I turned it, pulled it out and placed it on the table.

We took all our clothes off and piled most of them on the table too. Daniel put his new, black, shiny shoes on the floor by the door where we'd be able to see them and admire them from the bed. I folded and hung my blue corduroy trousers over the back of the chair. They were an early birthday gift from Miss Blackburn and Miss Lily, who had shortened them for me and put two pleats in the waist so they fitted just right.

We slid into the bed, me on the side by the window, which we hadn't even looked out of yet. The sheets were pink, slippery and cold, the blankets were heavy, and there was a dampness in them that made us shiver. Daniel wriggled over to me. I put my good arm across his back and pulled him close.

We'd never made love in a bed before, and I never did again – I don't know about Daniel – but we christened that chilly bed the love-bed because we loved in it so silly much.

When we were warm and heart-slow next to each other, we lay and looked out of the window at the grey sky and the rain, which was belting down now. There was maroon lipstick and sticky spunk on Mrs Perkins' sheet, but what the heck.

I retrieved the Benson & Hedges packet, which I'd stuffed into the deep side-pocket of my trousers. I gave the soft corduroy a stroke, flattening the nap perfectly. The trousers made me think of Lena Macintosh and her long, FANY legs, strong through the soft material of her trousers, even stronger bare and brown, crossed at the ankle, stretching out from the spindly deckchair. My own thighs were hard with bone, not as scrawny as Daniel's, but only one of mine had proper muscles. I could see my head in the mirror above the table. Head, neck, shoulders, arms, boosies, belly and the curly hairs at the top of my dark, wet cunt. This mirror was old and had the sort of dirty marks that all the polishing in the world wouldn't remove. It made me small, but perhaps not so badly formed, after all. I pulled out the chair and stood on it to get a look at my legs.

'What on earth are you doing, Grace?'

'Leg-up,' I said, and, for good measure, I added, 'in Lydd.'

Daniel rolled over in the bed, kicking his legs with laughter.

'Leg-over, leg-over, you twerp,' he sniggled. 'What the flip are you doing?'

My legs were like splinters of wood in the reflected grey sea-light. My cunt, in the mirror, looked shabby and dull. I sighed and clambered down off the chair. The rain was so heavy now that even though it can't have been later than ten, the room was as dusky as the apple-house. I walked across to the door and switched the overhead light on and off a few times. I left it on and walked back to my side of the bed.

I lay down and rearranged the bedclothes over us.

'Shall I tell you a bedtime story, my darling?' asked Daniel, squirming over so that we lay side by side like sunbathers. There was no shade on the overhead light, and you could see the word 'Osram' and '25W' in dark veins on the dim grey bulb.

'Yes please,' I said for the second time that day, and pressed the back of my good hand against Daniel's hip.

'It's your birthday, so I'll tell you a birthday story, shall I, Grace?' Daniel kissed me on the cheek and lay back on the bed. If he had arms, he said, he would have folded them behind his head, he felt that comfortable.

'Okay. Let me think. I imagine a pretty sound sort of start for you, Grace Williams. A rattling good birthday.

But first, you know, I see a staccato dawning. A line drawn on the map from Stettin in the Baltic to Trieste in the Adriatic. Your parents making love, making you, one early morning in early spring. One egg, one sperm and, one thousand, nine hundred and forty-six years after Jesus Christ, you, Grace – the footnote, not the headline, but all the more important for that.'

'More, more.'

'In May, I believe, an airport opened in Heath Row, Hounslow.'

We're neighbours now, Heathrow and I. But Daniel will never know that now.

'Summer saw bikinis, and your father probably snickered at the pictures. "You're snickering," says your mother. "Am I?" he snickers. "I'd love to see you in one of those." In September it was Vespas, Grace.'

Yes. Mother cut a photograph of boys on bikes in Rome from the newspaper and stuck it to the larder door. It was there for years, nearly as brown as the tape which still held it in place, but had curled and frayed.

'Pay attention, Grace.'

'I am.'

'You're not. You're improvising.'

Remember, remember.

'Next month,' I said.

'I know, sweetheart. October, November, bonfires and birthdays – yours, sooner than expected, November the tenth. You were destined to be premature. Grace Williams, the prima donna of the nursery. Small but apparently healthy. Eight fingers, ten toes, two unsucked thumbs.'

I put a thumb into Daniel's mouth and he nibbled it.

'Your birth, Miss Williams, was normal,' he continued. 'It went something like this – "Miranda. Run down to the station to meet Father. He's on the early train today. Tell him Mother's gone to have the baby. Take John with you."'

Daniel kissed my thumb. I removed it, put my hand on my belly and pressed my thumb into the empty pool of my belly-hole.

'Miranda ran.'

Across the grass, across the field, along the path, pixie-legs pedalling.

'You lived in muddy Oxfordshire, remember?'

John would have panted and tripped to keep up with his sister. They reached the lane. She took his hand. The lane was splodgy with wet leaves, grey puddles, fallen, sodden twigs. Half past three and already the air was chilly and darkening. They arrived at the tiny railway station, silent and deserted, and crossed the track to sit on the long wooden bench, which scratched their thighs with its flaky brown paint.

'What's the time, John?' Miranda pointed to the clock suspended from a bolted girder outside the station master's office, so large that if you looked long enough, you could see the big hand move.

'Twenty to four.' John scuffed his new winter lace-ups back and forth on the ground.

'Not yet.' Miranda remembered Mother teaching her to tell the time with this clock, last summer, when John was still in the pushchair.

'Listen.' Miranda put her hand on John's cold knee to stop him swinging. 'Can you hear?'

Both children cocked their heads, like robins, waiting to hear the railway track vibrate and hum. But all they heard was the rattle of keys, a door opening, footsteps and the station master walking towards them.

John nudged Miranda.

'Is it going to be late, d'you think?' he whispered.

'No.' Miranda smiled at the station master. He nodded as he passed them. He rarely spoke, even when Mother was there. Miranda glanced at the clock.

'Now,' she said to John. 'Look.'

'Twenty to, twenty to,' he crowed.

They stood up. The track was buzzing. The station master stood at the end of the platform, flags in hand. Round the corner came the train, louder and louder until it reached the station and, hissing and squealing, stopped. A door opened, right in front of Miranda and John, and Father stepped down, holding his briefcase, coat folded neatly over one arm.

'Father!' cried Miranda, rushing forward. 'Mother's gone to have the baby.'

'Gone to have the baby,' echoed John, hopping from one foot to the other.

Father smiled, put down his briefcase, pulled on his coat.

'Well, jolly good. Good news. Did she send you to tell me?'

'Yes. She said to run down to the station to meet you. So we did.'

'We did, Father, we did.'

Daniel and I lay very still. All I could hear was our window rattling, and the rain and the wind outside battering against it.

'I like to think of that scene. Don't you, Grace?' Daniel moved his foot so it lay, like a hand, against mine.

'And then your first few weeks at home.'

Mother holding me backwards over the stone basin in the kitchen, John passing the soap, Miranda christening me with bubbles, Father holding a camera. Cousins, congratulations, grown-ups sipping sherry. Cocoa-ey smiles, a glowing log fire. Mother's unbuttoned blouse. The chilly shadows and icy sharp echoes of children chasing each other – all through the snowy English winter that followed, cold and sunny, before the inkling inside my mother turned a ting-a-ling ringing and she took me to the doctor, who sent me to another, and all the trouble began. I see that winter as clear as crystal, cut with laughter and filled with fresh snow, toast, honey and endless rounds of Happy Families.

Here's Miranda, sparkling like the Christmas tree as she rolls a snowball bigger than her head. John digs an igloo. Mother winds me to her side in an old crocheted shawl and helps him. Miranda sculpts a hump of polar bear, and Mother brings prunes for the eyes. John and Miranda invite Eskimo mother and baby Grace to tea in the igloo. I lie wrapped in wool on Mother's lap while she tells fiery stories with Trojan horses and long voyages – odysseys, she called them. Stories with lovers named Menelaus and Helen, the most beautiful woman in the world. Apart from us, of course. Mother would smile and wink at Miranda, hug me closer.

Mother seemed to make the stories up, but she said they were old stories. While she spoke them, the cold, still air inside our igloo was alive with the flashing of oars and hooves, swords and sunlight that made John and Miranda's eyes glitter and crinkle like sweeties in their pale round faces made even rounder by balaclavas and, for Miranda, on top of her balaclava, one of Mother's Italian silk scarves tied over her head and under her chin. When Mother had finished, we went indoors and she made John and Miranda take off their boots and run up and down the stairs while she fetched wood, lit the stove, filled the kettle.

Snow lay on the ground for days. When the roads and railway lines were blocked, Father would stay at home and smoke his pipe, which made it seem like Sunday. After lunch, he would go out into the garden where Mother might be clearing snow from the path or chopping logs for the fire. I, propped in the old pram, would see him approach, hear him clear his throat so as not to give her a fright, then ask, shyly, if he could help. Mother usually shooed him away, not unkindly, telling him to get back to his books or his music. One afternoon, however, she smiled, shrugged and held out the heavy chopping axe to him. He took it from her, put it down on the ground, then put his arms on her shoulders, and they both bent their necks so their heads touched. They looked like two circus horses with sparkly heads. They remained for a long time like that, only their feet moving, making slushy craters in the dirty snow around their shoes.

Sometimes Father had to stay in London at our cousins' because the trains were so unreliable, and Mother became busier than ever, then, in a dashing, happy sort of way. She scarcely sat down from morning to night, except to feed me.

The first thing she had to do, every morning, was climb the ladder to the loft. She had to free the frozen ballcock in the water tank up there. The entrance to the loft was a hinged square of wood in the ceiling of the bedroom I shared with John and Miranda. It was a large, light room with two dormer windows and white-painted beams. My cot was by the door. John and Miranda had beds in the far corners. Mother would come in.

'Coo-ee. Anyone awake?'

She put two cups of milky tea on the low wooden table next to the nursing chair, lifted me out of my cot, settled herself comfortably and let me suckle while Miranda and John woke up.

There was condensation on the inside of the window and dampness in the air. Miranda said her nose was so cold she couldn't feel it.

'Come and drink your tea and get dressed.'

Miranda and John shivered over, drank their tea quickly, then pulled off their pyjamas and struggled into layers of vests and sweaters. They were allowed to wriggle back into bed for a few more minutes while Mother changed me and tucked me into John's bed. Miranda said it wasn't fair.

'Life's not fair,' Mother invariably replied.

Sometimes Miranda stuck her tongue out at Mother, behind her back, when she said this.

Soon it was time for the climb up the ladder. Up Mother went, dirndl skirt swaying, the muscles on her shins rippling like a swimmer's above the thick men's hiking socks she wore instead of slippers. She hauled herself through the hole and we heard her move carefully across the rafters, and then a tapping and scratching in the corner. Sometimes she cursed. Bugger, damn, damnation. Sometimes she put her head back through the hole and told Miranda to fetch the hammer. And to bring some flapjack from the kitchen while she was at it.

Miranda scuttled off, and Mother hung her head upside down, rolling her eyes, making silly pink faces at John and me. Later, they ate the flapjacks, Mother cuddling in with Miranda for a few minutes.

'Put your hands under my armpits, darling. It'll warm them up.'

Little bits of golden oatcake fell from John's mouth and crumbled next to me on the white sheet.

Tick tock ballcock.

Adding its echo to the following hot, hot summer of 1947, with its 'Greensleeves' through the open French windows, Mother and me on the prickly rug, and Father with the other two, asking for lemonade and ginger beer because they'd been playing pat-ball on the lawn, or something like that.

'Something like that,' Daniel finished off. 'Although we don't know the end of the story yet, do we, my darling?'

And we lay in silence for a long time, both of us looking at nothing in particular, alone but together in the best of birthday ways.

When there was a knock on the door, I unlocked it, and Mrs Perkins wobbled in with lunch on a tray. Bowls of soup, cheese crackers, two packets of crisps and a jug of water.

'Up to you what you do. But you're welcome in the bar later.'

We left the tray on the table and took the packets of crisps back to bed with us. There were little twists of salt inside, wrapped in blue paper. We tore open the twists and screwed them into balls, then flicked them like bogeys towards the brown wardrobe opposite the bed. Even with his feet, Daniel was more expert than me, but a toenail caught in the sheet, laddering it like a stocking.

In the afternoon we went for a walk. Rain still pelted down from the sky, thick enough to seem to pelt up from the sea.

'Look at all the lighthouses, Grace. How many there are.'

I held my good hand to my face, bending my thumb and finger into a circle and putting them around my eye.

'Good idea. Binoculars. Pass them here. My turn.'

I curled my finger around Daniel's eye. He gazed, then made out he was focusing on something in the distance. I followed his gaze out to sea.

'France,' he said. 'Take a look, Grace. If you look hard enough, you'll see.'

I brought my hand back to my own eye.

See what?

'The coast? The long, Normandy road? Papa in the van blowing smoke-rings?'

I shook my head.

'The Eiffel Tower, the Sacré-Coeur, *la Joconde*? Can you see them? Or let's go south – Troyes, Dijon, Geneva? The mountains, Maman, snow? What can you see, Grace?'

Turin, Milan, Florence, Rome? Yes, no. Trieste? I shook my head again.

'Never mind,' said Daniel. 'We don't need to pretend today'

We walked in the rain for a long time on the vast, empty beach, not talking, not touching, sometimes not even really walking. Neither of us went very near the sea, which was frothy and loud, rushing and sucking. The downpour hadn't ceased, and as the light began to fade, the air thickened with an autumn mist. A strange, yellow-grey glow was spreading across the sea from the horizon towards us, making the rain seem to fall in green scales. I was wet through, Daniel was shivering. We walked back along the untarmacked road between the shore and the straggling row of dilapidated houses, keeping ourselves warm by singing about dragons, knights and ladies, diamond rings, noble kings and all things bright and beautiful.

Into the pub, upstairs, and another lie-down on the love-bed, by which time it was quite dark and the wind was raging. But when I looked out of the window, the light-houses winked and flashed, friendly and steady through the angry night.

Mrs Perkins knocked on the door and told us we needed to wash and dress.

'I put your clothes to dry next to the boiler,' she said, and she handed them, damp, to me round the door. 'Thank your pa for the money, Daniel. He's a fine man.'

We pissed in the dodgy toilet and washed in the grimy hand-basin in there. We put our not-quite-dry clothes back on and went downstairs to the bar.

Mrs Perkins stood behind the bar with George next to her. There was a jukebox in the corner rolling out dance music, and fairy-lights strung across the windows. The door kept opening and closing, bringing in more and more people, along with gusts of sea air. Mrs Perkins came round from behind the bar and led Daniel and me to a small table in the corner, by the Gents.

'Sit quietly and be good. O'Reilly won't be here for a couple of hours yet.'

'I know,' said Daniel. 'It's part of the plan, Mrs P. You know I want Grace to see what a really good night out can be – a night at Mrs Perkins' Rising Sun.'

'Well, you've seen enough of them here, in your time,' Mrs Perkins smiled. 'I remember your pa bringing you here when you could scarcely walk. He used to sit you on the bar – you can't have been more than two – and you'd yatter away like Lord Montagu of Beaulieu himself. An entertainment, you were. And now look at you.' She looked from one to the other of us, and it wasn't a look of my how you've grown, but, 'My how grown-up you are.' Admiring.

Daniel and I scriggled with pleasure, and accepted, with pleasure, the two half-pints of beer Mrs Perkins slopped down on the table along with two more packets of crisps.

The jukebox music became loud, and people started clapping. Jigging and tapping.

'Go, go, go,' people chanted above the music.

A lady was hoisted on to one of the tables at the far end of the bar. She wore a beautiful ballerina skirt with sequins, and high gold shoes that glittered and clopped. She had ladylike feathers on her head and attached to her bum, and a proud-lady look in her big, sad, painted eyes that grew bigger as she danced, and less sad.

Fast and alone, the lady danced. Then fast and together, whirling and clopping, we all seemed to dance. Like never before. We shuffled our feet, clapped the beat. Faster than on the radio. Elvis Presley, Dusty Springfield, Cilla Black, the Beatles. The music made me feel like an aeroplane taking off because of the twirling propeller-lady and all the people swaying, leaking heat, sweating, and humming, half-singing, windy sounds.

'Happy birthday, Grace,' whispered Daniel, kissing my ear and sucking on the wisps of hair around it.

O'Reilly arrived at ten. The bar was emptying by then.

The lady had climbed off the table and, with her back turned, was helping herself to a drink. The feather on her bum floated up and down, reminding me of Miss Blackburn when she wrote on the board.

Mrs Perkins introduced us to Mr O'Reilly and handed him two small blankets. O'Reilly led us out of the bar and across the road to his van. He opened the back doors. Mrs Perkins hung the blankets like scarves around our necks and told us to climb up.

'Shutting you in, now.'

The back of the van had dozens of pictures propped and tied against the walls, but there was a gap in the middle, just wide enough for Daniel and me to squeeze into. Daniel lay down first and I covered him with a blanket. I lay down next to him and tried to pull the other blanket over the both of us, but it tangled with our feet and there was nothing I could do about it. The van started moving, and we both started muddling and fussing our blanketed feet. But we soon settled down as the van steadied into a soothing mutter around us, and we didn't actually need the blankets, because it was as warm as the boiler room in there. We spooned through our clothes and the prickly covers, my face resting on the back of Daniel's neck – the fragile white batty bit – feeling my own hot breath bounce back at me from his skin, like smoke from a windscreen. I fell asleep with the taste of dried salt in my mouth and to the sound of Daniel's voice. He was wondering aloud about the pictures in the van.

'We could unwrap one, Grace.'

Noodle. It was dark. We wouldn't see a thing.

Wondering if they were valuable, beautiful, useful. Did they tell stories? He started telling me one, about a ballerina, or a bluebird, but I fell asleep before he'd really got going.

There was no stopping on the journey home, and back at the Briar, it was nip, hush, piss, no wash and slip into bed. Three a.m.

Twenty-four hours on the road. Can you imagine?

A machine attached to the floor with bolts as big as the roots of a tree, and the machine itself a sort of tree – hinges and arms tilting and swaying, and a tray on one arm with tools in rows, like silver twigs. A moon of a mirror swung down from an overhead branch. The mirror was round with a white light around and as if behind it. When Dr Bulmer pushed it away, you knew he was nearly through with you, and a little sink would click out from the machine. The sink gurgled when you spat into it, and afterwards you rinsed all the red in your mouth and the sink with pink slippy water from a fizzing glass.

Over the years, Dr Bulmer had acquired a certificate, a budget and a drill, which allowed him to work by himself. So for some time now, it had only been drilling and filling for big-mouthed, sweet-toothed me. No pulling at all. Pushing, yes, and shushing too, because the drill made me shrill, and longer-lingering fingers. No more than that. The winter jasmine continued to flower.

But I no longer needed accompanying everywhere at the Briar, and it was my hand alone, now, on the brown-painted door of the room marked 'Medical Examination'. No more arm-swinging, witnessing Nurse Jameson. Not a whisper of mothering.

'Hmm. Eighteen, I see.'

Dr Bulmer removed his apron when he'd filled my tooth. He pumped on the chair, raising me, strapped and padded, to a sitting position. He threw his apron on the pile by the door. Then he went over to the sink in the corner, unbuttoned his trouser-fly, flipped open his underpants and pissed. Afterwards, he turned round, holding his dick in one hand, cradling it underneath with the other.

Rub-a-dub-dub. It didn't take more than a couple of minutes, but as he rubbed, willing his dick to harden and thicken, he was looking at me, my mouth, so longingly that I almost felt sorry for Dr Bulmer then. I know about longing.

He finished off at the sink – an anguished spurt, a judder, squeeze and the last few drips. Rebuttoned, he washed his hands, poured himself a brandy and released me from the chair.

'See you next year, Miss Williams.'

Next year, it was the same, and although the door was repainted green, and Dr Bulmer's hair went grey, it was the same every year, until the pulling.

Back. Back to the last few good bits before all that.

The hairdressing salon upstairs at the Briar. Preparing for Daniel, a dance, the choir. Chaperoned outings to Woolies in Watford for handcream, your own. Soap, shampoo, a brand new comb. And picking and mixing – Embassy records, Liquorice Allsorts, dozens of different red Coty lipsticks.

Payslips and visits to the hospital post office.

'Cash or savings?' asked the handsome young clerk behind the counter.

He looked like George Best, but his name was David Osborne, and he was engaged to be married to Miss Joan Walsingham.

'Cash, please,' I said every Saturday, until Dave explained that I could save my money as well as spend it.

I still preferred 'Cash, please', preferred the clinkle of coins wrapped in bank notes that dampened the palm of my hand. But I did manage to save, sometimes, for optional holidays, day trips and visits to palaces, factories and places of interest. Blenheim, Buckingham, Hampton Court, four and six. Five shillings for an evening at the Birmingham Hippodrome. Ditto for a swizz of a trip to the tulip fields of Lincolnshire. We went in winter and the fields were nothing but a windswept mass of pale brown soil.

In 1966, I saved for a ticket to watch the World Cup Final. A flickery, trickery, 'trust me' new orderly said he had several. He took my money every week and promised me a front-row seat.

'In the day room,' he said on the morning of the great day itself, 'Not Wembley Stadium, you stupid girl.'

There were televisions on most of the wards by then, and two in the day room that were never switched off. Eric kept a small television on an empty oil drum in the Nissen hut. His television had the best pictures and scarcely ever went wrong. But Eric, along with all the crazy fitters, including Daniel, was off with Major Simpson and his Scouts watching the World Cup Final at the St Albans City Football Club.

I didn't want to watch the match in the day room. Without Daniel, I'd hate the noise and the nurses making as much as us, everyone leaping up and down, preventing me seeing the cheering crowd, the nippy men with their beetling legs, and the heavy ball like a polka dot – on a foot, in the air, in the goal.

Miss Blackburn and Miss Lily had a large television which they kept in a wooden cabinet in the corner of their sitting room. It was on that grand television that I watched the World Cup Final.

'You're invited,' said Miss Lily at lunch. 'So's Toby.'

And Miss Blackburn added, 'Do come, Grace.'

I sat by myself on the velveteen armchair. Toby and Miss Blackburn sat on the settee, and Miss Lily flitted from one seat to another. At half-time we had cold mutton sandwiches, coffee for Toby, tea for the ladies, and when it was all over and Miss Blackburn brought out victory-sherry on a tray with four small tumblers, I was glad I wasn't one of the squashed, waving spectators at Wembley Stadium. Ninety-eight thousand, Daniel told me later. And four hundred million people had watched the match on TV. Four was enough for me.

Five and threepence for a trip that Christmas to see the London lights. The extra threepence was spending money. After gazing at Harrods, Hamleys, the packed London streets, we all piled out of the coach and into a shop near Oxford Circus. The shelves were stacked with Union Jacks, ashtrays, tea towels, badges and ornaments – miniature Big Bens, red double-deckers, the Houses of Parliament. Six pence each.

I spied a tiny bottle of perfume, shaped like the Post Office Tower. Threepence halfpenny, said the label.

'Threepence halfpenny,' said the man at the till, 'but I'll overlook the halfpenny. I've a mate with a kid like you. Poor blighter.' He shook his head as he took my money.

The bottle of perfume lasted for months. I kept it in the apple-house, moving it from shelf to shelf as if it were an apple. By midsummer, there were only a few drops left in the bottom of the bottle and they were cidery, sticky and brown. I rinsed the bottle as clean as I could and gave it to Miss Walsingham when she married David Osborne later on that summer.

'She smells.'

Sarah was right. I smelt.

'I don't want to sit next to her. Can't I sit in the front?'

'No. Be quiet.'

We were in Mother's nearly-new, olive-green Austin, Sarah and I together in the back. Across both our laps lay a half-sized cello in a dun canvas case. We were going to Leighton Buzzard to part-exchange this cello, which belonged to Sarah, for a three-quarter sized one. Sarah, nine last March, was growing fast.

Leighton Buzzard lay only an hour away by car from the Briar, so Mother, Father and Sarah had picked me up, before lunch, en route. They'd come right into the workshop, which was unusual, but I was expecting them because Sister had hurried me into clean clothes that morning, issued from the going-out box.

Spastics don't wear bras, but I wore ladies' knickers with elastic, not pins, a green serge skirt with a short-sleeved, slippery, flowery blouse and a big beige cardigan which still had all its buttons. I also wore two nearly-white socks which nearly matched except for the cable pattern up the side of one of them. I was twenty years old, but I still wore children's socks with grown-up skirts and dresses. All the ladies did. It drew attention to my not nearly matching legs and the clumpy, built-up shoes, but socks were more practical than stockings or tights, better for weeing us, cheaper, easier to wash. They were cold, though, especially in October.

Sarah, next to me in the car, wore scuffed, pony-brown

sandals with blue ribbed tights, a corduroy pinafore dress, pillar-box red, and a padded, hooded anorak, also red. My coat was thin grey wool with a silvery lining. I'd taken it myself from the going-out box.

'Harrods,' said Sister, reading the label. 'Very smart.' She eyed it. 'Probably Eleanor Maitland's. It's far too small for you.'

I wriggled and sucked my breath in to make the thing fit, and in the end, Sister let me keep it, but warned, 'You won't be warm enough. There's a cold east wind getting up. Still,' she added, 'you're a lucky lady, Grace Williams. Nearly a whole day out.'

I'd just finished slotting together two plastic panels into the side of a green transistor when the door to the work-shop opened, and in walked Mother, Father and Sarah, in that order. I dropped the radio. Everybody stopped work and stared. Sarah hid behind Father's back. The male nurse in charge that day strode across the room and shook hands with Mother, then Father. He pointed to me, unnecessarily, and Father chucked his head, a pale imitation of those long-ago days on the terrace – music, chit-chat, curls and ribbons of smoke.

Mother walked over and picked up the radio.

'There, darling. It doesn't matter.' A bright, make-believe-me-not. 'All set?'

'My coat,' I said, remembering. My coat was in the lobby. We fetched it on our way out.

'Goodbye, Gracie. Cheerio, Grace. Be good. Have a lovely time,' people were shouting.

'Why were they shouting?' asked Sarah as we walked in a windy foursome along the drive to the visitors' car park. It was a sunny day, but cold, with white clouds puffing fussily across the sky. Mother ignored her.

'Day out,' I said.

'What?' Sarah peeped at me from behind Mother's back.

I peeped back. She was still holding Father's hand. Mother held my arm.

'What did you say?' Sarah mouthed.

Nearly a whole day out, I wanted to say, but, 'One, two, three and away.' Sarah turned away, swung Father's arm and grabbed Mother's free hand. 'Come on. Please, Mum.'

'You're far too old for that.'

'But.'

'No. Not today.'

The four of us sat in silence in the car. Then I farted. A quiet but unmistakable bum burp. Which is why I smelt. Splotted my bottybook. Blop – another one.

'Poo! Grace stinks.'

After being told to shut up, Sarah pinched her nose between her thumb and forefinger, then twisted away from me and stared out of the window. With the fingers of her other hand, she drummed on the worn canvas, paused, then, with her middle finger, began to trace shapes which I could tell were letters. And the letters, I knew, made words. Daniel and I had our own version – fingers and toes on bare backs and bums.

Grace stinks, Sarah spelt out. *Poo*, then *ha ha. I hate Grace.* She stopped and kept her hand still, splayed on the belly of the cello. I could see how her thumb was shrivelled from sucking, and also how her nails were bitten and the skin all around them rough and raw, worse than some of the laundry girls. My little baby sister. She kept her hand still like that and her head turned away – so I couldn't help looking – until Mother pulled into a lay-by and said it was time for lunch.

Mother poured sweet tea from a big tartan thermos. The lid of the thermos turned into a cup, and Sarah drank her tea from that. Mother poured my tea into a plastic beaker which had a spout moulded into its lid.

'That used to be mine,' said Sarah.

I offered her the drink, very grown-up.

'I'm not a baby.' Sarah was cross. She was always cross when she thought people treated her like a baby. I only did because that's what she was to me, that's what Father called her in his letter. Your little baby sister, Grace, Sarah. That's what she would always be.

What was I to her?

I'd been home several times, overnight, that summer. Sarah had a friend called Katy who often popped round for tea. One afternoon they were outside playing 'Emil and the Detectives'. Sarah was Emil. Katy had to be Gustav and all twenty-four detectives. Their voices drifted in through the open window to the room where I was supposed to be dozing.

'How many brothers and sisters have you got?' asked Katy, who had an older sister and a new baby brother.

'Well, I've got a brother,' Sarah began. 'And two sisters. But one of them doesn't count.'

'What do you mean?'

'She's mental. Defecting.'

'What does that mean?'

'I don't know. Something to do with poo. She's ill. She lives in hospital. She never . . . I never . . . I don't ever see her.'

'Never?'

'Hardly.'

'Oh.' Katy sounded puzzled, but no more was said.

'More tea?'

Mother unwrapped sandwiches. Ham or jam? Jam, Mum. And butter, please. I chewed, mulched and gulped the soft red bread until,

'She's making a mess.'

Jam in my mouth, but jam on my hand too, and, worse still, jam on the dull canvas neck of the cello. Mother had to get out of the car, pull and flip her seat forwards, then lean into the back of the car to wipe everything clean with her hanky.

'See, she's the baby, not me.'

'Stop whining, Sarah,' said Mother. 'This is meant to be a treat. For both of you.'

'I hate the cello.' Sarah kicked both her feet against the seat in front. The cello wobbled. Father coughed. Mother made a noise that was part hiss, part sigh.

'For goodness' sake. Look. Custard creams. Lots of treats today. Joe, pass the biscuits.'

Father passed the packet of custard creams to Sarah, who was allowed to open them. She ate three, one after the other, while Mother wiped, climbed back into the driver's seat and started the engine.

'Share, Sarah,' she said.

'Yes,' said Sarah, but she didn't. She glanced sideways at me, unzipped her anorak and popped the opened packet inside. Mother and Father were bickering about which road to take – A1, A5 or 41? – so neither of them noticed.

We arrived at Leighton Buzzard via the A505, but the house we were looking for was on the other side of the town. There was more spattling, and Sarah said she was going to be sick if we didn't get there soon. Eventually we pulled up outside a crumpled, red-brick house. It had half its roof missing, and the blackened rafters underneath were bent and broken. The small, charred house was detached and set back from the road in a large, overgrown garden with a brambly path leading to the front door.

Sarah, pleased to be out of the car, led the way, skipping up the path, then standing on tiptoes, jumping to reach the knocker. Mother and I followed more slowly. Father brought up the rear, carrying the cello. Mother knocked. There were noises within, muffled voices, then the door opened and an old man appeared.

'Mr and Mrs Williams?'

'Yes. How do you do,' said Father.

'Come in,' said the old man, opening the door properly. 'You must be Sarah,' he said to me.

'No,' said Father apologetically. 'That's Sarah.'

Sarah had darted in ahead of the rest of us.

'Oh.' The old man smiled at me. 'So what's your name?'

'This is Grace,' said Mother.

'Well, come in, Grace. Mr and Mrs Williams. Please.' The man led us along a narrow corridor to a room at the back of the house. Sarah was already there.

'Look. Look. Chickens,' she said, giggling and pointing.

'Shhh,' said Mother. 'Behave.' And she put a finger to her lips. But I could see what Sarah meant. Violins in various states of completion or repair hung upside down from the ceiling like chickens, nine in a line. Their strings were broken or loose, so they splayed earthwards in quivering fronds.

A double bass and four cellos leant against the wall in a dark corner by the door. Two more cellos lay on their sides on a long workbench next to the window. There were armchairs and upright chairs, an old sagging sofa, a low table, a stool, bookcases piled with music, and two music stands, three-legged and spindly, like Sarah's – look, Grace, it folds – not the sturdy, tubular sort used by the hospital band.

What a clutter, Mother was bound to say later. Maroon carpet and striped wallpaper, brown and cream, made the room gloomy. It was chilly too, damp, even – we all kept our coats on – and through the window you could see a wintry lawn blobbed with wet black leaves. There were empty flowerbeds along each side, and holey hedges straggling into the distance beyond two squat, gnarled trees.

I sat between Father and Mother, all of us in a row on the sofa. Sarah was directed to one of the upright chairs. The old man sat next to her. He placed Sarah's half-sized cello on his lap and carefully unzipped it from its canvas case, taking care to remove the bow first. He passed Sarah the bow, let the case slide to the floor and spent a few moments just looking at the instrument on his lap. Then he picked it up and held it at eye-level. He tilted it this way and that, peering in through the curly holes on the top. Finally he unscrewed and pulled out the long metal pin that was supposed to jab the floor, and placed the cello between his legs. The pin didn't reach the carpet, but it didn't matter, the man just gripped harder with his knees. He took the bow back from Sarah, tightened the silver nut, pressed the horsehair several times with the flat of his thumb, then played a few notes. He was a big man, and the small cello could have looked silly between his legs, but he played so slowly and surely, increasingly surely – closing his eyes like people in the chapel choir – and he seemed so comfortable with the curved, lady-shaped wood, which he hugged, stroked and fingered, that he didn't look silly at all.

'There,' he said. 'Finished tuning. Your turn.'

Sarah took the cello and the bow.

'What shall I play?' She frowned and pouted.

'Scales. Anything. He just wants to hear what it sounds like,' said Mother.

'No,' said the man. 'I want to hear Sarah.' He spoke softly but firmly. 'Play your favourite tune,' he said.

Sarah complied. She played a tune we both knew well. Some French gavotte from her grade three book. A simple lilt, but her nibbled fingers moved nimbly, the sound was clean, and she had a natural sense of rhythm. Her left foot, crêpe-soled on the maroon carpet, tapped in time to the tune, and the pout of her mouth softened and swelled. You could see her tongue like an eye between her lips, because she was resting it there, focusing, like Miranda used to.

'Not bad,' said the man when Sarah had finished, and

you could tell that, as an expert, he was sparing with praise and not bad meant quite good.

'What now?' asked Sarah.

'Now you try out the cello I think would suit,' said the man. 'It's tuned and ready.'

He stood up, took Sarah's cello from her and laid it flat on his workbench. Then he brought over one of the cellos that had been lined up in the corner.

'And what about Grace?' he asked, addressing Father and Mother but looking at me, assessing my reaction. 'Does she play?'

'Well, she's . . .' Mother hesitated.

'She's damaged.' The man said the word neutrally, still looking at me.

'Yes,' said Mother. 'Defective. Physically handicapped, mentally defective.'

Mother had developed a way of saying these words that made them roll off her tongue, smooth and slippery, like the 'Wrigley's double-mint chewing gum', chanted and chewed – when she thought no one knew – by Sarah.

Wriggly gommy. Physically handicapped, mentally defective. Subnormal, abnormal, ineducable. Unbearable.

Sarah started playing the same tune as before but on the new cello. It sounded terrible. She stopped.

'I can't,' she said.

'You'll get used to it, grow into it. Start again. Just play the first few bars. Let your fingers adapt.'

Sarah did as she was told, but fiercely now, over and over, the same few notes, trying to get them right, trying to obliterate the pain that had unfurled into the room with the man's question and Mother's response to it.

'Do you like music?' the man asked me directly.

'She loves it, doesn't she, Joe? Your records. Remember.'

'That was a long time ago.' Father spoke for the first time. 'Do you still like music, Gracie?' He turned to me.

I looked at my father, swung my head from side to side, surprised. I'd be twenty-one next month. He was old. His lips, which had always been thin, drooped now, his mouth a pale loop of split grey skin. The lines around his eyes were from age, not laughter, these days, and the blue eyes themselves, smaller than they used to be, were squashed and dry. His face was creased and closed.

Father would have raised his eyebrows, surprised too, had he known how eclectic my tastes had become. Skiffle, jazz, the Beatles, rock – what did they mean to him? The hospital's concerts and music nights were the highlight of my week. Ditto the radio, TV, Major Simpson's LPs.

I enjoyed chapel at the Briar, too. Not because of God, or Jesus, or even the excuse it provided to say hello to the people who disappeared overnight into other wards or work teams, but because I liked singing the hymns in the grown-up chapel choir, hearing the rhythms in the King James Bible and listening to Eleanor at the organ.

There were snatches of music everywhere at the Briar. In the films we watched, at the dances we attended, in the chopsticky chinklings from open windows and doors, in the whistling, singing teams of workers, even in Daniel's jigging, itchy feet and Miss Lily's low, sewing, Irish humming. Not enough, though. Never enough.

More, more.

I wanted to shout, shake Father, spit in his eyes to moisten them. He couldn't have forgotten our warm afternoons and the radiogram, could he? The records. Our singing. Anything that sings.

But looking at Father's face in Leighton Buzzard, I saw a great sadness, the sadness of no bridge across time for him, no me trotting along it, nothing, not a thing hinging, clinking now and then together. No music. I had become someone else entirely to him, someone who might not like music.

'I do,' I answered, too quietly, looking down at the floor, hoping to stop the plopping tears.

'She does, I know. I've seen,' said Sarah, surprising us all.

'What do you mean?' said Mother.

'Nothing. Not a thing.' Sarah played the tune again, scraping the bow clumsily, too hard, across the strings.

'That's enough,' said Mother. 'Isn't it?' Looking at the man.

'Yes, I think so.' He took the cello from Sarah, wiped the fingerboard with a pink rag, laid the cello on its side on the carpet.

There was a quiet knock at the door.

'Come in, pet. Don't be shy. You don't need to knock.'

The door opened and a girl, or woman, appeared.

The clouds had thickened and darkened since the morning, but at that moment they parted and sunshine slid into the room, making it hard to see properly. I could, however, make out a tall, female figure, poised in the strange sudden light, with dust particles spinning around her in wide silver cones. The figure wore black slacks and a tight black polo-necked top which showed her pointed boosies.

'My daughter,' said the man. 'Helen. Meet the Williamses. Mr and Mrs Williams, Grace and young Sarah here, who's come for the three-quarter.'

I saw Sarah grimace.

'I hate the cello,' she muttered, putting her feet on the rung of the chair and leaning her elbows on her knees.

Helen stepped further into the room, out of the blinding light. We all looked at once. Her face was scarred, nearly as badly scarred as the faces of some of the old soldiers at the Briar slowly dying off in the back wards. Although Helen had long hair, it grew in messy tufts, like Toby's. There were bald patches on her scalp, and some of the hair was brown, some grey, some white. You could see that it had been carefully cut to the same length, but no amount of arranging or dressing could hide the damage to Helen's face.

'There was a fire.' The man gestured vaguely around the room. 'All that wood. The instruments.' His voice tailed away.

Sarah slid off her chair, scrambled on to Mother's lap and buried her head in Mother's shoulder.

'I'm sorry,' murmured Mother.

'I'm so sorry,' Father's embarrassment echoed.

What were they sorry about? Who were they apologizing to?

'Will you play, Helen?' The old man gestured to the three-quarter-sized cello lying on the carpet. 'This is – was – Helen's cello,' he explained. 'It's a good cello. Not the best, but we were all very fond of it. The fire . . . It killed my wife. Helen hasn't spoken since.'

'Oh, I'm sorry.' Father again.

'No. Nothing to be sorry about.' The old man waved any sympathy aside. 'We're travelling to Paris next week, Helen and I, to try out a better one, full-size, a gift. Tortelier heard her play.'

'Goodness,' said Father.

'Yes. This summer. In London. He wanted to help.' The old man hesitated. 'Helen's won a place at the Royal Academy.' He sounded more worried than pleased. 'It'll cost, though. And I don't mean just money.' His voice petered out again. He was looking at me.

'It's not any easier living outside, you know.' He paused. 'Better, perhaps, but not easier. That's what people don't understand.' Then, 'You do like music, don't you, Grace?' suddenly doubtful.

I didn't want this man to doubt. Helen must go to the Royal Academy. I was going back to the Briar, for now. But I wanted to banish the doubt in the man's voice, restore the light, or at least the smile, to Father's face. So I boomed in a big-belly voice, much louder than necessary, 'I do,' which made everybody laugh, even Helen. Which made me wonder about her muteness. There were dozens of dumbos at the Briar, but were some of them just pretending too? Noodles.

'You do? Good. Come, then, Helen. Play.'

The old man sat on the chair vacated by Sarah, while Helen moved around, first setting up a music stand and placing two loose sheets of music on it, then fetching rosin from the workbench.

'Why's hers wrapped up in blue?' asked Sarah.

'Shhh,' Mother put her lips to Sarah's ear.

'I'm hungry,' Sarah grumbled, pulling on the zipper of her anorak.

Sarah used to lick and bite her own rosin as if it were a giant boiled sweet.

When I stayed overnight at home, I slept in the sitting room, on a couch that doubled as a bed. It was here, in the sitting room, that Sarah practised the cello. While she practised, I pretended to snooze in the corner, on my couch pretending to be a bed.

'I know you're pretending, Grace,' she would say. 'You're not really asleep.'

And when I continued to close my eyes,

'You're not really asleep. Wake up, spazzo. Don't think I don't know.'

No response, which infuriated my little baby sister. She came up close.

'Spastic, fantastic. Nincompoop. Poop, poop!' Then, 'Ugh. You smell. Rotten apple,' she would say, pushing, doing wide-eyes, rubbing noses with me. Eskimo sisters. Dig us an igloo. Fill it with John and Miranda too, and the flashing oars of Mother's stories.

Sarah was right. I smelt. So did she, but she smelt of

baby – even though she was nine, by then – delicious little-sister baby. Soap and ironed, aired clothes. Sugar Puffs, toothpaste – or chewing gum – and rosin, which Sarah held in her hand, a russet disc, much darker than barley sugar, but with the same sweet semi-see-throughness, and stuck to a six-inch square of crimson velvet.

Sarah stood back and rubbed the rosin from the heel to the toe of the bow. Swipe, swipe.

'Look. Head over heels, Grace.'

All smiles now, she twirled the bow into the air.

'I'm an American cheerleader. A Yank,' she laughed.

I chuckled.

'Ha! I knew you weren't asleep, creepyhead.'

And then she would play. Scales, chords, gavottes. But often, she stopped. 'Look, Grace, it folds, the music stand. Watch out for your fingers. Ping. *Pizzicato* – funny word, don't you think? There are dozens of them. Funny words. Italian. I'm supposed to learn them off by heart. Write them down in a notebook. Look, there's a special pocket on the cello's cover. Mum made it – she loves the words – for the notebook, my rosin and a pencil. But I put other stuff in. See, you can hide things.

'There. Now put your hand on the strings. Feel. Can you feel them buzz? Put your head on the soundboard. Flat. No, your cheek, not your forehead, ninny. Like this. Like that, yes.'

Sarah said the rosin tasted sharp and nasty – 'I call it sharsty, Grace' – but if you sucked long enough and got enough spittle in your gob, you could put your tongue on the oval of rosin and you'd know what the word smicky meant – smooth and sticky at the same time.

She tried to persuade me to lick the rosin, but I was far too grown-up for such shenanigans. She considered forcing the rosin into my mouth. She brought it so close to my nose and mouth that I could smell its Christmas-tree sweetness.

But when Sarah did that, I opened my gob and let my tongue drool, which made her back away and wrinkle her nose.

Helen removed the wrapped rosin from its box, unfolded the blue velvet and swiped her bow with gusto, like Sarah, but slower, more measured, the movement of someone older. How old was she? Older than Sarah, not older than me, by the looks. When she'd finished swiping, before refolding the rosin and putting it back in its small round box, Helen held it up to the light for a moment. The rosin made a dent in the shaft of grey light, an orange glow like a sunset. The real sun seemed to have gone for good. Only small patches of blue remained in a sky that was filling with darker and darker rain clouds, lowering and pressing on the world, on this strange, shadowed room in Leighton Buzzard with its rows of broken musical instruments.

Helen put the box back on the workbench, sat down with the cello and began to play straightaway. I don't know why she bothered with the music stand and the sheets of music. She didn't appear to be following them or to need them at all. She played Bach's Suite Number One, in G Major, the Prelude.

That's what it was, and I knew what it was because of my job as the Major's assistant. We had a growing collection of LPs in the Major's music club at the Briar, including two by the Swingle Singers. One of the records had lost its cover and was scratched and jumpy on the turntable, but the other had a bright turquoise cover with a big yellow whirl on it, which I knew was the scroll of a stringed instrument, but could have been somebody's fat thumbprint. Major Simpson was fond of this music, and since he was in charge, we often listened to Jazz Sebastian Bach. At the end of the evening, I helped Mrs Simpson put the records back in their covers. Sleeves, she called them. She too liked the Swingle Singers.

'Now, which is your favourite, Grace?' she would ask, running her finger down the list on the back of the turquoise sleeve. 'I prefer side two, don't you? Shall we ask the Major for it one more time?'

More, more. So I wasn't alone.

But Bach at the Briar bore little resemblance to what came out of Helen's cello. No cosy double bass and percussion jazz combo this. No, it was something else altogether that leapt from between Helen's arms and legs, but seemed rather to leap from between her toes and her fingertips, pulsing out of her skin, splitting her black, skinny-rib sides, sparking along her scorched hairs and – whoosh – out of their electrified ends.

While she performed, Helen's mouth slanted in concentration, making the scars on her cheeks twist in frayed, ropey ridges. She, like her father, closed her eyes, which made it easy for us to stare at her. I could see Mother staring above Sarah's head, and Sarah, who was sucking her thumb, turned her head sideways and looked too. Helen swayed her own head, but not exactly in time to the music – she swayed it as if in thrall to some private, secret calling. I'd seen such swaying, often, on the disturbed wards. Mostly women. Women hunched on the floor, in corners, hugging their knees, rocking, swaying. But men too, more usually standing, leaning on the wall, clutching their genitals. Daniel called it the swaying of memories.

Helen's over-long body sat thinly against the rounded depths of the cello. It wasn't an especially beautiful cello. The wood was yellowish, veined with grey, brown and black. It reminded me of London brick. But it did have a warmth, even in its colour, the warmth of a house well lived-in. And the sound it made was lived-in too – an old sound, filled with many voices, aching, especially when Helen played more than one note at once, pressing on the strings and indenting them like skin. The noise echoed long after her fingers moved on.

I watched her fingers – how they leapt like the paws of a cat up and down the ebony fingerboard, sometimes shivering in wait, but sometimes pouncing, pinning the gut, clinging to sound. And then lightly off again.

I watched the bow in Helen's other hand, the way she dashed it over the strings, rosin like sea-spray whitening the wood beneath. The tailpiece quivered. The bridge seemed to shake. Back and forth went Helen's bow, making shapes in space that matched, or nearly matched, the patterns of the music. Lots of things clashed, seemed out of control, but the whole made perfect, indescribable sense.

When Helen had finished, and she only played for a couple of minutes, just the Prelude, she leant forwards, offering the cello to Sarah. But Sarah, more babyish than ever, turned her head away, burrowing into Mother's shoulder again. Helen shifted, held the instrument out to me.

'Thank you,' said Father, taking it from her. 'That was—'

'No need to thank,' interrupted the old man. 'It's a pleasure. At least, I hope so.' He looked anxiously at Helen. She sat with her head bowed, like mine when I didn't want the teardrops to plop.

'I've brought a cheque,' said Father, passing the cello back to Helen. 'I hope that's all right.'

'A cheque's fine. There's some paperwork, though. Come through to the front room. You can leave the girls here. Helen will keep an eye on them.'

But Sarah didn't want to be left. She wouldn't even get off Mother's lap. In the end, after a lot of kerfuffle and to avoid a scene, Mother asked if Sarah could go into the back garden to let off steam.

'Of course,' said the old man, closing the door behind them. 'We won't be long.'

Alone with Helen, I didn't know where to look.

Through the window I saw Sarah wander on to the lawn. She scuffed at the dead leaves and tuggled the hood of her anorak around her face. She came up to the window and made ape faces by pressing her nose against the glass.

Helen stood and took a step towards me. She twiddled the cello on its pin, then she leant it against me, its neck on my shoulder. The cello lay at a flat, precarious angle. Gently, Helen eased my knees apart. The green serge skirt rode up my thighs, which were unnaturally white in the dullness of the room, and my shrivelled leg looked more like an arm.

The body of the cello was between my legs.

Helen walked round to the back of the sofa. She stretched across and placed the bow in my good hand. Nelson was tucked behind the cello's back. Helen bent lower. I could feel her breath in my hair, by my ear. She put her fingers on the black fingerboard. We both held the bow, Helen's hand covering mine, taking the strain. Then she played, or we did. The Prelude to Bach's Suite Number One in G Major. Again. And again. It wasn't the virtuoso show of a few minutes ago. Sometimes there were only fourteen or fifteen notes in the sixteen-note runs because Helen couldn't reach high enough up the fingerboard, what with the back of the sofa and our heads getting in the way. And the music was slower, much slower, because of both our hands on the bow, and my arm, thick and feeble in its layers of clothes, dragging, acting as a brake. The tipped curve of the cello's waist dug into my knees, Nelson was squashed, hot and hurting with the pressure of Helen's fingers, and the neck of the cello knocked against mine. But as we played, the music went in and out of my belly, through my whole body, not just my heart, in vibrating waves, like the waves on the sea, each one different, each one part of something else. Towards the end of the Prelude, the music rises higher and higher like a tide, sucking at the open G, then D strings. Helen pressed hard. Rosin spurted. There was harmony, a climax and me. A funny cunt-wee. All over.

Helen moved away, took the cello away. Sarah was still at the window but she had stopped making ape faces. I heard Mother call her name and she disappeared. A few moments later, Mother, Father, Sarah and the old man came back into the room, and we prepared to leave.

We hurried down the garden path because it was raining now and the new, three-quarter-sized cello didn't have a cover. Mother said they would buy one in London, or she would make one. Would she remember to add the special pocket?

Back in the car, the cello lay naked across our laps. This time, I had the heavy end, Sarah had the neck.

I plucked the D string, then the low G. Sarah put a finger on the D string, turning it into a different note. Then another, and another. More, more. We passed the journey like this, while Mother and Father chatted.

'What a clutter,' Mother began.

The windscreen wipers wiped, the air in the car was fuggy, but Sarah didn't say that I smelt, even though I knew I must.

'Let's put a tiger in our tank,' sang Sarah as an Esso garage came into view beyond the Hemel Hempstead bypass. Mother said we had plenty of petrol, and Sarah knew perfectly well that Mother preferred Shell, but she drew in to the garage.

'Oh, all right. It'll give us a chance to de-mist a bit.'

By the time we turned into the road that led to the Briar – 'Will you stop that racket, you two.' Mother again – it had stopped raining. The clouds were still grey, but there was blue visible behind them and an evening sun making their edges white. Mother even had to pull down the hinged flap above the windscreen in order to stop the sun going in her eyes.

'That's autumn for you. That's England,' she grumbled, but not too unhappily.

'That's what I like about autumn,' said Sarah. 'The weather, the way things change so fast. Things are never what you think.' She lowered her voice. 'Like Grace,' she whispered, then nudged me to make sure I'd heard. I nudged her back.

'By the way, I like your coat,' she said.

We nudged and shared the last of the custard creams, which were warm and crumbly from being inside my little baby sister's red anorak all afternoon.

'Good day away? What d'you do? Have fun, Grace? How was it, your day out?' people were shouting.

'A treat,' I shouted back. Loud.

Sarah was right. Things aren't how they seem. I should have known. Secrets, leavings, without so much as goodbye.

Daniel finished being a weekly boarder at the RTS in 1968 and returned full time to the Briar. He'd passed some more tests, public examinations, and there was talk of college and further education, but nothing came of it. Daniel's dad needed to be consulted and he'd disappeared. I hadn't seen him since Lydd. He'd visited Daniel at the training school, but not regularly on Thursdays, like before, and not at all, said Daniel, for more than a year.

Packages for Daniel came less and less often, then stopped. There'd been the World Cup Willie mascot, which Daniel sold to a nurse for seven and six, and a Beatles record the same year, for Daniel's twenty-first. After that, just envelopes, *par avion*, with bonbons and jits and a couple of books – a pocket world atlas with a fold-out eyeglass, and, in 1969, a book that looked like an encyclopaedia to me, but Daniel said it was more like a dictionary.

'Papa's old *Petit Larousse Illustré*.' Daniel toed the patterns on the spine.

It was a mild, early autumn evening, and we were hot by the stove in the Nissen hut. Just us. So we'd taken some of our clothes off and stretched out comfy on a piece of felt salvaged from the hospital roof, which was being repaired.

That summer we'd had men on the roof of the Briar – patients.

'Protesters,' said Daniel. 'I wish I'd been up there.' He'd been down with the flu.

Men on the moon.

'Heroes,' said the nurses, waking us suddenly in the middle of the night to watch TV. 'History.'

And men on one of the women's wards.

'Male nurses with special training,' said Dr Green. 'A simple experiment.'

A simple experiment to queue early, eat quickly and nip, unseen, from the refectory to the Nissen hut – a woman on one of the men's wards, said Daniel, toeing the *Larousse* towards me. Daniel reckoned we had a good ten minutes before Eric and the crazy fitters returned.

I looked more closely at the book. Its hard cover was made of worn orange fabric. The wide, fraying spine had letters and a leafy border stamped in brown on it, and a dandelion, in brown and white, shedding seeds.

'Dad kept it in the flat in Paris,' Daniel continued. 'On the windowsill. I remember kneeling on it to look out across the place Pereire, waiting for him to come back at night. The place was like a fairground, Grace. Cars, mopeds, all sorts of odd-shaped little vans, some of them going round and round the roundabout, just for fun, the drivers tooting their horns, signalling and shouting at each other.'

Daniel smiled at me.

Whirly eyes, excitement inside.

'The bars, my darling. You'd have loved them. Their crimson-red awnings, glowing lamps and people going in and out of the revolving doors, or sitting outside, ever so late, at tiny circular tables with spindly red and gold chairs. People everywhere.'

The door to the Nissen hut opened, letting in Charlie and three of his mates, but Daniel was in full swing.

'The Metro opposite, arched and green, its sign bright red with lit-up letters, white all night. The tabac next door with a red sign too, Monsieur Esposito-Levi's shoe shop, and the chemist on the corner, woody, curved, crimson-red and gold, pretending to be old. Lights in all the buildings, four, six storeys tall, the shutters rarely closed. And the roads. Those were the best, Grace. Stretching out in every direction, like a gigantic firework or ferris wheel. A galaxy.'

Daniel seemed to settle back into the Briar, the Nissen hut, the crazy fitter team, Dr Green's experimental regimes. He became Eric's right-hand man.

'He says I'm indispensable, now his hip makes it hard for him to get around.'

Will Sharpe had started a line in bespoke footwear.

'For a gentleman's outfitters. Jermyn Street. Very fine repair-work. He says he doesn't know what he'd do without me.'

The Briar without Daniel was unimaginable.

But I should have known. Secrets, stories, ours, cut.

Daniel left the Briar in 1970.

Saturday, 11 April.

I saw the white Commer van as I crossed the visitors' lawn on my way to lunch. It bounced at speed along the drive, turned and braked, making the gravel squirt, then pulled up outside the main front door. Daniel's dad sprang out and rang on the visitors' doorbell. He paced up and down, waiting. He was as tall as ever, but less solid than in Lydd. Crinkling black hair, still very thick, and a yellow cravat at his neck, but his suit was loose, and he wore old workmen's boots on his feet, not French polished shoes.

Mr Smith coughed. He glanced at his watch, stopped walking and looked up at the clock tower on top of the hospital. He pulled a lighter and cigarettes from his pocket. There was a clicker-flip of silver, big, cupped hands, then the cigarette held with his thumb, sheltered under his fingers, even though it wasn't raining. He coughed again.

The front door opened. Mr Smith bowed, but his hair didn't touch the ground, nowhere near, and when he stood up, he looked dishevelled, not debonair.

Daniel was summoned during lunch. He slipped from his place at the end of the crazy fitters' bench. As soon as he'd gone, Charlie, next along, swiped Daniel's plate and spooned up the remains of his stew.

After lunch, we went back to our wards, and I saw that the white Commer van had disappeared.

No Daniel that night at the Beetle Drive.

No Daniel, the van or his dad on Sunday.

And Will Sharpe looked surprised on Monday morning

when there was no Daniel at the head of the queue outside the industrial units.

At three o'clock, the phone in the industrial units rang. The phone hung on the wall by the door and was mostly used for outgoing calls – reporting disturbances, requesting assistance. The only other time it had rung recently had been to tell Nurse Ogilvy she'd won twenty pounds in the staff sweepstake on the Grand National. Nurse Ogilvy had brought in packets of peppermint creams the next day and handed them out to everyone.

We all downed tools, hopefully.

Will lifted the receiver. He didn't say much, but he nodded and frowned and wound a stumpy index finger in and out of the glossy black curl of the telephone cord.

'I see. Yes, Mr Maitland, I see.' He pushed the cord against the wall and rolled it up and down. 'Yes. Of course. I will.'

He replaced the receiver and told us to take a tea break. After the tea break, Will moved one of the regular leather-workers from his seat at the electric hole-punch to Daniel's high stool next to his, by the lathe and the Jermyn Street shoes.

When I went to the Nissen hut later that evening, Major Simpson was there, with Eric, both of them busy by Daniel's bed. The crazy fitters were all at the far end, crowded round the oil drum, the TV, Apollo 13.

The bed was piled with Daniel's clothes and possessions. Eric was sifting through a stack of books. The Major was emptying the pockets of Daniel's old duffel coat.

'Nothing,' said the Major.

'Not a clue,' said Eric.

So I knew. Daniel had gone.

IV

May,

'Tantrums,' said Sister.

June,

'Sulking.' Dr Young.

July,

'She'll get over it.' Mr Maitland wasn't interested.

Dr Green was, briefly.

'Regression,' he said.

'Shoddy work. Sorry, Grace, but it won't do.' Will Sharpe looked sad, but there was nothing he could do. I kept slotting the panels back to front into his radios.

At the end of July, I was transferred to Ward Eleven, OT only – Occupational Therapy.

August, September. Case conference, Grace Williams.

'Significant deterioration. There's not a lot we can do, Mr and Mrs Williams.'

October, November. Remember, remember.

I went home in December for Christmas. The house was empty. Just Sarah and me rollocking around in it, and Mother not bothering to get cross because Father was in hospital.

'Angina,' said Sarah on the phone in the hall to a pal. 'Funny word, I know. Yes, sounds like—' She stifled a laugh. 'No. I don't know. Something to do with a broken heart.'

Father came out of hospital for Christmas. Parched and blue, he lay on the couch, eating half a grapefruit for breakfast instead of toast and marmalade, and turkey broth instead of the roast.

On 1 January, he went back in to hospital, and the next day the house began to fill up with people, because Father died.

The funeral was a cremation, which I didn't attend, followed by a do in our house, which I did, although Mother put me to bed before I was through with the doodle-do food. Crustless white triangle sandwiches without much inside – one at a time, Grace. Tiny cheese tarts, spinach swirls, and bacon rolled up on cocktail sticks – she'll hurt herself, Mum.

There were colleagues – musicians – and cousins Norwegian. Neighbours, friends and the three of us. Plus John.

'From America, Berkeley, UCLA.' Mother introduced my brother as if he were a stranger, but John was the same as ever, except he had new glasses, big Californian ones, which made him less shy.

Miranda couldn't come, Mother explained – too busy doing God knows what in the back of beyond.

'Too busy doing good,' Sarah interrupted. She cocked her head and smiled a pretend-Miranda smile. '"I know,"' she imitated. '"I'll make it better. In Nigeria."'

People laughed at Sarah's performance, but Mother said Shhh and changed the subject.

John stayed for a week, then returned home.

'Home?' Sarah snorted like Mother. 'You're not a Yank.'

'It's where I live,' said John, picking up his briefcase, which used to be Father's, and pecking us each on the cheek goodbye.

On the way back to the Briar, we dropped Sarah off, Mother and I, at Paddington station. The platform was teeming with trunks, bags, satchels, hockey sticks and different-sized girls in yellow and blue. Sarah moved stiffly in her new, cardboardy uniform, with her flyaway hair flattened and tied. She was quieter than usual and climbed on to the train without a fuss.

'Will you be all right, Mum?' I heard her say.

A quick hug and a neck-peck, but no answer from our pushing-her-away-from-her mother.

I saw Sarah make her way down the carriage and duck neatly under a teacher's arm to nab a seat by the window. As the train departed, Sarah pressed her nose to the pane, but she didn't make ape faces.

And Mother didn't talk for most of the rest of the journey, not even to ask, was I warm enough, did I need weeing?

At Watford, instead of taking the B route that led to the Briar, Mother went off in the direction of St Albans. She only realized her mistake at the roundabout with the Shell garage.

'Blast. I'll have to go right round. Damn. Missed again. What on earth's the matter with me?'

By the time we turned off for the Briar, the traffic had increased and it was dark. There were strings of red lights on the road ahead of us. The cars slowed, almost halted. Mother dropped her hand from the steering wheel and put it on my lap.

'Grace,' she said, and her voice was as hollow as the crescent-shaped gap between her wedding finger and its ring. 'I'm not myself. I'm sorry. I—'

She took her hand off my lap as the brake lights of the car in front of us winked. We crept forwards and, all the way back to the Briar, Mother tapped her ring-finger on the steering wheel. Left, left.

'I may not be able to visit, Grace,' she said as we pulled up at the gates. 'Not for some time.'

Not even gingerbread left, then.

I flailed like the spastic baby I'd always secretly be, waiting for Mother to scoop me, bitter-sweet, up from the warm rug in our hot, Oxfordshire garden, where Father, Miranda and John played with a ball that seemed to arc and roll for ever, like the old English songs on Father's radiogram.

'Sumer is icumen in.'

Miranda whooped her way across the grass to fetch refreshments – home-made elderberry or Rose's lime cordial, something like that.

With ice, everyone? My pixie-sister's voice.

'Lhude sin cuccu.'

Cuccu, cuccu.

'Gone cuckoo, have we, Grace Williams?' Nurse Halliday's sharsty laugh.

Not half.

I snarled when anyone came near me, gnashed my teeth if they touched.

In 1972, lockers arrived at the hospital. I hid in mine and used it as a toilet.

In 1973, we received radios, one each, above our beds. I tore mine off the wall, but the others on the ward, tuned in wrongly and to different wavelengths, drove me bats. I gnashed my teeth.

My teeth were pulled in 1974.

On the desk in the sun, the two matching pairs of silver pliers, which, it was said, Dr Bulmer wielded ambidextrously.

My gob was stopped with long strips of wax.

'Making an impression,' the doctor informed me.

Long strips of reddy-brown wax, making me retch.

'You're a lucky lady,' Dr Bulmer added. 'A brand new set of teeth. Free.'

Gas. The reddy-brown mask making me gurgle and sleep.

Feet on snow. Not Mother's, no. Hobnailed boots. Deep packed snow. Pliers in. Teeth – crunch – out.

'Wake up.' The doctor congratulating himself. 'Thirty-five seconds, twenty-five teeth. Not bad.'

The sound of running water, a chink of liquid gold, brandy on my lips and the colour of Lucozade replacing the bubbles of blood in my mouth.

There was no kissing, stroking, washing, dabbing, soothing, bandaging, cooing, no, but oh, the hospital grounds were lovely that year. It had been a mild winter. The almond blossom was already out, and Mr Peters had been busy. Jasmine. Scilla. Daphne. Camellia. They were waving at me, weren't they, my party-frocked friends? Come, Grace. You're invited. *Répondez, s'il vous plait.*

True, my head was still yellow and silly with gas, but true too that under the old cedar tree sang crocuses, all colours, and little blue scillas, brighter than bluebells. The grounds of the Briar were a choir of colour. Even Mr Peters' evergreen shrubs had pretty pink flowers peeping out of them. And – why hadn't I noticed before? – on the shady north wall, Christmas roses. They must have been there for years, interlaced with the winter-flowering jasmine.

Clutching a wad of Izal to my shredded gums, I made my way slowly back to the ward.

There was pissing, shitting, fitting, screaming, hitting, weeping, wailing on the ward that night. We all went under the reddy-brown mask. Twenty-four lucky ladies.

Forty-one seconds, thirty-one teeth. Thirty-five seconds, twenty-five teeth. Thirty seconds, thirty-two teeth – that was his record, nimble-fingered, ambidextrous Dr Bulmer.

Two weeks later, I was back in the chair for checking and collecting my first set of dentures.

Dr Bulmer wasn't wearing his apron. He didn't strap me in or fasten the pads. He didn't flatten the chair. That addled man climbed right into it, on to it, straddling me.

Leisurely, he undid his trousers, pulled down his pants, and stuck his dick in my mouth. At first, just the tip. It slipper-dipped in, fleshy and fat, like a chicken leg. The doctor used his hand to guide himself. My tongue swept, my lips blew. I couldn't spew him out.

Dr Bulmer gripped the top of the chair above my head with his other hand, wedging me fast, even my good arm locked by a tweedy knee.

I tried to keep my eyes open, but it was dark in the doctor's crotch – brown skin, damp black hair, shirt-tails tickling my eyes – and Dr Bulmer began to force more of himself into me, covering my eyes, my cheeks, my nose with the cotton twill of his freshly laundered shirt.

I'd have sprinkled salt on Dr Bulmer's dick if I'd had any, like Mr Peters sprinkled salt on the slugs that damaged his plants.

I'd have bitten it off, that dick, if I'd still had my teeth, and if it weren't for my lips drooping like broken knicker-elastic.

Dr Bulmer started knocking the middle of his body against my face. He thudder-shuddered into me, squashing me, hurting me, making my chest squeak and sigh. I'd heard my breath like that before, in the iron lung and under Mother's pillow. Dr Bulmer breathed noisily, pumping out mad, meaningless words,

'Yes, yes. Now, now. Oh no. Oh God. Nearly.'

He was taut and shivering. He removed both his hands – yes – put them on my forehead – yes – stroked backwards – now – ow, not like Mother, no – oh no – flattening my fringe – oh God.

I left the room marked 'Medical Examination' with a set of vulcanite dentures.

Some nurses found me in the hospital grounds, wandering by the shady north wall, sniffing the flowers, kissing them, sniffing. I don't remember. One of them took my arm, my good arm, but I shook her off, they said.

'My name? My name?'

That's what she whimpered, said the nurses. Again and again. But I don't remember, oh no. No words. Just sound.

1974–84

i

Father told me that when Gustav Holst's *Planets* was first played at the Queen's Hall in London in 1918, there were some cleaners at work in the corridors outside the auditorium. And when jolly old *Jupiter* started, Father said, the women all put down their scrubbing brushes and began to dance.

Father liked that music. He often picked up the needle at the end of side two and replayed the very last bit – watery *Neptune*, with his secret, hidden women. An off-stage chorus, Father explained. You can hear their voices – listen Grace, wait – right at the very end. No words, just sound. Yet music, a sort of singing, all the same.

I listened. I waited. But for a very long time, there was no music at the Briar. No singing at all.

I sank.

ii

It was *The Planets* playing the day I went down with poliomyelitis, Father in his study, working, Mother and John at the library – back in time for tea. Miranda, eleven, was in charge of me.

'We'll go to the rec,' she said.

I was six, but still too small for the old pushchair, which stood rusting in the shed at the end of the garden. I'd heard John ask Mother whether he could have it. He wanted to use the chassis to make a go-kart. When Mother said no, I heard him whisper to Miranda, 'She'll never be big enough to go in it. The boys at school say she's mental. She'll never grow. Mentals are all midgets.'

'Shhh,' said Miranda, putting her finger to her lips as if she were Mother.

She bundled me into the pram, which, like the pushchair, had been hers before John's. Although I was too big to lie down in the pram, I sat comfortably enough at first, cushioned by a blanket and folded towels. But on the way to the rec, I began to sweat. It was a warm summer's day and the London air lay heavy and thick on my skin.

'It'll be quicker this way,' said Miranda, bumping the pram off the pavement, steering it round a corner and through a gate.

We were on the path next to the railway track. There was a wire fence on the railway side of the path and a brambly hedge on the other. I could see tiny pale strawberries nestling near the ground among the nettles and the big, dusty dock leaves. Higher up, foxgloves clustered in shocks, twenty or so to a stalk. Miranda stopped the pram, reached out and pulled off one of the puffy blooms.

'Fairies live in foxgloves,' she said, putting the flower on my lap. 'Go on. Have a look.'

I scrabbled and picked the foxglove up. It weighed next to nothing, and its purple skin was marked by small circles of white with tiny dark dots in the middle.

'Well? Is there a fairy in it?' Miranda took the limp flower back and shook and poked it open. 'No,' she stated, matter-of-fact. She picked another foxglove off its stem and peered inside. She tutted. Another, and another. 'Hmm,' she pondered. She plucked a few more and put them carefully at the end of the pram. 'You look very hot, Grace,' she said as we set off again. 'You're all pink, and your neck's red.'

We met a man with a scythe, swiping at the hedge. He stopped swiping as we approached. He smiled and said hello. He wore heavy canvas trousers and was naked from the waist up. Sweat ran from his dark armpits, along the smooth, brown skin under his arms one way, and down the sides of his chest the other.

'What's your name, pretty?' he said, looking at me and putting a big dirty hand on the handle of the pram. The tops of his fingernails were black, there were cuts on his knuckles and scratches on his wrist.

'What's wrong with her?' he asked Miranda when I didn't reply.

'She's hot,' said Miranda.

The man edged his body next to Miranda's. He put down his scythe, and now he had two hands on the handle of the pram and was standing directly opposite me. The sun behind him made the wet spikes of his hair seem to spark and fizz. His eyes were sliced blue smiles.

'She looks retarded,' he said, glancing at Miranda for confirmation. 'We had a little girl like that. Annie.'

The man leant towards me, so close that the handlebar of the pram tucked into the crease of his belly, so close that I could see the pain hiding in his smiles. He brushed my cheek with the back of his hand, then pressed with his fingers around my neck.

'You are hot, aren't you?' he said. 'Aren't you going to tell me your name, pretty?'

'She can't talk,' said Miranda. 'Not really. Not properly.'

'Do you believe that?' asked the man, still looking at me. 'What about these?'

He gathered the scattered foxgloves and held them out to me.

'When you next go to sleep, put one on your finger. Like this.'

He slipped a foxglove over his little finger and stroked my nose with it.

'Make a wish. If the foxglove's still there when you wake up, your wish will come true.'

He straightened, stood back and twisted to face Miranda.

'She's too hot. She's not well, your sister. Do you live near here?'

Miranda was frightened.

'Help me turn the pram, please,' she said, breathily swivelling and jiggling the pram. I toppled sideways against the sharp, closed hinge of its hood. The man righted me and put the hood up – 'It'll give her some shade. God help her if it's the summer plague' – before manoeuvring the pram round.

Miranda pushed the pram quickly, looking thoughtful and worried. She, too, was hot and sweaty by the time we reached home. She fetched Father from his study. He came down, looking nothing but worried. He must have left the door to his study open, because *Mars* throbbed through the house so loudly, it almost covered up the pounding in my head.

Father carried me into the sitting room and laid me on the couch. Miranda brought water, but I couldn't drink it. She dabbed it on my lips and it ran, unwiped, down my chin to my chest.

'Best let her sleep,' said Father. 'Keep an eye on her, though. I'm going to phone the doc. Then the library. Call me if you need to. Mother won't be long.'

Miranda sat in the low armchair opposite the couch. The sound of *The Planets* continued, but more quietly. *Venus, Mercury*, jolly old *Jupiter*. Miranda counted the foxgloves. She put one on my finger and the others in a row on the arm of the chair. She took off her shoes, leant back in the chair. She pulled a length of string from her pocket and twiddled it round her fingers.

'A sailor's trick, Grace, look. I can do cat's cradle, too. And angel hair, see. Snake in the grass. Or is it the jungle? Who cares? How long is a piece of string?' She yawned. 'How long will Mother be? Will she be longer than this piece of music?'

Saturn, Uranus.

I let myself drift. Miranda's short white socks had frothy bits of lace around their tops. The toe of one of them hung off the end of her foot, and each time she flicked the string, the sock twitched and swung, like a pendulum.

Neptune.

I watched Miranda but I couldn't hear her any more, just a ticking sock, a stopping clock, silence and sound.

When I woke up, I was sweatier than ever and there was sick down my front.

'The doctor will be here soon.'

Mother picked me up.

The softness of her touch. A scorching hardness in my head.

'She'll have to go to hospital.'

An ambulance. The word poliomyelitis, spoken gravely. Mother's face. Mother, Father, Miranda, John. All gone. 'Nobody's fault.' 'Saved her life.' 'Darling.' A closing-in.

At the hospital, it was all I could do to breathe. They wheeled me in my hospital bed down corridors, through a hall, into a room with rows and rows of big steel drums on their sides. A girl's head stuck out of each cylinder's end, and mine did too when I was pushed and pummelled into one of them. Switches flicked, fingers adjusted, faces and voices floated above me. 'Air pressure, air flow, respiratory failure. Close the chamber.'

And then I breathed more easily, with something like bellows sucking on my chest. In, out. In and out. The noise was soothing. Like waves on a beach. Three dozen pumping iron lungs. In – whoosh. Out – whoosh. Shush, Grace, shush now.

'We'll have to cut her hair.'

'Shame. It's the one nice thing.'

'What's that in her hand? On her finger?'

'Open your hand.'

'She can't.'

'Looks like a flower. A foxglove.'

And when the nurses had gone,

'You. Can you hear me?'

It was the girl next along.

'I'm Shirley,' said Shirley, already shorn.

'Alison.'

'Amanda.'

'June Brown.'

And so on. Little girls without any curls, except in our slow, frozen muscles.

We wept a lot.

'It hurts.'

'I hurt.'

'Nurse.'

'Mummy.'

'Mother.'

There was no touching. Almost no movement at all. Our necks were wrapped tightly with stretchy black rubber. I could see if I looked down and nearly shut my eyes. If I looked up, I saw the world of the ward in the enormous mirrors, hung for our benefit above the cylinders. Bright and bitty by day, busy with nurses, doctors and silver trolleys. Eerie at night, the light from the night nurse's lamp weakly reflected over and over in the row of mirrors, like distant stars or dying eyes.

Alison died and Shirley too. Then June Brown. Their iron lungs stopped bellowing. Not mine.

More's the pity, said nurse to nurse.

I left my lung and was laid on a bed in the recovery ward. I ignored the flotsam and jetsam around me and continued my long roar to be heard.

She's a nuisance, said the nurses. A noisy cretin. As ugly as sin.

By October, I was as better as I'd ever be, they said, and I was sent home with my shrivelled leg, hairpin arm and a scribbled prescription for iodine.

'It could scarcely be worse,' said the discharge doctor, taking a photograph of me sprawled on the floor like a giant insect. 'My advice, Mrs Williams? Institutionalize. Try for another child. This one's ineducable. A write-off.'

'Grace Williams,' went his report, 'shows no interest in books, apparatus or pictures. She allows other children to do as they will with her. She does not take part in any activity. Apart from her physical handicap, which makes it extremely difficult for her to attempt anything educationally, there is complete lack of mental alertness.'

Complete lack of mental alertness. It was around this time that Mother and I lay on the slippery eiderdown with the pillow on her face, on mine, on hers. Drowning.

iii

I was eight before I was big enough, just, to go in the pushchair. Mother fetched it from the garden shed, cleaned the seat, oiled the springs, tested the brake. She cut the worn rubber from the handle of the pushchair using a sharp kitchen knife, then she whipped new string around it, like she did around the handle of the kettle and our chipped enamel saucepans.

'It's a sailors' trick, Grace. Watch.'

I watched – her fingers firm, her face set, she hadn't written me off, yet.

On our riverside walks, which Father called constitu-
tionals, Miranda grew out of begging 'Let me push', and
John stopped asking to ride on the footrest, where he used
to stand facing me, his chin lifted so high that, beneath
his glasses, I could see the stumpy lashes round his small
grey eyes. He remained a puny boy, and Miranda called
him a feeblosity. But John had his strengths, definitely.

The same Christmas that I, still tiny at ten, received a
baby swing, and Miranda and John their red and blue
books, we all had new balaclavas, knitted by one of our
Norwegian aunts. Mine and John's had the same snowflake
pattern in black and white. Miranda's was green, with
reindeer, in a row, around the neck.

'I'm fifteen, for God's sake.'

Miranda slouched out of the room, leaving her balaclava lying on top of the small pile of presents.

That was Christmas 1956.

A few days later, Mother was resting upstairs. The rest
of us were in the sitting room, reading. Even I had one of
Mother's home-made learn-to-read books propped next to
me on a cushion. It was about an adventurous pencil. The
pencil got lost and then found. All Mother's books were
about objects that came to life. There was the clever light
bulb, the naughty toothbrush, and – my favourite – the
dancing book. The stories were simple, with plenty of
pictures, made by Mother, drawn, painted and stuck using
different sorts of paper torn-up and rearranged. The book
in the dancing-book story was made to look like a skirt.
Mother had created the skirt out of tiny strips of paper –
words and unfinished phrases – taken from magazines and
newspapers. When the skirt-book danced, which it only
did if the little girl who found it and fitted it sang the
right tune, it swirled so widely, so grandly, that just for
that page, if you looked very closely, some of the words
on the skirt made sense.

Miranda didn't wear skirts any more. She sat darkly on Mother's chair at the sewing table by the window. She wore navy-blue slacks with elastic flaps that went under the heels of her navy-blue socks. She had kicked off her shoes and was wriggling her toes and rubbing the arch of one foot on the rung of the chair. Her new red guidebook lay open on the table before her, and on her lap was a small white paper bag of lemon sherbets. From time to time, she rustled the bag and crunched the sherbets. Once or twice she did goggle-eyes at John.

I was settled on the cushiony old couch, sitting with my back against one end and my legs stretched out, crooked but comfy. John sat at the other end. His feet, in brown polished lace-ups, were flat on the floor. He wore long trousers, but you could still see his thin knobbly knees inside them, squeezed together. He read with his book held like a prayer book, high in front of him, elbows tucked in, nose wrinkled to stop his specs sliding down. He couldn't see Miranda's bad imitations of him.

A hiccupping cough made me start. Three squeaky sniffs. Not Father crying? Father was sitting in the low armchair opposite the couch. He had been reading the newspaper, but now he held it folded on his lap. His head was bent and jerking, and the flimsy hair on it shook and flipped. I couldn't see his eyes, but there were drips on to the newspaper, and the crying noise became a moan. Father's breath kept catching in his throat.

'Fetch Mother,' said Miranda, pushing her chair back from the table and splattering the lemon sherbets on the floor. But John kept his eyes on his book. In fact, he held the book higher, blocking his view of Father, Miranda, the whole scene.

Miranda left the room. I heard her climb the stairs, two at a time.

'Mother.' Socks on carpet. Running. 'Mother.'

Father crying.

The bedroom door opening. Mother's voice,

'Go away.'

Shouting, screaming.

'I said leave me alone.'

Father crying.

Me crying. A noisy cretin. Screaming and shouting.

John closed his book and laid it flat on the arm of the couch. He stood up, took my good hand in both of his and pulled me to an upright position. He led me tottery-jittery out of the sitting room into the hall, where my pushchair stood, blocking the front door. John sat me in the pushchair and I didn't resist. He tried to put me in my coat, but it flapped, I squirmed and nothing would fit, so he wrapped the coat around me, tucking the sleeves under my arms. He took his dark-blue gabardine mac from its hook, slipped quickly into it and buckled it firmly at the waist. Then he tugged our new balaclavas over our heads. He was careful to pull mine down at the front so that it didn't cover and prickle my mouth, or get wet from my slobber. He opened the front door.

'Come on, Grace. Time for a constitutional.'

John pushed the pushchair slowly. We crossed the road at the zebra crossing and took one of the side streets that led to the river. John walked even more slowly once we were on the towpath. I quietened. The air was cold and the wind whippy. The wheels of the pushchair clicked against the stones, and twigs flicked in the wheels and sometimes up near my face or on to my lap. We passed men with fishing rods, and fish in buckets next to tubs of maggots. Seagulls squawked overhead and swooped towards the river, where ducks paddled and swam between the pleasure steamers and the long, thin rowing boats. John didn't say a word, and when I peeped at him, all I could see were the glassy bits of his specs, like shields.

Suddenly the pushchair jarred and jolted. The twigs fell out. I nearly fell out. The pushchair had skewered right round. It was at the very edge of the towpath, facing the river. The tide was high and still coming up.

'Let me at least put the brake on.' John's polite voice.

I twisted my head to look over my shoulder, and I saw John standing between two boys much bigger than him. They held his arms, one on each side, and they kept pulling at his arms as if he was trying to get away. He wasn't. He was trying to get to me.

'Whatever you do, keep still, Grace. Just keep still.' Urgently. 'Don't look. Not at me.'

I turned my head back to the river and did as John said.

'Give us the dosh, poshie.'

'I haven't got any dosh,' said John.

'Get some, then,' one of the boys hissed.

'I'm not leaving her.'

'The spazzo.' Spit hit my cheek.

'My sister.'

Two sculls skimmed swiftly upriver, pulled by the tide, pushed by the cold east wind. A Port of London Authority tug chugged downstream towards the landing stage by the railway bridge.

'Is it catching?'

No reply.

'He said, "Is it catching?"'

John remained silent, so they beat him up.

All I heard was scrabbling on the stones, like the wheels of the pushchair, and boys punching and making crowing, groaning noises. I think John put up quite a good fight for a feeblosity, but in the end it was two against one.

'You're beaten, weed.'

'Give me back my specs.'

The boys muttered together, then,

'No,' said one of them.

'You go or she does. Over the edge.'

'No.' John's voice quivered.

'Okey-dokey. Bye-bye, spazzo.'

The pushchair shook, tilted and tipped. My coat slipped out from under my arms. It fell in the river and disappeared in a muddy swirl of dead leaves.

'No.'

The pushchair shaking. A pulling back.

'No. Leave her alone. Damn and blast you. I'll go.'

The three boys lined up next to each other on the bank of the river. John took off his mac and laid it over my legs, which were chilly and pimply because my coat had gone and my skirt was skew-whiff.

'Do you want your specs?'

John shook his head,

'Give them to Grace.'

The boy – the spitter, I think – folded the spectacles and placed them on my lap. He glanced up at my face as he did so, and I spied shame in his eye, just a speck, too small to stop him seeing this through, but a speck, nevertheless.

John removed his shoes, then quickly jumped. It was all very quick. The other two boys jumped back in surprise.

'Blimey. I didn't think he'd do it.'

'Blimey. D'you think he'll drown?'

'Dunno. Let's scram.'

They ran.

John didn't drown. He appeared at my side a few minutes later. He was dripping wet and looked like a seal because he still wore his dark knitted balaclava. He put on his shoes, put on his specs, left the gabardine mac on my lap, and began to wheel the pushchair back the way we'd come, slowly and squelching. Before turning off from the towpath, he paused by a bench, facing the river. He positioned the pushchair at the end of the bench, pressed on the brake and sat down. He was higher than me, but he'd angled the pushchair so that I could see his face and he could see mine.

'I don't want to go home, Grace,' he said, and shivered.

It was cold, ever so cold.

Terns and heron gulls whirled in the wintry air, screeching and hollering a private language. Terns and heron gulls, mallards, divers and crested grebes, sycamores, willows, poplars and lime trees, sculls, pairs, fours and eights. Plus the cox, Grace. Don't forget him.

We saw these rivery things, and John named them for me.

Cirrus, cumulus, nimbostratus – imminent rain.

We stayed where we were until the rain became snow, and flakes lay like polka dots on the gabardine mac on my lap. All I could hear was the knocking of John's knees and his teeth chattering.

iv

Clackety-clack.

'Don't do that, Grace.'

I was jawing my false teeth, which always drove the nurses mad. I did it some more. My gums were sore.

We took our false teeth out at night, and they all went together, plippety-plop, for cleaning, into a pail of water. It used to be Diana's job to take them from the water and match the numbers printed on their undersides to the numbered compartments of a special plastic tray, but Diana moved to the disturbed ward in 1981 – she said she was marrying Prince Charles – and the nurses forgot after that. So for the last three years, when we queued for our dentures in the morning, we'd been making do with whichever set came out of the bucket first. Receiving your own set, the set that didn't make your gums sore, was like winning at bingo, hitting the jackpot, fitting the slipper. Otherwise, the false false teeth turned us into clackety old crackpots.

'Stop it.' The nurse raised her voice and her hand. 'Shut up, Grace.'

Smackety-smack.

Shut up, shut up, shut up, shut up.

Silence? Definitely not my thing.

Clackety-clack.

'If you don't shut up, Grace Williams,' the nurse yelled above the racket, 'I'll tell your visitor to go away, shall I?'

Clack.

Sarah.

'It's me.'

We went for a walk, or rather a wheel, for I was a wheelie, temporarily, having slipped in some piss on the toilet floor.

'Twisted, not broken,' said the locum doctor. 'Strap it.'

Swollen, throbbing and bandaged, my ankle made walking a palaver.

For half an hour, Sarah practised pushing me in the wheelchair up and down the main hospital corridor. 'Bloody hell,' she said, several times, under her breath, and, every time we got stuck in a fire door or banged against a wall, 'Shit'. When she'd got the hang of it, she pushed me through the hall, where I used to polish the door knobs, and out through the big front door. We made it all the way along the gravel drive to the gatehouse. The top of the gatehouse was offices now, and Toby's bottom bit had become a sort of shop, run by the Friends of the Briar. You could buy newspapers there. Magazines, cigarettes, birthday cards, flowers and a small selection of sweets.

'That reminds me,' said Sarah.

She turned the wheelchair and we lurched across the visitors' lawn in the direction of the visitors' car park.

'Here we are,' said Sarah, wheeling me towards a small

blue car, alone at the far end of the car park. 'The Ford Fiesta. Over there.'

When we reached the car, Sarah took out a key and opened the passenger door.

'I forgot.' She pulled from the glove compartment a large packet of barley sugar. 'Mum said to give you these. She said you liked them.'

The see-through packet crackled in Sarah's hand.

'Do you want one?' she asked, holding the packet up in front of me. 'I don't like them.'

Nor me. Not any more. My barley-sugar days were long gone.

I replied by clacking my false teeth and making sucking noises through them. As ugly as sin.

Sarah backed away.

'Sorry,' she said. 'I didn't realize.'

She put the packet back in the glove compartment.

Mother, said Sarah, as we set off back to my ward, this time via a path through the orchard, had been very ill – stressed, depressed, advised to rest. Something like that.

'A sort of breakdown. Sounds like a car, I know. She's better now. Home, at least. Though she won't drive. She rents a small ground-floor flat in Richmond with a shared garden. She sends her love. But she still needs to rest. That's why I'm here.'

Sarah stopped pushing and walked round to the front of the wheelchair, facing me. She'd grown so tall and wore such high-heeled shoes that even if I hadn't been a wheelie, I'd have had to tilt my head up and she bend her neck down in order to see each other properly. As it was, she had to bend her knees, her waist and her shoulders too.

Even so, we couldn't do any eye to eye because Sarah wore sunglasses. Even though it wasn't sunny. I stared at the reflections in them while she started talking again.

'So yes. That's why I'm here, not her. This came.'

Sarah produced an envelope. I looked at her fingers as she drew out the letter and unfolded it. Her fingernails were longer than they used to be and varnished a startling red – did she still play the cello? – but the skin around them was as gnawed and raggedy as ever. My little baby sister. Pretending to be grown-up.

Before reading the letter, Sarah pushed back her sunglasses, raking her thin, pale hair, cut short like a boy's, into wisps above her forehead, and there, at last, were her big fishy eyes – sky-blue, sea-green, changing all the time.

We stared at each other, diagonally, surprised by a sudden sun flashing aslant through the orchard trees, making us scrunch up our faces – not apes, not Eskimos, definitely sisters.

'Briar Mental Hospital,' said Sarah, pointing to the words at the top of the page. She moved her finger down and, with her red fingertip, underlined the single word below.

'Closure.'

1985–86

i

Hounslow or Hillingdon? Where would we go? Haringey, Acton or home sweet home? Would it be London or local? Round the corner, or over the hills and far away? North, south, east, west? Which was best? Words flew like birds before a storm. Closure. Resettlement. Care in the community. Who next? Where to? Who cares? Cuckoo.

People departed in fits and starts.

Some patients left, only to return. 'Failed to adapt' was the official term. Others went and got into trouble. A few even had their picture in the paper. Rick, who stabbed a man in Hammersmith and then tried to set fire to him, did. It was Eric who provided it. Eric still lived in the Nissen hut, though alone these days. His hip made it hard for him to get around and sway decisions like he used to, but he still made plans and had projects. When he heard that the Hospital Management Committee had appointed an official archivist to write the Briar's official history, Eric set about writing his own. His, he announced, would be illustrated, and he busied himself in the Nissen hut sorting out the photos from his old photography-club days.

We OT-onlies had 'Low Priority' stamped on our files. After an assessment, question marks were added and labels stuck on. Rehabilitation. Refer. Regional Health Authority. The wards around us emptied – first the people, then their beds – but we remained LP.

During this time, Sarah visited. Not frequently. Not regularly. Not really as if she wanted to – 'I hate this place' – but she put a good face on it. We would sit in the day room, drink tea and pretend to watch TV. Twice she brought Mother. Once for a Public Meeting, held in the refectory. Mother and I both fell asleep. The second time, July '85, we went to the Briar's centenary exhibition, also in the refectory, where some of Eric's photos were on display. Mother felt faint. She sat on the chair that Eric provided, and she stayed on it, near the door, while Sarah and I, accompanied by Eric, looked at the pictures. I was searching for me in a black and white group by a grey and white sea – not Torquay – when, suddenly,

'There's me,' said Sarah. 'Isn't it?' She stooped and peered more closely at one of the photographs.

The Briar summer fete, 1960.

'Those awful fetes. But I remember that day. I wandered off and got lost. I was terrified.' Sarah looked at the picture again. 'I'm sure it's me.' She pointed, without touching, to a small figure in the background of the photo, also pointing. 'And there.' She stretched her thumb to the middle of the picture, making an L-shape with her hand. 'The boy. The one with no arms. What was his name?'

'Daniel Smith,' said Eric, nodding at the photo of Daniel and his dad, cheesing for the camera in front of Roger's Dodgems. Behind them you could see the bumper cars, and, in the distance, the visitors' lawn, with stalls, bunting, groups of grown-ups and the tiny, pointing blob that Sarah said was her.

'That's right. Daniel. I remember now. What happened to him?'

'Didn't he write?'

The traffic lights changed from red to amber, and Sarah released the handbrake.

I tried to shake my head, but a loop of seatbelt rubbed against my neck and I could only manage a droop.

'Surely he wrote?' She glanced at me. 'No? Are you certain? Eric said he could write. Sort of. With his feet.'

I looked at Sarah's feet on the pedals. Soft, black-leather shoes – flatties, she called them. Car shoes. One was still on the clutch. The other hovered above the accelerator. She stored her flatties in a special compartment on the car door. What else did she keep in there?

'Not a single letter?'

Not one, I could have said. Instead, I muttered, grunted, improvised. There were hundreds in my head.

Dear Grace,
We're at Dover, in Calais, just north of Amiens. Back very soon.

Or,

Grace. Arrived. Flat unchanged. Paris beautiful. Business booming. Back soon.

Dearest Grace, On the road south. Dijon, Geneva, the Alps. Back as soon as poss.

Dear, dear Grace.

Letters, like bunting, strung across the globe. Hundreds and thousands.

'Left?' Sarah indicated, accelerated and turned – 'Why not?' – all at the same time.

I turned my head and stared out of the side window. We were passing through a town I didn't recognize.

'Let's go for a drive,' Sarah had said at the beginning of this visit, her next one, after the ones with Mother, and – though we didn't know it then – her last one to the Briar.

'Anywhere rather than here', and, 'At least it's something to do', I'd heard Sarah mutter and followed her gaze around the day room, which was nearly empty – just some old skitters sleepy and twitching in the corner, a group of wheelies watching telly and two nurses, in armchairs, with folders on their laps.

Sarah clunk-clicked me into the front of her Ford Fiesta – very uncomfortable – and off we drove.

We sped along lanes sprinkled with frost and bright in the January sun, then down roads and through towns and villages further away. We even went for a spin on the M25, just for a mile – just for fun, said Sarah.

'Soon it'll stretch all the way round London,' she told me. 'Can you imagine?'

Sarah tried to chit-chat, but she hadn't got the hang of my two-word replies and didn't have the knack of filling in for herself. Plus, she asked me questions I couldn't have answered, even if I'd had the right dentures in that day, and all the words from John's blue dictionary in my big mouth too.

'Eric said you knew each other very well. You and Daniel. Is that true?'

What could I reply? He didn't write. The flipping boy didn't even say goodbye.

I kept my gob shut, my head turned and my wetting eyes on the windowy whirl of houses, people and cars. There were more cars than there used to be – on the roads, at their sides, in people's drives. More makes, more colours. Daniel was wrong about all that.

'Sorry,' said Sarah. Again. Why?

We drove in silence until the roads became streets with shops as well as houses and, at the junctions, signposts.

'Actually,' said Sarah, 'what Eric said, when I talked to him last summer, was –' and she lowered her voice to a stiff rasp – '"Grace and Daniel? A perfect match, God bless".'

We both laughed.

'There. I knew you weren't asleep.' Sarah sounded pleased. 'Stop pretending, Grace. Now. Which way here?'

The town I didn't recognize turned out to be an outskirt of Watford, not far from the Briar.

'Try right,' I tried, but my tongue bow-wowed out, as usual, and Sarah didn't answer. She switched on the car radio – the afternoon play – and we drove back to the Briar on the Hemel Hempstead road.

Sarah stopped at an Esso garage and filled up the Fiesta.

'Now we've got a tiger in our tank,' she said, settling herself into her seat.

She twiddled the knobs and pressed the buttons on the radio.

'It's a cassette player too,' she said. 'Broken, though. It chews up all my tapes.'

She tuned the radio to cheerful pop and didn't ask any more questions about Daniel, or say anything else, until we'd parked in the visitors' car park and it was time for her to go.

'Here,' she said, at the door to my ward, reaching for something in her bag. 'Custard creams. I thought they might be okay. With your teeth, I mean.'

She thrust the packet towards me. I took it, and she took off down the corridor.

I was restless that night. No shut-eye for me. Six custard creams stirred into my tea, plus a few more in bed, may have had something to do with it. My innards gurgled, my head churned and figures flickered across my eyelids. Their voices trickled between my ears. Send her my love. I'd always come back for you, Grace. Here, custard creams.

There were crumbs on the bed-sheet and I could reach them.

Children on back seats waved goodbye.

When the night nurse came on at ten and shut herself

into the office for changeover, I climbed out of bed, dahu-ed to the door of the ward and slowly slippety-skipped down the stairs and out into the hospital grounds via the side entrance by the refectory.

It was a night with no moon and no stars, clear but dark, and – what with just my nightgown and no shoes – cold. I went to the rock garden. It was still private there. Not as peaceful as before. You could hear traffic behind the trees in the distance. Beyond the trees, if you looked very carefully, you could definitely see the Lucozade glow of London on the horizon. But the bench on the highest hillock had split and was splintery, and the plants had spread across the rocks, slippery and uneven.

I went to the tool-shed. It was so dilapidated you had to climb over broken timber to get in. The roof leaked and the place reeked of mice, dead and alive.

Up to the attic, which was locked. I sat on the staircase outside and waited for the chimes from the overhead clock tower. Eventually, I went downstairs and out into the grounds again. The cedar tree was still there, but I didn't crawl underneath its low-hung branches. The ground was crusty with frost, my feet were numb and the hem of my nightgown dragged. My ankle was as better as it would ever be, but it ached, and when I knelt, pain hot-knifed up my leg.

I wandered back to the patch of land beyond the orchard where Mr Peters' apple-house used to stand. I stood where it stood. Once upon a time. I was in the apple-house. There weren't any apples, but I counted them anyway. Five, eighteen, thirty-nine. Rows and rows of them. It was dark. I couldn't see. I felt along the slatted shelves. Each apple sat differently in the curved palm of my good hand. Each apple had its own smell. The rotten ones smelt the strongest.

I paused in the corner where the strawberry punnets used to be. I was about to pull down my knickers and piss on the punnets. But I remembered Miss Lily and her strawberry teas. Passports, manners and etiquette. And I remembered the apples. The ones I hadn't counted yet. So many. Arranged so neatly on the slatted shelves according to type. Pippin, Russet, Worcester Pearmain – Daniel used to mix them up, just to annoy Mr Peters. Cox, Idared, Gala, Fiesta. It was dark, but I didn't need to see. Beauty of Bath. Discovery. I knew it all by heart.

iii

February was Brentford. March, Shepherd's Bush. April, Hanwell.

Ealing, Isleworth, Hanger Lane, Chiswick.

In the end it was Hounslow for me, that May. But I'm telling you now – and I've been here a year – it's Eastbourne every day in Hounslow High Street.

V

1987

I've been here a year. I go to the high street once a week. Shops with awnings line both sides. They sell everything under the sun. Market stalls stand in the middle. Their goods ripple like rainbows in an off-season sea of people, pushchairs, wheelchairs, bikes, buggies, dogs and trolley-bags. There's a small fairground ride outside Woolies. It turns very slowly and plays nursery-rhyme tunes, very slowly too. Little kiddies lift up their arms, and mothers hoik them on to horses and aeroplanes, into cars, rockets and the two-seated boat.

Beyond Marks, BHS and no less than three shoe shops is the shopping mall, with glaring lights, as bright as a seaside amusement arcade. When it rains, we go to C&A in there, and order coffee from the help-yourself café on the top floor. You can see Heathrow from the seats by the window, and, if you look down, the swell and swim of Hounslow High Street.

Coffee and a smoke – nothing better, says Carole, my carer. Her cousin, Bet, works behind the counter in the café and slips us free Danishes. Carole takes her coffee black with two Hermeseta sweeteners which she shakes from the tube that she keeps in her handbag. We eat our pastries, Carole wipes me with a Kleenex, then, 'Time, I think,' she says, and we both light up.

The high street's only a bus ride away from Acacia Road, where I live at Number Ten. It's a semi-detached house, like the others in the road, and, like them, it has net curtains at all the windows. Ours has a built-on extension, there's a minibus in the drive, and two wheelie bins with 'London Borough of Hounslow' printed on their sides. The front door is wide, the top part semi-see-through with frosted glass. There's a doorbell, which pings the beginning of *Match of the Day*, and above it a typed notice, covered in polythene, which also says 'London Borough of Hounslow'. The rest of the words are blurred and run together from the weather.

Every Tuesday, instead of letting herself into the house and knocking at my room – 'Coo-ee' – Carole rings the bell and waits at the front door until Martin opens it. Martin's in charge of us. He lives in a ground-floor flat attached to the house with his wife Pat, who helps out in the evenings and first thing. My room is also on the ground floor. Next to Cynthia's. Opposite the bathroom.

Harry, Reg and mongy Christopher sleep upstairs, where there's another bathroom.

'Ready?' says Martin every Tuesday as I rush past him at the door.

It's a joke, because I'm still a slug-a-bed most mornings. When Pat comes in with my mug of tea and to open the curtains, 'Hello, sleepy-head?' she says, or, 'Who's a dozy bear today?' Except on Tuesdays, when she eager-beavers me into my clothes, through breakfast and a quick top-and-tail.

'Not stopping for a hug?' Carole laughs and hurries after me.

Carole's a hugger. She's slight and bony, golden-brown all year round from visiting her sister in Fuengirola and the tanning salon in Slough. Her Silk-Cut skin is loose and crinkly at the edges, soft and warm as a hot-water bottle. I stop.

We walk to the Bath Road, and Carole takes my arm, my good arm. There's no hop-skipping, because Carole's busy digging in her handbag for a ciggy. But it's not a bad imitation of Mother.

While we stand in the bus queue – 'not quite so close, sweetheart, people aren't used to it' – I count the cars, wave at the taxis and stare at the sudden scuddering aeroplanes. Whoppers. They fly so low, they look as if they'll land on Acacia Road. From my bedroom window, I can see their great gleaming underbellies, their engines, landing wheels and the unhinging flaps of their wings. From the bus stop on the Bath Road, you can see which airline they belong to and how colourfully they're patterned, how carefully painted with flags, faces, bows, arrows, crowns, wreaths, rings and ribbons. The noise they make takes a bit of getting used to. The house shakes with it, and you can't hear the radio or telly, let alone what anyone's saying. And in Hounslow High Street, every two minutes, the babbling stallholders stop in mid-flow while a plane goes over. Martin belongs to the Heathrow Association for the Control of Aircraft Noise. He pins HACAN posters to the noticeboard in the kitchen alongside our schedules, the cooking rota, *Desiderata*, the house dos and don'ts, notes to himself, to Pat, to the key-workers – 'key-worker, codswallop,' says Carole. 'I've always been a carer' – and a shopping list, which anyone can add to, but is mostly in Martin's handwriting. Bog roll, J-cloths, sugar – gran. WD40, Sparkle, Weetabix, pee-pads, things like that. Teabags. Carole adds Nescafé, if it's not already there. Pat thinks Carole lets me drink too much coffee – it doesn't help with the nights, and the peeing, she says.

'Have you spent a penny?' whispers Carole on the bus. 'If not, we'll pop into Marks, shall we?'

I nod and finger the fabric purse hanging round my neck. It was the first thing I bought with the spending allowance I receive in Hounslow. Carole said I should, and helped me pick it out from one of the market stalls. I've also bought a nylon moneybelt since then, three wallets, two leather-look handbags – and a partridge in a pear tree, according to Pat. Carole says my room's a veritable Aladdin's den.

Carole stands at the door every morning, except Tuesday, and surveys it proudly. She and I redecorated it ourselves. The walls are Homebase Magnolia – you can't beat off-white, Grace. The curtains, new, are green with pink swirls and match my duvet, valance, overhead lampshade and the cushion on the vinyl chair by the door. I've a brown chipboard wardrobe full to bursting with clothes, and a matching chest of drawers, ditto. The top of the chest of drawers has my telly on it and some of my high-street buys. Three Japanese bowls, a chunky, cut-glass ashtray, two snowglobes, a pyramid paperweight, three rose-scented candles, a plastic candelabra that looks like silver, a teapot in the shape of a cottage, a money-tin in the shape of a phone booth, a miniature windmill, a wind-up music-box, tiny and tinkly with *Für Elise*, my electric-blue ear-muffs, a wicker basket containing pot-pourri and a jewellery chest covered in fake red velvet and real gold braid.

I fluff up the velvet, making shapes and letters by changing its colour, before opening the chest, which is crammed with scraps of red and orange wool. I don't snitch from people's jumpers any more. Pat saw me take what I wanted from her knitting bag. She didn't let me keep the balls of wool, but she snipped lots of bits off their ends for me. I scrunch, suck and untangle the scraps, mapping and remembering.

More goodies crowd on the shelf above the radiator, between my cuckoo clock and the window. There are my books – Littlewoods, Freemans and Kays catalogues, plus a Bible, four files and an album, wedged between two wooden clowns sitting down. A teddy is propped against the back wall, shoulder to shoulder with a puppet. Carole has arranged the puppet's legs so they dangle off the front of the shelf. The rest of the shelf is taken up with a set of glazed figurines – sheep, a shepherd, two dogs and a milk-maid – a china thimble, a thermometer glued to a minia-ture lighthouse, and my photos, in frames. I buy the frames in the shop next to Dolcis – Save'n'Save – where Carole buys suncream and moisturizer in multi-packs. I also bought my ashtray there, the cuckoo clock, two batteries for it and, at the counter, two disposable cigarette lighters. I gave one of them to Carole, because she lost her fancy gold refillable in the sand last time she went to Spain. She'd had it for nearly a decade, she said. Jim, her old man, gave it to her for her thirtieth. But Jim's a drinker and a bad lot these days, she says.

When we couldn't fit any more frames on the shelf, Carole hung three clip-frames on the wall above my bed – me on a horse, me and Carole at the Beehive, all of the Acacia Road residents and our carers at a barbecue last summer in the back garden.

In November, for my birthday, Carole gave me a photo-cube. We spent ages choosing the pictures, then we slipped them in and put the cube by the basin on my vanity unit – uppermost, me in the kitchen at Acacia Road, blowing out the candles on a cake from Greggs.

We placed the thick ceramic picture-frame, knobbly with sea shells, which I bought before Christmas, next to the radio-alarm clock on my bedside table. The frame contains a photo of Mother, also at my birthday party, sitting beside me at the kitchen table. You can see old Reg, grinning, and half of Harry's beardy face too, as well as the back of Carole's brown bobbed hair and the flash of Martin's camera in the window by the sink. We're all wearing pointed paper hats.

Mother visits Acacia Road. Regularly and frequently. It's a train and two buses from Richmond – quite a journey – but she manages. She sits in the kitchen with Carole and me, and we drink coffee from mugs which don't match, but have pictures, cartoons and words on them – the London underground, a heart, an apple, the Royal Botanic Gardens, Kew, I Love New York, Majorca, You. Cynthia has a mug with her name on and won't let anyone else use it.

I help Carole make the coffee. I spoon, she boils. She pours the water, I the semi-skimmed. Then I stir Mother's sugar in for her, because of her shaky hands.

Carole and I smoke. Carole tells Mother what we've been up to.

'Gracie's doing brilliantly,' she says about all my activities.

She shows Mother my schedule.

Self-Care, Healthy Eating, Keep Fit, Craft – 'You're a star there, Grace.'

Communication, Cookery, Relationships. 'Not a problem. We get on famously most of the time, don't we, Gracie?'

Carole and I chuckle. Cooking's neither of our fortés, and Carole gets on famously with nearly everyone.

Church Social, the Acorn Club – Grace loves that. The Beehive Pub – don't we have a laugh? Mencap meetings, the Cranford Mental Health After-Care Group, the Disability Centre at Heston School. And In-house Leisure, which means whatever you fancy. Martin's keen on participation, co-operation and group entertainment. TV and high-jinks in the lounge. Me too. But I'm keen on my room as well.

I show Mother my room. She sits on the bed, and I bring her my things, one by one. She fingers them, half smiles and passes them back to me, even when I want her to keep them as presents. I take the album, a catalogue or file from the shelf. Mother and I sit next to each other on the bed, and we flip through the pages. Mother doesn't say much, and her smile isn't curly – 'Lovely, Grace. Yes, lovely, darling' – but she leans in close to look at the pages, and I stroke her wavy white hair.

I often sit like that with Carole. I don't stroke her hair, because we're too busy choosing clothes from the catalogue, sticking photos in the album or fitting another certificate of achievement into its file.

If, on the bus, I reach out to stroke someone's hair, Carole takes my hand, holds, strokes and squeezes it with both of hers. 'I'll give you a manicure this afternoon, Grace,' she says. And she does. Nelson, especially, looks beautiful these days.

As the bus jolts into the bus station behind the shopping mall, I definitely need a pee, so we go to Marks & Spencer, and that's where our morning in the high street really begins. It ends, when it's not raining, with coffee and cigarettes at Greggs bakery. If it's sunny, we sit outside. We buy two cut loaves for Number Ten in there, whatever the weather.

Sarah also visits Acacia Road, occasionally. Miranda's too busy. Doing good, I expect. In the Third World, according to Mother.

'In Geneva nowadays,' said Sarah. 'A desk job that drives her mad. She'd far rather still be fairy-godmothering about.'

Carole asked Sarah if Miranda would send a photo for our Life Project at the Acorn Club, but all she sent were some torn mucky snapshots of the back of beyond – her, flitty and blurred, in a moving mass of different men, nurses, flies, army trucks and half-naked, big-bellied children with sores on their heads. I didn't stick any of them in.

Since then, though, Miranda's been sending postcards from her jaunts around Europe – breathers, she calls them. Mountains, snow, nuns on skis – 'Can you see me?' Pigeons in Venice – 'even the shit is beautiful'. The leaning tower of Pisa, with a group of tourists leaning against it – 'trick photography' written on the back. A vague cloudy sea, lilies by Monet, a man with a hat and a big apple on his face by René Magritte, 'for Gracie, from René (like the tummy tablets)'.

Mother provided plenty of photos, and John sent a tidy batch from California. At the top right-hand corner of each picture, he'd attached – carefully, so as not to spoil the gloss – a neatly hand-written post-it. I peeled them all off and Carole helped me stick them in the project too. 'Us at the Grand Canyon', 'Us, Thanksgiving', 'B's 45th', 'B and JJ on the beach', 'JJ First day at school', 'Me reading', 'B and me at home (taken by JJ)'.

JJ's a speccy, moon-faced mini-John. Sarah calls him 'the little professor'. John and B are real professors.

'And I'm just a jumped-up Avon lady,' Sarah told Carole.

Sales and marketing, wheeling and dealing – not that exciting, she knows she's lucky, she has flair for languages, she's not at the top of the tree, though, and is it really what she wants to be doing? Something like that.

'But,' she smiled. 'I perform well. I reach my targets. And it has its perks.'

Business-class flying being one of them, several times a year.

When she goes to Heathrow, Sarah parks her Fiesta in Acacia Road, or very nearby, and takes the tube from Hounslow West. On her way home, if she has time – it's a fiddly route to Clapham, she ought to stop off in Richmond, rush-hour's coming up – she drops in to Acacia Road. She too sits in the kitchen and drinks coffee with Carole and me. Carole and I smoke. Sarah tries not to.

'So where's our jet-setter been, this time?' asks Carole.

'Nowhere very glam,' replies Sarah, but we don't believe her.

She brings us chocolates. Duty-free ciggies for Carole, and, for me, the freebies from the aeroplane and her hotel. I store them in the cabinet above my vanity unit. There are more chocolates in the car for Mother, she says, the same as ours. Boxes from Belgium, tied up with bows. Red Suchard bombs, six to a pack. Big black bars of Lindt. Gold and white tubes of dark Dutch pastilles. Hershey's Kisses, all the way from New York. And starry, blue-silver Bacis, Mum's favourite.

I make a mess eating mine, but it doesn't matter, everyone makes a mess with their wrappers and the wrapping on the kitchen table. Carole licks her fingers. Sarah twists and folds the mess, rolling the foil into nuggety balls, tearing the tissue into narrow strips, which she pleats and leaves dangling on the edges of things.

Carole tells Sarah what we've been up to. She says I'm doing brilliantly at all my activities, but she also mentions a few hiccups. I muck about with Harry in Keep Fit. I become impatient with the wheelies and cripples in Craft, who can't wield the tools as well as me, and I'm a tad too social, says Carole, at Church Social.

At Acacia Road, I have the odd run-in with Cynthia, thieving and hoarding are ongoing issues, and Pat doesn't like it if I let Harry in my room after the nine o'clock news. Martin says I'm grumpy and unco-operative when Carole's away, and he's concerned about my inappropriate noises – muttering, grunting, clacking – at inappropriate times.

'Just hiccups, though,' says Carole. 'Nothing to worry about.'

'Nothing to worry about,' she said one day. 'But there's something I'd like to ask you, Sarah. I hope you don't mind.'

'What's that?' Sarah took a sip of coffee from her all but empty mug.

'It's about Grace talking to herself,' said Carole.

'She's always done it, I think,' Sarah answered.

'I know, but the thing is –' Carole lit another cigarette – 'it's not the talking, exactly, or even the doing it in public. We're working on that. Martin says you're just attention-seeking, Gracie – grumbling and moaning when you're bored or fed-up. But I think. I don't know. You do go on, don't you, Grace? When you're alone, too. In your room. Do you remember the other day?'

Carole doesn't normally mind my improvising. She replies as if she understands, even when she couldn't possibly. Codswallop, she told the teacher at my Makaton class, who said my motor skills might be up to signing, but he didn't think I had the cognitive ability to grasp the Makaton system of symbols. Who are you to judge? Carole added. Gracie talks the hind legs off a donkey to me, given half the chance. Give her a chance.

On the day Carole meant, we were in my bedroom, curtains already drawn. Carole was sitting in the armchair between the vanity unit and the door. She was filling in her time sheet before catching the coach to Swindon for a residential training course.

'I'll be back next week. No fretting, and no silly biz while I'm gone.'

I was lying on my bed. We'd switched off the radio, and I was listening for planes through the January rain on the patio. *Countdown* counted down through the wall from Cynthia's room. I didn't want Carole to go.

Martin knocked on the door. He asked Carole to give him a hand with Reg, who was stuck in the bath again. Carole followed Martin out of the room, leaving the door wide open.

When she came back, she said, more sharply than usual, 'No, Grace. Enough. Don't. You're spooking me. I could hear you as I came down the stairs. Jabbering. Blabbering. I thought you had a visitor. I thought something must have happened. You weren't crying, but you sounded so . . . oh, I don't know.'

Then she hugged me and cried a bit herself and said she was sorry for seeming cross.

'You sounded so sad,' she said.

To Sarah, she said, 'I haven't spoken to Martin, but it occurred to me ... it might seem a bit far-fetched ... but perhaps Grace has – or had – an imaginary friend. She says no.'

I shook my head.

'See? Adamant. But I was wondering. At the Briar, did Grace ever ... you know, talk to anyone ... someone who wasn't there?'

'Not that I know of.'

'Not when she was little? Are you sure? Well, you wouldn't remember, would you? But something ... Lots of children do. A doll, or a blanket, even? A make-believe friend.'

'No. Just the boy, the one with no arms. Daniel Smith. And he was real.'

That got them started, and they pooled what they knew about Daniel Smith. It didn't amount to much, but enough for Carole to say, 'Why don't you find out? Someone ought to know. It shouldn't be hard.'

'I suppose not,' said Sarah. 'There must be records.'

Next time she visited, Sarah said she'd written to the Briar but drawn a blank. Official records of the relevant years had been transferred to a central archive in London, she told us. Many had gone astray on the way.

'What about people? Aren't there still staff at the Briar?'

'Only a skeleton. I phoned. The geriatric wards are functioning, apparently, but that's about it now. They're planning to put the whole thing up for sale as soon as poss.'

She'd asked about Eric, she said, but he was in Watford General Hospital following a stroke. She'd rung and spoken to someone on the ward – bedridden and gaga, she'd been informed.

'So we're stumped.' Sarah frowned.

'Shame,' said Carole.

'But I'm curious now.' The faraway, fishy look came into Sarah's eyes.

In March, Sarah had to go to Zurich for work – a bugger, she said, because it overlapped with her birthday.

'Still. I could fly via Geneva. Go and see Miranda. That might be fun.'

When she returned, she phoned from Heathrow. Would it be okay to call in? Carole had picked up the receiver from the payphone in the hall. I could see and hear her through my open bedroom door. She cupped her palm over the handset.

'It's you-know-who,' she mouthed, unnecessarily, to me.

Sarah arrived half an hour later. Nearly teatime at Acacia Road, and the kitchen was busy with Harry and his temporary carer making cottage pie, Cynthia sticking her big nose round the door and asking 'When'll it be ready? I'm fucking starving', and Martin popping in to keep an eye on things.

'I told Miranda,' said Sarah. 'About Daniel. She remembered him too. Much more than me, in fact.'

Tell me, tell me, tell me.

'Tell us,' Carole said.

'About the fete, the photo. And Daniel's dad. She said he owned the bumper cars.'

I shook my head.

'Really?' said Carole. 'Are you sure?'

'"As sure as eggs are *oeufs*." That's what Miranda said. "Try tracing the dad, Mr Smith," she suggested. "With a name like that? You must be joking, sis," I said. We'd had a couple of glasses of wine by then.'

Sarah took one of Carole's cigarettes – may I? – and lit it with my disposable.

'We were about to go out, buy some more cheap fizz

and a Chinese for dinner, when the phone in Miranda's flat rang. It was for me – John, getting JJ to sing "Happy Birthday, Aunt Sarah," down the line.'

Harry began to lay the table for tea. Carole and Sarah shifted our clutter to make room for his layouts of cutlery. He made the right shapes with the knives, forks and spoons, but in the wrong order and much too large.

'So then what?'

'Then I got the giggles. Miranda, at the grand old age of forty-six, was doing goggle-eyes, you see, dancing about the living room with her fingers round her eyes and her elbows clutched in. Like this.' Sarah did Miranda's bad imitation of John – well – and the three of us burst out laughing.

'Sorry to interrupt the fun,' said Harry's carer, who wore an agency uniform and his key-worker badge, 'but would you mind not smoking? Lounge only. That's the rule.' He nodded to the board's 'dos and don'ts'.

'You're right,' said Carole. 'Apologies.' She winked at me, and said in an undertone to Sarah, through sideways-twisted, lipsticky lips, 'Sad sod.'

'Sorry.' Sarah stubbed out her cigarette. 'The point is, Miranda and John had quite a chinwag on the phone, in the end. John's certain that Daniel's dad drove a small white van made by Commer. Daniel told him that day at the fete, John said. Plus a lot of guff about the make, horsepower and so on. And John, being John, remembers some of it. Not the number plate, but he did see the van. Daniel showed it to him on the way to the cricket pitch. A battered old thing, John said, with writing on the side, too far away to read, but the van stood out in the visi-tors' car park, even at a distance. Otherwise he probably wouldn't have remembered. What with the fracas later.'

She paused and looked at me.

'I've no memory of what happened at the dodgems. I

know I was there. Like I said, Eric told me about it, and now Miranda's described it pretty vividly. By the way, she also said you only started muttering, grumbling – whatever – to yourself when you went to the Briar.' She put her stubby fingers on Nelson and pressed. 'I didn't know that. Sorry, Gracie.'

'You were very young,' said Carole.

'Yes.' Sarah took her fingers away and nibbled the skin by her thumbnail. 'Apart from getting lost, I only remember after the dodgems, eyeballing this funny-looking boy – Daniel – held in the arms of a very tall man. And the car journey home. Me, sleepy, between John and Miranda in the back, John reading, arguing coming from the front. Miranda suddenly bent down, lifted my feet out of the way and tied John's shoelaces together in a great big knot. "Silly ass," she said and took his book away from in front of his face. "It's all your fault." I started blubbing, and Mum started yelling. Oh, and someone's watch, smashed, lying on the grass. Anyway . . .'

Sarah crossed her arms and tucked her hands under her armpits.

Harry brought a stack of six tumblers to the table and began placing them in a flower-pattern around the water jug plonked down by his key-worker.

'Anyway. Smith, plus some details about the van, plus approximate date – year, at least . . . I bet they keep records for ages at the vehicle registration place.'

'Yes,' said Carole. 'Let's get on to them as soon as possible.'

March passed. Harry had an operation on his varicose veins and we all went in the minibus to Ashford Hospital to cheer him up. I took him some daffodils from the garden and a pouch for his specs. The pouch did up with Velcro – a godsend, says Carole. Reg and Christopher have it on their shoes. It doesn't work with built-ups, but when I buy a skirt or pair of trousers – I still can't manage dresses – Carole removes the buttons, poppers, hooks and zips and replaces them with Velcro. She's not an expert. Her stitches are wonky and big. It's worth it, though, for the splittering sound the Velcro makes when you pull it apart, like Eric striking a Swan Vesta.

At the end of the month, Cynthia won two goldfish at the Acorn Club Spring Fayre. On the walk home, she and I collided as we were crossing the road. The goldfish fell out of their plastic bag and flipped through the grid of a drain in the gutter. We all crowded round, blocking the traffic. Christopher knelt on the ground and peered down the drain. I thought it was funny – goldfish doing a Jesse, wriggling through pipes, swimming invisibly beneath roads, houses, parks, schools. So did a group of boys and girls on the opposite pavement. They were pointing and laughing. Cynthia didn't think it was funny. She blamed me and she's still blathering on about the flipping fish, in fact.

On 2 April, a Thursday morning, Sarah called in unexpectedly. We'd just got back from Heston, and I was in my room unpacking my photocopied pieces of paper – not purple, smelly, smudged and drooled over, but not that different from the ones in the COU, either – plus the thick felt-tip pen I'd removed from the classroom. The teacher leaves them on the metal ledge at the bottom of the slide-along whiteboard – a doddle to lift and place in one of Nelson's nooks. While Carole was answering the door, I put the felt-tip with my others, in a pop sock under my bed. Every so often, Pat has a clear-out under there and calls me a squirrel. 'Squalid,' she says to Carole with her hand over her mouth. 'They all do it.'

'I can't stay long,' said Sarah. 'No. Not even a quick coffee. Thanks. I need to check in by midday. But I've got some news. Nothing earth-shattering, I'm afraid. But since I was going to the airport, I thought I'd let you know.'

The rest of the Acacia Road residents were still out and about, doing activities. Martin was having a meeting in the lounge with some people from the council, so we sat in the kitchen – quiet, except for the fridge, and the birds on the feeder outside the window, and the planes. Sarah took some papers from her briefcase and put them on the table.

'The van,' she began, 'was registered. In the name of Leslie Smith. To an address that exists, in St Albans, but has never – as far as anyone knows – had any connection to a Smith. The registrations go all the way up to 1968. There's no record of registration for 1969. Or 1970, the year Daniel disappeared.'

'Is that it?'

'No. The DVLC didn't really get up and running until the seventies. They were trying to gather together – up in Swansea – the masses of admin, including police paperwork, previously scattered between the Ministry of Transport and all the different, local authorities. At the same time, they were starting to computerize. It was a nightmare.'

'Still is, by all accounts,' said Carole, whose old man drives minicabs when he's not on the booze or off sick with his back. 'Jim's always getting bad news from Swansea,' she added.

'Yes. Anyway. Because they've never received a Certificate of Destruction or Sale for the van, the file on the Commer is still, technically, open. So they've been able to send me copies of the old local authority registrations that made their way to Swansea, and some documents relating to various brushes Mr Smith and his van had with the law. Here.' Sarah patted the small pile of papers on the table. 'They arrived in the post this morning.'

'Do they tell us anything?' Carole took some of the papers and began to glance through them.

'Only that Mr Smith was prone to speeding, drink-driving, and not paying his parking tickets.'

'And not just in this country, by the looks of things,' said Carole.

'That's right. France, mostly. The bloke I chatted to on the phone said there's actually quite a sizeable police file on Mr Smith, here and in Europe. Obviously they can't divulge any of that. France, though ... God knows what he was up to. And see – an address in Paris. The place Pereire. There.' Sarah pointed to one of the forms, signed many times, ornately decorated and rubber-stamped. 'At the bottom. An ancient, overdue fine from the French road police, I think.'

We all stared at the pretty photocopy.

'Do you think it's worth a try?' said Carole finally. 'Paris, I mean.'

'I could write a letter. But, to be honest, no. It was so long ago. And I think the address, even if it exists, is fake. Like the St Albans one, I'm afraid.'

She turned to me.

'Sorry, Grace. I haven't been a very good Emil, have I? But I've given it my best shot.'

Easter came and went, with beautiful weather and three stay-up-late videos on Good Friday night instead of the usual Friday-night two – *Casablanca*, *ET*, and – Cynthia's choice – *Rocky IV*. Mother visited on Saturday afternoon.

On the Sunday, between church and lunch, Martin organized an egg hunt in the back garden, and we all sat on the patio afterwards for coffee and a smoke. The sun shone, bright but gentle in our eyes, the aeroplanes were quiet, and the back-to-back gardens of Acacia Road, dotted with a few old fruit trees still in blossom, were clotted with yellow forsythia. Fluff-balls of forsythia drifted around our feet and the patio furniture.

The children from next door peeped over the fence. All you could see were six dark eyes and three black top-knots. Martin invited the boys to climb the wooden fence and find the Easter eggs we'd failed to spot.

'We don't believe in Easter,' said the tallest boy.

But they came nevertheless, plus a little girl wearing slippers. She was too small to see over, let alone climb the fence. One of the brothers helped her, and she snagged her silky clothes sliding down our side of it. I saw she'd scraped her arm too, but she didn't blub and was the best egg-finder and eater of the lot. She and mongy Chris had a game of marbles on the patio with the mini-eggs, while the boys sat divvying up in a row at the edge of the patio, with their feet in the fronds of the enormous pampas grass that explodes across the path and that I can see from my bedroom window. Eventually, Martin – You can play here any time – gave the children a hand climbing back over the fence.

'Love thy neighbour,' he said to us, sitting down again. 'Second Commandment – very important.'

Martin believes in Easter, Christmas and the Power of the Lord every day of the year. On Sundays, as well as driving us to church, he uses the minibus to pick up other believers and bring them to sing with us in the squashed, hot worship hall in Perivale. There's a sermon and praying too, but it's mostly singing, and not just hymns – soaring, stomping, put-your-hands-and-hearts-together songs led by a huge swaying choir and no organ. 'Lord of the Dance' makes some people, including Christopher, dance, and even Harry, who says he's not a believer, enjoys singing low, 'Sweet Chariot'.

Our neighbours on the other side at Acacia Road look like Martin and Pat, but the only thing they believe in, says Martin, is getting us evicted. No chance. They've written to the council and our local MP. Now they're organizing a petition.

On Easter Sunday, they put down their gardening tools, came over to the privet hedge and complained again about Reg, whose bedroom upstairs abuts theirs.

Reg is a gentle old thing. Nobody knows much about him. He doesn't have any visitors. Everybody says he's no trouble – quiet, content, cheerful even – during the day. At night, though, Reg rages, weeps and talks in his sleep. I wish he wouldn't. He goes back like we all do from time to time, in our different ways, to where we came from. I'm the only ex-Briar patient here. But Reg replays scenes I've seen – and I think the others have too – and it could have been yesterday.

'No, Charge. Don't do it. Please, Charge. Don't.'

And then, in a different voice, 'What are you?'

'I don't know, Charge.' Reg's own voice again. 'What am I? Don't hit me, sir. Please.'

'What are you?'

'Tell me, Charge. Tell me. Ow.'

'You're nothing. Say it.'

'I'm nothing, Charge, nothing. Ow.'

'Nothing. Not a thing. Less than nothing. Say it.'

'Ow. Ow.'

'Die, you bastard. Die.'

'It takes time, Charge.'

Martin explained to the neighbours, yet again, that swapping the rooms around upstairs wasn't as easy as pie, but yes, he sighed, he'd see what he could do. Not a lot. Harry snores – like a fucking hyena, according to Cynthia, whose room is underneath his. And Christopher, who needs to pee three or four times a night, whistles while he pees and slams the toilet seat up and down – just for fun, I suppose. The upstairs toilet also abuts our neighbours' bedroom.

When we go to the Beehive, Martin rips down the posters the neighbours have taped to the lamp posts along our road, and the next one too.

'Bloody troublemakers', he says.

'Love thy neighbour, my arse,' shouted Cynthia once, through more than one letterbox, on Fern Avenue. Martin told her she'd be sent home unless she stopped, but we were almost at the pub by then.

We go to the Beehive every last Monday of the month, so we were due there the Monday after the Easter bank holiday. I didn't go, because that's when Sarah told me Daniel had died.

Carole had left early for a doctor's appointment. It was Pat who put her head round my door and said, 'Your sister's on her way. She's just rung. From Arrivals. How about that for a lovely surprise? Come on, cheer up, cross-patch.'

I was lying on my bed. It had been gusting with rain most of the day, our picnic in Osterley Park had been cancelled, and we'd been cooped up and cranky all afternoon in the stuffy lounge. My room was cool and pleasant, and by half past five the clouds had lifted and thinned and the sun was coming out between splatters of blown rain. Sunlight flickered in my room and sparked off all the silver things at the same time as it hit the wings and windows of the descending aeroplanes.

The doorbell tin-tinned *Match of the Day*, Pat hummed down the hall, and a few seconds later Sarah knocked on my door. She came in carrying a large squashed brown-paper package – no writing, no stamps, no string.

She sat on the bed, where I was still lying, and placed the package between us. The music for the start of the six o'clock news filtered through from Cynthia's room.

We didn't open the package until the cuckoo from my

cuckoo clock, flying nowhere on its battery-operated spring, cooing two notes, again, again, again – a tame, recorded calling – shut up. All but the echoing, echoing in my head.

And not until the two fat little figures – a man in blue breeches and a wide-skirted red and white woman – stopped jiggering and flicked back inside. You can't tell which is which while everything's whirring. The mechanism slows, the shutters close on the quivering bird, and the weather man and woman stand still for a bit. The woman always sticks out further than the man, except at night, when they stand side by side, because Martin's turned the central heating down. Finally, with a few plasticky clicks, they judder backwards, jolt into the house, the front door closes – flickety-flick – and all you can hear is a two-beat, hop-skip ticking from the quartz within. The ornamental weights and pendulum – pine cones and a leaf – only move when a jet flies particularly low, or when I'm dusting.

We didn't open the package until at least twenty aeroplanes, including Concorde, had landed at Heathrow, and everyone had set off for the Beehive, apart from Pat, who put her head round the door, raised her eyebrows at me, then Sarah, then went away again.

We didn't open the package until the wind had dropped, the rain had ceased, and the sun had stopped slivering between the aeroplanes and the parting, joining, reshaping clouds and begun to cut a dash through the sky, changing the light in my room and making the windowpane shimmy with diagonal, drying raindrops. The wind had blown water-logged lumps of old brown forsythia into one corner, and the glass was splattered with clusters of dead blossom, like giant, sprawled insects. As the sun, dropping lower, burnt away the clouds, it shone through the feathery pampas grass by the patio and threw spotty shadows of its plumes on to the wall above my armchair, opposite the window

– moving, watery, fading shadows, because it was evening by then.

Not until after Sarah told me Daniel had died.

'Ages ago. I'm sorry, Grace. 1976.'

Sarah left the package on the bed and went over to the armchair. She sat down, and the grassy shadows on the wall above the chair seemed to grow out of her head.

'I changed my mind,' she said. 'About having shot my bolt. I almost wish I hadn't now. But I was in Paris. I hadn't got round to writing a letter and I felt bad. I was free for a couple of hours between meetings, so I looked up the place Pereire. It wasn't far from my hotel. I walked there. Paris was beautiful. Lovely weather, windy but clear. Girls in pretty summer dresses already. The trees were in blossom on the Champs-Elysées. The place Pereire itself was busy, but not as seedy as I'd imagined. The address was an apartment, in a building with a concierge.'

Concierge? Wassat? I raised my head.

'I don't have to tell you any of this, Grace, if you don't want me to. Perhaps we should wait for Carole to be here. It's not a long story, but it's a sad one. Do you want to hear it?'

I grunted and banged my head on the pillow, making the bed, me and the package joggle and Sarah jump. Of course I did. I settled my head back and crossed my good arm over Nelson. All I could see was the ceiling with its swirly light-shade, and, out of the corners of my eyes, bits of the room, including Sarah.

'Okay. He was a student, I think, the concierge – very young and not very interested. Try the landlord, he said.

'Monsieur Esposito-Levi lived in a ground-floor flat at the back of the building.

'I knocked, and a small, smiling man opened the door. He was old, with several gold teeth and funny eyes. "You want my brother," he interrupted when I began to explain.

'The landlord came and stood behind his brother. He was small and old too, but not smiling. He wore round, silver-rimmed, brown-tinted glasses and groped the wall with his hand when he took a step forward. As if to get a better look at me. He let me in, though, and actually seemed quite eager to talk. Naturally, he began – in heavily accented French – he knew Smith and son. Certainly he remembered them.

'Monsieur Esposito-Levi had bought the building for two *sous* during the war, he told me, when he and his brother settled in Paris. Shop, workshop, offices, apartments, the lot. Mr Smith was one of his first tenants. He'd rented the flat to Mr Smith since 1944.'

Since Daniel was born.

'Until 1970, which is when he last saw Smith and son, he said.'

Smith. And son. So they made it to Paris, Daniel and his dad. Three cheers for the white Commer van.

The landlord remembered hearing Mr Smith and Daniel arrive at the flat late one night in the spring of 1970 – Mr Smith merry and unsteady, *le handicapé* tappety-tapping on the floorboards, unsteady too. He remembered collecting the previous quarter's overdue rent the next day. Then seeing Daniel's face at the window, on and off, all through the summer of 1970. Mr Smith's path and his didn't often cross. Mr Smith kept very odd hours. But, "I don't ask questions," Monsieur Levi said.

At the end of September, due more rent, the landlord knocked on the door of Mr Smith's flat. He knocked again. Finally, hearing noises that alarmed him, he fetched a key and let himself in. 'I have the right,' he added. He found Daniel, a shivering, gibbering, emaciated wreck in a corner of the bedroom, and Mr Smith dead in the bed.

'A doornail,' according to the landlord.

'Could have been dead for weeks,' according to the

317

retired man of medicine – another tenant in the building – to whom the landlord turned for help. The English *Monsieur* was riddled with disease – lungs, liver, *le tout*.

Monsieur Levi, with the help of his tenant, organized the removal – and disposal – of the corpse. Not cheap, he emphasized. And not easy. Daniel blocked the door and, in what Monsieur Levi described as a state more execrable than a starving street-dog, Daniel threw himself on the rotting, stinking, *dégueulasse* dead body. They'd a job pulling him off and could do nothing to calm him.

That same afternoon, the landlord handed Daniel over to the authorities – 'what else could I have done?' – who sent him to a refuge for *handicapés*, run by catholic nuns, somewhere in the country.

That's all the landlord knew.

But when Daniel died in 1976, Monsieur Esposito-Levi received notification from the authorities. Daniel died during the summer heatwave, following a massive fit. And a few weeks later, a parcel arrived, via the authorities, for Monsieur Levi, from the nuns. It contained Daniel's possessions.

The brown paper package. I nudged it with my thigh.

'Yes,' said Sarah. 'But there was more originally. All rubbish, Monsieur Levi said. They threw everything away – clothes, old and useless, a wooden crucifix, a sort of armband, legband, I suppose, a garter, with Daniel's name and a number sewn into it, some sewing needles, a rusty old Opinel knife, a few other bits and pieces. He didn't really remember. Everything went in the bin. Except this.'

Sarah pointed to the package on my bed and stood up. She came and sat, like before, on the bed, but this time she lifted the package and held it on her lap.

'Monsieur Levi wouldn't tell me what was in it. "You'll think me odd," he said. "Or sentimental. But we all have our stories." Monsieur Levi did smile then, sort of.'

Sarah patted the package.

'Shall we open it?'

We pulled off the outer layers of paper. They weren't Sellotaped or done up with string, just wrapped. Inside were sheets of French newspaper, old and yellow, folded and tucked. More brown paper inside them. Then a brown paper bag. Sarah opened the top of it and looked inside.

'Shoes,' she said. 'Oh dear. Just smelly old shoes.'

She shook a pair of black men's lace-ups on to the bed. Fine Italian handcrafted shoes. Worn but polished, they'd been re-heeled, I could tell, and there were small brown stitches – sixty-four? – around the welt of one of them.

'How disappointing,' said Sarah. 'Sorry. I don't know why, but I must have imagined at least a biscuit tin or shoebox stuffed with I don't know what. Documents, photos, passport, a birth certificate?'

Conkers, camellias, a pencil stub or two, mother-of-pearl dress studs, seven, and cufflinks, pure silver.

'No. That would have been silly.'

A Daniel, make-believe-me world.

'Mementoes. I don't know. Private, secret things.'

Of course – what else?

'Not . . .' she paused. 'Smelly old shoes.'

I couldn't help myself. I guffawed. Couldn't she guess? Didn't she know what might be inside?

'Why are you laughing, Grace? Really. I don't know.'

'I do,' I said, as loud and clear as any old echoing cuckoo, and a darn sight louder than the aeroplane coming in to land, at that mo, overhead.

When Sarah had gone, Pat suggested I have a bath. She ran the water, squirted body-wash in, helped me off with my clothes and fixed the suction frame over the bath.

'I'll leave you to it,' she said. 'Have a cry, pet. Have a good soak. You'll feel better. Buzz when you're ready.'

There was a sliding lock on the door, on the inside. I slid it back and forth a few times, but left it unlocked. Only Cynthia has reached Level Three at Self-Care, which means she's allowed to lock the bathroom door.

I swooshed the pink plastic shower curtain out of the way, climbed into the bathtub and sat down quickly because my ankle hurt. I sat with my head at the tap-end of the bath, facing the door in case it opened – people don't always see the sign we hang on it when one of us is in there. With my good hand, I paddled the water and made a few bubbles, but they didn't last long.

I slid further into the bath until the water lapped my neck. Lying on my back in the bath is difficult because of my hump. I rolled on to my left side, shifting until Nelson anchored me firmly. I brought my good arm over and pressed my palm flat on the bottom of the bath, feeling the thin metal chain of the plug with my fingers. I slid further down, bending at the knees and waist. Slowly, I lowered my turned head. Ear, hair – my crowning glory – and one half of my face. The bath water lapped and tickled my nostril, so I held my breath and let my whole face sink. I opened my eyes, then shut them again – the water was murky and stung. I counted. The air in my lungs began to harden and hurt. I counted some more, came up for air.

I don't think swimming's my thing. All the residents of Acacia Road, except me, go twice a month to the Fountain Leisure Centre in Brentford for swimming lessons. I went once, and although Carole came with me, and we'd both bought blue stretch-nylon swimsuits from BHS, once was enough. I hated the cold chair that winched us up, then down into the water. I hated the rising of the water up my legs, over my belly, chest, neck. I hated the looseness of my skin and bones underwater. Swimming, or floating, is good for us and is supposed to be fun, said Carole. But my body flabbed heavily, and the water pushed too hard against me, making me feel locked in, like Daniel said it would, in the sea.

It was different in a bath. I've always liked baths. Only a baby could drown. And the bath at Acacia Road is worlds away from the sluices at the Briar, where you shared the big tub with two others, and the water with ten. So down I went again, and this time I didn't stay underwater for long, but I opened my mouth and blew, gently agg-agging like you do for the doctor, sending the sound humming from my throat to the surface of the water in bubbles that were still there, some of them, when I heaved myself up and took several panting breaths of air.

I'd never have beaten Miranda and her friends around the fountain at the rec. But I spat the gummy water out and went down one more time.

Did Daniel make friends in the refuge run by nuns? Did he lead them into other worlds, all the while plotting, himself, really to escape? And if – if only in his eggy old head – he escaped, did Daniel come back for me?

I prefer to think he made his way back to the city of light. Found work in the ninth arrondissement. Saved and set up a market stall. He's waiting for business to boom, that's all. He'll be sending for me soon.

Or perhaps he hitched a lift, first, in a lorry going south. Dijon, Geneva, the Alps. He ran to the mountains, seeking shelter, magic, the *famille Dumont*. And when he found them, 'You must meet Grace,' he said.

I can't wait.

No. I think the woodcutter rescued him and he became an elf.

Don't be silly, Grace. Don't be a fool. Fairies don't live in foxgloves, do they?

The woodcutter must have taken Daniel back to his hut in the forest. And there he was fed on home-made bread

– warm, soft, soaked in fresh goat's milk – and given clear, alpine water to drink from a pure mountain stream.

The woodcutter raised the boy kindly and wisely, showed him the abundance of the forest, taught him the beauties and dangers of the mountain, and educated him gently in the ways of the valley. When he grew up – into a fine, handsome young man – Daniel was apprenticed to the village cobbler, and there Daniel stayed, cobbling away, until one day, the most beautiful woman in the world walked into the cobbler's shop.

'*Maman?*'

'"*Oui. C'est moi. Oui, Dani*".'

But it could have been Mother, Miranda, Helen, Sarah, Carole. Or me. Why not? Me in a cream satin ball gown, with ribbons to match in my hair. There's a red rose between my boosies, and I'm wearing a bra.

I tried to imagine high heels like Sarah's, but built-ups were better for dancing all night. Everyone watching our wedding gavotte. I don't want to step on the bridegroom's shoes – such fine Italian handcrafted shoes – do I?

Still underwater, I tugged at the bath-plug. I dangled it on the suction frame when I'd got myself to a sitting position again, and pulled the buzzer-chord for Pat. While I waited for her, I felt the water suck away down the plug, behind my back, but there was plenty of it and I didn't get cold, because Pat arrived in two shakes of a lamb's tail, and the towel she wrapped round me, once I was out of the bath, was fleecy and warm from the tumble dryer and my radiator.

Back in my room, someone had cleared away the wrapping from the brown paper package and put the shoes on the carpet, next to the radiator.

Before getting into bed that night, I moved the shoes to by the door, so that I could see and admire them from the bed.

I'll find a way of unpicking the stitching, and when the words tumble out from their soles, flying and fluttering like snow, I'll catch them on my tongue. And if they don't melt, I'll piece them all together. Carole can help.

'Get a good night's sleep,' said Pat, switching off the overhead light. 'Tuesday tomorrow. You'll be an early bird. I know you.'

We're into May now. Whitsun next week, and camping in the New Forest with the Perivale people. When Martin told us, way back, Carole said nothing would induce her to sleep in a tent. But Martin explained it's huts, not tents, and a canteen, not campfires. And I think Carole's quite keen now. There's a preacher coming from Camberwell. And the Perivale people, says Martin, are planning an all-night sing-a-long vigil. It's up to us whether we join them. Harry claims he won't. Claptrap, fruitcakes, over my dead body, he says repeatedly. I think I'll wait and see. Harry might change his mind.

Before then, Carole and I have shopping to do. We're buying cagoules in Millets, a throwaway camera, plus travel toiletries in Superdrug, and, from one of the market stalls, torches and a tiny sewing kit – a hussif, like Miss Lily's, with needles, thread and pins, and a little quick-unpicking hook.

We're also buying a present for Martin and Pat. It's their wedding anniversary the day we leave. Carole says a new gift shop has opened on the high street where Parminder's Shoe Repair used to be – Parminder cut keys too and engraved a bangle for Carole once. We might try there.

Sarah visited again last week. She wasn't in quite such a hurry as usual. We went for a drive. I sat in the back, next to Carole, unbelted. The front seat was a jumble of chewing-gum papers, cigarette packets and cassettes, in and out of their cases.

'Sorry,' said Sarah. 'I've quite a collection.'

She doesn't play the cello any more, she said, but she listens.

'I've got some of those classics I used to play in easy arrangements. Do you remember, Grace?'

She's having the car MOT-ed and the tape-player mended in June.

'So when I next come . . .'

And over the summer, she's planning to put Father's records, which she says Mother has kept in boxes under her bed all these years, on tape.

'Even the old 78s.'

We drove to Heston Services and had coffee in cardboard beakers and chips in cardboard cartons. We sat in a special smokers' section, but there were no ashtrays, not even cardboard, so we used our chip cartons and made sizzling noises in them with our stubs.

On the drive home, Sarah said John was due over for a conference in August, and if they could persuade Miranda to make the journey, Mother was thinking of having a small do in the flat.

'Of course you're invited, Grace.'

Bowling tonight, and our postponed – twice since Easter – picnic in Osterley Park tomorrow. Plus another trip to Homebase soon. I need a lamp for my bedside table, and Carole's redoing her conservatory. You can't beat off-white, Grace.

When I lie on my bed, these days, looking around my room or out of my window at the cream-coloured blossoms, I wonder whether she's right – it's definitely whiffy with an off-white sort of happiness around here.

On the other hand, what's wrong with wood, eh, Nelson?

And when shadows stir, or a bird echoes, I cry out for the Briar. Not all of it. Just a few of its buildings, the grounds, our secret places. I've plenty of hidey-holes now.

Cupboards, drawers and boxes galore. I've even a case for my new, perfectly fitting dentures. And I haven't begun to fill up my jewellery chest yet, except with Robert. Yes, I improvise. The Briar. Eric and the rest of them. Mr Peters' gardens. The tall, dark cedar tree and the thick-walled apple-house. Its stink. Our excitement. And the stink of leather. Daniel and all those shoes – the journeys he gave them. Just a butterfly-boy with pale tufty hair. His unstoppable whoppers. So debonair. 'So many people. More than two thousand, Grace – the size of a small village.'

They'll never be counted, but I can hear them.

Acknowledgements

I would like to thank the following people: Véronique Baxter, Julia Bell, Lucy Brett, Martin Brett, Tania Brett, Jo Broadhurst, Franck Chapeley, Candida Clark, Jo Forbes Turko, Pat Gilliland, Jocasta Hamilton, Rik Haslam, Mary Henderson, Cordelia Henderson Moggach, Mimi Khalvati, Elissa Marder, Charlotte Mendelson, Tony Moggach, Corinne Morland, Jean-Michel Morland, Blake Morrison, David Osborne, Michael Read, Jon Riley, Lenya Samanis, Susan Wicks.